THE MAN DANCE

A Novel

LESLIE M ROLLINS

This is a work of fiction. Names, characters, places, and incidents are either from the author's imagination or used fictitiously. Any resemblance to actual persons living or dead, events or locales is entirely coincidental.

Published in the United States by *Wishing Star Press*

Cover design by *the*Book Designers

Editing by Rogena Mitchell-Jones, RMJ Manuscript Service, LLC, www.rogenamitchell.com

For Carrie and Maddie

PART I
Part One

NEW WORLDS

1955-1959

ONE

"Let Yourself Go"

(IRVING BERLIN, 1936)

BECAUSE HE WAS an adored ten-year-old living a fine, active life, fear came slowly to George Carveth. It was a tingling sensation during a telephone call on a cloudy Saturday in November.

The remains of bonfire night were scorched on the ridge. The kitchen phone rang so rarely it made anyone close to it jump. As the eldest of the household, Grandy Morwen answered, then hustled through the halls, importantly, announcing a ring-up from London.

Aunt Sally called from upstairs. "A ring from London? Who for?"

Grandy bent to an open window. "Gerry, quick! It's London on the line for you. Get going, man."

George's father loped into the house. George and his cousins followed him to the wall telephone. Why would London ring Dad?

UNTIL THAT INTRUSION, home had been a crowded house on a hill, a run from the school, a climb from the village.

There'd been a day the summer prior, in 1955, when George had flooded with a sense of his good fortune, the sea a jeweled expanse, the billowing land salted with houses. He'd seen an opposite life in newsreels—gray cities where children huddled in damp rooms with empty bellies. The war had stopped a year before his birth. No air raid siren would embed itself in his bones.

It had been a typical Saturday for the Carveth clan, with the uncles bringing out the bicycles. George climbed onto his dad's bike, awkwardly in front, bum in the basket, as did the others with their fathers. Only the elder cousins manned their own rides. It was shaky going until Dad got up speed and the wind pelted.

The cyclists followed the ridge road past the last of the houses and hillside scatterings of sheep. They slowed to park at a divot in the landscape. From there was a careful descent over rocks and grass shelves. Ocean spray cooled his legs as George backed down. Surf roared below and washed the sand clean, leaving it baked in sunlight.

Their garments were gladly thrown off. Bare bodies danced through fizzling foam, the hip smack of surf, that was nut-shrink cold; George needed moments to absorb the shock of it. Then he plunged, boring through waves as if he were a dolphin, all muscle. He popped out beyond the breakers where Dads and cousins bobbed nearby, grinning. Then everyone jostled shoreward in a mad race to body surf. He tried not to get a salty mouth or a tumble with water drilling the nose.

He'd been swimming for most of his nine years and knew the dangers of rocks and riptides and first-aid for swimmers. The Cornish coast was a rocky landscape, which was why the family favored pocketed coves and the slope of the beach. If a wave looked fearful, he was to mind the feeling, Dad saying, "Don't tell yourself you're not afraid when you are. Fear comes for a reason."

George knew not to swim in rough seas and was a good deal braver than many of his mates. Dad could get awfully worried about things happening for having been a soldier in the war.

Dad's head was a glossy cap in the distance. No children were allowed past him. When he returned, the uncles called "Gerren," and tried to dunk him, but his father sloshed free, body slick as if pulled from a shell, hair black and shiny as he sleeked it, the handsomest of the men. He was tall, but not too tall, not hairy like Uncle Arthur, more strong looking than skinny. Little ones cavorted on the sand as Dad shaded his eyes.

George knew Dad searched for him, and barked like a seal before diving into the murky green underworld. Supposedly, a sea goddess named "Calypso" lived in the deep. He once saw the ripple of her long hair as she fled. Only now he was distracted by the hum of water in his ears. It sounded like a piece of music by WC, the composer with initials. Bubbles gushed out of him as Dad swam up.

George gasped. "That music… 'Claire of the Moon'… I heard it. D'ye think WC swam underwater? He has them just-right notes."

Dad grinned with hair in his eyes. "Just right, are they?"

"They tickle my ears and make me dance."

"Oh, sprite. Don't be tellin' your uncles about this music."

"I needs to dance."

"Later, boyo. Ack, these wrinkly fingers. To the beach with you." George whooped as Dad threw him high.

Released from water to greedy sunshine, WC's notes swirled in his mind. It was hard not to dance a little on the flat, shiny surface of the sand.

Uncle Arthur called, "Butterfly Boy. Is that you flitting about?"

George ran over hot sand and climbed to a grass shelf. His uncle reminded, "Older lads oughtn't to behave like butterflies." The music blew out of his head. Little Ethan taunted, "Butterfly," so George kicked him, causing a wail. An uncle snapped, "Shut it!"

Everyone sprawled like biscuits baking on a rack. George tanned a honey hue in summer because his mum had "dark blood, half-Asian," and the blood showed in him, apparently.

Cousin Margie propped as he fell in beside her. She was a year older, tough as a lad. He confided, "There was music in the water."

She grinned. "Your eyelashes look like stars. I could kiss ya."

"Don't you dare!"

"Nor would I." She gave him her grass-stained back.

Dad spoke sharply with Arthur at the rocks.

. . .

THE FAMILY LIVED on the outskirts of St. Ives in one of the large detached homes that were high up and overlooking Porthmeor Beach. In the back garden, the grownups poured beer and neighbors climbed the ridge. Sheep clustered like gossips along the fence of a nearby farm, their dung scent wafting.

Aunt Sally strode past with a tray. "Clothes on! Folks are here."

The cousins tore naked over the grass too energized to care about clothes. George smelled of salt and sunshine. Air teased his skin like bristles. He just missed crashing into Aunt Tiffany in her wide-brimmed artist hat. She hooted. "The freedom of childhood."

"Them little Carveths is brown as berries," said the sheep farmer.

George lagged. Sweaty bodies bumped him, but he lost the fantasy. The fiddles were out. A melody started. The uncles and their mates tried a jig, a lively stepper. The older people clapped along.

The kids switched to dancing, little naked adults at the town hall social. Margie flailed her arms like a loon. George could hide in a group dance, where no one would call him a butterfly. Until an adult voice was overheard:

"Ho-ho, Gerren! Your boy has it down. Look at 'im."

It was more the jig had George. The other children fell out to watch. His heart opened like a bird on the wing. Here came the feeling! He could find the dance in any bit of music. Drunk from his swim, in the heat of the afternoon, with bees in the air and sweat on his skin, the sound was a wire, and he, a high wire artist. Though it twanged and swayed, he stayed with it, his footfall light and sure.

"A sparkler to music, that 'un," Grandy Morwen shouted.

A neighbor said, "Lucy in him there, with her Oriental ways—"

"A pretty lad," agreed another.

Someone said, "Little naked devil. Little wog."

The tune ceased, and the ground flew up.

Dad caught George as cheers erupted. Faces encircled, beaming, Mum radiant, Dad ruffling his hair. Uncle Arthur squeezed his neck but not in the hard, come-look-what-you-did way, calling out, "We got ourselves a Fred Astaire."

Was it good to have danced? He never knew anymore. Who'd called him a devil?

Margie charged through, yanking him from the crowd of grownups and straight between a scratching hedge— "Ay, me front bits!" —down to the rose trellis along the side of the lavvy.

Having donned trainers but nothing else, she kicked him in the shin. His leg collapsed in pain. "Show-off! They were looking at me until you started flipping your willy."

She stalked away, angry buttocks working, her springy hair floating with her stride.

He hobbled alongside the stone house to a side door entrance. The kitty mewed from a cement perch. "*She's* the show-off."

The kitty blinked, impartial.

He entered a dark interior, through the fishy scullery with its filleting knives, butcher block, and rows of boots on the floor. The large kitchen was fragrant with the baked scent of pies. He switched to his toes on the sticky floor. Grandy Morwen had told him to "stay on his toes," and that he did whenever possible. Behind him, the door banged open and cousins flooded in, Aunt Sally following.

"Clothes on this instant. No more playin' until 'ee do."

George was herded with his older cousin Timmy to the bedroom they shared. On the wall was a fisherman's net artfully arranged by Aunt Tiffany, who'd helped the boys attach various prizes: shells, starfish, pieces of hammered silver, an image of Saint Ia, the patron saint of the town.

The boys pulled on shorts from the dirty clothes pile. Timmy blurted, "Aunt Lucy."

"Aunt Lucy," George repeated.

His mum kissed Tim, then pinched George's ear. "Who am I?"

George winced. "You're Mum." But everyone called her Aunt Lucy.

Alone, she snared him against her warm, damp blouse. "You smell divine, my ocean lad."

Black hairs clung to his cheek as she pulled back. He liked her long hair. His was a curly mop, like most of the others. He'd been told he had her sly "cat eyes" and sunny smile. He'd seen how his mother could dazzle. Folks noticed her, not all of them nice about it.

And he remembered. "Some'un called me 'wog.'"

Her brow creased. "I swear we'll get you out of this small town."

There were shouts outdoors. She snagged his arm before he could flee. "You'll rise above them all. You've a spark, crumpet. All they see is Darjeeling."

That was his other grandmother's home. She was dead. He liked the name of the place, though it was too far to visit. He'd been to Truro, Penzance, Plymouth, even all the way to London, briefly, where he'd seen broken buildings, rubble and gray dust, and no one to give a smile. None of those places were nicer than here.

HAPPINESS WAS music filling his head. George couldn't remember when he'd come to love it so much. It just seemed a part of him, like being able to swim. As a young tyke, he used to hang around well after bedtime staring moony-eyed from a doorway as the adults laughed and played records on the gramophone. Someone always noticed and shooed him back to bed.

He'd been the first to take to certain children's songs—that is, until the day he couldn't stand another minute, so often did they repeat in his head. He held his ears and screamed to make them stop. He did it when Aunt Sally led a sing-along with the cousins, and most voices veered off key. He did it at school where they sang even worse than at home. The matron sent a note to his parents about his "fussing." He could only say, "The songs sound bad. They has to stop."

The singing went on, and he spent an hour in the headmaster's office while his class did their distant hoots along with the piano, the timing off. It was decided he had a "tin ear." At home, his family kept quiet.

His father played *South Pacific* at night on the gramophone. George was tantalized straightaway with "Bali Ha'i" from the Overture. *Come away,* it entreated, piercing his sleep. He would rise from his bed past sleeping cousins and stop in the darkened hallway, where he slid to the floor and listened to the world that unfolded.

For a time, Dad played a record of a woman singing to a skylark. George felt near to crying hearing it. The Fred Astaire records were a safer listen. He sang the song about joining the navy to see the sea.

Aunt Sally faltered at the piano whenever he passed through the main room. Dad egged her on. "Play Irving Berlin. Try Gershwin."

Then came wonderful tunes that stopped him in his tracks. Dad scoffed. "Tin ear, my eye."

His cousins were mad for "Happy Talk" from *South Pacific* and played the song daily, until he cried, "No more, *no more.*"

Sent to bed for spoiling the fun, George wailed when the ditty resumed. Someone thumped up the stairs—Mum, looking cross.

He told her, "It don't stop playin' in me head," and sang it to her, knowing the words, aping the singer's accent, as tears dripped.

Mum's mouth fell open, almost, but not quite smiling. After, he heard her tell the others, "We'll give that song a rest now, children."

Timmy shouted, "He's a loony!"

There was much debate on whether he should be allowed to see *South Pacific* at the local cinema. Aunt Tiffany said she'd take him out during the "Happy Talk" sequence, which she did, and confessed in the lobby that she didn't care for the song, either. George had been willing to stay after seeing Mitzi Gaynor. He'd never seen such a marvelous looking, golden-haired lady.

Music was played openly again. George skipped and twirled to a song about a swan and another one about biscuits: "Swanee" and "Puttin' on the Ritz." One record was nearly all drums and had the daft title "Sing Sing Sing." He wiggled the moment it started, which made his parents laugh. They called him "wiggling monkey."

The family enjoyed an evening sing round the piano, songs started with a quick look at him. Mystifying, how often they bungled lyrics.

During a struggle with "Skylark," George took over—and finished to cheers. He merely imitated the record. Dad scooped him against a damp cheek. "What a sprite you are."

Sometimes Dad plunked the piano keys, mostly hitting wrong notes. George was worse on piano, his two hands like mallets. He couldn't focus on his fingers and the dense markings of sheet music at the same time. Whereas, Aunt Sally was called the "penis" of the family. Amazing how *that word* could also mean "good at the piano." He winced when anyone called her that. She played the grand in the main room, working pieces that were long and haunting. He would slip beneath her piano to catch the resonance. Even outside, his hearing detected the quiet notes of the "Moonlight Sonata." Not only Beethoven, she played a concerto from a fellow named Grieg or a lullaby from Brahms or pieces from Chopin, and recently, WC.

George, his dad, and his aunt seemed to understand a language the other family members did not. He nearly floated to and from school, so much did this music play inside him. Uncle Arthur complained.

"Gerry, your lad is going to get thrashed. Can you not teach him to climb or build things?"

Uncle Arthur frowned at George putting on dance gear for his ballet class. Amazingly, after the dance on the lawn in front of all the family and neighbors, Mum enrolled him in a ballet school to attend after regular school. No one was to say *anything*, she announced to the family, her cat gaze sparking.

No one said a word at first. Even George didn't know what to say about it. He was the only lad in the class.

Grandy said, "Him with his bedroom eyes in a room full of lassies. I bet you're the star there, boy, are ye?"

"They hate me."

They teased him in a girly way, not like the football gang, who kept his face in the grass. As in that situation, Margie sidled close, "Who are they? Shall I go after 'em?"

Which only made things worse. It was bad enough she threatened girls he talked to in the schoolyard.

"Margaret Susan, you've chores in the kitchen," Aunt Sally snapped whenever Margie tried following him to the ballet school.

George didn't want her seeing him clumsy. He was used to moving any way he liked. It was hard to do certain steps and always be on one leg. The teacher, Mrs. Treadwell, chided the giggling students. He was a big laugh at this place.

Until Mrs. T played "Swan Lake" on the gramophone. After, he danced with wings on his feet. None of the girls teased him.

He could scarcely stop the surge of joy that happened whenever he danced. But he did get better at paying attention in the lessons and learned how to loosen his body. The advice on balance was spot on. He stopped wobbling, stomach in, and lifted his leg higher than the lassies. Soon he could spin across a room and not get dizzy.

By winter, everyone in his family had an opinion. The uncles said, "It weren't good for a boy to be whirling and pointing his feet."

It upset his cousins. George got to be special; anyone could dance. They teased him in his tights, told him he had a fat bum and fat calves.

"Pay them no mind," Mum said. "You've the strong legs and buttocks of your father."

Was that why his shorts were tight and his socks never stayed up?

Dad grew doubtful. Perhaps the school wasn't a proper place. Strange, his son was the only male child there.

Some of the boys in the neighborhood didn't want George playing football anymore, which was batty. He eluded tackles better and scored goals.

The adults decided this "Frenchy dancing" had gone far enough. An uncle grumbled, "I never trust them French, aligning themselves with Hitler."

George pointed out that Hitler was dead. Cousins glared at him as Uncle Arthur reared. "And you'd best be thankful for that, my lad! We rid the world of evil."

But what did the war have to do with dancing? His pleas came to nothing. Even Mrs. Treadwell coming to the house to say he was the best student she'd seen in years didn't help.

Mum was furious for him, Dad awkward. Grandy Morwen said he'd best look ahead. His cousins were glad all the fuss was over.

BUT CHANGE OVERTOOK him that dark November day of his tenth year. George would tally his enjoyments—chasing Cloud, his favorite lamb, as she ran bleating around the farmer's pen; darting up steep, cobbled roads as the summer tourists panted, fish-white and crowding the town, though Dad said they brought in money. He'd been happy on Uncle Dan's fishing boat jostling the salt-flecked sea, going out to where the gray seals speared water off Godrevy Lighthouse. He'd even been happy in Aunt Tiffany's art studio in the Warren where she painted her pears and empty bottles.

Why would London ring Dad?

Dad shouted and grinned through his telephone call, nattering on until the adults drifted off and the young ones went outside. Mum rolled yarn, her attention sharp on Dad. George felt oddly tingly as if the call had to do with him, though, clearly, it did not. Grandy sewed. Cousin Margie had been roped into darning, a task she hated.

The phone pinged as Dad rang off. "A mate from the war."

Grandy said, "A rich mate to talk to ye so long."

"Aye, he's that. A peer."

Dad gaped like a half-wit. "Lucy, he went on about my saving his life and wants to help our family. He's offered me a—job—in London. I told him I had to talk to you—"

Mum squealed. "Say yes, say yes!"

His parents leapt like baby goats. George crouched behind a chair. Margie joined him. They gripped arms and regarded each other with worried eyes.

Dad said, "Ma, it's a great opportunity. I'd be a fool not to consider. There'd be more pay."

Grandy said, "Aye, but you ought to consider all aspects."

His parents giggled as if she hadn't spoken. Footsteps thumped the stairs. George rose. Grandy stared at him with upset eyes.

His parents didn't come down. Aunts and uncles marched upward.

Outside, the temperature dropped. Clouds rushed in from the ocean, blowing off smoky remnants from the ridge. The boys played jacks on the pavement step. George couldn't focus on the game and banged the doorjamb going inside.

Margie wailed from the kitchen. "They wouldn't move, they can't!"

His dad was in love with the sea. He'd never leave their *home* to go to a broken-down city.

Uncles Dan and Arthur clattered downstairs. "I'll miss her witchin' eyes, our half-black maharani."

"Hush now. She's always wanted out of here— Hey, whatcha doin' there, young George? They're waiting for you upstairs."

George bolted outside, flew down granite steps, then leapt to the grass, nearly tumbling down to the path and the switchback, and two more switchbacks. Until he was staggering on dry sand, catching his breath. Darkness gathered over the bay. He tramped the hard, wet surface of the beach, not much of it, the tide rushed him. Who cared? It was too much. Cold water swamped his ankles, skated his feet. He laughed over his ruined shoes. His mother was half black—

"Laddie, look out!" a woman shouted.

Surf knocked him down and yanked him out. He paddled to right himself in the force of it, to spit, to breathe. But a wave smashed him down again. He floundered beneath fizzing clouds, directionless. His heel broke the surface. He sought his toes through a spray of bubbles.

And gasped blessed air. Salt rimed in his mouth, his eyes stung. He flicked away hair. A woman danced in the distance. Swells rocked him, the water nearly opaque. Another wall was coming. He nudged off the impediment of his shoes and swam hard. With perfect timing, he bodysurfed a thrilling ride.

The world flipped. Water knifed his sinuses. As the deluge released him, he gulped air like drinking it. The snot glopped out. The ground was back then away, with nothing to grab. Surf barreled him as if he were seaweed.

His shoulder burned; he was hoisted and climbed a grownup who had him. His lungs expanded noisily.

His two uncles ran across the sand. The woman sloshed out and dodged them. "Such a helpless little seal in the waves."

Uncle Dan waved. "We're his uncles, miss. You can let go."

Arthur said, "He knows how to swim, miss."

She shouted, "He nearly drowned!"

George screamed to stop everyone pulling him apart, and with that, the woman let go. Uncle Dan carried him like a sack, hurting his ribs and stomach. "Put me down," he squeaked.

His uncle stopped, but George fell across an adult knee and got his backside swatted, the smacks stinging.

"That's what 'ee gets for doing a crazy thing like that!"

Uncle Arthur said, "Easy, Dan-o. The lad won't be doing it again."

George panted, blood burning his face. He tried walking with the men. His legs gave out.

Uncle Dan hoisted him, soothing now, his big body keeping the shivers at bay. In the distance, the woman watched them.

THOUGH IT WASN'T a bath night, George sat in the tin tub by the kitchen fire. His madness forgotten, the family were gathered in the main room where a wireless program sounded faintly. He didn't care about missing it. His shoulder was sore, his head addled by water.

Mum mixed shampoo from a packet. Not that he needed cleaning. The sea had scoured him. He could still hear the roar of it in his ears. Dad always said, "The Sea can turn on you. Don't think she won't."

A stream of hot water from the kettle made him cower to the side and swish his feet, chanting "Hot, hot," like a little one. He didn't protest when his mum started on his hair.

She said, "London is one of the great cities of the world. You'll get to know your Uncle James, my brother. You should know the Hartley side of your family. We're not all Carveths here."

He did want to know the Hartley side. Yet didn't want this talk.

Should he tell her how the uncles spoke of her? She hadn't even been upset about his lost shoes.

He felt the pitch of waves and gripped the tub. Odd how the land never swayed with the ocean, not even in sympathy.

He told her, "It's war-torn in London. No one is happy."

She stopped. "Crumpet, how can you remember? That was years ago. It's been rebuilt. You should be out in the world. The blood of many lands runs inside you. Don't forget my mother was part Tibetan. We have her good bones."

Did the "many lands" make them black? She doused his head with water. He blinked, the soap stinging. "Dad is in me, too."

She hugged his wet shoulders. "He most certainly is. You have his curly hair and long eyelashes, his sweetness."

He squirmed from her nuzzling.

She handed him the soap. "Finish up."

"Doesn't Dad care about Mr. Clemo's store or keeping his books?"

"He'll be keeping books for his friend now. For greater pay. It's a chance Daddy and I never thought we'd have."

"Can't you ever like it here?"

She dried her hands with a tea towel. "Lovey. It's hard to be away from a cultured place. I had a gay life in London before the war."

Her former life felt a precipice, sometimes, one that made her go quiet for hours.

He thrust out his chest and pitched his voice like Uncle Arthur: "I's a fit fellow in the war, mate. I showed them mountaineers a thing or two about scrambling up a cliff, no lie I did."

She hooted. "Wicked thing! *You* ought to be on the radio."

She held a towel at the ready. "Nothing will happen soon. Daddy will see his chum. There's time yet."

That's what he needed to hear. He'd put this muddle far out of his mind. Though the grownups talked of it for days after. His cousins cornered him, wanting to know why his parents were keen to leave.

"They're not. Dad's going to talk to his rich mate, is all. It may not happen."

Life went back to normal, sort of. Margie became fun again. When he happened to talk to a wary girl from his class, Margie drifted away, allowing it to happen. Mum cleaned out her and Dad's bedroom and began packing things in a trunk, "summer things" they didn't need, and did the same in his and Timmy's room, "making space," she said.

She proposed a project for George, saying he should write an essay, which didn't sound fun at all. She insisted he teach her about a favorite subject. Of course, she rejected most of his topics, but approved one, which was how he came to labor over a paper called "What to Listen for in Music." She corrected it, and Dad made it longer by saying, "Explain this more." Grandy thought it awfully clever.

A part of him was proud he'd written it, as if putting words on paper eased the torment in his head, bedeviling songs from the wireless, adverts repeating. He wouldn't have minded reading the essay aloud in school. But Mum posted it somewhere.

The essay project no sooner ended when he was told he'd be sitting a special exam—on a Saturday, no less. The schoolmistress met with him weeks in advance, saying he needn't be perfect at it, just to do well enough. (His grandy would never have approved such lax advice.) Still, it was surprising being the only child in the room on examination day. The schoolmistress started a timer, then quizzed him on arithmetic, writing and problem solving, none of it easy.

Back home, Mum asked how he'd done on the Eleven Plus, the dreaded national exam.

George scoffed. "Those are at the end of the year."

"Dream boy, what do you think you just did?"

"Some tests? But I'm not… eleven yet."

Had he really sat the important, future-deciding exam already? He'd been told not to mention it to his classmates who would be taking it later on. How odd to be ahead of them.

He could feel puffed up about it, especially when he learned he'd passed, and the schoolmistress called him a smart lad.

But he suspected it was to do with London and moving.

The adults had discussions in low voices. Grandy prepared his favorite meals, like ray fish with boiled taties and butter. Worried, he hid inside the kitchen pantry as the women washed dishes.

Mum burst out, "You must be joking. Not on your life."

Grandy said, "It's an option, Lucy. He may be happier."

"We'd never do that. You know we have plans for him."

Silence followed but for the clink of plates.

Too soon, Dad's job was secured and a London house found. George kept remembering the city as a huge, broken-down place. He asked if Farmer Hale would let Cloud come to London.

Mum laughed. "Cloud stays with her mother as you stay with yours."

Dad said, "You don't separate sheep, son."

"But you separate children?"

Dad blinked his soft brown eyes.

Mum snapped, "Enough. The world isn't coming to an end."

George called her "Aunt Lucy." It had the right effect. She flapped her arms at Dad. "Do you see? This is why."

His last day came in early February when he left the schoolhouse forever, everyone knowing about it and being awkward. Irked, he did an imitation of the master as he walked home with a pair of lassies. They laughed. For moments, he forgot the situation and chattered with them. Maybe one lass would become his girlfriend.

"George Carveth, you sorry toad!"

Margie ran at him. The idiot girls screamed and clung to each other. He bolted. Then lagged in case she was going for the girls. Margie came like a fury. He was a better fence climber than her and chose a shortcut, veering through back gardens, upsetting a cow in one—fortunately tied. He nearly crashed into an old-timer coming from the privy.

But what his cousin lacked in speed came out in bull-headedness. Just as he thought he'd lost her, he met her fist in surprise.

Then she was pummeling. "You talk to others when you're leaving me? You'll take a black eye to them girls in London."

. . .

ON A CHILLY MORNING, a lorry was loaded with trunks, his parents' bed, and other furniture from the big house. Neighbors stood outside, watching. His vision was partly blurred. Margie scowled nearby, the wind blowing her curls.

George asked for the fisherman's net from the wall of his room, but Timmy declared it his net, too. Dad said perhaps his auntie would make him a new one.

Aunt Sally gripped his shoulder. "Well, child. You're going to have an adventure."

Aunt Tiffany blinked. "London is a nice place, all built up."

"There's music in London. Your pa will take you to concerts."

"There's so much to do. We're all envious."

He clutched his aunties. The uncles came over to tousle his hair and thump his back. Uncle Dan said, "Those in London will look at your shiner and know you're not to be trifled with."

His cousins hung in a group and gawped as if he'd become strange. "Say goodbye to your cousin now," Grandy spoke in a hoarse voice, "Tell 'im you'll write."

The children repeated her words. How wrong this was!

Grandy squashed him to her bosom and used his Cornish name. "Ah, we'll miss you, Jory-love. You've always a place here."

Tears shot in, painful in the bad eye. Grief clotted his throat. But Uncle Arthur signaled him to silence.

Margie, Timmy, and Uncle Dan joined them for the short, cliffside train ride from St. Ives to St. Erth, where one caught the cross-country to London. Margie took his hand. George jerked it away.

Shocked by her look of dejection, he offered his hand. Besides, he had more important things to do, like memorize the retreating view of his seaside home. A green spit of land jutting into blue like a promise. No longer would he greet the sea. *I'll not leave you,* said his heart.

But losing his home was only the start.

TWO

"The Big Hurt"

(WAYNE SHANKLIN, 1959)

PADDINGTON STATION WAS FIERCELY LOUD, the locomotives screeching and rumbling. Smoke choked the air. Mum dragged George through a crowd worse than catch day on the island. Dad hustled them outdoors to a taxi stand with its queuing black vehicles.

His parents chattered about places not seen in ages. Flanking row houses looked sturdy with the business of living. A few buildings showed war damage. One turn and the view opened, streets wider, as they joined tides of cars and people. Skeletal trees were glimpsed in parks. The city was a flat ride, though George recalled that from his previous visit, not that he could get a proper view of any distance with his pummeled eye. His strained vision took in what it could.

Lights flashed on marquees. He'd heard there were cinemas every-where, "Picnic" on the one they passed. That could be a fun picture. People danced in an upper floor window. Ballet, was it? Perhaps he might be allowed to take classes again. Snatches of music came from somewhere. But, of course, there would be lots of music in an active place like this.

There were a good many stoplights. He didn't mind, as there was so much to see. A song blared at a speedy tempo from a car alongside. The driver jerked as if having a fit, his hank of greasy hair bobbed. The singer sounded crazed about the "Rock Island Line." George and his parents stared until the man's car sped forward.

Dad muttered, "All types."

They passed famous areas, though it was hard not to watch, instead, as people poured out of a red double-decker bus or swung onto the pole of it just as quickly. How wonderful to dash through a city and know what to do.

With Big Ben in the distance, they crossed the Thames River, reeking of sulfur and old fish—George had to pinch his nostrils— heading south to an area called Clapham, where the railroad went.

Mum urged the cab driver to take them round the Common, a huge park, "with a great children's playground," she added, roping George with her sunniest smile.

"Through there is the Long Pond. Over there is the old Victorian bandstand where my father took Jimmy and me to hear music."

George craned to see it through the stretch of winter greenery. The High Street was broader than the one at home. Neighborhoods looked patchy with the old and new. There weren't many children about. Though, of course, they'd be in school. How wicked to *not* be in school. The taxi turned up a street of row houses similar to ones at home, only these were brick, not stone.

The cab slowed and idled. Dad spoke the words, "Here we are."

Yet there was no house on a hill nor any place separate.

His parents hastened from the taxi. George was the last to slide out. The wind blew fiercely as if to say, *Go back.*

Dad fussed with a key. They entered a hallway as cold as the outdoors, then opened the door to an empty front room that smelled of old fires. Floorboards creaked. Dad peered in the coal scuttle. "Not empty." He gestured wide. "A fine bay window. It's not like home, but it'll do, eh?"

What good was a bay window with no bay to see?

They moved to the back room and the kitchen, that also had a burnt reek. Mum brushed soot off her gloves. Dad went to the gray humpy boiler in the corner attached to copper pipes and smacked it. "Modern times."

Up narrow stairs, George had a remarkable thing, his own bedroom with no cousin pushing to claim the best part. It faced the gray street with look-alike houses.

Dad said, "See the lavvy in the hall? No going outside, not for us."

Wouldn't the house smell of their business?

Mum would never abide this prison. But she gazed about, soft-eyed and smiling. "We'll make it right smart, pet. Don't worry. Help Daddy bring in the bags."

As his father clattered downstairs, George lunged for her lapels. "Mum, we can't stay here. It's cold and mean and dark."

She yanked off his grip. "What a spoiled thing you are. You'll get used to it."

The taxi had chucked their pile of suitcases and fled, the lorry with the furniture had yet to arrive. Dad hummed on the front stoop, his trim figure bulked in a coat, hair greased. His breath came out a mist.

"This is supposed to be an up-and-coming neighborhood. Who knows? In another five years, it might be quite the place."

"But where shall we swim?"

Dad squinted around as if there must be a body of water behind one of the houses, then gazed skyward.

"Funny to be here without worrying about bombs."

Bombs? George gawked at the leaden sky. His father went to collect the bags.

Something vibrated beneath his feet. An ominous rumble gained in volume and froze him on the step. "Dad?" he called out.

"Ah? Oh. Those are the trains at Clapham Junction. Pretty great, eh?"

· · ·

GEORGE DREAMT a bomb dropped from the sky, crashed through the ceiling, and fell like a weight on top of him. He jerked awake. All was dark.

Then he clearly heard, "Why in *hell* did we get a place near the station? I keep thinking it's…" and Dad's voice trailed off. Mum's tone soothed, too low for words. Odd to hear his parents so close. He hadn't heard a train sound at all. Though he felt the faintest vibration, a dying rhythm in the rails.

Shapes loomed in the room. Jammed-in furniture and boxes. It was mad cold, the hot water bottles unfound. Still in his coat, George burrowed in covers up to his eyes. On cold nights at home, there was always a cousin or two to warm a bed. Mum and Dad had offered a share. But why should he crawl like a babe between them?

The next day, in a break from unpacking, they explored the area, his parents seeming to need the walk and air as he did. It was raw out with a faint burning smell. A city smell. There seemed to be a constant din of noise going on. No more the music of seabirds. George was drawn to the junction with its thundering cars, but Mum said it's only a train station, they needn't go there.

They saw bomb ruins in nearby Lavender Hill. A pile of rubble in the overgrown grass was dubbed "the old Pavilion Cinema." Mum showed where houses once stood and winced at the sight of the damaged Shakespeare Theatre.

George did not feel comforted over cream buns in Lyons Tea Shop, where the tea lady said, "Got a little fighter, 'ave ya? Or did your dad have to knock some sense into you?"

His dad said, "No, no," and muttered, "as if I would ever hit my kid," and two girls also stared at his black eye. His parents assured him the war was all so long ago. The world was a different place now.

Cousin Timmy said adults lied to children to keep them from getting upset. Everyone knew bombs were far worse. The "Gerries" might be quiet, but what about the Commies? At least St. Ives was small. George saw that now. Why move to a big target? Hadn't his parents considered that? Perhaps they were no good without Grandy and the others weighing in on things.

For the first time in his life, George realized his alarming state as an only child. Why hadn't his parents ever thought that one through? They were growing short with him, especially Mum. He shadowed them from room to room, easy to do in a limited space with the unnerving thumps and echoes of neighbors on either side.

Dad roamed the upstairs newly bathed, scented and handsome. George breathed in the smell of him. Donning a suit and tie for the new job, his dad looked important. His wet hair made inky curls on his head. He squirted a bead of hair cream, rubbed his hands vigorously then swiped them through his hair, muttered, "That'll never hold," and knocked into George. "Lad! Need 'ee be in the way?"

Dad relaxed for a hug, his voice vibrated beneath George's ear.

"All right, love. I've got my appointment. Go and help Mum while I'm gone. Find your bat, and I'll bowl for you later."

"Can we listen to records, as well?"

"The gramophone has to be set up. We may not get to that and the records is all packed still."

A distant train rumbled with brakes squealing. Dad paused on the last stair and touched George's cheek. "I'll make a point to set it up. Our music is important."

George beamed. "Right, Dad. Mum!"

"Lucy, I'm going!"

George found his mother out back in trousers and smiling at their tiny garden. "Mum, Dad left. Can I ring Margie?"

"Long distance, he wants? Telephones are dear. You'll write a letter." She brushed past, her loose hair trailing a whiff of the outdoors. "I saw children out front, yah? Go, baby. Make friends."

By himself?

Children noticed him as he squinted from the front stoop. He stepped down casually. They looked to be sidling away. Perhaps he seemed fierce with his eye. Or odd. One girl watched him. He stared at her, and his gaze said he would take her hand and run with her to the grassy common, if not to the sea. But he never got to meet her.

"Son, you'll not be going to school around here," Dad said that evening, his eyes alight in a funny way. He'd yet to plug in the gramophone or find the box of records.

George aided in the search, needing music like blood. They would play "Sing Sing Sing," and he would do his wiggling dance to make them laugh. If he didn't dance in this house, how would it ever feel right? He certainly wasn't dancing outside.

Dad paced. "The thing is, we're sending ye to a grammar school, a really good 'un, out in the country it is. Remember that essay you wrote? The exam?"

His stomach flipped. "Sending me?"

A parental look was shared. "Well. It's a boarding school—"

His legs gave out.

Mum dove to the wood floor and scooped him up. "It's too soon. We needn't send him yet. He has to get used to this."

"It's best he gets used to it all at once, Lucy. 'Take the medicine at once,' Mum says."

"We're away from your mother, we can do what *we* think is best. Poor lamb."

"My eye," George moaned. It was one thing to brandish it in front of a few neighborhood kids, but an entirely new school?

"The term has started," Dad shouted over the thumps of an accelerating train. "We have to get him there as soon as possible. This is a privilege. You'll thank me in the end. I'm spending our luck on you, lad. Ack, these bloody trains!"

THEY RODE a train from Clapham Junction. Dad tried a pep talk, but George would have none of it. Dad pointed out the new motorway being built. They chugged over a bridge, passed towns and hamlets. George couldn't take in anything, and didn't want food from Mum.

He flashed on his tumble in the waves. Had water got inside his head? On a hillside was a sprawl of buildings with a tower. His gut knew it was the school.

A chatty fellow in a taxi drove them to the campus. Gnarled trees were bent with loneliness. There was nothing bright here, no wildness. At a sudden bell, the place bled students, motley figures in gray surging out. Masters collected in black. Crows tending pigeons. All of them chattered like wireless announcers.

George plainly didn't belong here. How could his parents not see? They were no good without the others.

Dad hoisted his trunk. George refused his mother's hand. Lads gawked as they came up the walk, with most eyes on Mum as she clicked along in her prized fur stole. A lout whistled.

Through the doors was confusion and blur, a slip underwater, with echoes and tones and forward movement down a hall.

After the horror of arrival in the headmaster's office and meeting the grand Lord Kettering, who went on about Dad's bravery in the war (which George normally would've loved hearing), the headmaster *saluting*, and meeting Kettering's snot of a son Edward, who sneered at George, the headmaster calling George "a fighter" because of his eye, and Mum offering to dab makeup under it (he batted her hand away), then her going tearful like she was sorry now, and Dad holding him when George wanted to kick him—as if that hadn't been bad enough, when the adults left, Edward scoffed, "Cornish boy, fend for yourself," and deserted him.

The undertow sucked everyone clear. Only an assistant scuttled back for a tour, brusque now, no respect. George ought to have guessed after her *don't worry about unpacking, leave it for later*, knowing they'd be sending him off. His insides shot up his throat, he leapt to a hall dustbin. The assistant said, "Oh no, oh dear," and snapped at a laughing student to take the fouled bin away.

George was given tea and a "buck-up" lecture. He had no appetite. He was issued clothing and shown to a bed in one half of another lad's room, his trunk already crowding the space. Sometime later he heard the boy arrive, mutter, "Great," walk out, and never realized if the boy returned, so sunk was he in the deep.

BELLS SHRIEKED IN DARKNESS. George sat bolt upright, head ringing. The air was frigid. The wall bumped, a stirring of bodies from the other side. Feet pattered, doors slammed. His roommate was out of bed, his whisper harsh. "Come *on*."

The floor was icy. George pawed for the nearby uniform of shirt, shorts, blazer, and tie and fumbled into them.

Outside, boys pressed into military formation, everyone clad in pigeon gray, all heads capped. George barely made the lineup after his desperate search for a privy. A headache pounded, not that anyone cared. He shuffled along the first day with a guide, a decent sort, who walked him from the chapel to the dining hall, from one large classroom to another, back to the dining hall, then left him in the evening at the lavatory with its indoor toilets and exposed urinals. Lads shouted and brushed past him. Like the new home, the sinks had hot and cold water taps. Next door was a room of bathtubs. After a bit of a search, he found his original room with his unopened trunk and wary occupant.

The numbing ordeal was repeated for days without an escort. George was forever in long, turning halls, passing anonymous doors. Lights shone through transom windows up high. His vision better, he still had enough of a tinge under his eye that fellows gave him a second look or a smirk. Not that he wanted to be noticed. Keep walking, gaze down, follow the brown shoes. Until the ranks thinned and he didn't know where he was. One classroom was absurdly far from the last. He found it well after the bell, and had to master his frustration before entering and admitting, "I'm sorry, I got lost."

The master said, "'Oi-oi-loose'—what? Have you got something in your mouth?"

Everyone laughed. The master said, "Come in, creature. You're a good deal behind. I don't know why you were admitted so late."

Warm-faced, George sidled to an empty desk, all eyes on him. If only there were lassies here to smile a welcome.

After dining hall, lads rushed to check the afternoon post. His assigned cubbyhole held a gift already, a long letter from Margie forwarded from the new address in London. George forgave her the black eye and escaped outside with a torch. His socks fell as he ran, exposed legs seared and pinged with sleet. The building behind him echoed with activity. He shielded the precious pages.

Margie's letter was on delicate sheets of blue. Sleet marked it like tears. Her handwriting was bad, but she spoke with the voice of home. *How could Uncle Gerren do such a thing? Does he not love his family? The sea was rough today. I'd best get over and feed Cloud, as promised.*

George resented her doing what had always been his favorite chore and clutched the letter from his wild-haired cousin, the only nourishment for his heart.

Back indoors, his legs burned, cold as marble to the touch. No sense entering the dining hall late, though his stomach growled in protest. Better to use the quiet to find his room again.

His bed was a mattress atop a set of drawers. There were more drawers and shelves taken over by the other occupant, who was well stocked on his side of the room. Each boy had a small desk and chair.

With the hiss of heat coming in, George shed his blazer and stretched on the bed to write his cousin before the dining hour ended. During a pleading letter to Mum, his roommate entered, a grim, freckled lad, who announced, "You weren't at tea. Everyone saw."

"I weren't hungry."

"'Hoon-gray.' You talk funny. You'll get in trouble."

The lad hovered by the open trunk. "Aren't you going to unpack? I say, what's this? You ought to display it. It's ripping."

It was a model of an old pilchard fishing vessel given him by Uncle Dan. The lad leapt with it, the boat bobbling in his grasp.

George threw down his pen. "Don't scat 'un, will 'ee!"

"What?"

There was a rap on the door. The lad flew to his bed, stashed the boat under covers, whispered, "Barlow. You're in trouble."

Schoolmaster Barlow opened the door. "Carveth? Come with me, please."

His model boat was on the wrong side of the room. *Loony wanker taking personal property.* George slid from the bed, his murderous gaze lowered for the master.

He softened his footsteps in the hall, especially as other nosy knobs cracked their doors to watch. His scalp prickled. No cap!

Down a stairwell, the air got colder. George had forgot his blazer, as well. He was shown to an office and sat in one of two chairs facing a desk. Barlow squeezed round the desk to sit. He was a baldy fellow who peered over black-rimmed spectacles.

"You weren't at the dining hall, Carveth. Are you ill?"

"No, sir. I weren't hungry." He tried to say it clearly. An electric fire glowed in the corner, too far for the gooseflesh on his legs.

Barlow sighed. "'I *wasn't* hungry.' Whether you were or not is beside the point. When the bell rings for meals, you attend unless you are dying. Think you're some sort of pugilist then?"

"Sir?"

"More likely set upon, I'd wager. You do not get to choose your own rules here, Carveth. I understand you're the new boy, Kettering's boy. I'm sure his lordship meant well, but this is a prestigious school, and we don't care for little Cornish lads who choose to hide out in their rooms. You're a dark boy—are you Irish or Welsh?"

George was in his light stage, what with winter. "Er, a bit of Irish, so Dad says, and Indian. Mum's mother, she were from India, a place in the mountains, Darjeeling," he said it slowly, "like the tea."

He was about to add the Tibetan part, except Barlow gawped in a way that stopped him. That reminded him of being thought "black." He tried a smile. Grandy said he had a smile to melt an angry heart.

It didn't appear to be working. The glow faded from the bars of the fire. The cold clutched his legs like hands.

George looked down. "I never met her orn account of she died. When Mum was a girl. I weren't born."

Barlow's pen scratched paper. "Are you hungry, boy?"

"I am, sir."

"Too bad. Now go to your room. Next time you break our rules, I will send you to the headmaster."

HIS MODEL BOAT had a part broken off. His roommate claimed, "You didn't use the right glue."

On the other hand, a sixth-former acting as the house prefect came to check on George and ordered his roommate to "make space this instant." He told George he'd best serve an older lad, though everyone was probably paired up this late in the season.

George didn't intend to serve anyone. He wouldn't be here long enough. He awaited his mother. She'd have to fetch him after his letter about the broken boat.

He was summoned after classes to the headmaster's office and made to sit outside. Mr. Barlow's voice piped within. "Set a new precedent? We don't allow colored boys."

The headmaster's response was muffled.

"Yes, his mother," Barlow added. "Darjeeling."

They wanted to send him home!

The headmaster said, "He's here? Send him away at once."

The pink-faced assistant appeared. "Go on. Go back to your room."

"Shall I pack?"

The man frowned and pivoted back to the office.

George wrestled his trunk from the cupboard even though his roommate complained. The lad shut it when George said where he was going.

Soon the headmaster approached him in the hall between classes. (Here was news, at last.) "How are you getting on, son?"

George answered, "Well enough, sir."

"Fine. That's fine." The man clapped his shoulder and moved on.

A letter came from Mum with no mention of fetching him. She said he sounded dramatic. Quills pricked his heart. Each letter from his parents was a punch in the stomach. His own parents had become strange to him. Alone in the lav, he snapped at his image in the glass, "You're the dramatic one." Then he mimicked his mum's film star glower, trying to raise one eyebrow.

His roommate said, "You're not going anywhere. I asked at the office."

George kicked his trunk, killing his toes. He threw out its contents and forced the cumbersome thing back in the cupboard.

An irksome word, "colored." He only had dark blood. He noticed lads noticing him, which stopped his urge to greet them.

On 4 March, he turned eleven. His parents sent him an apple cake and a card promising gifts the next time he was home. The prefect came to his room and ate large chunk of the cake, as did George, and declared George's roommate oughtn't to have any. The prefect mentioned pairing up again. George said he'd spent enough time serving Timmy, meaning his cousin. The older lad misunderstood. "Ah, Lydcote? We only use surnames here, Carveth." When he left, George gave his dour-faced roommate the last piece of cake.

Margie's next missive arrived with handwriting etched into the paper. She demanded her mum send her to his school.

His eyes smarted. Being in an all-boys school hardly mattered to that daft girl. His multi-page response was hard to fit in the envelope.

Sport was played on Wednesdays. A team leader chose him, but when the ball came his way, George botched the play.

Lads taunted, "Hey, Carrr-veth! Talk for us, Carrr-veth." This was followed by lunatic gibberish meant to sound like him, supposedly. Someone said, "Call him 'Corny,'" and the gang agreed it was perfect.

The shock of arrival had blasted music from his head. Now lovely tunes seeped back, memorable refrains, danceable bridges. Perhaps it was kid-like to want to dance. Grandy had said he'd grow out of it.

Yet George felt his body had sprouted wings he couldn't try out. There was so much inside him to express.

In a rare moment of privacy, he thumped in his room alone. The commotion in the hall ceased. He heard whispering.

He leapt onto his bed, frozen. A burst of laughter sounded behind the door. His cheeks flamed.

Seconds later, his roommate entered. "Is there a mouse? Hang on, I'll find it."

George sensed the scrutiny, after. His roommate decided, "You're a bit fey."

He didn't like the sound of that.

He sought the outdoors with its grazing air. The grounds were littered with "mines," black turds from deer, hell to get off one's shoes. A large wood bordered the campus. Mischief-makers roamed, the ones who'd called him Corny. George sped for the forest.

He'd never actually been in a forest before. His heart pulsed in his throat. Did something move? He stared hard at menacing trees. Here lived witches, goblins, wild animals!

You're a bit fey.

Really, 'twas only cluttered like a cupboard. Stay at the edge and keep the school in view. Would Fred Astaire be this soft?

George tried out dance moves, soon shucking the blazer. His socks puddled his ankles. He whirled with amazing skill and danced until his shirt went damp and the skin was scraped on his palms from bouncing off trees. A witch's shriek chased him out.

Or was it a bird cry? He darted back for his blazer. His mad, running feet tramped lumps that weren't grass.

It felt worth the cold that followed, and going to see Matron, one of the few women, who smiled over specs, a thermometer in hand.

"Master Carveth. What a pair of tea-brown peepers on you, lad. I'll bet you get away with the dickens."

"I don't get away with nothin'—anythin', missus."

She stuck the thermometer in his gob. "Then you must have good parents."

That was hardly true.

~

FOR SOME REASON, Mr. Barlow transferred George from the class of one schoolmaster to another. Since he left the one who'd called him a creature, he was glad of the change. The new man didn't whinge on about how much work he'd already missed, and wasn't going line-by-line over boring *Henry V*. Instead, George was given a shocking text to read on the weekend, *Lord of the Flies*. He read enough to not entirely fear a Monday discussion.

Rowdy lads were quick to undo the lesson. Kids at home were never so cheeky to adults. Schoolmaster Wilburn put his head in his hands as the students filed out. George couldn't help pangs of sympathy. Grandy used to say, "Do a kindness, if ever there's a soul in need."

"I thought your lesson was good today, sir."

Mr. Wilburn looked up, eyes pale and surprised behind amber-rimmed specs. He had prominent cheekbones, and untidy strands of hair plucked loose from its oiled-back style.

George said, "Some of them boys on the island really tried. Like you said, Human Nature were—was—against them. I could see some of the boys in this class bein' like them wild ones, the ones that kill."

"'That kell,'" Mr. Wilburn echoed, "And you would be Ralph."

"Oh, I—Sorry, sir." He started, but the man put a hand out.

"Decent Ralph, trying to make things right. I hear so few regional accents in my classroom. You are the latecomer. What is your first name, lad?"

"George, sir."

Mr. Wilburn smiled saying the name. "How... very..."

George didn't know whether to smile. "What, sir?"

The man laughed. "Very-very—forgive me. I heard about your situation. It won't be easy, you know, in this bastion of privilege. Is that a southwestern accent you have? Lovely country. You must have been sad to leave it."

Tears shot in. Did Mr. Wilburn know his seaside home? Could they talk about it? The master rose.

"My kindhearted fellow, perhaps you'll join me for the lunch break? We'll quit this rabble. You must tell me all about yourself."

GEORGE CHATTERED LIKE A LITTLE ONE:

"Aunt Sally would play the piano after dinner, or I would climb orn the ridge—my lamb Cloud would be there—she's more a sheep now, lives with Farmer Hale—an' I would do shows for me cousins. 'Fred Astaire,' they called me that."

Mr. Wilburn *had* been to St. Ives, once, on holiday, and declared George part mountain goat to live there. George circled the confines on his toes, so pleased to be with a friendly adult again. It had been a long trek out to this farthest building. The man's digs were above an old milking shed. Sadly, the school had got rid of its cows. In a display of lavishness, Mr. Wilburn not only started the gas heat but plugged in an electric fire. For the first time in forever, George felt warm. Like his host, he shed his blazer. His hand brushed the spines of books, a globe on a stand, a framed picture of a house. Mr. Wilburn brought in Spam and butter sandwiches.

George dared to say, "I been working on a new dance. Would 'ee like to see it?"

Mr. Wilburn eased his big body into a creaking rocker. "Did you say 'dance'?"

It was a risky move. Yet this grownup seemed all right. George did his version of a soft-shoe to "Mr. Sandman," a song Mum used to sing him. He sang and danced as if, like Fred Astaire in an early picture, he'd just sprinkled sleepy dust and was gliding over it, tapping lightly, careful to avoid the shaky stand with the globe. He muddled some of the lyrics about his hair being like some Italian word, then sped up the finish to make it big, with a spin and a burst of taps. The globe rattled dangerously. Mr. Wilburn laughed and applauded.

"Delightful. How did your parents ever part with you?"

George would certainly include that quote in his next letter home.

Mr. Wilburn beckoned. "Let me fix your socks."

George sprang forward. "They won't stay up. My legs are fat."

Mr. Wilburn looked surprised. "You have very nice legs." He patted them. "Harder muscles than other lads. Too much, I fear, for these over-laundered socks. You will need sock suspenders as an adult."

Yes, his dad wore them. With a creak of the rocker, Mr. Wilburn went to the kitchenette and cut the string on a box. George alerted at the Victoria Sponge withdrawn from it.

A slice was set before him. His host said, "A superior sponge from a cafe in the village. My indulgence. Go on, lad."

Mr. Wilburn cleaned his specs by window light. "You can carry a tune. You should try out for the choir. Surely, you have a few years before your voice changes. I'm guessing you've had training in dance."

"Went to ballet for a time. I was the only lad. But the family would have rows. Uncle Arthur said I'd turn into a swan."

"The short-sightedness of some people."

"Oh no. Uncle Arthur doesn't wear specs."

Smiling, Mr. Wilburn opened a case that turned out to be—! "Do you mind if I listen to music? I find it calms me during the break."

George could scarcely contain his joy at the gramophone. "What… what do you listen to?"

"Then you like music? I thought as much. I prefer the classics."

"Do you have the C Minor Concerto?"

"Rachmaninoff? I do, indeed." The man shook his head. "Splendid."

Mr. Wilburn was careful with the needle on the record, then settled with tobacco and a pipe.

The piece started with a middle C chord, played in a minor key, an afternoon with Aunt Sally at the piano had taught him that much. "Oh, thank you," he said at building chords.

The relief of it! And minor keys were unfinished business, they left one wanting more, the "page-turner notes," Aunt Sally had called them—that he'd written in his essay. Sounds swept him off. He closed his eyes, his brain recording notes for use in the forest.

By the end of the first movement he rocked in a sea of bliss, even as he knew Mr. Wilburn watched him. The tobacco scent had waned. Movement Two gathered, an impending sun shower. He admitted, "I dance in the forest."

"Good Lord. Is that your favorite thing to do?" He heard the man's surprise.

"Here it is. At home, I dance without clothes by the sea."

"Lord…" Mr. Wilburn echoed.

The melancholy of the second movement jabbed his heart. George missed his father. They'd be swimming back home, even in the cold, building up their heart and lungs. Should he write about hearing this piece? Dad would want to know he'd met a music lover. But then his parents might think he'd forgiven them when he hadn't at all. He'd never forget what they'd done to him. It was hard not to rage about it still. He looked at his shoes to staunch the feelings. He mustn't go off in front of his new friend. How kind Mr. Wilburn was. He hadn't shot up with "Get back to your rooms," as George half expected, but slouched angular in the rocker, listening with a thoughtful look, hairs loose on his forehead.

Sometime later, the needle slid to the center of the record and bounced. Mr. Wilburn reached to stop it. Rare sunlight speared the window. His specs flashed as he leaned forward.

"Remarkable. I've never known a child to stay silent through a piece of music. Where did you come from, George Carveth? No need to answer. Rather a comic name for an angel. Forgive my nonsense."

There was a trace of scent—cloves, was it? George leaned, too.

"There's much I should tell you. Don't let the older lads push you into slavery. It's not allowed. The headmaster frowns on the practice. You'll want to avoid Schoolmaster Bing, known as 'the paddler'—you can guess why. I so hate to end our fun. What is your next class?"

"It's PE. Only PE."

"I haven't got a next period."

Both grinned at the same time. Dare he miss a class? What an outrageous thought. Mr. Wilburn knelt. His warm hands enclosed George's hands. His eyes were mossy green.

"You can dance here, anytime, I shouldn't mind at all. You can even dance without clothes."

George hooted. "How bollocks! Sorry, sir." He was horrified by the word slip.

"Why do you like dancing without clothes?"

Everything felt hilarious all of a sudden.

The master shook him. "*Tell* me, batty kid." Yet his face was kindness. His breath pelted tobacco.

Only mad people laughed so. George shuddered to control himself. He shut his eyes to think.

"It feels free, I guess. Like I'm an animal in nature."

An arm squeeze startled him. Mr. Wilburn grinned. "But you are. Why don't you? To the third movement. I'd like to see this animal."

Mr. Wilburn went to the gramophone. George blanched. Why had he confessed dancing starkers? "I'd better not."

"Don't be embarrassed, son. We're both males. I've already seen how well you dance. I'll start the record, shall I?"

"Can I dance like this?"

"Looking like a schoolboy? Is that worthy of the music?"

He understood at once. It felt a slap.

Mr. Wilburn persisted. "You are an artist. You don't trust me."

"I do." George had never been called an artist before.

"Artists don't think. They act. I sense greatness in you, George. Show me your greatness, not your fear."

I'm not fearful! Yet his heart pounded, his face was on fire. "Fear comes for a reason," Dad said. *What did Dad know?*

The sunlight had faded, the sky pewter with clouds over his missed PE class.

George hitched his sparking jumper over his head, his hair standing up. He tugged loose his tie, worked off his shoes and socks. An old part of him loved shucking his clothes. Yet why did his stomach clench so? It must be like going on a stage. He should be honored. The room couldn't be this warm. He paused with his cotton Y-fronts, bunching the waistband in his fists. Mr. Wilburn averted his eyes.

George pushed off the idiot garment. It was unworthy to dance about like a schoolboy. Mr. Wilburn was right.

Be great. Think of the sea.

On the record, the piano ran up and down like a spray of rain, too maddening for a dance. George's arm caught the strings in what he felt was a very Russian gesture, but still, the piano swirled, crazed. This was useless! He closed his eyes to block out the bookish room and awaited the next melody.

I am a gull catching the updraft.

He leaned when it came, riding it, holding his arms aloft, doing movements from ballet and his own creation. The music crested with gorgeousness, telling its story—possessing him. He sailed like a diving seabird, then banged his thigh and hit the hard floor.

A chair was knocked. Mr. Wilburn loomed over him.

George meant to laugh. But his "hah" trailed out like a sob.

Mr. Wilburn scooped him up as if he weighed nothing. The rocker screeched with their weight. George clamped his mouth to stop a wail. The man pressed him close. And with that firm embrace against a warm adult body, George was seized with the most violent crying that made his gut ache.

Yet it felt good to let go. Hiccups popped like explosions in his chest. The record caught on a skip, repeating notes. Penning George, Mr. Wilburn turned off the gramophone.

George squeaked with burning spasms. His teacher's voice was velvet-soft.

"There now. Hold your breath. Your poor thigh. My God, you were marvelous, right with the music."

He couldn't believe the words. They sunk deep, like "artist."

"I wasn't." He hiccuped, "I fell."

"You're getting a bruise."

"I," he shifted, "dance better at home. I couldn't get it right." He was on something hard. Mr. Wilburn's pipe?

"Be still. Quiet now."

"Aren't I heavy?"

"Of course not. Your body is perfect."

The large hands brushed in a ticklish way. George said, "Don't," and they settled and soothed.

His fit seemed to be passing. The next hiccup never came. He collapsed against Mr. Wilburn's damp neck and clutched his lapel as if it was all right to sit this way with a schoolmaster.

They rocked and said nothing. A clock ticked on the mantle. Shouts from his class were faint in the distance.

His heart brimmed yet Mr. Wilburn's touch eased him. There was the scent, sweet and peppery, that seemed to be coming from the man's hair or cheek. He did not feel cold and hugged the close neck, eyelids heavy. All the while, his body lit to the stroking hand and being so beautifully petted.

He knew what he was sitting on.

George flew off. "I have to go!"

The man's protuberance was obvious. George snatched his school clothes and ran to the loo. His own willy stuck out. His eyes in the glass were large and mad. He splashed cold water on his face.

Mr. Wilburn stood waiting for him, hands clasped in front. "Are you all right? You're not ill or…?"

George mashed his cap over his unruly hair, fringe in his eyes, his shirt half out under the jumper. "No, sir."

"I very much enjoyed your dance, young sport. Please don't be—"

"I'd better go."

A clock chimed three with a miniature tune of Big Ben. The simple tones struck him in the heart. The great clock was bonging now, back where his parents were. He could hardly recall that London house, and it seemed he might wail again as if all that misery of before hadn't been enough.

Mr. Wilburn spoke softly. "Off you go."

Snowflakes greeted him like hot points as he walked. They danced in the air and melted on the grass. The tower bell rang late, or perhaps Mr. Wilburn's clock had been fast. George was lightheaded with a relieved-from-crying, faintly sick sensation. Strains of the concerto filled his head. Yet shame burned his cheeks. Only babies cried like that… and to take off his clothes! George nearly ran—and with his lit master no less! He kept his eyes on his moving feet, walked faster along the path to get away from the feelings, that knob of a grown man's—

SLAMMED.

He was banged flat on the grass, his second fall in less then an hour. His nose hurt, books gone, mind awhirl.

"Watch out, Corny, you twit!"

George blinked at the swirl in his eyes. His thick eyelashes caught the flakes like stars on the edge of his vision. The grass was wet-cold. He detected clusters of boys, curious, stopping to see. Perhaps he would become The Boy Who Lay on His Back. His schoolmasters would have to come out here to teach class.

A ruckus sounded. A "V" of geese passed noisily overhead like chattering relatives. He followed their movement and saw them sail down. An upside-down Mr. Wilburn came running. George got up immediately, and gathered his books that were everywhere.

The man said, "Are you all right?" then clapped his hands. "Move along, lads. Clear off now."

The boys were slow dispersing. "Don't you have studying to do?" he added, glaring at George.

George fled and didn't stop until he reached a twisted old tree on the north end of the grounds. He let go of his books and hugged a low branch and winced. The nail of his index finger was crusted with blood. The other nails were ragged. When had he resumed that disgusting habit?

He headed to his house trailing a stink on his shoe and scraping the soles on the stairs. His cap was gone, though he dared not go back to search. A letter had come for him. His father's homesickness nearly choked him.

Without the sea, I can't even tell the weather no more. I miss all the color, don't you? The blooms... that bank of honeysuckle at the bottom of the hill.

I heard your aunt Tiff is in Mrs. Sawle's gallery again. Remember the pears? You should write to her. I know they're friends, but it's quite an achievement.

I know we've done the right thing. Though it's hard sometimes. And we miss you so much, chickbird. But there's ever so much to do here, you'll see. Your mother's a different woman. Do well at school, son. You're our smart lad.

MEMORIES DANCED. Mum soaping him in the bath... Squashed in a chair with his back-scratching dad as both read together... How nice to be bare and touched. Why must it stop because he was older?

Only it wasn't the fingers of Mum or a grabby cousin, but a grown man's large hand, that big blackbird of a late-morning teacher. His pinky nail hurt. *Stop chewing.*

The roommate shuffled in and dropped books on a desk. "What ho, Carveth? Daydreaming again, I see."

George lay on his prison bed, his father's letter curled in his hand, the room a cold box even with the hiss of gas heat. Thumps and voices sounded from the neighboring pens.

His roommate wrestled with drawers, then settled on the opposite bed. "Are you going for tea?"

"No."

"Don't you ever get hungry?"

"I had sponge."

"No, we had trifle today."

"I had sponge."

George watched the boy ponder how that could be possible. There was a whiff of starch from the sheet beneath his cheek. Grandy at home spraying starch and working the mangle…

"You weren't at PE— What did you say?"

"Clever, clever dick."

The boy rose threateningly. "I could tell Barlow, you know."

"Go ahead."

"How did you get that bruise on your leg?"

"I fell into a chair."

"Hah! You are the clumsy one."

George sprang from the bed, fists clenched. "You take that back, or I'll knock your gob in."

"Hah, hah. Steady on, old chap. I take it back."

"I'm a better athlete than most anyone 'ere. You'll all see."

He was in the boy's face, quaking to hit him. The boy knew it, his freckles standing out more.

George said, "You ask too many bloody questions."

His roommate edged along. "We're not supposed to say 'bloody.'"

"Bloody, bloody, booger and puss!"

The boy grappled for the door and fled. George laughed out the doorway. Then scowled at staring faces in the hall.

He darted back in, slammed the door, and collapsed on the bed, bracing for the knock of the prefect to go "See here" and write him up for door slamming.

IT WAS FINALLY HERE! His half-eleven with Mr. Wilburn! George got out his *Lord of the Flies* text and waited for eye contact, a familiar word. After all, he and Mr. Wilburn were mates. In a way. Had their time meant friendship? What an odd time it was. *He saw me without clothes.* Could an adult and child even be friends? The man looked right at him. George flinched and stopped a giggle by leaning his mouth on his hand. Too many unwanted sounds were coming out of his mouth.

The schoolmaster strolled as he taught. George doodled a page in his notebook to appear studious then froze when a shadow hovered. A question was put, then:

"Carveth?"

George took his hand away. "Sir?"

"Well?" The voice was behind him.

His heart banged. "Right, um, sorry?"

Boys snickered.

"Did you read the chapter, Carveth?"

Chapter? He'd forgotten last night's reading entirely. The master strode to the front, saying, "Samuels, what do you think?"

Humiliation surged. The man hated him. The other boys clearly saw him as thick. George tried to look alert yet could scarcely stop the burning in his face. He'd never forgotten a reading before. When class ended, he fled.

He ate quickly during the lunch break then ran outside where the sting in his cheeks changed from internal heat to external cold. Yesterday's snow had thawed. He leapt black bombs but hit slush. Wetness seeped in his shoes. He ought to be in boots. At home in winter, people lived in wellies. He scarcely noticed his raw legs anymore, what with stinging feet. The wood was a blanket of silence but for the sound of dripping. The damp bark was intensely colored, as were the greens. His red fingers reached to touch. He settled on a log, and he recalled the shock of Mr. Wilburn's "stiffy."

Of course, that happened with males. He'd had a few and had joked about it with his cousins; their erections were small in comparison. Not like the hump he'd been sitting on, that grew in his imagination. And George had seen enough displays in the animal world to know what that stiffness was a prelude to. Not that a grown man would mount a little boy! The idea was preposterous. In a way, he'd almost rather be sitting on the hump than be so alone. Would Mr. Wilburn warm his toes?

In the days that followed his lit master scarcely paid him attention. George fantasized telling him in a grownup voice that he was "otherwise engaged." Yes, they'd shared a love of music, but he was no baby, he didn't sit on people's laps. He made his own way, minded his own business.

He used to crave privacy at home, fleeing his cousins to hide amidst sheep or to dream on a lonely bluff. Here, he couldn't stop his mind from worrying and jumping. His mind seemed to dance when his limbs could not.

Tall and hawkish, Mr. Wilburn kept to himself in the dining hall, shunning the pots of tea, choosing black coffee and reading his modern books. Other masters laughed in a group, cups clinking on saucers, their looks sidelong. No one approached the lit master. The headmaster greeted him once. Mr. Wilburn seemed awfully glad of the interruption. Tears sprang to George's eyes and he smiled at the headmaster, though the man didn't see.

Some blighter was always gawping at George. George wiped his face to make sure nothing was growing out of it. If anyone spoke to him, they did so covertly. He was still called "the late boy," and that was the kindest name. Evenings, upperclassmen prowled the halls with young ones in tow. One of the leaders stopped dead, stared at him and called. He escaped through a clot of students. His age group tended to be the followers, acting proud of it. Yet he'd seen them frantically washing socks or stealing cakes for their "owners." He was only too glad to not be a part of that nonsense, to be free.

"How are you, sir?"

It was the end of lit class one week later. George stood warm-faced before his teacher, a link, a representative of his goodhearted fellows. If his fellows had been that way. He fully expected Mr. Wilburn to scoff. But he said, "Hallo, George."

Tears were stupidly near at the sound of his name said so kindly, the "G's" softened just a bit, the timbre of the voice matching the look of the hazel eyes behind specs.

"Good lesson today, sir. Well, I'll be off."

"It didn't look as if you were paying attention."

George slowed. "Oh, no, I was… I was having deep thoughts."

The man's face was too kind to bear. Mr. Wilburn shuffled papers. "Are you free to join me for the lunch break? I'll play music. No need for you to dance."

He couldn't imagine doing a dance. Back in the faraway flat, with the gas heat on, the electric fire aglow, George sat in a chair while Mr. Wilburn sat in his rocker, two music-lovers relishing what many people ignored. He kept closing his eyes to keep back the joy. Rachmaninoff again—how the piece moved him. And how warm in here.

The *adagio* started. Mr. Wilburn beckoned. George slid from his chair and crept, his gaze on the wood floor. The rocker creaked. A spicy scent wafted. The request was whispered.

"Wouldn't it be better if you took off your clothes?"

George hiccuped. He veered door-ward and knew a part of himself ran. A different lad wrenched off his sweater and tie and fumbled through the jitters that jumped his hands and stuck the zipper of his knee pants. What a muddle having clothes. Soon he would feel the big hands.

Mr. Wilburn scarcely waited for him to shuck his underwear, dragged him onto his lap and moaned as if it was all too much for him as well. George's circuits came alive, his exposed skin sang beneath hot-palmed caresses. He pressed his face in the man's scented collar. Mr. Wilburn handled everywhere he shouldn't. The kisses were like suctions on his neck that bent back his head. *He was going to be eaten.* His own voice made sounds, whimpering. His bum cheek hurt. Mr. Wilburn squeezed it too hard. He carried George across the room, threw him on the bed and kissed down the front of his body. Feelings boiled and raced to his privates. Then Mr. Wilburn put his *mouth* on him, and sucked him completely in. It was lovely. George almost couldn't stand it. Something bad— He was dying! Feelings surged. A cry shot out of him.

Mr. Wilburn clapped a hand over his mouth. "Stay. I'll be back," The man spoke as if he were alive.

But... he was alive.

Cold air filled the room. What had happened? His body had come loose like butter in the pan. A tiny spider scurried up the wall.

Mr. Wilburn returned from the loo and coughed. "Righto, then? You can't sleep, lad. You've afternoon classes."

He hauled George to a sitting position, eyes agleam behind the amber specs. Green and worried they looked, reddish points of beard on his cheek, mouth twitched into a smile. Tobacco fingers skimmed George's hair.

"Come on, son. You must dress."

His garments were scattered. George was amazed his body worked, that it moved without help. Not even an hour had passed. Afternoon classes sounded impossible.

MOONLIGHT LIT THE ROOM. His roommate buzzed with snores as George tossed with memory, falling inward to grabbing hands, a kissing mouth, then waking, pajamas twisted. His penis that used to be pretty was dark and hard, obscenely piercing the front of his trousers. The only relief was imagining Mr. Wilburn's mouth on him. He'd survived something huge today, something dangerous.

"CARVETH. A WORD, PLEASE."

His schoolmaster sounded severe. Was there to be a punishment? What happened yesterday ought never to have happened.

It played over George like a movie on the skin. It stole his attention, homework barely completed, masters disgusted by the lame effort. He knew Mr. Wilburn wouldn't harm him. It was only kisses the man had given him, hugs and kisses. Yes, George was new, and no one liked him. But a grownup had loved him. Why settle for a haughty fifth-former when he had a master?

When the last pupil filed out, Mr. Wilburn shut the door and returned to his desk. "Come here, child."

George stood, though his legs were jelly and his heart wanted out.

Mr. Wilburn indicated "Right here."

Surely, he'd crept close enough.

Mr. Wilburn seized him. George cried out.

"Hush, dear thing! Hush..." Kisses mauled him this way and that. Hot breath pelted his ear. "Barely got through the class... what a gift you are, a gift."

Tentacles... suction kisses... How many arms did the man have? George dropped beneath the embrace, crawled along the floor, found his legs and ran.

THREE

"Teach Me Tonight"

(GENE DEPAUL & SAMMY CAHN, 1953)

GRANDY MORWEN WINKED AT HIM. "It's trouble you'll have with that face, I fear. Especially with the ladies."

The adults laughed. Margie huffed and dragged George from the main room. "See what I mean?" Grandy said to more laughter behind them.

Who could figure adults? It was great to be in his cousin's grip again, not that he'd tell her. There was still that awkwardness.

There'd been awkwardness at home with his parents. Luckily, the trip to St. Ives had been the focus. He'd had to endure their sloppy emotions and steel himself not to cry or pull away. Their surprise at his reserve had been gratifying, with Mum saying rather sadly, "My, what a grown-up eleven you are." Hard, too, to resist Dad wooing him with music, showing off the blanket meant to cushion the gramophone from the rumbling trains.

They hadn't liked his grades, with Mum calling it "the shock of first term."

Dad expected better. "Lord Kettering used his good name to get you into that school. You're not a boy of means. You must try harder."

Dad was hardly a man of means.

Soon after fetching George from school, it was back to trains they went, lugging suitcases. Instead of the Junction, they walked through the park of Clapham Common and took the underground. George was thrilled, alarmed, as they descended. How could one go so far beneath the city? Beneath the *river!* His parents hastened him to the subterranean train. How did the tube not crack or spring a leak from all the weight? Other people didn't appear to be bothered. The noisy ride was soon over. Instead of surfacing, they walked tiled halls and switched to another line, the Bakerloo Line. The cars thundered and rocked. Lights blinked on and off as they barreled along. Impassive strangers rode and exited. Dad showed their journey on an overhead map. George was glad to emerge at Paddington Station, and irked when he realized he'd missed the entire city in the process. Yet the sooty, outdoor air was welcome. The great train at ground level, with its look-at-me whistle, was ready to crank westward. The right direction. He brimmed with joy.

With a fine sea breeze on the ridge, the large stone house was bedecked with flowers. The cat skittered along the fence, tail up in recognition. Uncle Arthur frowned at the front door. "No London visitors allowed. Except for this one."

George was pulled inside. Aunties fell on him with kisses. Grandy was there, murmuring, "Jory." His parents were dragged in, also set upon. Young ones squirmed below. Margie hovered, grinning. They were given tea and cake.

Grandy Morwen declared George more handsome though he looked exactly the same. He blinked to see the fresh flowers on the piano, the old photos crowding the mantle, the gull statue on the sideboard. A new fisherman's net was draped on the wall beyond. Aunt Tiffany's pear painting held a central spot. Otherwise, it was the haven he knew, with its sea views and the whole group talking at once. Certain cousins weren't there. Margie said they were waiting.

George used the outdoor lavatory. How quickly he'd gotten used to the luxuries of indoor plumbing. Thank goodness for the clearing breeze and the trellis of roses. Sheep called from the farmer's pen. He rushed to greet Cloud and her sisters and breathed in their mucky wool. Reassuring, the fug of animals. Margie's patience was at an end. She tugged the shirt from his waistband.

He followed her gingham figure. Even her frock was dear, as was the strong body within, now with bumps in front. That thought stirred the crux of his trousers, even as he laughed at the thought of Margie as a woman. (Stop trying to see her bum through the fabric.) Beyond, the vibrant sea was emerald, starred with sunlight. Butterfly bushes spilled cones of violet blossoms. Butterflies danced away as the two cousins followed the granite wall. Flocks of gulls sang incessantly.

Margie assessed the crowd on Porthmeor Beach, her hair fanning in the breeze like its own unique flower.

"Typical summer madness. We're off to Lelant. I've a suit for you. I 'spose you forgot how to swim."

"Not likely."

He raced her through steep, winding streets past the old school-house, innocent and small, where once he'd been "a smart lad," and into the town with its meandering tourists. Margie panted to keep up, saying, "You're quick now."

They ran to the train station he'd come from. After huge Clapham Junction it seemed a toy station with its one short train that went back and forth. They rode the cliff-side trip to neighboring Carbis Bay, also crowded, and wended down to the near-deserted beach at Lelant. His other cousins splashed in the surf. One beachcomber was tiny in the distance.

George shucked his clothes and donned one of Timmy's old trunks. "There's no one about," he said in protest of the garment.

"Mum said we must. They can see us from the train."

"We can wave at 'em with our willies," shouted Cousin Ethan, gripping his own small handful. The lads hailed George from the water.

He ran through easy waves, glad to be doused and held. A seal in its home. He nearly swam out of the annoying trunks. Surprisingly, it was a struggle keeping up with the others. His swimming had got weak from starting so late in the season. He stayed a long time in the water, determined to get strong again, and finally staggered out to his squinting Marge.

"You're in need of the sun, boy. I'm darker than you."

Her limbs were honey gold and sparkling. Conical tits budded beneath her suit.

He flopped on his stomach before the stiffness came.

She rolled close. "D'ye like me bubbies? I've some hair, as well."

Younger sister Irene huffed nearby. "Margie thinks she can boss everyone because she has bubbies."

George smiled through his discomfort. "Reenie, t'aint bubbies doin' it."

Irene crawled in. "Timmy has a big willy now. He'll show you for a penny. He shows it to a fisherman for half a crown."

George blanched. Then gawked at his older cousin bodysurfing the waves. "Does he have to do anything?"

Margie said, "Nah. He just whips it out for a big Norwegian. No one we know."

That evening, with the grownups laughing and getting tight, Margie pulled him into the dark pantry and pressed her new body against him. He bucked at first. Then gave in to the surprise of her, her butterscotch breath and beachy hair. He even let her kiss him, though she just passed her candy into his mouth.

"Tomorrow," she whispered, "let them go to Lelant. We'll bike to the inlet."

THEY SWAM naked at the inlet, going beyond the breakers, where they assessed each other in the cool depths...then surfaced in time to see bratty children stealing their clothes. Margie roared out of the waves threatening the removal of limbs. Their clothes were dropped on the rocks. George negotiated the dicey retrieval. With garments secured, the two cousins moved to sunbathe on a grass shelf.

Margie's body had certainly changed. He'd never wanted to gawk at her before. She grinned, noticing. He asked her to put her mouth on him, and she hooted. "You're disgusting! I shouldn't even be with you, a younger lad."

"Why are you, then?"

She cut him a side look. "Don't know."

Was she going to ignore him now? It was just as well. Whenever that ticklish, swoony feeling came on strong—the kind that might pitch him over a cliff—he stopped it.

She said, "'Course, I don't know why you're with me. I'm such a lump."

He turned. "Not hardly."

"Really? Thanks."

Both shut their eyes to the searing sun. Its power weighted him with drowsiness. Though he heard the faintest whisper:

"So lovely, Jory. Do you even know? Not like other lads…"

He squinted her into focus. "What do you mean I'm not like other lads?"

She scrambled to her feet. "Quit listening to private thoughts. Grow up!"

"Why are you bein' a cow?"

She threatened a punch, then marched away. He sprang for her. She came down with a thump. They rolled like snarling cats amidst the dirt and grass, their bodies finding the sharp edges of rocks. She shuddered in his arms, laughing now. They both were, vibrating with it. The swoony feelings rushed up. Both let go.

That evening, George felt unsettled. Naughty games made everything a muddle. It was naughty what they'd done, just like at school. His stomach clenched. He oughtn't to spend so much of his holiday with her. With a shock, the bedroom looking glass showed a changed boy. His all-over burnt butter hue and dark tousle of hair, his honey-gold eyes rimmed in black lashes. Was this who others saw? Was he a looker now?

Daft! He'd never been one to peer at himself. He ought to be kicking a ball with mates or riding in Uncle Dan's boat. That's what regular lads did. In his shared room with Timmy, George asked if the Norwegian would pay a crown to see both their cocks.

"You're still little," Timmy said with his new low voice. "He wants to see 'em man-sized on a young bloke. He wouldn't pay for yours. Come back in a few years."

George breathed with relief. Timmy raised an arm and showed sparse hair as he reached to click off the light. The darkness soothed. A brine scent wafted through the window.

George dared, "There's a man at school who likes to...to touch. Me." His heart pounded. He wasn't supposed to talk about it.

Timmy's drowsy voice said, "Odd ducks in the world. I've met a few. No one ever tells you. I don't do nothing for free."

George couldn't imagine asking his schoolmaster for money. Perhaps when he was older, with new hair and muscles. Yes, he quite fancied that image. *Pay up.*

HE GREW dark and fit as a seal, spoiled on his grandmother's pies, delirious from Aunt Sally's piano and the happy nights of singing. Urges that might've gone to Margie sent him out of the house to dance, to fling himself with joy. Until his cousins noticed, calling, "Butterfly Boy."

Most afternoons, they joined Timmy for his delivery job, the group of them roving through town, assessing the tourists. Just as the old life felt snug and right again, the summer break was over.

It was another wrenching departure from St. Ives, followed in London by the grim preparations for school. George ranted about that dungeon of snooty kids, mean adults, and stupid rules about everything. Mum was fed up, said it was a hiding he needed. Dad joined him on the train ride north. As the sprawling structure came into view, both were silent.

The taxi idled as George fought for the shocking weight of the trunk, leaving Dad empty-handed. He hauled the giant thing to his assigned house and would not look back. Inside, the sadness hit. He bolted outside, but the cab with his father had gone.

What would the new term bring? The air braced with coolness, some of the trees already dashed with color. A cry like a baby's echoed. The headmaster was in the far garden trying to feed a peacock. The bird skittered from the man, unsure.

George laughed, heartened by the jittery newcomer. He needn't be yellow anymore. He'd had a good summer. He greeted familiar lads in the courtyard. One said hello, another gave a quiet "Carveth."

"It's Corny," a lout shouted. His mate sneered, "We know about you being let in with luck. Piss off, farm boy."

"I don't live on no farm!"

George pivoted, shamed by his accent coming out and the mimics that followed. Lord, he'd have to fight this time, he'd have to fight *someone*.

That evening, he sipped his cocoa at a table with a pudgy lad and the runts in thick specs. Even this lot stared like he didn't belong. Dog's balls! Just let them try and move him.

A voice spoke behind him: "He's colored. Did you know?"

"I didn't know they allowed coloreds here."

"They don't. He shouldn't be here."

"Devilishly pretty, though," said an older voice. "Eyes like a girl. Might make a good slave. Carveth, fetch us a cocoa, would you?"

George didn't move. The mean voice said, "I'd like to push his face in the dirt."

He left. They could pick on someone else. However, as bad luck would have it, those same lads were in the queue for baths that night. George blanched with realization.

An older one called St. Clair stopped his escape. "You can't run out of here buck-naked. See here, Carveth, is that your skin color or are you just tanned?"

A squawk went up at the answer. "Where are your swimsuit marks?"

"He's a liar!"

George took the first tub by the door. The water was cool and cloudy from the last bather. *They're not here. They're nothing to me.* He ripped open a new bar of soap.

St. Clair shouted out the occupant of the adjoining tub. George never washed quicker, then tried to emerge. St. Clair had his arm.

"Why the rush, Brownie? Unless you're coming into my tub?"

The white body vaulted over and perched. The boy jigging his penis as others in the room crowed. George braced for a shove under-water. But the lad whispered, "Has anyone claimed you? Be my slave. I'll be good to you. You'll never have to worry."

St. Clair looked expectant. George inched upright, then dashed. The rotter handled and pinched him.

The next day, in the crowded hall between classes, his cap came off and his hair snagged on something—the hands of Schoolmaster Barlow, as it turned out.

"See here, Mowgli, doesn't your father take you to a barber?"

"He said that? Oh, cripes." Mr. Wilburn turned away and hissed. George thought he heard "Arse."

The big man's tie was askew. His shirt billowed loose from his belt. His eyes flashed concern. "I'm sorry you're subjected to petty bigotries, especially from a—well, never mind. You could use a trim. I have barber scissors. Come, let's wet your head."

George's feet had run for the faraway digs even as his mind lagged. *Wait...don't know...must think.* Now here he was.

Music played low in the room. There was a faint smell of toast. Mr. Wilburn smiled. "I bet you're peckish."

He was given lovely toast with butter and jam. His heart quickened at the neatly made bed in the corner. He wouldn't take anything off. The man suggested George strip to his vest to spare his school shirt. George did so warily and bent over the washbasin. His hair was gently doused. *Feels good. Don't cry.*

Anyone being nice near did him in. Mr. Wilburn was no longer his teacher, and last term had been odd—the bliss and feeling sick. Mad that those feelings should go together.

And yet, under the man's humming, snipping attention, with the wireless lit up on the bookshelf, the BBC's midday program on, and Mr. Wilburn commenting, George forgot the sick part. His barber brushed away damp curls.

"There, that's better. Not that you could ever look ordinary."

Run. George peeked through his lashes at the one inspecting him. His bare knees abutted dark trousers. His shortened breath came out a gasp. The man noticed and drifted behind him. Big hands claimed small shoulders, starting a massage. George's body broke apart.

AS CLUELESS FELLOWS played field games outside, all the backed-up feelings of the past year flushed out of him in a great emptying. A hand muffled his wail, as the moment pulsed on. The man bolted for the loo, after.

Going over the cliff hadn't killed him. Yet he felt split. Surely, his smart-self had fled long ago, even before the entanglement of last term. Who was this one who stayed?

Mr. Wilburn returned, trousers deflated. His big weight punctured the bed. George was trapped in an aroma of peppermint and body odor, long arms closing him in. "Mmm, your skin. If I could, I'd package the stuff. Watch it, monkey."

George wriggled free. "Would 'ee like a dance? I'll do a dance then, shall I?"

"All right, I'll have a dance for that haircut."

George paced the room, mentally scanning his Fred Astaire repertoire, launching into "Putting on the Ritz," using Mr. Wilburn's rolled umbrella in lieu of a walking stick. He felt more himself, dancing. Only it was no good tapping with bare feet. He spied a hat, put it on, and switched to "A Foggy Day." Mr. Wilburn said he looked sexy in just a hat.

George frowned. "Sexy like a girl?" *I'd like to push his face in the dirt.*

"You stand out and they know it, that's the trouble."

He shuddered. "Is that the time? I'd better dress. "

"Drat the clock. Thank you for coming, sport. You're always welcome. I hope you'll come again."

He would never return. Back in his uniform, he tore up to the main building and tried paying attention to afternoon classes, but kept thinking of how Mr. Wilburn had undone him, and the release that went on and on and on. A voice inside him laughed.

He shocked you, and you went off like a firecracker.

George squinted at the chalkboard. This master had tiny hand-writing. He would have to move closer next time. He volunteered a correct answer. No one would view him as thick this year. His schoolfellows yawned.

Back in his new room that looked the same as last year's room, but for being on a different floor, his new roommate said, "How was your day, Carveth?"

"Well, Horace Winston Palmer the third—"

"I told you, call me 'Winnie.'"

"It went like this, Horace Winston Palmer the third…" and George went through an imitation of the vicar, of Barlow, and every teacher he'd encountered, but for Mr. Wilburn, who did not feel mimic-able. He was hyped up, especially as his roommate laughed, and said, "That's him all right, that's cracking. You're awfully funny, Carveth."

Funny! He managed a "Thanks, Winnie," and ran to the lavatory to calm down. His heart was racing. He'd never get through homework. Another dance would do.

He fetched his cap and blazer, and ran to the forest, leaping deer poop, the air searing fresh. An inviting smell wafted. The groundskeeper was burning leaves. The sun's rays slanted low. The wounded cry of the peacock echoed down to the haven of trees. George danced in what he imagined was Hungarian style to the remembered music of "List," a queer name for a composer. He danced until his shirt felt damp. Not a bad day today. He'd made someone laugh. He hadn't died. Hadn't even been in danger.

Bloody silly you were, said the voice in his head.

He barely made supper. A boy in the queue sneered, "You're all sweaty." No one sat close to him. In the baths, St. Clair taunted, though George managed to slip out.

He lay awake in the dark. He would have done his homework by torchlight but for waking Winnie, who was a light sleeper. Winnie had a folded picture under his pillow of a lady in a brassiere. It was comforting to think of a lady in a brassiere bending over him, smelling of powder, tucking him in.

Mumbling started from the other bed. Winnie's dream talk.

At some point, George slipped under.

Then came the doctor fingers. Mr. Wilburn brought skin bags to class. He'd packaged the stuff.

HIS HANDS SHOOK as if he were an old person, usually before the lunch break. It happened no matter what he was doing, even when just offering directions to a lost lad. His pointing hand started a quiver. Trying to eat in the dining hall was a trial what with hiding this new affliction.

He would go to Matron. What if he had an aging disease? Boys would stare as he walked the halls, wrinkles popping out all over him. He'd die early, serving his parents right for sending him away.

Of course, he wasn't going *there* anymore.

Why didn't the absence free him? How could he have imagined being normal here, doing normal activities? Who would crave that nasty business? He'd made himself sick from all the trouble it caused.

He gave in after a week. That doctor knew the problem and the cure. ("Don't resist, child. Your body wants what it wants.")

And there was a sort of relief. Symphonies played on the gramophone. Mr. Wilburn made him surge with that lovely, all-over melt. And stopped running off to the loo. The sessions got scarier. Mr. Wilburn shushed him. "Who knows your body better than I do?" George mustn't make too much of it all, like "an oversensitive girl." Didn't the trembling always stop?

George was grateful leaving the faraway digs, his shaking gone, his gait swerving like he had no balance.

HE SAT IN COLD BATHWATER, the room redolent of moisture and rank bodies. Utterly quiet. Matron peeked in.

"I didn't think anyone was still here. Out, out, love. It's late."

Embarrassed, George came to and pawed for his towel on the rack. Was she watching him? She turned away. He dried himself quickly.

She thwarted his exit, drew him in front of her, "A birth mark?" towel lifted.

George twisted away. How could she look at him?

Her face flushed pink. "How did you get a bite mark?"

An idiot's grin claimed him, even as his body burned like an effigy. It was here, the moment to confess. He hadn't realized there would be a moment, as he hadn't realized the man had left a mark. There was something fierce about Matron. Yet her motherly appearance made him whisper the name.

Her smack staggered him.

"You dare accuse a master, a kindly man? It's filth you've been up to, and with an older lad, no doubt." She balled her fists. "Those rumors are *not* true. Get out of my sight!"

George grabbed his clothes and hid in a toilet stall. The washroom door banged.

He'd grabbed his uniform, not his pajamas, and here it was bedtime. He must've been mad to rat on the one friend he had.

He will punish you. Keep away.

FOUR

"All Shook Up"

(OTIS BLACKWELL & ELVIS PRESLEY, 1957)

GEORGE SHIFTED at his desk while other students read aloud, then popped up at his turn to read aloud, smooth in his pronunciation because he imitated his fellows so perfectly. No one noticed or smirked. It was over too soon. Hard to be caught here when he could be out running and running and running.

The master snapped, "Carveth. Be still and sit properly."

Prickles teemed down his legs like tiny ants. It was hard not to laugh in this dull, dull class. Other kids bored. The blighter beside him was picking his nose.

Don't laugh, don't. Concentrate. But concentration only happened in spurts. Was this how madness started?

"Great scot, boy, shall I send you to Matron?"

George froze as the master scowled over him. "No, sir."

He and Matron had been avoiding each other. It seemed, incredibly, Mr. Wilburn had yet to hear of his betrayal. His stillness held as if the master had turned him to stone.

Afternoon PE, thank God. Crazy, wild! What if he were an American boy? He was mad for Elvis Presley. Elvis songs stayed in his head. Elvis was racy and made lasses swoon.

At least PE was a relief, a place to kick balls or hang upside down from bars. Today, the lads were herded to a lower level. The air grew heavy with a wet scent. There was a huge swimming pool with lanes marked out; George and others whooped at the sight. He knew pools existed but had yet to swim in one. He couldn't believe there'd been a pool here the whole time. That changed everything. It smelled of bleach.

Someone explained about the chlorine. Lads were issued woolen trunks. George could've walked on his hands with glee. A swim well before summer. It was the first of March on the 1958 calendar, three days before his twelfth birthday. He'd been here more than a year.

The shimmering water threw light to the ceiling, the whole room tinged green. Two older students rounded the far end, lifeguards probably, though awfully skinny, the fair-haired one familiar…

Drat, bollocks, crap on a stick. St. Clair smirked with his chum. With a whistle around his neck, he noticed George with a slow spreading grin.

The gym master strode out, hairy-legged, in a dark shirt and shorts, and shouted, "Is anyone going to need these?"

St. Clair and his chum brandished white flotation boards. No one in the class said a word.

"Right. Pair off and show me a race. Swim as far as you can, but don't kill yourselves."

George snorted—that was fine swimming advice.

The older boys moved through the ranks of students, saying, "You, you." St. Clair stopped with a leer. "Humpty and Corny, now there's a match."

"I don't want to be paired with him," Humpty cried—real name Giles—whose white body bulged in the tight trunks.

St. Clair got in his face. "What, Beast? You don't like your Beauty? I think it's inspired."

George flushed, muttered, "Come on," to Giles, and joined the racing queue.

Giles lagged. "But, I don't— Bother! I hate bloody swimming."

How could anyone hate swimming? Why should he be paired with someone so utterly wet? Yet something in the boy's tone alerted him. "D' ye need a board, Giles?"

"Course not."

Hilariously, the first lads across were losing their shorts hoisting out the far end. Even the master laughed. George smiled, but hoped his scratchy trunks would stay on. Giles still looked worried.

The pair ahead of them splashed in and floundered across. Only a few could dive. George had leapt off of rocks at home. Plunging into this tub would be easy. The master made notes on a clipboard. Lads cheered their favorite from the sidelines.

George couldn't imagine himself or Giles getting a cheer. Would the place go silent? He quaked for his chance, legs shivering. He'd beat anyone, even his scrawny nemesis with the whistle, who watched him more than the swimmers.

He likes me. Bad George flickered like a shadow inside him, the fearless one who came out when naughtiness occurred. He looked boldly at St. Clair and muttered, "Wanker," for Giles's benefit. Giles didn't react.

The master cried, "Girls, what's the problem? Let's go!" and blew sharply on his whistle.

George flew forward, piercing the water.

No dive sounded behind him until he was halfway down the pool. It came heavily. He took a breath and flipped back. Sure enough, Giles sank like a sack, eyes popped in fear. Someone plunged in and wrestled the boy, blocking the view with a snow of bubbles.

George burst to the surface, cried, "Board!" St. Clair gaped at him. "Board!" The older boy caught on and threw one in.

George swam the board, then bounced on it to get it below the surface. Giles was climbing the teacher. George thrust him the board. The teacher knocked both boys in a mad rush for air. Giles spun, but floated upward. George flapped up, lungs burning, burst out and gasped. From the side of his vision, he caught the slick white body being hauled out.

He hoisted out the side, grabbed his sliding suit, cried, "Give way," to the crowding students. Giles coughed out water. But pinkness flushed his skin. Panting, George braced his knees with relief.

The master spoke to Giles in a soft, frantic voice, "Are you all right? Thanks be to Christ," then snapped, "Fetch Matron." One of the dry lads ran.

The class was forgotten as Giles was seen to, all students transfixed by the drama. George shivered, too keyed up to grab a towel. One was draped around his shoulders. St. Clair backed away, eyes averted. George gripped the towel in disbelief.

The master in sopping wet clothes nearly deserted the class to follow the ailing boy. But he wheeled back to glare.

"Basic swimming starts tomorrow. There will be no more pretending. That boy is lucky to be alive. Carveth!"

George stiffened. The master softened his tone. "Carveth, quick thinking, lad. Well done. You should sign up for lifeguard training, but not until you're thirteen."

He sneered at the two older ones. "You rotters were useless. Do the world a favor and train for something else. But don't waste my bloody time, you posh kittens."

The older lads wilted. George's mouth fell open in shock. Yet he turned with pangs of sympathy. It was easy to panic in that situation. His dad had told him as much on the beach long ago. St. Clair bolted for the locker room. George moved to follow. "St. Clair?"

The youth whirled, eyes shining. "Big hero. I'll smash you. My dad paid for that pool. You watch out."

THE SPRING BREAK CAME. George wasn't so sure he wanted to return to the rumbling house in the city and the supposedly loving parents. How could Shadow George go, his bad self? *He* didn't belong. Perhaps he'd stay on campus. Some lads always did. He did not join the Friday afternoon departures.

On Saturday, Mr. Wilburn spoke from his shuddering car, ready for his own hometown visit. "They miss you, sport. Go."

He grinned in his jaunty clip-on sunglasses. Greasy strands of hair danced on his forehead. He looked more like a "Willy," as George privately thought of him, though that was partly for the rude connotation. He reached out to stroke, voice quiet: "Just remember you're my boy, too."

Matron faltered coming down the walk. She carried a suitcase. George backed off then headed for his house.

Mr. Wilburn called out, "Hello, Iris. Are you ready?"

George turned to see him load her bag in the boot of his car.

THEY WERE there on Sunday when he rode through to Clapham Junction. His handsome parents scanned the windows, expectant, Dad in a slim-cut suit, Mum in a yellow hat. Unseen, George stepped down to the platform, playing it cool.

Mum cried out. She enveloped him in her gardenia smell. "Lamby. You're getting so tall."

George flinched when Dad grabbed him. Then he clung to his dear father who didn't have a stiffy. Dad squeezed like he didn't want to let go. "Darlin' child."

Mum pulled them apart. "Let me look at you."

Her cat eyes were lined in black like a film actress. Her net gloves cupped his face. "Are you eating enough?"

George said, "I suppose I don't always like the food."

Her eyes widened. "Your posh accent." She looped her arm in his. "Come. We're having our tea out."

There was confusion inside the teashop, an encounter on the way to the table that made his father groan and his mother laugh, saying, "You are very attractive."

Dad was pink in the face as they sat. "Hush. He was smiling at you."

Mum beamed. "It's the price you pay."

"Hush now, the boy."

"Oh, he'll find out soon enough, I can promise you that." She winked at George.

George smiled too, flooded with happiness. "Find out what?"

Dad winced. "Ach, never mind. It's just…" He leaned, and a greasy curl flopped loose, the scent of hair oil so welcome. George was slow to catch his father's words, "…men who like men. It's not natural. It's sick. You steer clear, lad."

George blinked rapidly as if he couldn't stop. He gazed at the table. Mum said in a singsong voice, "My brother, darling."

"Jimmy hasn't found the right woman, that's all."

"He may never find her."

"You don't know that. Here's your tea, son. Anyway, discussion over. It's givin' me the creeps. Whoa, now—"

George coughed on his tea, some spattered his sleeve.

Mum thrust a paper serviette. "Easy, lamb, it's hot. Are you all right? Gerry, he's pale."

"You're tired, son. Are ye feeling poorly?"

"He should see a doctor. His skin is sallow."

George wrenched away from her scratching gloves. "Don't! I'm all right." He glared at his cream bun.

No one said a word. From a radio, Connie Francis sang, "Who's Sorry Now."

Why did I come home? I'm more his than theirs. He recalled that strange pair driving off together. What in the world were *they* up to?

There were sips and clinks of the spoon. Patrons came and went. Dad gathered the untouched buns into the serviette.

"We'll take these home," he said. "We could all use a rest."

HE DISGUSTED HIS FATHER. No surprise there. George looked at the sallow skin of his arm, expecting blackness and rubbed until it made redness. But for supper, he hid under the covers in his chilly bedroom pretending to read but mostly listening to the trains. Their faint rumble was almost like a roaring sea.

Dad knocked. "How many symphonies did Beethoven write?"

George sat up. "Nine, I believe."

"You've heard the Seventh?"

"I think so."

"Oh, you'd know if you heard it. Come."

George didn't entirely want to come, comfy as he was in his socks and dressing gown. But the lure of music was strong. He shoved on slippers and padded down the creaking stairs.

A fancy carpet was laid out in the front room, an item from the Indian grandmother, previously rolled up. Traces of soot lined edges and corners in the room. The chimney sweep had been by. A coal fire snapped in the grate. Mum brought him sweetened tea, drew down the shades, and stroked his cheek on her way out.

Dad handled records by their edges, as Mr. Wilburn did. George steeled himself. Concert music affected him differently now. He was not so easily seduced. And since his parents had purchased a telly, he would prefer to watch that. Everyone knew the better programs were on at night.

Yet the notes piqued his interest. He shifted forward. What started as a pleasing melody gave way to a rollicking dance; he couldn't help swaying. His dad tried not to watch him though he grinned in his chair, the wily devil. It took all of George's effort to stay seated. His younger self would have been cavorting. There was so much to be excited about. Even the bass violins had a solo.

"Bass violins," he mouthed to his father, who nodded.

He sprang from his chair at the finish, but Dad signaled silence. With the opening chord of the second movement, twilight unfolded. George backed to his seat.

The hair rose on his body. Unreleased tears singed his eyes. Even the trains were silent. Like a scalpel slicing him open, this new music played his secrets.

Willy mustn't hear this. And yet his presence haunted the notes as if they were written for him. George gripped the chair arms to stay tethered. A counter-melody danced outside the main theme, dodging

Willy, staying apart. The melody climbed to a higher place, staying out of reach. George rode the melody as it soared, until—oh my God... He was in a bliss state.

George. Go away. *George.*

There was his body below in a plaid dressing gown. Mr. Wilburn couldn't revive him. George liked him less being away from him. He liked being away from him.

"George!"

He came from blackness to his dad shaking him. The music was loud, the room vibrating. Dad's eyes were bright with alarm.

Dad said, "What happened? Your eyes rolled up. I thought you'd fainted."

"I...was just...inside the music." The symphony sounded off as if the notes had rearranged themselves.

Dad cupped his face. "Oh, love. Is it hard for you there?"

Tears shot in. "It's, ah, better...than it was." Was he back, this protective, seaside father who made everything all right?

Dad's eyes were cow soft. "I went through my own hard times as a lad. I know how rough it can be. Is anyone hurting you?"

George laughed; it came out a mess of snot and tears. He mopped his nose in embarrassment. Shadow George panicked. *Don't sicken him. He doesn't want to know. It would give him the creeps.*

"Some blighters..."

Dad offered a hankie. "Sprite. You've always had a sensitive way. Some will see it as soft. Show them you're not. And if it's too much, tell a master, or talk to the headmaster. He seemed a decent sort."

George hooted. Dad rightfully smothered him against a warm woolen shoulder, his hand on the back of George's head. Mum's voice sounded frantic behind them.

Dad said, "I've got it, Lucy. We're okay now." A cool kiss on the forehead. "Life is a hard business. But know you are loved, son."

He wouldn't love me, said Shadow George.

· · ·

GEORGE FELT off in the morning as if he'd been whacked in the head. Mum made him Bubble-and-Squeak. But the eggy pile and glistening bangers made him queasy. She allowed him to creep back to bed, where he slept for another two hours.

His second awakening was gentle. A memory stole in sweetly like the light in his room: he was with his parents.

In the afternoon he and Mum walked to a doctor's office in town. The day was cold and squintingly bright. He held his cap at the wind gusts. A lady's hat spiraled into the street. Hemlines billowed, and flashed another lady's suspenders. His mother was fortified in a straight skirt, black hair knotted under a headscarf. She'd provided him with long trousers for their outing, clearly forgetting his raw legs in shorts had made it through most of the winter.

The elderly doctor was all smiles for Mrs. Carveth. He called her "flushed and windswept."

She thrust George in front. "I've come for my son."

Her mention of his breakdown with Dad sounded worse than it was. The frowning doctor sent her off so he and George could have a manly chat.

The man asked about studies and meals, as he listened to and peered at George's person, and mused about "secret ceremonies among schoolboys." Shadow George sniffed something amiss, which seemed confirmed when the codger asked how things were "in the John Thomas area." "You can tell me, lad. I won't be shocked. Things are going on there—"

You're not kidding.

"You may enjoy, well, handling yourself, as it were."

Or someone else might.

"Do you think about girls, Carveth?"

It was hard not to laugh with Shadow George there. "Sometimes. There aren't many about. I've seen a few pictures of film star ladies." And he flashed on the memory of suspenders seen earlier.

As if reading his mind, the doctor said, "Indeed. They get you riled up. It happens, it happens. You've a few years yet before you succumb. That's the advantage of a boarding school, trust me."

Afterwards, they cut across the common where all was green and rustling. Mum said, "Pressure and puberty, that's what he told me."

"He asked me about my John Thomas."

"Did he? Well. He's a doctor. Would you like ice cream?"

"Nah."

"I'm buying one anyway. You need the fat. What else did he tell you?"

George had to mimic the old doctor, making her laugh. Soon, they were licking cornets and off serious subjects and approaching the old Victorian bandstand, a circular structure of cast iron.

Mum hailed a dark-skinned woman on a bench, who blurted, "Lucy, is this your handsome son?"

How queer that his mum should know such a dark person. The slight musical quality in his mother's accent was exaggerated in this round-faced woman. Mum made him do his doctor imitation again. He improvised a bit, what with having an audience.

The woman's laugh was hearty. She said, "Oh my God, you could be on 'The Goon Show.' He could be on 'The Goon Show,' Lucy."

As the ladies chatted, George ran to the bandstand, snatched up a stick from the ground for a conductor's baton, and pictured a brass band in uniforms with shiny buttons. The back of his neck prickled. A stranger passed beyond the pillars, a man in a gray hat who smiled. Embarrassed, George tossed the stick, ignoring a quiet "Hey there," and whistle, exiting rapidly, slowing as he approached Mum.

He flopped beside her on the bench. Gray Hat lingered near the bandstand. He had a camera. Perhaps he'd only wanted a photo.

Mum said, "Sorry, girl, we must go. I don't like the look of that staring fellow."

"Up to no good, is he? He wants to take your photo, Lucy."

The man approached and lifted his hat. "Hello. Might I take your picture?"

"What did I tell you?" hissed the woman.

"Your son is arresting, as you are, madam. I would be honored—"

"I think not." Mum snagged George's hand and jerked him past the man. The man raised his camera. Shadow George fancied a photo. Didn't he look smart in his cap?

Mum said, "Don't look at him."

"He's following. I think he snapped our photo."

"We'll find a copper."

"No, wait. He's heading for the south side."

They stopped to watch the man walk away.

She huffed and pulled him along. But George was too old to be holding her hand and yanked it free. "How can he call me 'arresting'? How can I arrest him? That's stupid."

"Never trust a man with a camera."

His shadow-self wouldn't have minded. He suspected he might be photogenic. They walked toward the Long Road in silence. Mum seemed withdrawn. In St. Ives, he always feared her dreaming of London. Where on earth did she go to now?

He kicked a clod of earth. "She was an odd sort, your mate. Rather dark, don't you think?"

"It's no good using that tone with me. You well know she was Indian, as you are. And don't think your British blood makes you better—"

"Three-quarters British."

"And one-quarter the world. I'm not raising a bigoted child."

She halted and grasped his chin. "And what part do you think he wanted, sweet, the man who wanted to claim you? It wasn't the English part, I can tell you that."

Her knowing voice shocked him. *The man wanted to claim you.*

She marched on ahead. He ran and took her hand, needing the connection, needing her grounded. Though she allowed it, she seemed far away.

THE TRAIN NOISE faded to the background. George was adapting. He rather hoped for a jaunt around the city, preferably above ground. Yet his mum, vague in her promises, had errands for the day and decided to drop him off to see her brother, an uncle he barely knew. Hadn't she implied in the teashop that this uncle liked males? How could she offer up her own son?

Shadow George thought it might be a relief to get some attention down below. *We should look handsome.* Shadow George made him reach for the black cap.

But the old man shakes seized him at the bus stop. It was midday.

Mum said, "Are you cold?" as a red double-decker came into view.

"Can I sit on top?"

"All right, but we're not going far."

In all the hubbub of moving to London, she'd failed to mention the profession of her brother, who ran a ballroom dance studio called "Fleet Feet." George's mouth opened when this incredible news was imparted. There was another dancer in the family.

James Hartley whirled a woman around a shiny floor as the adult students watched. After the demonstrated steps, the man skittered over. (George stopped a cry of panic.)

"My nephew! How marvelous. I'll take good care of him, sis."

George offered a weak smile. The man was black-haired with Mum's tawny skin and an off-putting pair of gray eyes. *He didn't quite get the looks*, noted Shadow George.

"You don't remember me, do you? I've just started a class, old chum. You'll have to wait a bit. Or join in."

He darted away. George crushed his cap, feet rooted. And yet... how marvelous to be in a room full of music appreciators.

And how badly they danced. What staggering before the mirrored walls. One fellow kept trying to trample his partner's toes. Many couldn't keep to the beat. When the class ended, and the chattering adults straggled out, unabashed at being so horrible, Uncle James signaled him over. A flutter started like a bird trapped in his stomach. George moved, as dizziness dogged his steps.

"I hear you're mad for dancing. Did you know it runs in the family?"

"No, sir."

"Oh, please, don't 'sir.' 'Uncle' is fine. Well, not only me but Mother was considered a fine Indian dancer."

Grandmum Kirati danced, as well? He loved how no one told him!

Uncle James said, "You couldn't, by any chance, show me some of the steps the class was doing?"

George dutifully showed the entire sequence, glad that they were at least going to dance first.

His uncle nodded. "Wow, right. Good memory. Rather good form. So, how about this?" The man danced a longer sequence, hands loose like Fred Astaire's.

George's interest was caught. "Can you show me with music?"

His uncle flipped through EPs. With an upbeat Petula Clark placed on the turntable, the dance made sense. George tried it out.

Uncle James grinned. The poor sod was probably unused to people getting things right.

George warily demonstrated. "Couldn't you also do it this way?"

"Ah, yes…one could. May I?"

George was grabbed from behind. (So soon?) Adult hands had his waist "Not so stiff, son. You've good posture from ballet. Yes, I know about the ballet, it keeps you lifted. But here," hands rubbed down his flank, "stay loose in the pelvis, the legs…" his back thigh squeezed. "You're like a rock, lad. Relax."

Shadow George had to flood through him to unlock movement.

"Yesss," urged the voice behind him, "that's right."

"What on earth are you doing?"

A lady stared. It was Miss Kathy, a fellow teacher from the class.

Uncle James said, "I'm trying to loosen him up."

"Well, it looks scandalous. You'd better let me try."

The uncle laughed and slapped George on the back. "Sorry, old chap. I didn't realize. A feminine touch might be better at this."

Wary of this short, adult female in a bell skirt, with a trim waist and pointed bosoms, George nudged out his shadow-self. He'd have to tell his roommate Winnie about this little number.

Her hands taking his were small and soft. "Let's learn to be a good partner first. Eyes up, please."

Maintaining a square of distance, she showed arm position and explained the subtle pressure of the fingers, the most important responsibility of the man. George nodded at "the man" part, inwardly thrilled. She was, however, tougher to please than his uncle and not impressed by his pushes and pulls.

She moved chairs onto the floor, then tied a scarf over her face. He had to guide her round the chairs using only the touch of his fingers, no talking. She wouldn't let him dance for the longest time. Only when he had correct partner form did they try an air-skimming waltz, a joyous, jubilant polka, a frustratingly slow foxtrot.

James said, "Master the technique, lad, before you add your own spin. Be considerate of your partner. She's not competing with you."

Kathy said, "Shoulders down, neck long. Use the mirror to correct yourself. Check how your body moves."

George had to dash surprising tears. His dancing was being *directed*. Perhaps his uncle wasn't going to fiddle with him. (Although, why not?) The hours flew by, so engrossed were three of them. Until the ring of a telephone.

James shouted into the receiver, "Come over and see this boy dance...Well, you need to see him again...Yes, now." He rang off and grinned. "They're coming."

The Carveths entered the studio with his dad saying, "You want us to watch our Fred Astaire?"

Mum's eyes were sly. "Is he any good then, Jimmy?"

Uncle James flipped through records. "Despite this poor fellow being raised by a pair of left-footers, I think even you, sis, will be able to answer that question."

George hadn't heard his parents teased since St. Ives.

James said, "Kathy will partner. She's very picky about partners."

Miss Kathy winked at George. "I only pick the best."

"We'll start with Louis Prima. Lad, use what you've learned," James winked, "and go all out."

Needle down, a crackling hiss came through the speaker. 'Jump, Jive an' Wail' stole George straightaway. He went loose as a noodle, took Miss Kathy's hand, and hopped her aboard the musical express.

Dad laughed. "We know this one. Wiggling Monkey."

Uncle James shouted, "He was already doing the Charleston steps. Heck, he was navigating the whole dance. We just gave him a road map. Look at him, look," he said each time George hit the beats.

Miss Kathy beamed, whipping out and sticking back, her skirt wrapping his legs. It was great how the song built. In the nick of time, his body remembered the right step, the right bit of flash.

James was near dancing himself. "Did you see that?"

George provided more did-you-see-that moves. The room felt so full of excitement. Everyone whooped at the finish.

Miss Kathy hugged him, mashing her bosoms to his chest. Uncle James cried, "The boy is a natural!"

"What fun." Miss Kathy was rosy. "He's completely uninhibited, probably his youth. Don't lose that, George. People get inhibited when they're older, especially men."

George said, "I just move how the music tells me."

"That's great, love. Stay loose like that. And he's…" she clamped his ears, "…when he dances. Did you see?"

"I'm what?" he asked. Mum nodded, Dad looked sheepish.

Uncle James bumped him, a glint in his spooky eyes. "Sexy. A good quality in a dancer. You've your grandmother's talent and her bit of something extra."

What bit was that? Amazingly, he was asked to dance solo. Gobsmacked by the reactions, George reached for a Cozy Cole record.

"Topsy, Part 2," was a great number with drums. Its beat sparked a walk, a plan. He tried steps and checked his look in the glass. Spurred on by his audience, but for one shocked dad, who almost made him flag, he kicked with the cymbals, threw in a turn, even grabbed Miss Kathy for a swing dance.

He couldn't remember such an evening of fun since leaving St. Ives. Shouts and applause filled the studio, an addictive sound.

Uncle James said, "Do you know what you have here? I want him every break. And you'd better start thinking about a talent scout."

Mum blurted, "A talent scout? Dear God."

George bounced on the balls of his feet, scarcely believing this talk.

Dad clamped his shoulder. "Easy, son. That's plenty to think about, Jimmy. He is only twelve. We don't want to move too fast with him."

Mum, James and Kathy bubbled with ideas. George wrenched from his dad to hear them.

FIVE

"Tears on My Pillow"

(SYLVESTER BRADFORD & AL LEWIS, 1958)

ALARMINGLY, Mr. Wilburn answered the door in his dressing gown. "Quickly," he pulled George in by the arm, "It's been a trying morning."

"But—I'm hungry. I count on having a bite here."

"Oh, all right. I'll fix you a cheese sandwich. Get that gear off."

George shrugged off his sopping mackintosh. He didn't want to do anything on this miserable day. The gas heat was low, the electric fire down to two bars. His reddened legs were damp gooseflesh. While a relief to scrape off wet shoes and socks, he left on his school shirt and Y-fronts. It was too cold for all-over access.

Shadow George flooded in with a devilish thought. He fetched the 45-rpm record from inside his chemistry book and slipped it on the gramophone. A quirky Cuban riff started. Mr. Wilburn squawked from the kitchenette.

Dancing, George stopped him in his tracks. The beat of the music was slippery and infectious. "'Beware of the Blob…'" he sang and popped his cheek with his finger. He'd won the 45 in a bet and had been dying to play it. If he kept moving, would he stall his audience and hear the song straight through?

Mr. Wilburn couldn't hold a stern face. His body seemed on the verge of twitching. How badly George wanted to see him dance. Whole worlds would break open if only the geezer danced. Big hands grabbed. George ducked out beneath.

The master pouted. "Don't be a tease."

George sidled from another attempt. The man charged forward and switched off the gramophone. Fun over.

"What gem have we here? 'The Blob' by The Five Blobs. A real work of art you've found. No more Fauré for you. Now we have The Five—"

George snatched it from him and placed it in his chemistry book.

"Pardon *me*, Highness. What I endure for your lovely bits."

Eager for his sandwich, yet cornered in the kitchenette, George faked darting round, but was nabbed trying to dash. The man pushed his head crotch-ward. George sank to the floor, went through the hairy legs, pounced on a side table and offered the pipe and tobacco pouch. Mr. Wilburn rarely turned down a smoke. Though George had been in trouble with other masters for "reeking of pipe smoke."

He didn't have to do what was asked. Not if he was smart. He and Shadow George were newly fourteen. The body was taller, legs longer, calves still big, though he had a good football kick, a high toe raise. His hands and feet seemed large, though Fred Astaire had large hands. George would learn to be graceful with his affliction. His school uniform had got snug just about everywhere. Mum promised adjustments in the next break.

The rocking chair creaked as Willy settled, lit up. "Don't succumb" —*puff, puff*—"to rock-n-roll. It's tribal. And unhealthy."

George was on tiptoe liking the stretch of his arches. He sniffed the precious bottle of Old Spice cologne atop the bureau. Mr. Wilburn had a seafaring cousin who bought the cologne in New York City. He snatched up a fedora on a hook. It was large and reeked of Mr. Wilburn's hair oil. The hat made him feel like a Bob Fosse dancer. He was mad for the Fosse style. He dipped before a glass case, noting his reflection, smoothing the brim of the hat.

"Look at you." Willy smiled, peaceful with the pipe.

George tipped the hat, suave like Sinatra. Dancing either worked well, ideally followed by compliments, or backfired. He parked the hat and flopped in a chair.

"I saw a Rock-n-Roll picture in the village. Some of us danced." Before the usher made them stop. Ever since the reports of aisle dancing to the film *Rock Around the Clock*, dancing at the cinema to swinging music was the In-thing.

"With that gangly bunch? That's twice in the village."

"New Matron lets us go. She wants us to have fun."

His former lit master frowned. Old Matron had left last term. George still wondered about that time after spring break when he was twelve, and Mr. Wilburn had mostly left him alone. He'd heard one or the other of that pair had been summoned to the headmaster. Or perhaps he didn't want to know about their business. Back then, he had wished Matron would marry Willy.

"Don't pick your feet."

George thrust his leg down. "Jayne Mansfield was in the picture."

"I must say I find that woman grotesque."

"I find her dishy. We mainly wanted to see Little Richard. He was in the movie."

The pipe tapped empty. "Is he a child star?"

George hooted and tucked his legs beneath him. "You would think that. You'd probably be after 'im. He's from the States and plays bashing Rock-n-Roll."

Mr. Wilburn flinched. "The way you talk these days I'd never know you were educated. If you're going to start swooning over actresses, try a real one. Audrey Hepburn is an endearing—"

"She's flat." George, his ex-roommate Winnie and a few others had created a list of starlet bosoms. Audrey was not high.

"Christ, the sex hormones are here. You'll become bony. Pimples will erupt on your perfect skin. You'll get a mean curl to your lip."

Not this again. George vaulted from the chair and pulled on his knee pants. "You're potty."

Mr. Wilburn leapt up, the empty rocker going back and forth. "Always a smart mouth in the end. I should have dropped you at the first sign of hair."

George froze tucking his shirt, mortified by the fuzz around his genitals. His joy at becoming a man was too often tempered by his fear of becoming ugly. Sometimes the older man would look at him and sigh.

Mr. Wilburn seemed to read his mind. "I don't mean that, sport. I suspect you'll be a brilliant butterfly. It is just, well…I prefer the caterpillar phase. You're leaving?"

"I've a report due."

They gazed at each other. Butterflies, caterpillars… What on earth was he talking about? George pulled his tie over his head. He didn't relish putting on the wet socks.

Mr. Wilburn darted to the kitchenette. "Your cheese sandwich. And, here, take this." He plunked the fedora on George's head. "It suits you. Sexy kid."

"Honest? Thanks, Will." George flicked the brim.

Early release was a victory. He shielded his two gifts from the downpour.

He skipped several days after that and felt a rakish sort of boldness in his action. It seemed an adult action, choosing not to go back. The master would plead for his return. Only George didn't know whether to forgive him. He couldn't stop his body growing.

Mr. Wilburn usually sent a note of summons. Nothing appeared in the cubbyhole. After previous breaks, George had been fawned over for returning. Unless the man found him ugly. He stared at himself in the washroom looking glass.

Some weeks later, irked by the whole business, he ventured down the long path and knocked on the familiar door.

Mr. Wilburn greeted him with joy. Then his face clouded.

Wary, George said, "I'm back. Don't be cross, if you are."

But the man stopped his entrance. "I was rather impressed you stayed away. I think, perhaps, we might keep it that way."

A laugh shot out. "What, you don't want me?"

Shadow George hissed, *you didn't do what he wanted.* He reached for the master's crotch.

The master darted back. Alarm showed in the amber specs.

George staggered down the steps in surprise.

Wilburn called, "I just think it's best."

George whirled. "I'm not returning. You're too old!"

He nearly ran past an impromptu match on the green. Oh, hell. Who cared if the players didn't want him? He scored one easy goal amidst the gobsmacked boys. The next two were more of a struggle with clots of lads ganging up. But George was even angrier over years of being denied star status on a football field, as if having a Cornish accent meant he couldn't play or being "colored" meant he *shouldn't* play. The field was viewing distance from Mr. Wilburn's window. Did the man look out at the shouts? Did he see George get hoisted in the air, euphoric by the end of the game, knees dirty, shoes caked in mud?

The leader said, "You're a scrappy player, Carveth. Join us again."

Surely it was better to be free between lessons, to finally have time for studies. No more weekend demands. George had his rock-n-roll mates, the "gangly bunch," who tuned to Radio Luxembourg on a wireless to hear the latest hit songs from the States. Every night on the floor below his room a lad named Edgley played square music at full volume, tolerated by faculty because it was Pat Boone or Edgley's favorite tune "High Hopes," Frank Sinatra singing with children. It grated George's nerves. He couldn't play Little Anthony to the grounds and surrounding rooms, schoolmasters smiling in comfortable satisfaction. *Here is a good boy, one of us.* And too often the absurdly catchy "High Hopes" stuck in his head, his brain making it a torment.

RAIN PUMMELED the campus for days. All occupants were restless inside. George was not well. His shaking hands and prickling limbs had subsided, but he felt chilled as if something worse were coming.

His new hair seemed a dirt smear, his groin felt heavy. Were his balls darker? He was not yet afflicted with the skin eruptions that plagued others. How could his blank skin not show a map of hands and teeth? Self-relief was a common outlet for most of the inmates. He suspected some of his fellows were being coerced for the pleasure of older lads. Why was he not approached?

Shadow George scoffed. *They know we're for masters.* The thought of a new master was frightening.

Dog's balls, and now he'd wandered in the wrong direction. A tide of young ones surrounded him. The first-years. Misery emanated from their work-loaded bodies. He caught one sad sack by the sleeve. "It will get better."

The child blanched and squirmed away. He stopped a pale lad in specs. "You will be all right, honestly."

Days later he noticed each lad again, their faces lifting familiar. One had wavy brown hair and a closed-down look. The other was a weedy blond with thick specs. George smiled at each; both gawped as if they thought him daft. Though the third instance brought return smiles. Mission accomplished. That game was done.

One day the maddening rain lightened to a patter, then halted. George bolted out with others into the wet, fresh air. Maybe someone would start a match. A strange lad drifted alongside him.

"I've been had by old Willy, as well."

George flinched. "Pardon?"

"About a year ago. Let's have a smoke."

The boy headed for the wood. Stunned, George followed. It was slow going on the spongy ground. Their shoes squished mud. They entered the clearing where George sometimes danced.

Lighting two ciggies, the youth shocked him further. "There was a third who went mad. Headmaster in a tizzy. Suitcases, parents. Gone."

"Who'd turn mad over, over that?"

George paused with the cigarette. He'd never actually smoked— and this lad's time had overlapped with his! He'd presumed himself the only boy in Willy's life.

The kid cut him a look. "Been watching you. I knew he set you free. Do you miss it?"

George coughed violently. "No," he managed through tears.

"You ever smoked before? Don't hold it in."

The lad took an impressively casual drag, smoke leaked out the side of his mouth. "He liked me because I have a way with words. 'Cyrano' he called me."

George blurted, "I was his favorite." What a daft thing to say. "How did you know there were others?"

"I asked him. I can see why he picked you." The boy twitched his brows.

George flushed. "I dance."

"I recite poetry." Which he then did, showing off, tapping ash while George fought nausea. How could anyone stand smoking?

Maths homework gave George the means to escape. On the trudge back, sensations flew to the top of his head. He felt dizzy-silly, not bad. In the relative warmth of his room—his feet dry in slippers—he had a giggle with his two roommates and did master imitations. He was known for his imitations, including master walks and manner- isms. His roommates laughed easily, attracting the attention of neigh- boring lads, who gathered in their larger corner bedroom. George was made to perform again. More boys laughed.

He threw in a twirl, a shuffle step, an elegant gesture as if his doddering subjects had developed grace, which prompted one room- mate to cry, "Wow, you could be a dancer."

No one else heard the fun because "High Hopes" started below. All groaned. George cried, "Argh, that song will be stuck in my head all night. If he plays it tomorrow, I'll get him."

The next day started well—a swim before classes in the subter- ranean pool where George was now a lifeguard. He had no problem leaping into water first thing.

But late morning was chemistry, his worst class. His chemistry master startled him with a grasp that made George knock his goggles to the floor. Mr. Gyllen bent to retrieve and clean the goggles. He kept glancing at George from across the room and told him to stay after class, so they could "discuss his progress."

Lord. Shadow George flashed out. *Is this the new lover?*

He couldn't help revulsion. And wasn't there a Mrs. Gyllen? Yet how many times had he not been keen on Willy? If this one was mild in manner, he might be a tiger in other ways. And Shadow George could do with a bit of relief.

Mr. Gyllen delayed him with senseless chitchat. Shadow George worried his hair, which felt long and wild. Chlorine wafted from his fingers. He chewed a nail. *Stop that.* He sat alert and tried to look interested. Would the man ever make a move?

Mr. Wilburn's instruction flashed in. *Look down: it shows off your lashes. Now slowly, eyes up. You must learn to meet an adult gaze. If you can hold a gaze then, my lad, with those peepers, you'll undo anyone.*

"Carveth, what *are* you doing?"

Shadow George held the gaze, answered, "Listening, sir," with a forward lean even as his heart banged.

The master tilted backward. "Are you hard of hearing?"

"No, sir, not at all. I've not a thing wrong with me. I'm quite healthy and fit. You might want to see if I'm lying. You might check…"

Mr. Gyllen blinked, not catching on.

Shadow George pressed, "You might take me to your room."

The man gasped as if that were the wrong offer or he was incredibly stunned—and *eager* as he pulled George from the room. "We could do whatever you want to do, sir."

But George was pushed down the long hall. Most students had dispersed, though it only took one to start a gossip. But here was the headmaster's corridor!

Mr. Gyllen pushed him past the secretary and into the office. "Headmaster. He's just behaved like the—worst sort of—fairy, inviting me to— I give him to you."

The headmaster went around and shut the door. Shadow George grappled for a chair, his heart going like a pinball. How could he have guessed so wrong? How did one *tell?*

Headmaster paced. "I'm shocked at you, Carveth. You should know not to— Those are wicked feelings. You must resist them. Don't let me have to inform your parents."

George flinched. No, his wickedness was his own affair.

Headmaster muttered, "All his lads go wrong in the head."

"Sir?"

"You boys are loved. But...not in that way. I fear you get confused being singled out by him. I've told him not to play favorites. His methods are—he assures me it's all above-board. I shall have to decide —but that's not your problem. I know you're a good lad, if not a stellar pupil. I so enjoyed your entrance paper, the one on music. And your father, such bravery. Focus on your studies, Carveth. That is why you're here. Those other feelings are not for you to, or not at your age, not yet. Perhaps you didn't know what you were doing. No. You most certainly did not."

He released George for the dinner break. It felt like an escape. Light pierced the hall windows. The sun was back.

When classes ended for the day, George resisted the urge to run to the wood and instead loped the stairwell to his room. He mustn't have another year of bad grades. Dad had threatened to ban him from dancing with Uncle James in the summer.

One roommate was well into his studies. George sat at his desk and opened a textbook. From now on he would be normal. Professors would single him out for his superior mind and athletic abilities.

His other roommate burst in. "Look out, lads. Edgley's at the gramophone."

"Oh *no*. If one more ant moves a rubber tree plant, I'll go mad."

"How does he get away with it? He's their darling, I'll tell you that."

George leapt up and paced, his body surging with energy. "I'll take care of this nonsense. I think it's time for a show."

His roommates brightened. George had spied the fedora and would do Frank Sinatra. But Edgley would probably love that and think it a tribute. What else?

Surprisingly, Edgley started with "The Impossible Dream" at full volume. George sneered. Frank was sure to follow. On the other hand, it could be a *rude* tribute. He worked off his shoes and socks, his uniform. The lads gaped.

George said, "Help me. What should I wear? I wish we had some-thing outrageous." He wrapped himself in his counterpane then threw it off, searching for a character to play.

A roommate opened the door. "Carveth is doing a show!"

There was a commotion in the hall. Fellows pushed inside. "You're doing it starkers?"

George mulled in his vest and Y-fronts, then said in a falsetto voice, "Whenever I hear 'High Hopes' I simply *must* take off my clothes."

If only he had a girl's wig. Yet everyone laughed, more boys crowded in. He donned the fedora and opted for fey. "I hope he plays it. Oh, I do so hope he plays it."

More laughter. Below them, "The Impossible Dream" built to its tremulous climax. George cleared off his desk and stood atop it. When the hateful song started, the group cheered.

He caught the beat in his hips and made exaggerated gestures of innocence: how *did* that ant move a rubber tree plant? His audience seemed delighted. He jumped down and made himself a pathway, stopping with a pose, a rakish tilt of the hat, the Fosse moves. How freeing to dance, even to such a daft song.

Someone said, "Wow. He's *good*."

He needed room to kick and used the outer hallway. Cool air enveloped his lightly clad form. More bodies filled the space. He mouthed the lyrics and whirled from St. Clair's swiping paw.

A roommate boasted, "He knows every word."

George danced his way down the stairwell to the louder volume and the oblivious record player. He bared his bum at the line of the ram "butting" the dam. Boys whistled, catcalled. He leapt the last few steps to whoops. Edgley opened his door and gawked.

But it was the instrumental part now. George gave the dance his all. His focus was the hat that he played with and never dropped.

He popped an imaginary balloon right with the record, tugged the hat brim at the finish, and said, "Ring-a-ding-ding, baby" to an appalled Edgley.

The stairwell erupted in cheers.

But the rowdiness changed as if by a gust of wind. Schoolmaster Barlow pushed through the crowd and froze George mid-bow. Face flushed, the master growled, "What's this?"

George flew up the stairs.

"Oh no, you don't," the man cried behind him.

Everyone flew. Doors slammed. George got to his room just behind his roommates. They blocked the door and cowered. Moments later, the door thundered on its hinges.

"Open this door at once!"

The roommates looked frightened. One said, "We have to open the door, George."

"No."

"We have to."

George had just managed shirt and shorts when they opened the door. Barlow burst in, wrenched his arm, snatched the hat, and dragged him into the hall.

Barlow snapped at peering faces, "Back in your rooms!"

They didn't turn for the headmaster's building but went up the tower, climbing around and around.

George was thrown into a different room and saw landscape far below. How could this be happening twice in one day? Barlow forced him into a chair and threw the fedora on a desk.

"I should expel you for that display." Spittle hit his cheek. "How dare you preen naked in front of this school. *Eyes front.* Don't look at me, don't you *dare* look at me."

George whispered, "Can I have my hat?"

"You're lucky the headmaster's gone out. I heard about you tarting it up with Schoolmaster Gyllen today. I'll not have you infecting these boys—"

"M-my dad gave me that hat."

George quaked. Barlow went silent, sidled close, and sniffed.

Cold nausea rose within him. Adult fingers gripped his hair.

"Oh, Mowgli, Mowgli. My little catamite. What is this smell you reek of? Think you're a seducer? I'll bet you were an eager pupil in the old perv's hands. Parents didn't even take you out. Now you can be a little brown concu-boy." The hand pushed his head.

He knew about—?

Barlow strode to a cupboard and opened an array of sticks and switches. "I think a riding crop might be appropriate."

"I only danced."

The red-faced man charged forward. "Only danced, sweetie? Is that all you did?"

George was plucked from his chair and hauled to a table. Barlow bent him over the edge. "How unfair for you. Trousers and pants down."

"No! Please, sir…"

"DO IT! Before I slice these garments—!" Barlow whipped the table leg.

George's cheek smacked the polished table as he struggled to comply. Everything went black.

PAIN! He fought to waken. Someone held him. Ammonia was thrust under his nose.

He heard Barlow's voice. "Are you all right?"

His vision hooded, George squirmed, grabbed his slipping garments, scrambled up and found the door. He tore down and around the coil of stairs, pawing the banister, and smacked the floor at the bottom like hitting a wall. *Oh…that hurt.*

He propped slowly. And rose on new colt legs.

The house prefect stared. Boys emerged from their rooms. St. Clair appeared and clasped George's arm.

"Are you all right? Can you walk?"

George swayed. His arse stung. "My arse…"

"Quickly." St. Clair pulled him into a room. Others crowded in. "Let's see."

George relaxed his grip on the unfastened shorts, the half pulled-up pants. There was an intake of breath.

"You only got one." A youth sounded resentful. "I usually get several."

Was it just one? George craned to look. There was a single hot stripe across his buttocks. What luck to have fainted.

St. Clair said, "You look wobbly. Sit here."

"Aaaaugh!"

"I mean you'd better stand. Sorry. Someone get ointment, quickly. Macky, you have some. You're always getting whipped."

"That's true," said poor Macky.

George said, "I think I fainted. That's why he only did one."

"Really, you fainted?"

He was urged to tell the experience. How queer to have an audience for this. He didn't mention the ugly name "Mowgli."

Another boy chimed in about seeing the cupboard of switches. St. Clair sneered. "That baldy perv likes hitting us."

George remembered. "He called Mr. Wilburn a 'perv.'"

The boys shifted. What was that other word Barlow used?

Macky brought the ointment. St. Clair snatched it. "Everyone, go."

One lad balked. "This is my room, too."

"Come back later. Listen." The bell was chiming for supper. "Go on. We'll be along shortly."

The others cleared out to join the chatter in the hallway.

St. Clair steered George from the door. "You mustn't be seen. You're famous now."

Famous? George couldn't imagine entering the dining hall *now*. Yet he wasn't entirely sure he wanted to be left alone with his nemesis.

"Lie on my bed, Carveth. It's all right."

George lowered himself warily. The youth helped work his pants down in the back. It felt better not to have fabric there, though he hissed at the touch of the ointment.

"Sorry," St. Clair murmured. "It must hurt."

George focused on the pleasant evening out the window.

St. Clair said, "I didn't know you could dance. You're really great at it."

"Oh. Thanks. I've always done it, just for fun." Did that sound stupid?

The older boy wiped his fingers with a flannel and stopped George from getting up. "Rest. You must let it dry."

St. Clair looked a little intense. They eyed each other.

The boy smiled. "You gave a bashing performance. No one will forget it for quite some time."

Pride mixed with embarrassment. The dance had felt fantastic at the time with everyone cheering. "I never should have, I mean it seemed a laugh, just a go at—*Cripes*. Is that a stiffy?"

"Wait, Brownie—"

"Don't call me 'Brownie!'"

St. Clair pushed him back, devilment in the eyes. George lunged, but the lad blocked him with knees and elbows.

The boy jockeyed to stay over him. "If you'd been my slave, I would have taken such care of you, given you sweets and favors. You've a great arse and legs. Let me kiss you, then I'll let you go."

George bucked with a cry of frustration. He didn't want to be kissed by this arsehole. He wasn't "Brownie" or "Mowgli." For moments his rage prevailed, he nearly toppled St. Clair. Until the older lad used his greater weight to bear down.

George slackened. His cut burned from the squirming.

St. Clair panted and loomed over him. "Your cheek. Red on one side. Where you fell, I think."

George shuddered from the experience in the tower. How Barlow hated him. He must never cross the man's path again.

Could St. Clair be the new lover? He had the temperament of a protector. And would soon be in the long trousers of an upperclassman, the sixteen- to eighteen-year-olds.

George endured the boy pressing his lips on him before shifting away. He could disappear in his head. Or take over the power and demonstrate a proper kiss.

St. Clair urged him for more, his mouth sweeter than an old pipe mouth. His enthusiasm even gave George a spark. Did it feel this way to kiss a girl? (But for downy facial hair and the pressing bulge.)

The lad sighed, as tamed as Mr. Wilburn used to get. "You smell like the pool."

George blushed. "Well. I'm a, I'm a lifeguard. In the morning."

St. Clair tensed. Then eased. "You deserve it. I've never forgotten how quickly you reacted. Stay with me tonight. Don't worry about Dog Breath, he won't say anything."

"I was whipped today. I'm done for."

"You kidding? Quite the opposite, I'd say. I'll bring you home with me at week's end. I can do that, you know. My room is far from my parents' rooms. We'll be together all night."

"You're mad." A trip to the family manse? Were they mates now?

The door thumped. "Let me in."

St. Clair shouted, "Piss off!"

"I've a paper due."

"Use the library."

But fear of Barlow reignited. George wriggled free, much to the protest of his new lover. "I have to go."

St Clair clutched his arm. "You're the most beautiful boy in the school."

George laughed. It didn't sound like an insult.

In the hall, the roommate smirked. "Had a good time, did you?"

GEORGE LOWERED himself carefully after the singing of the hymn. He felt the nearby attention like the flick of tiny insects. So many boys had smiled and given fond greetings. Others stared. He scanned the chapel but had yet to find St. Clair's blond head. How strange that they'd even been together. Would they really take off at week's end?

He couldn't believe he'd danced yesterday, openly danced, and everyone had liked it. Or almost everyone. Better think about history class coming up. He could be quite worried about history. There was New Matron looking younger and friendlier than Old Matron. Her bubbies were barely visible beneath her cardigan. She didn't rank high on the bosom list, though everyone liked her. They needed lassies here. Would there never be a dance with a girls' school?

Everyone rose. As usual, the singing was plodding and bad.

Chaps he knew grinned and slapped his back as everyone filed out of the chapel. Someone said, "Great dance." Another said, "Ring-a-ding-ding." Macky gave him a shoulder squeeze. A big fellow pushed past. "Poncy queer." George stalled in surprise.

In his cubbyhole was an envelope. No summons from the head-master, but a note from Willy.

I can't believe what I've heard this morning. You were performing publicly in your undergarments? My dear, come to me.

He would not. Word was going around fast if Willy knew. And who'd told him? Some other pet?

Someone said the headmaster was gone for a week. What splendid luck. George cut through the courtyard, pants chafing. St. Clair sometimes ambushed him here, usually to torment. Not today. He crossed the field with warmth in the air, the promise of another fine day.

A gang approached. The leader was the kind who'd push his face in the grass. George slowed and braced. The leader marched right up.

"I say, Carveth, we did a collection. There's three bob here if you'll repeat the performance." The big lad showed a bag of coin.

George loosened his fingers. "But I was whipped for it."

"We meant privately, you know, some place secret." Eager faces peered at him.

Payment for a dance! "Barlow has my hat."

"Oh, dash it all. You must wear the hat and, you know, just the hat."

"And pants." George colored. "I did wear pants."

"We heard you were starkers."

Now he wasn't so sure he liked the look on their faces. "Sorry. I've a class now."

Farther along, he was yanked and whirled to face a distraught Edgley. "Arse!" the boy shouted, "You ruined Frank Sinatra."

"Edgley. I like Frank Sinatra. I like to dance to him."

Kids laughed as if George had said something funny. An audience gathered. Edgley seemed near tears. Boys called out taunts—but at Edgley, not George—until the lad backed away.

Another said, "Don't worry, Carveth. You showed that nancy twit."

"Yeah."

"You did, all right."

"You were ace."

"No more crap tunes from him."

George half smiled and struck off again, blind to his direction. He could almost feel happy, if he didn't feel bad for Edgley.

The history master seemed preoccupied, another stroke of luck. He ordered the boys to read silently. After a while, he started a lecture, but mostly at the chalkboard with a lot of points striking the board, the chalk crumbling as he wrote. But when one lad volunteered a wildly wrong answer, the mood changed. George could see the spark alight in the master's eye. There were three targets: himself stuck in a front row, fat Humpty, and Gilbert Wall, a perfectly nice yet clumsy chap, who dropped papers and books whenever their master aimed his spotlight of derision.

The man flapped his arms. "Why bother reading our text at all? Perhaps you'd prefer we peruse magazines like housewives. Or torture small animals. Or watch the lovely Georgina dance in her knickers. Darling, you didn't."

The master braced George's desk. Face burning, George pressed back in his seat. The master shook the desk.

"Don't keep us in suspense. No show for us? You thought it appropriate yesterday. Burlesque awaits. Or wait, I don't think they have burlesque for boys. Or perhaps they do, but we don't talk about that in polite society. Still, darling, you have a career ahead of you." He creaked the desk, big face close.

He and Barlow must be best mates.

And with that thought, bold Shadow George looked up slowly and met his teacher's gaze.

The man's smirk disappeared. "You dare look me in the eye?"

"Oughtn't I, sir?"

A ripple seemed to go through the class. The master reddened and shoved George's desk into the desk behind him.

The master darted past him. "Gilbert! To the board."

But there was a clap from Gilbert's book hitting the floor. The poor lad quaked. The master flew over, scooped up the book and smacked it on Gilbert's desk.

George leapt to his feet.

The master whirled on him. "Do we have a problem, Carveth?"

"No, sir."

Shadow George trembled yet held the man's gaze. As the man turned to Gilbert, Shadow George spoke up. "Why don't I write on the board, sir?"

"Because I don't want you to."

"I've got better handwriting than he does."

"*No one* is writing on the board, you pack of hellions… Enough nonsense! Chapter 28, read it now." The history master strode to the front and sat at his desk.

Gilbert flashed a look of thanks. George sat lightly while his insides roiled. He mustn't vomit from years of blackness coursing through him. Oh, God…not here. Lightheadedness came over him. He was in the sea, in cool water, beneath a warm sun. There was a dim sense of his master at the periphery writing on the chalkboard. Still, it was better to stay below. Safer.

He came to at the bell, body tingling to be back in air, and staggered out with everyone else. Fellows squeezed his arm. Gilbert held up his notebook. "If you need to copy the assignment?"

In the safety of the crowded hall, an adult voice summoned him. It was the art master, who was generally nice. The underwater feeling still buzzed. George went warily to his office.

"I heard about your performance, Carveth." The art master threw him a pointed look. "I won't tell you how wrong it was since I'm sure you've been given that message. However, it was impressed upon me how good you were. How you kept to the beat and had a high kick. And that you used a hat as a prop."

The man smiled, said, "Where did you learn to dance?"

George shrugged. "Always done it. I've had ballet and ballroom. Not that anyone here knows."

"Nothing to be ashamed of, sounds grand. We could use a lad like you. I work with a theater group and I advise the drama group here. I advised them to stop doing Greek tragedies. As you see, they didn't listen. We need lighter performances. Something fun. I assume you can dance in clothes? Marvelous. I'll arrange an audition and send for you. Bring a song and the hat. Off you go."

George left, euphoric. He belonged on a stage, right as rain. But what to do about the hat? A kid got in his way. It was one of his smile recipients, the brown-haired pint. The child was pink in the face.

"I-I heard about your dance with no clothes. I heard you're going to do it again. Some chaps were talking about it. They say you told off Barlow and that you dance for schoolmasters."

What an eager little face peered at him. George didn't know whether to laugh or be horrified. "What's your name?"

"Wells. Martin Wells. If you do it again, um, can I be there?"

"Wells. I'll see you around." George pushed towards an exit and bolted outside.

Young Wells called, "Yeah. See you around."

George cut across the garden where the peacock used to be until certain boys set it free or perhaps killed it. Headmaster had gotten angry for the first time ever. But wasn't that St. Clair smoking in an alcove, the shock of blond hair and the knobby knees? George called out. The youth strode forward. But there was something on his face… his eye purpled.

"What hap—?"

George was banged off his feet, books loose, and hit the ground without air, his gasp kicked away, his side burning. He could only curl as St. Clair shouted in a ragged voice, "Stay away from me, you fucking poofter!"

IT WAS Shadow George who came to and got treated by the nurse. He moved through the days much slower. A bruise marred his cheek and stained his ribs and side. Yet kids gravitated as if he had all these mates now. He didn't trust the attention. And George, who was better with that sort of thing, was completely gone. Two younger ones tailed him—an eager pup named Wells and a skinny blond in specs who gazed as if he were a marvel. It was unnerving.

The history master noticed but left him alone. Of course, Shadow George stayed well away from St. Clair, not that he'd ever trusted that lout to begin with.

Too sore to dance or join a match, he eluded his matey fellows by taking the old, familiar path to the farthest digs. He picked off a willow switch swiping it as he walked. Then remembered Barlow and dropped it. What if the old geezer had company, like that chatty bloke Cyrano? Shadow George looked bad now, all blotched and slow moving. Willy might feel sorry for him. Willy was the one to go to when bad things happened. A crunch behind him, Shadow George turned.

There was the blond kid looking caught. And Wells strolled not far off, hands in pockets, with a casual salute as if just passing a good deal out of his way. Oh, this was rich. Why not have a bit of fun?

Shadow George walked backward, inviting them to venture closer. "I guess you know who I am." *Not really.* "And you are?"

The blond flushed, and stammered, "M-M-MacIntyre."

"Charmed. And this chap here is Wells. Hello, Wells. How are we today?"

Wells beamed. "Good, sir—I mean, Carveth." He flushed as badly as the other.

Shadow George grinned, which hurt the side of his face.

"You don't have to call me 'sir.'" He exaggerated his voice like a master. "I think you shall call me, oh, Zeus. You've read Ovid? The *Metamorphoses?*"

The boys hesitated. Wells said, "Mainly the naughty bits."

"Hah. Those are the fun bits, aren't they, Wells?" He spoke like Mr. Wilburn, an imitation at last. "I love being naughty. I'm good at it. I'm Zeus and I willed you to come. You must follow my power. Wells, you shall be Ganymede. And MacIntyre can be, hmm. Vulcan, I think. That's the Roman name. It's easier than the Greek. You don't mind being Vulcan, do you? He was the blacksmith of the gods."

"Oh n-no, th-that's fine," MacIntyre sputtered as they walked, still rosy in the face.

But he had a stutter. Luckily, George was a good sort who wouldn't make fun. MacIntyre smiled whenever Shadow George did. Did he? Yes, he did.

Wells said, "Pardon, Zeus, but who was Ganna—Ganim—?"

"Ganymede. He was Zeus's friend, his 'cupbearer.' If I wanted a cup of tea, you'd have to fetch it for me—"

"I could be your servant then?"

"Oh no. You don't want to *fag* for me. That's rubbish, older kids with butler boys." Shadow George shuddered. "No, Zeus adored Ganymede like a, like a pet. I suppose he was a bit of a servant." Wilburn had nattered at length about Ganymede only who remembered the boring details?

Wells grinned. "You sound like a master."

"Come." His voice squeaked in an unmasterly way. "We'll go to a secret place where you shall do my bidding."

He picked up the pace, though it tightened his side. The boys fell in beside him. He headed at once to the old milking shed below Wilburn's rooms. What if he led them straight upstairs? Two new gifts for the tall man.

The shed was musty, earthy, with stacked pails and dormant machinery. "Wow," Wells said, making it magical.

"We shan't be disturbed in here. You can scream and no one will hear you."

Shadow George colored. He hadn't meant to say that. Lord, he felt odd. He loosened his tie for air. His welt itched. He explained, "There used to be cows on this land a long time ago. All those tits would get sucked right here."

All lads collapsed in giggles that ran on for a while. It hurt the side of Shadow George's face. He sloughed off his blazer.

"It's warm. We can go barefoot too." He sat carefully on a milk crate, glad to work off his shoes and socks. The younger ones followed. The odor of ripe socks permeated.

MacIntyre was glinting specs. "D-did you get in a f-f-fight?"

"I did, Vulcan. You should see the other chap. And he was older."

Their two faces were moons in the dim light. They watched his outstretched legs.

Wells said, "Great Zeus, how did you find this place?"

"I like to go around and survey my lands. This is the perfect place for you, Vulcan. It's your smithy. No one else must know of it. But now, before I can trust you, we ought to do a secret ceremony."

Both boys seemed to anticipate this.

"Remove your shorts. We shall all remove our shorts."

"Remove our...?" MacIntyre said perfectly.

Shadow George stood with a wince. "For the ceremony. I, Zeus, command you to obey."

The two boys stared at him, then looked at each other.

"The magic words are: 'bollocks' and 'arsehole.' Obey me."

The lads fell out giggling. And complied. How naughty to shuck one's shorts.

Shadow George stepped onto the crate meaning to make a speech. But it was his body that spoke, hips and shoulders unwinding, trying a slow Fosse twist.

"This is how I danced on that day. Of course, I wore *nothing at all*.

But the hat." He touched an imaginary brim and swayed through his sore places like a cobra, as if he were his Indian grandmother with her sexy "something extra."

His audience gawked. He showed them his scar. "You see? Whipped, on my poor bottom."

Blood filled his penis. He flashed on the memory of St. Clair lusting...that rotter who'd turned on him. Shadow George leapt from the crate and shoved off his sticky pants staggering a bit. He felt woozy. But look how large he was splitting the front of his shirt.

"This is the Rod of Zeus. Let me see your rods."

Wells looked as if he might faint or flee. But skinny MacIntyre popped his Y-fronts. Shadow George presented himself to MacIntyre.

"It needs to be wet. Spit."

Hesitantly, Vulcan spat on the Rod of Zeus. Shadow George stroked it to make it longer even as he felt a wave of tingling. He braced MacIntyre, who was close and helping.

"Where's Ganymede? You're not playing, Ganymede. Must I do everything?"

Fighting dizziness, he knelt before the boy's covered crotch, moved away his hands and took the limp, urine-y bit in his mouth. Ganymede and Vulcan both gasped.

How small. Like a thumb. His mouth not stretched. What next? *Pierce him.* He sized up the trembling cupbearer.

Wells cried, "No."

Shadow George took down the boy with a wrestler's hold. The child bucked beneath him, the violence costing him breath. A darkening hood was coming over. He found a tight opening and pushed his finger up. *God, was this what he'd felt like?*

WHEN GEORGE BROKE THROUGH, he gaped at a bare bottom, a boy's anus. Wells, of all people, was crying in a corner. He saw his own erection. Had he penetrated someone? The bent-over boy turned out to be that blond kid, who glanced back at him.

A voice jabbered in his head. *They ought to know what can happen. But another took over, another did something.*

George gasped, "No, stop. Go away."

The two boys gaped as if he'd said it to them.

"Go!" he screamed and fell to his knees.

Wells grabbed his clothes and bolted. The little blond fumbled with his shorts, saying, "Zeus? Zeus?" George vomited and heard the child run out. He backed from the mess, his school tie dragging.

How had Shadow George taken over so completely? He was only a feeling, a voice. What had he *done?*

Outside was a pink-gold sky. Gilded stragglers pushed each other in the distance, late for the evening meal. George hid in darkness and donned the rest of his garments.

He crept the long route back. His building was thankfully deserted. Inside his room was a shock—the fedora on his bed. And a note.

Carveth,

I have taken the liberty of returning your hat since I understand your father gave it to you. I have also written your parents and informed them of your latest episode. You should talk to them. You are a very troubled boy. One more incident like this and I shall have to send you down.

Headmaster

George swept off the hat. His pillow took his wails, the weeping that so alarmed Wilburn.

But he wasn't the only one here. In the room below—that had been silent since the night of his dance—Edgely played "The Sunny Side of the Street," the Judy Garland version. He cheered Edgely's will to play records, though the tune lanced his heart. It was his dad's favorite song by his favorite singer. His good, kind, and ignorant dad. The song reeked of happiness and a home soon to be spoiled by the lump of shit coming in the post. He ought to throw himself in the sea. Who in the world would love him now?

PART II
Part Two

NEW FRIENDS

1960-1963

SIX

"Nice 'n' Easy"

(ALAN BERGMAN, MARILYN KEITH, LEW SPENCE, 1960)

GEORGE MET his first Yank girl, clearly a grownup, with full bosoms and corn silk hair, who said in the front room of his home: "Tupelo, Mississippi. But I could've been Japanese and known the answer to that one, hon."

Her voice was rough from a cold, not that he knew it then. She came with a husband. He was great too, if less compelling. It wasn't every day two Yanks stood in the stifling Clapham house, everyone shiny from the heat.

It had happened so fast, Uncle James nattering at Dad and Mum to find a talent scout, then Dad on the phone with a war mate, a Yank's brother was coming to London. It turned out this brother was looking for talent and starting a new career with a new wife and wanting to set up shop, and Mum saying, "You must invite him to tea, Gere-bear. It's fate, sweetie. Tell him to bring his wife. Georgie will dance."

Shadow George snorted. "Georgie" was not a performing monkey. Although, he was "on watch" this summer, no mischief allowed, and only allowed to dance with Uncle James because his grades had improved somewhat.

He'd endured a barrage of parental questions and handwringing at the start of the break. He'd nearly forgotten the dance in the stairwell so distraught was he by the Wells-and-MacIntyre incident and, worse, his lack of memory about it. At first, he'd assumed his parents were reacting to that. Why shouldn't an angry father have posted a letter? George had finished the school year keeping well away from those two. Though MacIntyre kept trying to seek him out. George never let the boy get close enough to get a word in. By contrast, dancing in his underwear seemed a trifle.

Luckily, Mum decided the school had overreacted. George had danced as he had in St. Ives, not even naked. Only small minds would find his display offensive.

Dad didn't share that view. Dad suspected there was more to it. George fit his responses to Mum's view.

The Americans were late if they were coming at all. Mum decided it was too warm a day to sit waiting in formal clothes. George bolted upstairs to change. In the bedroom across the way, his mother donned a lighter frock and his father shucked off his suit jacket. George thundered down the stairs. "May I ride?"

Dad called, "Not for long. Don't go far."

But George was already steering his new bike outside, a belated fourteenth birthday gift. The day was hot with clouds moving in.

He rode towards a large neighborhood lad named Thomas, who looked fierce but always nodded at him. "We've got Yanks coming over."

Thomas squinted. "How do you know they're real Yanks? Me mum said we'd have Yanks once. Only they were cousins from Suffolk who went to the States for two weeks. We had to look at their pictures. Dead boring it was. The States look like here mostly."

Disheartened, George pedaled off. When had Gerry or Lucy ever been to the States? Why should they know anything about Yanks? With a warm wind on his face, he accelerated for the common.

He was sweaty coming home. His hair felt wild, like clown hair. An insect bite was coming up on his arm. It was stifling in the hall where he parked his bike.

"There he is." Dad spoke from the front room. A fan whirred on the mantle. A fair-haired couple rose from the sofa, no doubt English.

Mum came over to flatten George's hair. He pulled away and did the flattening himself. Mum tugged his bitten arm. "Mind, pet. The Stuarts are here to see you."

He sidestepped her, eyeing drinks on a tray. "Are they *really* Americans?"

Dad said, "Saints preserve us. O' course they're Americans."

"Then where was Elvis born?"

He'd scarcely looked at the couple until the wife answered correctly, calling him, "hon."

She was tall and curvy, eyes summer blue and holding back a smile. Her skin was spattered in freckles, hair blonde and curled at her shoulders. "Whoa. Who turned on the lights?"

She seemed to mean his smile, which made him smile more.

The husband extended his hand. "Jack Stuart, New York City, born and raised, in the good ole U.S.-of-A. Pleased to meet you, young fella." The man was broad-shouldered with hair like a mown field, eyes gray and startled.

George hastened to shake his hand. "Begging your pardon, sir. I didn't think they knew Americans."

Dad flapped his arms. "The war? I met all sorts there."

The wife leaned in. "Parents can be so backward. But they get out more than you might think, cookie." She held out her hand. "I'm Jill Stuart."

Jack and Jill. George grinned, unused to shaking a woman's hand. Or should he kiss it? "Ring-a-ding-ding," he said stupidly.

She laughed. "The Rat Pack, eh?"

Her taller husband hovered. "So, kid, I hear you're a heck of a dancer. Can you give us a demo?"

George laughed. They sounded like characters on telly. He stopped at a look from Dad, then helped him push the furniture to clear a space. Despite being in a suit, Jack joined in the moving. George felt childish in his cousin's old knee pants and a short-sleeved shirt. How could he dance in kid-like shorts?

He kicked up the edge of the Indian carpet and rolled it, exposing the wood floor, and blushed at Jack's open stare, his smiling interest. Jack winked.

Dad said, "We've lately been listening to Brazilian music, the *Black Orpheus* soundtrack."

Jack nodded. "I heard that was good."

"Aye. This one here is in love with the rhythms. How 'bout a samba then, lad?"

They'd planned the samba in advance. Uncle James had advised, "Be flashy. Americans like that sort of thing." As partner, Mum was to follow his steps and try not to fumble. Dad started the record.

At the percussive opening, George snapped into the routine and heard surprise from Jill. He guided Mum out and back, feeling manly with his perfect form. Then remembered his kiddie shorts. Mum felt stiff down his arm; he focused on loosening her. Her smile bloomed at last, turning authentic. That was the best part of dancing with someone, seeing the joy come over. He flashed joy at Jill as if he could rope her in. A pretty lady was watching him. He wanted to be good. He managed spins in the tight space and threw in more complicated moves. A squeal snaked out of Mum as he dipped her at the finish.

Their guests applauded. Jack said, "Wow."

George wiped his face on his arm. "Did 'ee loik it, truly?"

"Diddy-do, what?" Jill said.

"Did 'ee—you—like it?" *Stupid.* Talk like at school. Dad's accent always rubbed off at home.

The couple agreed the dance was great. George smiled and worked his fingers. "Bet everyone sambas in America. They do everything there, don't they?"

Jill said, "You bet. I usually samba to the grocery store and the gas station." Her blue eyes teased.

Jack kicked her. "She doesn't samba to the *greengrocers* or the *petrol station.* Neither one of us sambas anywhere."

Jill flashed a frown.

George didn't want her upset. There was dampness on her blouse, with the faintest lace showing beneath on what was clearly a full bust. He smelled her sweat and powder. "I can do all the Latins, other dancin' too, any kind, cobra dancin.'"

"*Cobra* dancing?"

"All kinds, is what I mean." He blushed hotly. Cobra dancing was his slinky version of Indian dancing. His bite stung fiercely.

Mum said, "Don't hover, lamby. Sit. Everyone, please."

George and Dad hauled chairs back in place, Mum deciding they'd unroll the carpet later. Jack squeaked the sofa with his weight and dabbed his forehead with a handkerchief.

Jill said, "You must be glad Elvis is out of the army."

George nearly bounced with excitement. "I am. Though I'm worried he's gone square. He did the show with Frank Sinatra."

"The 'Welcome Back Show,' yes. That duet of 'Love Me Tender.' Hoo boy."

She was wonderful! "*Awful*. I wish he'd get back to rocking. The best Rock-n-Roll comes from America."

Jack frowned. "Rock-n-Roll is a passing fad."

George blinked, embarrassed.

Jack pawed for a packet of smokes and held them out. Dad cleared his throat, which stopped Shadow George from taking one.

Jack lit up. "What I mean is you'll find out for yourself. We'll take you there."

Jill said, "We will?"

"Hell, when this boy is famous, he'll be dancing in New York City."

George started, but Mum braced him down. "Then you liked him?"

George jerked up anyway. "I'd love that, Jack—Mister—I can do tap, ballet, anything. How 'bout it?" He offered his hand to Jill.

Jill sputtered, "Oh, I don't dance, really, in front of others."

"But how can you not dance?"

Mum dug her nail in the back of his leg. "Not everyone likes to dance, baby."

Jill stood up. "No, I can dance, that's not the point. I can take you."

George said, "Yeah? Dad, put on Little Richard."

Mum laughed. "Heavens. I'll not have that screaming man in this house."

Dad darted to the gramophone. "How about 'Sing Sing Sing,' eh, Lucy? We like that 'un and we know the boy does well to it."

George pushed back the chairs and swiveled around Jack, who'd got up with him and danced a bit. Jill watched them, hands on hips.

The drums pounded their signature beat. George shook himself out. Feeling suave, he beckoned Jill.

He was now an assistant teacher at his uncle's studio, and less shy dancing with ladies. He kept the moves basic, yet Jill stayed with him, her pleated skirt fanning. He slipped in a twirl for himself. "Show off," she mouthed, eyes bright.

Jack hovered like he wanted to cut in. "Step away. Let him dance."

Jill backed off. But George nabbed her and switched to Charleston steps.

Mum said, "Be careful. Don't stomp."

George steered their kicks towards empty space. He stomped and started the whips in time to the music, whirling Jill out and back, her soft breasts grazing each time. She laughed as he spun her. Glasses and objects shivered on tabletops.

Her hand slipped; she flew from him, flashed knickers and banged a table. Items toppled, crashed.

Dad leapt for Jill. Mum gathered fragments.

George was horrified. He'd never lost a partner before. He wiped his hands on his shorts, dazed by the flash of bare legs and lace panties.

"Are you all right, lass?" Dad helped up their startled guest. "Lucy, leave that. George, apologize, son."

"I'm so awfully—"

Mum said, "Only a plate. Jill, do you need water?"

Jack claimed his wife. "We should go. We've bothered you folks long enough."

Dad stopped the record. "Dear me. What a way to end our visit. The lad is all arms and legs at this age."

Jack waved it away. "No worries. We all got carried away."

The guests wanted out.

Dad followed them to the hall. "But were you pleased with the performance, I mean before …?"

Jack stopped and skimmed the short bristles of his hair.

"I'll be frank. I often don't need to take these performances beyond a living room." He turned his gray eyes on George. "But, kid, when you spark you move like water. Can you can dance alone? That's what I need to see."

George couldn't believe the words. "I can dance any way you like."

Everyone laughed.

Jack put his hands in his pockets then pulled them out as if he didn't know what to do with them. George dared a look at Jill.

Her freckles rosy, she seemed less accessible and took her husband's arm. Dad rang for a taxi.

Outside, a shower had started. Dad and George held umbrellas for the couple and watched the cab sizzle off in the downpour.

George wilted. Why had he done that second dance? He closed the brolly and didn't have words when Dad looked at him getting soaked.

Dad closed his brolly and turned his face up. George smiled, and did the same. Dad whooped and shook his head out like a dog. George loved the beats of rain, the crackle of summer thunder.

Dad said, "Well. Your uncle should be pleased. We made an effort. What happened to you back there?"

George grimaced. "I didn't mean to lose her."

"I think we can safely say she'll not forget you. Hoo, and you liked her, I saw that all right."

"I didn't."

"Sure, you didn't."

Mum shouted, "Fools!" and waved from the window behind them.

∼

THAT EVENING, supper was quiet. The experience of the afternoon faded. George needed it to fade, even though it had been exciting. How barmy to have hosted Americans. To his casual ask, Mum guessed Jill to be in her twenties. Dad cleared his throat, not quite smiling. They watched the telly after as they did most nights.

His prick took over at bedtime. No more the mushroom, it had become a sap-filled root. Sometimes, he thought of the ladies he partnered in his uncle's classes or the naughty ladies in magazines. Jill Stuart flooded his mind with her Hollywood voice, her full bust and lacy knickers, her freckles like beach sand, that had gone pink when she danced and made her eyes so blue, her whirling hair like foam on the water, blonde on brown. Lord, each time she bumped him during their dance.

Jack must be so content. If George married, he'd want a fun wife like her. Although, there had been that tension.

Yet married people were often sniping at each other.

He tried out, "Good ole U.S.-of-A. You've got talent. Kid, you've got talent." And added a cigar. "You'll be dancing in New York. Noo Yawk…daaancing."

What had Jill called him? "Cookie." He giggled.

SEVEN

"Blame It on the Bossa Nova"

(BARRY MANN & CYNTHIA WEIL, 1963)

A FAMILIAR VOICE on the phone said, "Is this my future star?"

George blurted, "Jack?" then, "Mr. Stuart?"

"Call me 'Jack.' You sound surprised. Couldn't you tell I liked what I saw?"

The Yank didn't hate him. His wife hated him for dropping her.

She ought to know he was a part-time dance instructor and school lifeguard. Shadow George nattered, *I'm so terribly glad he liked us. Tell him.*

Jack said, "Let me speak to Mister C."

"Who?"

"Your dad."

George winced at his stupidity. "I'm so *awfully* glad you liked me," Shadow George forced out of his mouth.

Jack gave a delayed chuckle.

George handed the phone to his frowning dad.

But it could happen. It wasn't a joke. He'd dance for money and be on "Sunday Night at the London Palladium."

Dad chatted with a slightly false note to his voice, then rang off. "Huh. I wasn't sure we'd hear from him again."

"What did he say?"

"Ohhh, well. He said your focus should be on school, of course. You should involve yourself with drama and music. He'd like to see you perform sometime." *This was sounding awfully dad-like.* "Your talent needs to be honed for a few years."

"He didn't say years. I'm sure he didn't say years."

"Well, it's not happening tomorrow. You're still a lad, and you're under my sway."

"He likes me. He wants me to be famous."

"And I'll tan your hide if 'ee speaks to me like that."

George knew his dad would do nothing of the sort. He jerked his bicycle down the front steps to the pavement—as he'd planned before the phone call—and set out for his day. It was a fine one now. A talent scout liked him.

Where St. Ives was sea air and flowers, with dung scents from the neighboring farm, Clapham had the burning tinge of soot and petrol. Vehicles shuddered up his street, though rarely enough to stop the play of children. George sniffed the air daily to get a read on its scent. Just as he had a whiff from a neighbor's roses, a lorry rattled past, trailing fumes. He steered his bike down an alley between the backs of houses, through a gantlet of rot and vegetable smells, past gardens and rubbish tips, and the tang of frying pork. Back onto another pavement, a gentle scent passed from high hedges and clematis-draped fences, then smoke and petrol as he pedaled towards crowded streets and the distant cupola of the Arding and Hobbs department store.

This busy area had been home for his mother. Her family had a history of drama wrought from the day Grandfather Hartley brought home his prized Darjeeling beauty, who had died young, no doubt sad to be so far from distant peaks and tea-growing slopes. Life had not been easy for her children—Mum and Uncle James often deemed as "foreign" despite being English.

Uncle James was great. Shadow George reminded that he was one of *them:* a ponce, a fairy, a nancy, bent. But George didn't know. Sometimes one could feel that sort of thing in a look. The glances from his uncle were more often proud. Usually, a man's attention made George's skin prickle. Women tended to smile at him, like the lady clerk in the corner greengrocers. But women weren't wicked.

George bought lemons, his errand for the morning. His mum cooked with lemons or bright orange powder from a precious bottle of saffron. Or she had him collect a sack of rice instead of the ever-common potatoes. She hadn't cooked much in St. Ives. Now she was keen on it, her meals getting stranger and hotter. George liked most of them but suspected his dad was just acting a sport. He was not to say anything if his dad slipped off to the pub for a meat pie. George added the lemons to the bag containing his brown trousers, secured in the basket of his bike, and pedaled on.

On a previous errand, he'd taken the trousers to the launderette, washed them hot and put them through the mangle to make them shrink. His mum would have been gobsmacked to see him at a launderette, but a boy at school had done his that way. George had to have one tight pair. Elvis wore tight trousers and dungarees like drainpipes, tight shirts as well, sometimes zippered.

He slowed his bike. Neon shoe soles flickered on the Fleet Feet studio sign. In the men's locker room, George shucked his shorts and pulled on the illicit trousers. They were still a bit damp but snug all right and high around the ankles. He liked his ankles showing and purposely wore white socks. If he had matching gloves, he'd complete the Fosse look—hands and ankles. *Watch me work.*

In softer shoes for the studio floor, he dampened his wild hair, pulled some curls over his forehead and walked out like a star.

Miss Kathy had left to have a baby, though some evenings she came in just to coach George. Old Mrs. Wren was the new female assistant. A tall chap named Cecil also helped.

George preferred assisting the adult classes. He was tall enough for most of those ladies. But his uncle made him a featured demonstrator in the junior classes. Lads his age had to be dragged to the studio. He had no empathy for those clods. They hated dancing, never practiced, and one called him a "poof." He called them "wankers." The lasses were keen, though they giggled and whispered. Did they know things about him? Were any related to Wells? MacIntyre? Mr. Wilburn? They sometimes threw off his partnering.

George wished Uncle James would play Rock-n-Roll records, but still enjoyed the girl singers, Big Band, cool jazz, and especially the Latin rhythms. Latin music taught him to loosen his spine. The Brazilian movie, *Black Orpheus*, had been a revelation. Why couldn't he live in Rio? Everyone there danced as he wanted to—all wild and free and full of life. The most percussive music was his favorite. He shimmied to one of the Carnival pieces between classes attracting a Jamaican woman, who joined him and gave him pointers. Their antics kept students from leaving and distracted the new ones coming in. Incredibly, she told him to make his bum talk.

"Fart?" he cried.

"No, fool. Use it."

Her point being to shift his dance weight to his seat. When she demonstrated, he hardened watching her.

Uncle James thought it best if they didn't dance like that in front of the students (though Shadow George had enjoyed the shock and attention). Miss Kathy told his uncle, "It's good Delia found him. She'll keep him limber. Let's face it, Jimmy. He'll soon be passing me by."

The Jamaican woman was Delia? He'd only seen her that one time. Had she found him attractive? He'd been all sweaty then. He fantasized being with her in the assured way men were with women.

Uncle James raised an eyebrow at the snug trousers. Ladies filing into the class glanced as George did warm-up exercises. He assessed them on the sly, heard their laughter, cigarettes held between fingers with fire-painted nails, glances passed to each other, different looks for him. Uncle James allowed him a show-off dance at the end of class. If the reactions were good, George would add a bit of flash—a flip or the splits. It impressed the ladies even more if he slid back up from the splits. Sometimes he was so infected with the zeal of performing he had to walk out on his hands.

"Jimmy, your nephew is amazing."

"What a talent."

"Your nephew is going to be trouble, my lad."

"Aye, there's trouble all over that mug. God help our girls."

Alas, George would not be doing splits in these trousers. He held himself with a grownup air, arms in an open frame, guiding hand on the middle of his partner's back. He led a cha-cha to "Rinky Dink" with Mrs. Althorp.

She said, "Ooo, look at them little 'ips goin'," making his face heat up.

She was shorter than him, with a wide face and eyes that squinted when she laughed. Eye contact was proper. But the way she pinned him with her two little beads made him want to move his gaze to a nice plain wall. Cecil and Uncle James were working the far side.

Suddenly Mrs. Althorp was against him, laughing. How wrong to break form! Her bubbies were squashed on his chest. Stiffness surged in below. Couples thumped past them, absorbed in their own steps. He willed his leaden feet to dance.

She breathed tea and tobacco in his face, "Little lovah." *Her red lips.* "So, you're not a fairy boy. Thought you were with them swishy hips. Your eyes are asking for it now."

She was mad. He must detach.

She pelted his ear with an invitation to her house tomorrow afternoon, before resuming the proper position. In the tight trousers, both noticed his bone in the four o'clock position. He fled to the loo.

Later, he practiced in the empty studio determined to be reserved in movement, no more swiveling. But Uncle James strode out, his light eyes upset. "What are you doing?"

"I-I'm trying not to move my hips. They call me a 'fairy' now."

His uncle grimaced. "What did Miss Kathy tell you?"

George couldn't remember, but his uncle cried, "Don't be inhibited. Never change the way you dance because someone said something stupid. If you do, you'll never be great. You think I didn't hear that? All right—yes. You'll hear we should be manly. We're not supposed to dance like women. Well-meaning instructors will tell you that. But, lad, that's when we lose the excitement. Men become mainstream. Men belong in the background. I'm sorry, but bollocks to that." He clasped George's arms. "You have a gift. You are not a background dancer. Remember your grandmother. She lives in you."

KIRATI WAS A DANCER. Kirati was removed from her home, as he had been. Had she known his pain? Perhaps he wouldn't live very long.

Right. He wouldn't go to her, Mrs. Althorp, who'd called him a "fairy" with her bubbies smashed against him. Now if sexy Jill Stuart had invited him over, that would be different. Uncle James was right to look out for him.

Once his mother left the house for errands, he ran a bath. A creeping, excited fear stole over. An adult wanted him for sex again. Shadow George was itchy for the bodily attention. And a female couldn't stick anything inside him—quite the contrary. Although, what would that be like? He mustn't black out or do something awful.

Uncle James had said she was "in her thirties" with an "oafish" husband. That seemed to imply muscles. Surely, she wouldn't invite him when the husband was there. What if she wanted him for her husband? George threw up his breakfast, barely making the toilet in time. Cold sweat beaded his skin. He flushed the mess and washed his mouth. Right. He would *not go*.

After bathing, he perused his father's toilet items. The cologne bottle was nearly empty. He wasn't to use the hair cream but for special occasions. George had been using some to keep his hair from standing up when he bicycled and used a bit now. A book from school had mentioned how 19th-century Frenchmen used to pomade their hair with lemon and vanilla to enhance their appeal to the ladies. He dashed down to the kitchen in his underpants, rifled the cupboards, found the small bottle of vanilla, and shook drops into his hair—ooh, he smelled like a cake! Nice, though. He paused at cutting up one of his mum's precious lemons. Perhaps she wouldn't be too upset if he just used half. In fact, it was best to use both halves and discard the evidence. He ran upstairs to finish dressing—and to pick out the pulp and seeds. He patted his armpits with Mum's powder puff and talc. For an outfit, his tight brown trousers, of course, with a short-sleeved, button-down shirt.

Too many scents wafted as he bicycled to her house. Let the wind take it away. What if she hadn't meant for him to come over and it was all just a laugh to see if he would?

"'Allo, my pet. You're looking flushed."

Her frock hugged her curves, her pronounced bum invited him into the front room. "How 'bout a nice glass of milk?"

He was rather hoping for a grown-up swig of ale or at least a shandy. He smoothed down his tacky curls. "Yes, please. I'll have that."

Her house reeked of stale cigarettes and a bit of the "footballer's fug," as Mum called certain smells. Obviously, Mrs. Althorp didn't burn joss sticks. George strained for any sounds of the husband. He'd better start lifting barbells.

She hummed in the kitchen. The front room walls were bare but for a Spurs pennant and a South Sea Islands poster. The furniture was a woolly plaid, with one orange chair, the whole effect a contrast from his home. A bookshelf was crowded with ceramic poodles.

Mrs. Althorp cha-cha'ed in with his glass of milk. He gulped it too quickly and coughed. Something sharp was in it.

She clamped his wrist and took the glass. "Why you're all a-shiver."

"No, I'm just, I mean sometimes I..."

"Relax, dancer."

His throat burned. Her mouth stopped his, her tongue pushing in. He tried not to gag. Cold tingles buzzed like flies eating his head.

She stopped and held his chin. "Kiss back, lovah. Here, do you smell lemon gateau?"

"No." What he'd done to his hair was stupid!

"Don't lean, sweetie-lovey. Let mama have these pretty lips."

He turned his head. "You like poodles but you don't have one."

"I did. Meet my Ginny."

She led him to a hallway painting. He barked a laugh at it, and felt so loose and warm now.

"What? She's gorgeous. Best doggie in the world, my Ginny."

She baby-talked at the painting. George wouldn't have minded a real dog weaving about his legs. He missed the presence of animals.

Her fingers walked down his spine and over his arse. He didn't pull away. She tried an easy kiss. The warmth inside him spread everywhere. Her tits grazed back and forth. She kneaded his bum, not crushing it like some. He dared to clutch her back handful and she let him. Oh, God. He was massive. She enclosed his root. He fell into her, unable to stop the spill and shudder.

She danced him to the stairs. "Early fireworks. We'll get you all cleaned up. Up we go."

"Where's Mr. Althorp, did you say?"

"At work. I swear somebody's baking around 'ere. Mind if I call you 'fairy cake'? You sure smell like one. Your Myra has a sweet tooth on 'er."

SHE MADE him feel as if he'd done something important, rather than more naughty business in a bed. No substance in the world was as silky as a female breast. And once he got over the shock of her privates, he saw a sea mussel with a red pearl. What heaven to be the one penetrating. To be held in her pocket.

For some reason, he had to promise never to become a delivery lad, where he'd "make a mint" among the housewives. He assured her he would not.

AT THE DANCE STUDIO, she pulled him aside. "Careful, love. With that blushing smile, you just announced to the entire class what we did."

It was hard not to grin. Even her fussing with his collar made him twinge below. He was eager for another round. But her little brown eyes seemed worried.

"I'm a bad person corrupting you. You shouldn't have tempted me."

"Sorry, Missus."

"Well, it's not your fault. I'd be the one in the slammer. We can't ever do it again."

"Why would you be in the slammer?"

"No reason, pet. Just being silly."

"It's not *against the law*."

"'Course not. It was fun while it lasted, eh? Are you my sweetie? My young man with perfect posture?"

But if they couldn't ever do it again, then Mrs. Althorp clearly didn't want him anymore. Shadow George howled in the privacy of his bedroom. To finally get a lover—a lady—and *this* again?

He could always try Jill Stuart now that he was experienced. But Jack hadn't rung but once. Jill likely meant to keep away.

How could he even think of making the end-of-summer trip to St. Ives? Yet his parents acted as if it was the perfect thing…the bracing sea air. His lungs expanded at the thought. And the final leg of the journey, the short train ride from St. Erth to St. Ives, with its increasingly panoramic vistas as the train hugged the cliff side, grabbed his heart still. His parents also pressed to the window.

"Lord, this boy has grown," was the tiresome theme of hugging relatives.

"*Fatla genes*, love?" Grandy murmured, her skin soft and powdery.

"I'm fine, Grandy." *And I don't speak Cornish.*

How provincial his uncles sounded as they orbited Mum, trying to make her laugh. They fancied her. Was that how George sounded when he first came to the school? No wonder lads had made fun of him. He supposed his mum had a good figure though she was more compact, not so in-and-out.

Plump, bosomy Aunt Tiff remarked on him being quieter. Where was his bright-eyed, smiling mug? Didn't he want to entertain them?

"Will we get a Fred Astaire show?" prodded Aunt Sally.

George coughed. How embarrassing that he'd presumed to be Fred

Astaire. Oh, he would do a show all right. He'd light a cigarette and sing "One for My Baby."

His cousins chattered like loons. There was Margie with her mad hair. She was taller, womanish, and practically flirting with his dad. She assessed him with narrowed eyes and didn't come near. George had never felt so alone in his favorite place. Remembering Mrs. Althorp, his prick pinged with life. He slipped away. But the outdoor privy dampened his mood. How backward to not have indoor plumbing. What an absurd bunch of relatives he had, laughing and shouting over each other. He would be inside if he didn't have this extension on his body craving relief. It was becoming ugly like Mr. Wilburn's. So Mr. Wilburn had used George to ease a craving. *I'm like him. He's made me like him.* Those poor two boys. He would go to hell for those boys. MacIntyre's frightened little voice: *Zeus...Zeus.*

The uncles proposed an afternoon bathe at the inlet. All the teens wore swimsuits. George wore his lifeguard one. Only the little ones shucked to the skin. The fathers started to, but Dad said perhaps they should keep their shorts on this time, and added, *Arthur,* right sharp, as Uncle Arthur flashed hairy balls.

His uncle muttered, "Eden ends with puberty."

Margie was curvy in her one-piece suit and seeming uncomfortable in it. She was well tanned. Even little Irene had sprouted. Cousin Ethan wouldn't leave off about her "mosquito bites." Timmy was shockingly handsome, with a tuft of hair on his chest, his body strong for being only four years older. Did he flash his tool for other sailors?

"Shall we find Calypso in the waves, laddie?"

Dad stood dripping and smiling, his flaccid penis partly visible through his saturated shorts. George imagined it engorged and demanding.

"Later, Dad. I'll come in a bit."

George knew from school that Calypso was merely a character in a book. How embarrassing that he used to search for her. He sloshed in and stayed at the surface and wouldn't dive under, even though he wanted to. He just wouldn't. Not anymore.

"CRIPES, LONDON, ARE YE PITCHIN' a tent?"

Timmy's curly head grinned at the lower bunk level. George stretched in bleary puzzlement and then sat up, mortified. Timmy laughed and strolled out. George was irked being called "London." Then decided he liked it.

Only Timmy and Margie had the luck of choosing their own clothes. He dressed in hand-me-downs, though the t-shirt and shorts were clean, soft with wear. With a cup of Grandy's cream tea, George climbed the ridge to a favorite spot. It was a lovely morning. Porthmeor Beach dotted with life below.

Margie appeared from the house in a frock. "Too grand to have breakfast with the rest of us?"

A dark tuft showed under her arms as she shaded her eyes. She climbed and flopped beside him. Her private hair should be quite filled in. A scatter of tiny moles flecked her shoulder, the only place she had them, but for two on her thigh.

He said, "I had a scone before."

"Lord, and she made you that tea. She goes soft when you come home. What'd you have for breakfast at your posh school, steak, and kippers?"

"Caviar and lobster." He laughed at her startled face. "Porridge. It's awful."

That pleased her. He felt her gaze and shifted, glad the goods were out of sight. She nudged his leg. He looked off and drank his tea.

He couldn't imagine kissing her anymore. Though he might if she wanted it. Would she want all the business Mrs. Althorp wanted? He'd never cared about other women in the town but now wondered about them, as well. If he became a delivery lad, he could service quite a few.

She pulled tufts of grass. "We may go to Bingo Palace later."

He scoffed.

"Ah, right. Must be boring to a Londoner like yourself. You'd raaather go to concerts and plays."

He snapped, "Yes, I would rather."

She huffed, and he said, "If you don't like me anymore, why did you come up here?"

"Who said I didn't like 'ee? You. Now you're making me talk all posh and stuffy."

"Proper English is not stuffy."

"Ach, listen to 'im. All proper now, is he? A gentleman, are ye?"

He rose. "At least London is not backwards like here."

He strode off, hating himself. After more strain with the others, Aunt Tiffany said it was his changed accent putting them off.

"Aunt Tiff, I have to talk this way for school. I'd be thrashed otherwise."

"And so you should, lad. You're educated. But I'm more a woman of the world than these others," which was a reference to Aunt Tiffany having lived in London to attend art school, though she hadn't lasted six months.

In the afternoon, George walked far from the house and shucked his clothes entirely. The sun would burnish him yet. He lay on the ground, bunched the T-shirt over his bits and let the scald pin him flat. Thoughts danced. His mind succumbed to images dazzling and heavy. Until he heard Uncle Dan's voice:

"Must be nice to lie in the sun."

He blinked at the silhouette above him. "Uncle Dan. I'm pale as a ghost."

"With all there is to do around here, I'm amazed to see a perfectly fit lad lounging in the sun. Best way to get a tan is doing a chore. You can stay naked. I've no problem with that. Keep busy, work your muscles. Then, before you know it, you have a fine tan. There's a hill needs mowing—"

George sputtered a laugh. "I'm not mowing starkers. That's mad."

"How'd you think Tim and Ethan got their tans? Not by lying around. 'Course ye might want to wear your shoes. I'm mending Farmer Hale's fence on the far side. He's at one of his shows today. Come along."

Scowling, George pulled on his clothes and shoes and went to Farmer Hale's shed to fetch the push mower the two households shared. Goats clustered in the way. He rattled the mower, and they scattered, voicing disapproval. By the time he got the machine to the far field, his shirt was sticking. He peeled off the garment and dutifully mowed.

Uncle Dan said, "I see you prefer a cottontail tan. Is that what city boys like?"

George glowered. Then ditched his shorts.

Ooo, this was potty. At least he was far from the houses. He wrestled a sideways mow. Then couldn't decide which was worse—controlling the mower downhill or forcing it up. Flipping grass tickled his ankles and collected in his shoes. He kept stopping to clean out the blades. Sweat cooled instantly. Better still, and he hated to admit it, was the balls-out freedom. No sticky garments. Mad to wear clothes in summer. He used to know that. Muscles popped on his arms. His legs handled the steep grade. Uncle Dan worked shirtless at the fence, his skin a rosy, shiny brown.

When George finished, he wiped himself with his T-shirt. Nicer still was the all-over, caressing air. Uncle Dan nodded in approval.

"All right, then? And you've a nice blush on you like a ripe peach. If I could, I'd always do chores naked. Feels good?"

"It does. Why don't you?"

"Well. I don't want to scare them girlies spying on you."

"*What?*" George looked about wildly.

"Pipe down. I'm only teasing."

George gripped his damp hair. "I could murder 'ee!"

His uncle laughed. "If any were watching, so what? Be proud. And quit skulking about like you don't belong here."

How mortifying that his uncle had noticed. A sea breeze carried the smell of shorn grass. George assessed his hill.

Uncle Dan offered a piece of straw. "Put it between your teeth like so. Your dad and I had to repaint the house one summer, about your age, we were. Did it starkers. Had quite an audience then."

George nearly swallowed his straw. Uncle Dan chuckled to himself.

WHAT AN ODD HOLIDAY. George felt more accepted by his older relatives than his wary cousins. He swam with Uncle Dan, just the two of them. Timmy denied doing naked chores. Though Grandy laughingly confirmed the house-painting story. "Danny and Gerry never lacked for dates after that. What a pair of Lotharios I had."

George mulled on the surprise of a boyish father and uncle during the train ride home. He was so preoccupied when he got off at Paddington that he became separated from his parents and engulfed by the emerging crowds. He looked all around until, out of nowhere, his father grabbed his arm and dragged him down a flight of steps to the Bakerloo Line. Why hadn't his dad done this when he'd become lost to them at school? George yanked his arm free and strolled along the platform, his pre-school anxiety rising. Young Gerry evaporated. At Charing Cross, they hauled their luggage out to switch to the Northern Line and home.

There was no point unpacking. George sat on the edge of his bed gnawing his thumbnail. He bit hard and licked metallic blood. His parents talked in their bedroom. The usual soundtrack played through the open window: street games and distant trains. The rain was coming, a dirty, city rain.

Mum's voice became audible. "Not the same...so quiet, somber. Remember our little sprite?"

"Just puberty...could take him to the doctor again."

"It's that school."

Yes, Mum, at last.

"Being a teenager, Luce, is more like it...went through it with his son...a bit rough, he said. Now it's our turn with 'im."

Their voices dipped and became muffled as someone walked around. They seemed perplexed with him now. And his dad had tried so hard at the beach. But George had preferred his uncle.

As a train accelerated, Dad entered his room like a wish coming true. George leapt up and embraced him. "What the—?"

Here was the man who'd taught him to swim so he wouldn't fear the water, who'd shown him the constellations at night, and given him wondrous music that was stitched into his soul. His dad had brought him to the neighboring farm to witness the birth of twin lambs, born in March, as George had been, and encouraged him to focus on the heartier female lamb, not the male, name the girl. George hadn't realized until years later that the males were killed for meat, the females preserved for wool.

How wonderful, this paternal love. The last man who'd embraced him like this was—George went hot and pulled back.

Dad blinked, eyes soft as a cow. "You surprise me, love. We had a fine time at the old place, eh?"

George smiled. "We did. They were glad to see us. I'm not unpacking. I'll be ready to go first thing."

His father looked woeful. "Aye, that's fine. Not worried about problems at the school, are you?"

George turned away. As if he'd tell his dad a problem. Hopefully, dotty MacIntyre would leave off this term.

"You'll be a good lad? I don't want to be hearing from the headmaster. Try and study. O-levels is coming sooner than you think."

St. Clair would be entering the sixth form. Not that it mattered. Shadow George whispered, *he'll see you in the baths and want you again.*

I don't want lads anymore.

"What about Lord Kettering's son? He said ye never wanted his help?"

George scoffed. "Is that what he told you? He dropped me as soon as you left and told me to fend for myself."

Dad blinked. "Why would he—?"

"I'm still low class, Daddy. And they call me 'colored.' I mentioned about Grandmum Kirati once. They've never let me forget it."

Dad frowned. "Why didn't 'ee say something? Where you going? It's near tea, your mother will be—"

George ran downstairs, mad to get out. He took his bike into the leaden afternoon and pedaled down the street. A sea of clouds drizzled shining up the land. Fat drops hit his face and plunked in his eye. Blinded, he nearly missed the curb jump, fought for balance on the grass, and then veered behind houses counting to see which back garden was hers.

The messy one, as it turned out. He parked next to a chair with a broken spring, stepped over discarded bottles, and peered in at the back door. He flew down when she saw him from the kitchen. She darted out.

"You got a nerve coming here, little man. Are you spying now?"

"I wanted to say goodbye. Is Mr. Althorp…?"

"*Yes*. He's in front of the telly with 'is beer."

She stood higher than him on the step. He could reach right out and pull her down. Her brown eyes were flinty. The name "Myra" was stitched on the bosom of her frock.

He blinked at more drops dousing. "Why did you, I mean— Someone at school also showed me things."

"Did they now?"

"Was it my dancing?"

Glancing inward, she pulled a smoke from her pocket. "We had a bet on who could take the virginity of this hip-twitching popinjay. Ah, don't look shocked, pretty. I'm joshing. Here, the rain don't half make your eyelashes nice."

A squint of the eyes, a crack of a smile. She thumbed his bottom lip. He felt it below.

She said, "You won't forget me now?"

"Never. I'm yours. We could do whatever you—"

But a shower released and she ran inside.

EIGHT

"Stranger on the Shore"

(ACKER BILK, 1961)

HIS COURSES WERE HARDER in the Lower Fifth. Old mates returned. The "Corny" name did not resurrect. Of course, now George spoke as well as the best of them.

St. Clair didn't acknowledge him. Still a tall, rangy threat, the youth in college trousers appeared severed from his old gang. He was spied walking the grounds alone or sitting behind a pile of books in the library. Not that George cared. He had his own research to do and papers to start.

George grew jittery not only from his mounting workload but from the curiosity of his fellows. Last year's dance had tagged him as "racy." He gave way more often to his shadow-self, who could stroll down a hall without care. Twice he had to tell younger lads he didn't believe in servants.

In the dining hall, came a baleful look across tables, a tentative smile from St. Clair. Shadow George broke the eye contact. It was no good, him smiling. *That* traitor could rot. George received odd gifts in his cubbyhole: a snail shell, a dead moth, a comic from a gum wrapper. One day, a note appeared, folded small, with a handwritten *I Miss You*. Three days later, *Dance for me.*

George flinched when St. Clair came alongside him in the hall between lessons. A crowded intersection forced them to stall. St. Clair said, "Going my way?"

George shook his head. "I'm down here."

"I'm in the house next to yours. Third floor."

The youth flicked his hair and backed into a younger kid and scowled as if it was the kid's fault. George hastened off, then slowed at someone calling for him.

Winnie Palmer scuttled up, pink-cheeked with pleasure. George eased in the company of his former roommate, who still seemed baby-ish, despite his rampantly dirty mind. Winnie's voice had yet to change. George's had dropped from having sex with Mrs. Althorp. They walked companionably.

Winnie said, "New curse word this week: bugger. I buggered; he buggered; she buggered—well, she can't technically bugger. My uncle told my aunt to 'bugger off,' so you can use it with 'off.' 'Buggery' is the noun, though it's also an adjective, like 'buggery shame.' It means putting your—"

"What?" Winnie's voice had gone too low.

Winnie pulled George into him and giggled. "It means putting your cock up someone's *arse*. I know! Who wants their cock all brown? Can you imagine? Do you think it feels good?"

"How should I know?"

"Oh, no, I mean— Isn't it the blazes? Sorry. Poor taste."

"No, it's funny," George said crossly, then added, "I shagged a lady this summer."

Winnie pushed him to the wall. "My God, man. And this is the first time you're telling me? Outside, quickly. You must tell all."

But outside a scuffle caught his eye, a glimpse of flaxen hair going down. He broke off for a better look. Something roared inside him. The younger lads were shocked by his charge. All fled. One glared before running off: Martin Wells. But why would he be picking on—?

"My specs," cried the victim.

George found the tortoiseshell specs. "They're not broken."

He passed them to MacIntyre and offered a hand.

Glasses on, MacIntyre gawked.

"Don't," George warned, itchy to flee. He yanked the lad up and stalked away.

"W-wait!" called the voice behind him, "Kuh-kuh-kuh—"

George bolted before his name was said. This wasn't his muddle. He scarcely noticed that Winnie ran with him. They slowed when MacIntyre was well out of their view.

Winnie panted, "Good man, Carveth. Jolly decent of you. But why are we running?"

TRUE TO HIS word from last term, the art master referred George for student skits. However, the chance to perform before the entire school came with a newly planned Christmas Talent Show. Parents and locals were invited. Dad wrote that the American couple, the Stuarts, would attend. Uncle James offered to coach George privately and worked with him during weekends home and for days prior to the show. Uncle James came early and stayed in the nearby village.

Backstage, George worried his greased hair. Curls sprang loose. Uncle James shook his head. A pacing lad cracked his knuckles. Another polished his already gleaming French horn. A short one was having a quiet row with his mum. The art master popped through and beckoned. George was on. His stomach shot up. Bowels clenched. Uncle James squeezed his shoulder.

The auditorium beyond was full. Out there was a real audience. Perhaps Jack Stuart wasn't among them. His wife had balked at seeing the sweaty boy. George was all in white, from the soft leather of his jazz shoes to his cricket sweater, for another ode to Frank Sinatra, only this time to a cooler song.

The headmaster announced him. George emerged to polite applause and smiled at the darkness beyond. Footlights blinded. A speaker amplified the crackle of his record starting.

The opening of the song was slow. He moved as he should,

careful with his hands. It felt a pantomime. Stiffness came into his limbs. The theater felt huge. There were so many people. His legs grew cold. Perhaps he wasn't cut out for real performing. Rows of bodies waited, ready to judge; rowdy boys set to jeer. There was no expression on his face. He raised his brows and probably looked a twit.

Someone called "Georgina." Laughter. He turned his back to the audience, distraught at the blue velvet curtain.

Shadow George reminded *you are a gull catching the updraft*. George turned for Willy, hands splayed on either side of his face just as Frank sang "your fabulous face." A bit of a dance stopped the hands. People stirred as the band picked up, the tune "I Get a Kick Out of You."

No one laughed now. And the song was a lark, a ride. Faces came clear. He dared to smile at those smiling at him. His feet skimmed the stage, white shoes kicked—pop, right with the drum. People liked that. Well, here was more for them to like. The song was in him now, the dance like silk. He held a pose and searched for Edgely to show him no hard feelings, only a bit of fun. Stepping lightly, he succumbed to the joy of twirling faster and faster.

Boys whooped and shouted "Carveth!" He relished his favorite parts of the song. Hands, ankles…then a leap with the drum…people cheered. Whatever he did brought a reaction. Oh, for another stanza. But like the dance in the stairwell, the ending was quickly here. He cooled the mood and glided offstage.

A clatter erupted. The art master stayed the headmaster and pivoted George out again. Whistles and applause came louder. Faces beamed. Amazed, George almost forgot to bow. Then he saw the two blond heads beside his parents. They'd come.

The talent award went to an earnest van Cliburn-wannabe. George would have chosen the same way but mistakenly said in the ruckus backstage, "It wouldn't do to pick me," which riled his mum.

"What do you mean? How could it not do? You were clearly the winner."

Happily, Uncle Arthur and Aunt Sally had come up from Cornwall. His uncle chucked him on the chin. "I'm eating my hat, lad. You were fantastic up there."

Aunt Sally hugged. "Some of us are not surprised."

He endured her affection, distracted by the two Americans, who looked so clean and tall. A golden couple. Jill Stuart squeezed his arm. "I like the new voice."

"Ah, what?" Did she have to notice *that?*

She said, "It was a very mature dance. Calling attention to your face—nice touch."

Uncle James piped, "I heard that line and knew we had to use it."

Her blue eyes teased. "You have a great smile, cookie."

George almost giggled. "I love the way you talk."

"Hey, *I* don't have an accent. *You're* the one with the accent."

Her ballooning frock crushed against him. Her chest was sandy freckles.

Dad said, "I agree with you, Jill. Jimmy, you did a grand job."

Uncle James said, "There was a lot of George in that dance. I merely refined it."

Jack watched quietly. George dared, "Mr. S. What did you think?"

"Ah, kid. It was super, of course. But can you sing?"

"Sure."

"I think you should have sung the song instead of playing a record."

George swallowed. He'd done it the easy way.

Jill gripped her husband's arm. "He's got the face and the footwork. Does he really need the voice?"

"That's why he didn't win."

A man in black slunk past. George lunged for him. "Mum, Dad, this is Mr. Wilburn, my old friend."

Everyone made room for the startled lit master, who tensed in George's grasp. Dad pumped the man's hand. "Pleasure to finally meet you, sir. We so appreciated your befriending the lad his first year."

Mr. Wilburn adjusted his amber-rimmed specs. "Oh, not at all. Your son is a delightful...a truly..."

"We think so." Dad winked at George.

Mr. Wilburn saddled his arm heavily on George's shoulders with a whiff of spicy scent. "Goodness, yes. A true talent. This chap will go far indeed. Jolly nice to have met you both, at last."

George balked. "You were the one never wanted—"

Wilburn jerked and bashed into Jill, who frowned at him. She stepped out of his way and gave George a questioning look.

He knew he should change his face. But there were his mates pushing through. "Lads! Over here. The Yank." He pointed at Jack then asked him. "You don't mind, do you?"

Jack shook his head, eyes wide, as St. Clair and the others crowded in. Jack said, "All right, who's coming out for Cokes?"

Boys clamored and raised hands. St. Clair gawked. "Cripes, your parents look like film stars."

Winnie sprang over to Jill, hand out. "Horace Winston Palmer, the third. I've heard *so much* about you, Missus—"

"Winnie!"

George had blabbed far too much about Jill Stuart's breasts. Winnie pulled back his hand with a giggle. Jill looked confused.

Mum said, "Lamb, is that a friend? He wants to join in."

MacIntyre had gotten backstage. George blurted, "No. Leave him out of it."

The little rotter slunk away. But George's ear was twisted.

Mum narrowed feline eyes. "Now, baby, why would you be so rude to that poor child? Go and fetch him."

Ear burning, George shuffled after MacIntyre. The lad glanced back. George erased his frown. "MacIntyre. Look sharp. You're joining us."

MacIntyre looked skeptical, so George added, "I changed my mind."

"R-really?" Pinkness bloomed on thin cheeks.

How bad off was this kid that he wanted time with a monster? MacIntyre grinned like a loon. George charged him with telling the others he'd gone to change clothes.

George dodged families on his way to the dressing room. People stopped their chatter to compliment him. It was wonderful.

Someone grabbed his arse cheek and dragged him backward. Mr. Wilburn hissed with peppermint breath, "Very slick, very naughty. I told you I don't meet parents."

"All right. Let go."

But the man squeezed until the tears came. "Still a nice handful. Hope there's no bruise. You did well, sport, your best yet."

George wrenched away. He'd punch this ape.

"Ooo, there's his fire. Aren't you lovely when you're angry."

Buggery arsehole! George flew towards the dressing room.

IN THE SUMMER, Uncle James freed George from his dance job because Jack Stuart required him. Jack started him on lessons with a singing coach, which was more trying than fun. George knew he was mediocre. In an office on Sloan Square, Jack took portfolio photos with a camera on a tripod. George squinted under a spotlight. A foil card angled nearby bounced more light. Jack turned him by the chin.

"You have a touch of the Orient in your look."

George smiled without comment. Mum said to stop volunteering about his heritage. It invited trouble. Jack peered through the lens.

"You remind me of Alain Delon, that hot new actor? He was in *Purple Noon* and *Rocco and His Brothers*. They're great pictures. You must see them. Don't just go to British films or American. What comes from the continent is equally important. And Japan, you know *Yojimbo* by Kurosawa?"

"I saw *The Misfits.*" This was the most adult film George could think of, and Marilyn Monroe had been heaven.

"John Huston. Good. Look here."

The shutter clicked several times. "You should know the directors. And see actors like Toshiro Mifune and Marcello Mastroianni. And Delon, a stunner like you."

George flushed, a grin breaking out.

Jack scanned national auditions, not just local, which was how George won a part in Bath, in a production of *The King and I*. Though he auditioned with a song, he was offered the non-singing part of the young prince. Privately, Jack shook his head as if that wasn't good enough. He booked a room for each of them for the play's duration.

Mum said Jack "came from money." Dad fretted about the expenses. But George loved how Jack took care of him.

His parents brought Jill to the play's opening. When George wondered why Jill shouldn't join them for the run, Jack scoffed. "These are working experiences. I don't want you distracted. And my wife gets a little too flirtatious around you."

Shadow George knew it. He would visit her on his own.

No, George decided, *she belongs to Jack*. An ace chap like him deserves a wife like her.

When the play finished, Jack took him to Brighton for the day and brought a London paper to peruse more auditions. With its long pier and gay atmosphere, Brighton seemed grander than St. Ives. They changed into swim trunks. The Channel sloshed in with mild crests. George inhaled the briny air. The pebble beach was a disappointment —one needed shoes to get to a beach chair.

Jack positioned two chairs in the crunch. "Just pretend it's the Riviera. I've heard the women there go topless."

George gasped. "We have to go. And bring Jill."

Jack laughed, then said, "Hey!" and swatted him with the paper. "You like my wife. She's no great beauty. Good figure, yes. But I'm a little mystified how much you—well." Jack smiled behind his sunglasses and snapped open the paper.

But Jill *was* beautiful. And fun. And nice. George slid down to thoughts of her. Eons later, Jack said, "You must have a girlfriend."

It arrested his doze. His eyes cracked to searing brightness. "No."

No, but we have a housewife, mused Shadow George, who'd managed a reunion with an eager Mrs. Althorp.

"I find that hard to believe, a worldly chap like yourself."

Shadow George smiled. "Well. I've had sex, plenty."

"Plenty, eh?" A page flicked. "You should turn over before you burn that flawless skin. I guess you don't get freckles."

They both turned over. Jack's shoulders were brown freckled, slightly printed with the bar of the chair, a vaccination mark on his arm. "Khrushchev and Kennedy," he muttered, switching to a *Life* magazine. Shadow George had glimpsed the ridge of a scar on Jack's midriff and wished for his own scar, or maybe a tattoo.

Jack said, "I bet you're the ladies' man at school, right?"

George sifted cool pebbles beneath the slats of his chair. "There are no ladies at my school. But for old ones."

"I think I understand. Fun with the lads."

Shadow George scoffed. "You won't guess. A schoolmaster."

"Ah…oh. Yeah?"

Shadow George used the suave term "affair." "It went on for a while. He was mad for me." He crossed his arms as if to sleep.

But for a "Huh," Jack went quiet. Perhaps he was shocked. He'd seen George as a naïve kid. Well, that image was gone. Shadow George peeked.

Jack appeared to be reading his magazine as if such affairs were common. Though he said, "Was this recently?"

"A few years ago."

Pity flashed in the gray eyes. Disbelief. The man thought he was telling tales. Mortified, Shadow George fled, leaving George to hide his face in his arms with a sudden wish to be riding his bike at home.

They toured Brighton Pavilion in the afternoon. But George dragged and yawned. He made Jack stop at a bar on a side road because Julie London was performing, only it was someone *pretending* to be Julie London. Jack reminded that her name had been in quotes. Her voice sounded awfully husky.

Jack ordered lemonade for George and wouldn't change it to a shandy, even when the bloke next to them said, "Go on, buy him a shandy." He kept saying "your lovely pet" to Jack.

Jack said, "Let's get out of here," then, "I hate men like that."

During a filet of sole supper, George finally realized about the man and the bar. Did Jack think him a pansy? The cold tingles made him put down his fork. Jack asked if he was all right.

He nodded. "'Course. A bit done in."

Jack smiled without disgust. "We've had a long day."

GEORGE HAD a week of freedom before auditioning for an important, young theater group, as Jack called them, and rode the tube to Chelsea, to the brick maisonette. Jill Stuart smiled in the doorway, a sunny vision in an orange frock.

"Hey, dancing boy. He's not here. Unless you're coming for me."

Was there ever a nicer girl? "'Course I'm comin' for you."

George had dressed with care. His new dungarees made his fingers blue. His clean shirt was sticking from the heat. Jill offered a bottle of "pop." She settled on a settee, long legs crossed, knees shiny and exposed as she drew sewing onto her lap. The Stuart flat was a mod gray and black with red accents. Patterned rugs covered a black-and-white tiled floor. Tobacco wafted from Jill's burning fag. George wished he could join her but still found smoking nasty.

"Talk to me," she ordered, poking a needle through a button.

"Jack thinks I'll be famous."

"Is the Pope Catholic?"

"Sorry? I…believe so." To her grin, he said, "You're too American."

"Doll, that's the risk you take coming over here. What?"

He giggled into a red pillow.

She squeaked and sucked her finger. "You've been beaming at me since Day One."

"You talk like the pictures."

He darted to inspect the hi-fi unit, the latest cabinet model. "Wish we had a gramophone like this. You probably hear so much better." The sound was clear and full, tuned to the BBC. He didn't recognize the piece that was playing.

She said, "Wait, you listen to classical music?"

He whirled on her, indignant. Was she ever serious?

He said, "You know that dancer from the Kirov who defected? He's supposed to be the best male dancer in the world. I hope he comes to London."

Nureyev, the defector, took over his body. Ballet moves shivered the tumblers on the drinks trolley. Until George remembered he wasn't at home. Nor homeless, like the poor Russian.

But wasn't Jill homeless, in a way? "It must be hard for you being in another country. You must get sad."

Jill looked up from her task in surprise. "It is. I do."

"I know how that is, sort of. Not a country but being in a new..." He turned, overcome. Too personal. But he wheeled back. "Do you know what frightens me? The H-bomb. Do you think we'll be alive in ten years?"

Her eyes were wide. "What if it's only five?"

"I wish they wouldn't always talk about it on the news. Can you imagine such a thing on a day like today?"

"It's like we're held hostage while they stockpile bombs."

"Dad says we may be back in the underground."

"Would that even be safe enough?"

"Lord, I don't know."

But the music on the wireless had switched to Beethoven. "It's the Seventh Symphony, the dancing one."

He turned up the volume and settled on a chair. Not that he would be able to keep still. This was the piece Dad had used years ago to pull him out of himself. Jill's foot caught the rhythm.

George sprang up to dance—or casually walk—or dance, just a bit. How could there be bombs in the world when there was this?

With the cigarette in her mouth, Jill applauded, saying, "*You* are like the pictures."

But the joy of the first movement gave way to the adagio of the second, its somber beauty stealing in. *Don't disappear. You're with her.*

Too late, the spell was cast.

A place in here, dark, with a piss reek, salt flesh pressing...

George opened his eyes. Jill pulled thread in the peace of the afternoon. His heart pounded. He leaned into the cushion.

But his lids succumbed to the drug of listening. Yes, the violin still teased, and he still rode it to keep away.

"That counter-melody," he said, "do you hear, beneath the main one? That's me."

"Why is that you?" She sounded amused.

"I am not part of this life. I complement so you don't notice."

"Why are you not part of this life?" she said from a distance.

SHADOW GEORGE STARTLED at the sound in the room. "That piece. He mustn't hear it."

He leapt and switched off the unit.

Jill Stuart stared at him, hands out in a tableau of sewing. "Who mustn't?"

"Beethoven is a bore."

"You're kidding." She stood and a jacket fell to the floor. Her gaze stayed on him.

Shadow George demurred with a bat of the lashes. "We own that record. I'm sure you could borrow it. Dad won't mind."

A flash of a frown, she went for the stairs. Was she deserting him? Should he follow? Ladies were a puzzle, one minute, warm, the next cool. Or perhaps Americans were a puzzle.

She reappeared, a book in hand. "I wonder if you like stories. I just read this."

She brought down *A Taste of Honey* by Shelagh Delaney. He said, "That's a play in the West End. Isn't it a girl's story?"

"It has a female protagonist. But it's more about teenagers struggling. It's edgy. You might enjoy it."

There was powder beneath her cigarette reek. He ignited his smile. "I like being with you."

"Why are you not part of this life?"

"What? But I am. I'm full of life." Did that damn George think he didn't exist?

"You don't want to talk about it?"

How she studied him, then broke off. "I believe Jack was stopping by your uncle's studio. Shall we meet him there?"

It was too nice a day for the tube. They opted for the open windows of a southbound bus. Shadow George urged her to the top deck. Young girls squeezed past with a giggle, "Did you see that boy?"

Jill quirked her eyebrows at him—did that happen a lot?

It happened enough. They rode over Battersea Bridge, the dead fish smell of the Thames churning beneath.

At Fleet Feet studio, a class was in progress. There was short Myra losing patience with some geezer, though she grinned Chinese seeing George. He couldn't help saying, "That one there. She's quite a mover, don't you think?"

Mrs. Althorp whirled by, gawping at Jill.

George pushed his guest into his uncle's office and shut the door. Jill protested, but he put "Tequila" on the turntable, its Latin beat infectious. Shadow George felt a swing coming on.

Jill said, "Okay," at his swaying.

Mrs. Althorp had told him he must be bold with women. He dove for Jill, dancing her to a wall, her breasts popping close. "Do you like my cobra dance?"

"What *is* that, exactly?"

"My body is a snake. You can't resist—"

She pushed him backward. "Stop it! You're not my type."

Shadow George staggered. "You think I'm ugly? I'm repulsive. I-I've grown funny, you see. I used to be better."

He fell to the wall, needing to sit or blackout. "I'll be covered in hair and, and spots. You're not attracted. I don't please you."

Her faraway voice, "*Please* me? Something's not right here..."

Jill Stuart crouched beside him, holding his arm. "Sweetie, you're shaking. Why are you shaking? Should I call your uncle?"

Bloody Shadow George must've made trouble again.

"No."

His uncle had yet to see this batty side of him. Now *Jill* was seeing it, how awful.

She plucked at him. He scrambled up the wall and drifted from her. "Please don't tell Jack. He thinks I have star quality."

She stopped the record. "You do."

He winced. And dared to face her.

Her look was kind. "Honey. What just happened? You have to tell Jack if you can't perform."

He smiled like an actor. "But I can. Performing is the thing I do well. Or one of them."

Her brow creased. "Are you feeling better?"

"Heaps. Sorry. Those old-man shakes, I just get them. It's an age thing."

"I hurt your feelings. Open the door, would you?"

He did so and squawked at Mrs. Althorp standing there.

Mrs. Althorp glared. But Jill got in front of him. "May I help you?"

Mrs. Althorp tried to go around her. "I need to see that one."

But Jill played guard. "I'm sorry. We're still talking."

She spun Mrs. Althorp out and shut the door! His lover would be furious later.

Jill charged for the cigarettes on his uncle's desk. "A bit old for *that* behavior. Clearly too soon to have— Let's stay put a minute. How are your singing lessons?"

"Um…yeah. Pure rot. I mean I never knew how bad I was until I started lessons. Jack wants me to audition for a musical. Is that mad?"

Her smoke went straight to his face. She said, "I wish your trips weren't 'men only.'"

Don't cough. "I've asked him to bring you."

"Oh yeah? I think you're going to land *Guys and Dolls*. Doll-face."

She elbowed him, her grin back. But she thought him bats, didn't she? Females were hard to figure.

NINE

"La Mer (Beyond the Sea)"

(CHARLES TRENET & JACK LAWRENCE, 1946)

BUT JILL DID NOT JOIN them for the Scotland trip, and the hasty learning of *Guys and Dolls*, which was just as well. When George finished the last performance in Edinburgh, he was ecstatic with relief. The director seemed pleased. The audiences had liked his Sky Masterson. Yet he'd barely hung on. He should have had a bit part with the popular New Lights Players, where all the actors were under eighteen. It was an honor just to be selected. His audition for them had gone long, with the director feeding him lead parts. The lead had nearly been promised to a Scottish youth, who was none too pleased when the director cast him in the supporting role. The lad clearly wanted to push George's face in the dirt. George had to tune him out and go deep within himself to learn the role. He ended up channeling Jack, complete with an American accent.

Applause was a godsend at the end of that first show. Jill and his parents were among the sea of heads. They found him backstage.

Jill pulled him aside. "You were imitating Jack, weren't you?"

"Don't tell him."

She punched his shoulder. "Of course not. Whatever it takes, right? I only wish his parents could have seen it."

She squashed her breasts on him in an embrace, which would've been nice if her presence didn't spark embarrassment. She'd witnessed his batty behavior. (And slammed the door on Mrs. Althorp.) He'd finished her book in no time. Why had she given him a story with a queer character?

Again, she wanted to stay and ride home with "the fellas." But then she was on the train in the morning with Mum and Dad. At least they wouldn't see him fall on his face in subsequent performances.

Yet that never happened. The director told him to come back next year. Even the Scottish lad offered a hand. "I wanted to hate you, but you slayed it."

"Sarah Brown" pulled George into a dark corner. Desired at last by this girl who sang so well—a confident lass of sixteen—she didn't fight him off when he mauled her lips and tender neck, her earlobe buttoned with a pearl. She nattered between kisses about letters, promises, and a boyfriend who was waiting for her. Perhaps George would win her favor?

He broke off. "Keep your lad. I'm still in school."

Alone again with Jack, the Royal Mile was alive with late-night revelers. They stopped at a coffee bar and listened to a cat play bongos. George loaded his java with cream and sugar; he wasn't allowed to go to coffee bars at home. Thrilled by the bongo rhythms, he walked on his hands on the pavement outside to the amusement of passing girls. An old man snapped, "Hooligan."

George flipped to his feet, offended. Jack laughed and shook out a smoke. George stood still to be lit. "But was I any good, really?"

Jack said, "This again? Kid, you pulled it off. Like Marlon Brando, it's not your strength. But most people didn't realize it."

"But *you* saw."

"I saw a novice keeping his cool."

"I faked it." He swallowed a cough. "I was sick before each show. I heard myself and winced."

"There were some rough notes. Your 'Luck Be a Lady' was top-notch."

"I aped Dad's Sinatra record."

Jack laughed, an infectious sound. "It worked, Frankie-baby. Relax. You have more musicality than you think. Big star." He tousled George's hair. "Hey, I sound like your Sky. Let's celebrate. What do you most want to do?"

George couldn't wave his cigarette wide enough. "Oh, I'm beyond happy. Even if it has been a summer without the sea."

"You'll have to give me a few hours to fix that one."

The next day was the return ride south. George had to pack for school. But Jack detoured them to Scarborough on the North Sea, instead, a last-minute treat. A cab dropped them at a busy hotel where Jack booked the last room.

How great being with this big American who granted favors. George now saw his life beyond school. In seven months he'd be sixteen, the age to legally quit. He'd likely quit after O-level exams. Dad wanted him to go the extra two years until A-levels and possibly university. But George had different ideas.

What a fine evening in Scarborough. They had supper at a local pub. A Frank Ifield song played, and Jack joined the crowd at the bar, half-singing, half-yodeling "I Remember You." George grinned. He *had* to have this record. Jack shouted over the commotion and a Brenda Lee song. George maintained a listening face, but tuned in to Brenda Lee, liking the sexy gusto in her voice. And Jack nattered to anyone who would listen. He caught the interest of quite a few patrons. The Yank was clearly likable. George felt a warm sense of ownership.

Isn't he a feather in the cap? Your *American*, Shadow George teased.

So. You're back now that the pressure is off.

What do you mean? You were handling it. You might need me now.

George scoffed aloud, catching the notice of a nearby drinker.

He and Jack walked back to their hotel via the beach, barefoot in the surf. Jack had procured two large bottles of beer. The brew was tingling gulps, bitter and gaseous. They finished with great, head-turning belches—too funny! Dad would never have allowed the drink nor the proffered cigarette. George was finally smoking like an adult, no longer sick. It was mellow, just the ticket, the cat's whiskers. When Jack said he looked good smoking, George couldn't help mimicking the adverts. Wonderful, making Jack laugh.

The sea roared restless and comforting, glinting lavender beneath a sky scarred in pink, the tide coming in. George tossed the butt, hiked his trousers to his knees, and danced through stinging waves. Debussy dwelled here (*La Mer*) with old spirits, old joys.

Jack called, "Wait. You have good calves. Mine are thin."

Jack stayed on wet sand, rolling shallow cuffs, and hooted when splashed. George giggled to see the big American scoot from the surf.

George's trousers were drenched to the crotch. Waves rushed him, with sand peppering back. He trod cool depths. He'd get used to swimming this sea in no time.

Jack was a swaying silhouette at the edge. "Come on out, Nijinsky. I have to return you in one piece."

"I'm a fish, Jack Stuart."

"Don't even think about it. Hey, have you ever tried dancing against the music? Like in a jazz band when a player goes off on an improvisation? Fred Astaire did it in this solo in a ship's engine room in 'Shall We Dance,' all rhythmic."

George sloshed out and grabbed the big man, who went mule-like about going any farther in the water. George broke away and shouted, "I love Fred Astaire!"

And he loved it when Jack challenged him. Dancing counterpoint.

The tide was hungry for the beach. The hero of the pub stopped to shove his wet, sandy feet back into loafers. George stayed barefoot and ran on the balls of his feet across the coastal road. They worked their way up the zigzag trail to their hotel, the hilly terrain less steep than St. Ives.

But Jack was soon panting. "Where do you get your energy? Oh, wait, you're fifteen."

They thumped, giggling and shushing each other up eight flights of stairs to their narrow top-floor room. Jack gasped, "Oh God… you're going to have to drag me."

And George did, hefting him the last few feet and laughing so hard he could have pissed himself. Both fell backward onto the wood floor. Half the ceiling was slanted in the hotel's one remaining bedroom. There was one double bed.

Jack staggered up. "Damn. They didn't bring up the cot like I asked. I'll take the chair. You take the bed."

"I can fall asleep in a chair. I've done it in school."

"I'll pretend I didn't hear that. Your feet are black."

Jack claimed the chair. George confirmed the state of his feet. A bath, it was. He'd need to scrape off his damp trousers.

The tiny bathroom was papered with brown and yellow flowers. Copper pipes throbbed and moaned at the faucet-turning demand for water. A tepid stream spilled into the deep bathtub. He yodeled, "I Remember You" through a quick scrub. After, he saw through a window that the tide had conquered the beach.

In their warm, smoky bedroom, George balled his clothes and threw them in the manner of one bowling in cricket. The force of it knocked a picture off the wall.

Jack flinched in his underwear. "What the hell?"

George dissolved in giggles at these nervous sides of the Yank.

Jack sighed. "Okay. I'm guessing you haven't had a lot of beer and cigarettes."

"Oh, I've had my share."

George shed his towel and burrowed into the bedclothes, bringing the sheet over his face. Though it was warm in the attic room. At least his head was still wet.

Jack commented, "So you're going to leave the picture on the floor and your clothes strewn everywhere. I didn't take you for an entitled little prince. But I guess you are one."

George hiccuped a laugh. Or…was Jack *really* being a mother hen about it? He threw down the bed sheet to check.

Jack's expression was cold.

The change in mood burned his skin. Woodenly, he retrieved his garments and tossed them at his suitcase. The bloody picture wouldn't go on the wall until he realized the nail was bent. He was far too aware of being naked and watched as he strained to straighten the nail.

"It's bent," he said stupidly.

"Do the best you can."

His body warm, George got the picture to hang again, crookedly.

Jack said, "Wait," before he could dash to the bed. "My artists have class. Remember that. You know…it isn't the worst thing in the world for your agent to see you. You're a strong-looking kid."

George barely nodded. Water dripped from the hair on his forehead. *My agent.* It was a powerful word. It drained the tension in his body. He looked at Jack.

Who looked away. "Go on."

George darted for the bed and its covers. Jack shuffled about the room then went out to the loo. George leapt for his suitcase to drag out pajamas.

HE WAS IN A HOTEL ROOM, impaled and crying that first weekend away. Mr. Wilburn trying to shush and kiss him. And all along, that splitting pain. *No, don't move.*

George forced open his eyes. Jack stood over him with an alarmed face. They were naked. A lamp was on. George said, "What?"

"You were moaning and making noises. You don't remember?"

"I-I was asleep."

"You looked at me when I spoke to you."

George frowned. His heart ricocheted in his chest. He had no memory of moaning. The bedside clock read half past one. Jack made noises like snorting through gritted teeth. "That's what you sounded like."

George bolted from the bed.

He thumped through the hall, into the bathroom, flicked on the light and raised the toilet seat. For a moment, it seemed a false alarm.

Then he was seized with a jet of bile and sour lager. The sensitive surface of his knees pressed the hard, cold tile. He gripped the toilet through another emptying wave.

He did a choked cry that stopped as quickly as it started.

Shadow George hissed, *He thinks you're crackers.*

I must have been dreaming. That first weekend with Willy. What a thing to remember after all this time.

Jack had woken him earlier, his hot-skinned weight crowding behind him. "I can't sleep on a chair. Move over. You mind?"

And the man moved him, being strong, his hands sliding right past the barrier of pajamas, freeing him from their cloying cover. Shadow George cried, *here we go.* George leaned against him to keep from flying apart. Jack was pulling him from the waves…whisking him from Clapham. And hungry like that other, hands taking, mouth seeking. George felt fiery with a dizzy, falling-in feeling, a familiar mania.

And things were off now. Way, way off. Even that was familiar. He rose from the floor and pulled the chain to flush.

WAKE UP!

He woke in another two hours but managed to drift back to sleep until the clock hands formed the line of six.

Wake up! Shadow George was nervous. *The morning erection.*

George came to, realizing, and slipped as carefully as possible from Jack's arms. Dressed and catlike, he departed the room.

Outside, fresh air grazed, ocean-scented. The best scent. The beach was exposed, silvery-sunlit and mostly deserted, except for a few dog walkers. He trotted down the zigzag path over the steep slope of the land, crossed the coastal road down to the sand. The North Bay was glinting and molten, the surf tumbling and thrusting the shingle with a gentle force. A waiting lover.

George stripped to his underwear, stuffed his clothes between rocks and ran in. Waves sliced up his legs, through his pants. He plunged the chill, dolphin-kicked through crests, blood pumping, limbs working, coldness dissipating, an easy force to master. Not like the restless bay at Porthmeor.

He didn't stop until well out. The sun blasted. He turned his back to it and flung his hair from his eyes. The coastline was a vivid green horseshoe of land, castle ruins on the high point, colored toy box rows of houses and hotels, people waking up now, making coffee, and frying eggs. One mere human he was, disconnected (packed up, sent off), cradled in seawater. Had he lived in a bubble in St. Ives, happy and naïve? How broken he'd felt after that weekend away with Wilburn. They'd gone to hear music in another town. Eventually, he adapted to the new order. And now the man waited at the hotel.

The sea rocked and slapped. He plodded sun-wards, toward blinding shards. What relief he would gain when his arms gave out. No more memories to frighten him anew.

But Jack waited, fool! Not that *other*. George reversed course and swam madly towards the land. Only perhaps he was in a current. His swimming seemed to make no progress whatsoever. He cut back on a diagonal, slowed, and tread water, gasping.

But was he drifting at all? Annoyance gave him the strength to press on and the fact that he'd look a right twit sinking in a calm sea. A ways down, closer to the castle ruins, he rode crests like hitching rides, floundering between, surfing another. An old man and a spastic terrier watched from the shore. George found the ground and staggered out. His sagging, soaked pants webbed his front bits. The little terrier barked and pranced, rightly mistrustful of creatures coming out of the sea.

"'At's a hearty swim you did there, young lad. Done it before?"

George scarcely had a voice. "St. Ives Bay, sir, when I can."

He collapsed to his knees, grateful, in the chilly sunny air and offered a hand to the dog. But now the man was taking him in, noticing the transparent underwear. George shrank. Water sluiced his bottom, tightened his scrotum and shifted his pants. The man clucked to his dog and moved on.

George scraped hair from his eyes and jumped since he had no means of drying himself. He was all right, better now. Sunlight scalded his skin. A shiver snaked through him.

Shadow George worried. *He thinks we're queer.* Queers gave Dad the creeps. Police took them away.

We're normal. We like lassies.

You liked it in the dark.

I didn't. I don't know anymore. We liked that dirty Myra.

St. Clair didn't affect him, not really. The big lout helped with studies, even if payment was a bit of the nasty. And George didn't go for Winnie Palmer or others. Had he ever pursued a lad? Other than… Please let dotty MacIntyre leave off this term. At least Wells rightly turned at the sight of him. Perhaps he'd stay on at the school through his eighteenth year, as Dad wanted.

After jogging a good distance George found his garments peeping through the rocks. He sloughed the wet underwear before dressing, and carried it balled up in his hand, and then stuffed it in his pocket as he approached the hotel. His stomach yawned empty.

"Hey, sonny."

The florid-faced owner called, who'd registered them in. "Your Yank friend was looking for you. Seemed quite worried."

"I had a swim."

"That feller, is he a mate of yours?"

George nodded, though the man narrowed his gaze as if he didn't quite believe him.

"How old are you, son?"

Cheeks prickling, George sidled for the stairs. "Fifteen."

"Wait up, hang on. I mean it's all right your being here? Your parents know? I don't want any funny business in my hotel."

George loped the stairs. When he flew into the top-floor room, Jack sprang from the bed.

"Christ! There you are."

"I was swimming, right? I told you I'm a fish. Do you have to run about the place like my mum?"

His voice shot up like a kid. Mortified, Jack's loafers filled his line of vision. The pocketed underwear dampened his thigh.

"Are you okay?" Jack's voice was gentle.

"I'm right famished if you want to know. Aren't they serving breakfast now?"

Not waiting for an answer, George about-faced down, taking a turn on the stairs away from the front desk.

The heat of the kitchen warmed the small dining room. The smell of the sea wafted from his hair and skin.

A waitress poured coffee. "Someone's had a swim."

He and Jack were silent through the service. George cracked open his soft-boiled egg, practically slurped it out, and wished for another. He pulled his tea forward. A piece of toast tasted like nothing. He worked a shred of loose skin on his thumb. His nails were mangled. He would even them out.

Jack cleared his throat. George lowered his hands. There was an anti-bomb headline on someone's newspaper. "Jill."

Jack alerted. Lines appeared on his forehead. "You won't say anything?"

But his eyes stung. How had he not thought of her before? "I can't see her again."

"Yeah, we'll talk in the room."

"How can you face her?"

Jack picked up his fork then put it down. George frowned at his piece of bitten toast. Jill would go back to hating him.

"Kid, listen. I'm not a…a homo." Jack mouthed the word.

"Nor am I."

Jack stirred his bacon through egg goo. "Great, that's good. Anyway. What happened isn't unusual. Throughout history, men would dally, even when they had wives. It's a phase, a thing."

A "thing." A dally.

Jack put down his fork. "You're young, I know, but experienced, as you said. We were horsing around. Last night was, it was just…"

But then came a lilt in his voice, the way some people would get after doing what they wanted, as if it were music now, their feelings, sad and yearning. He whispered low, "When we go back to the room, would you let me…?"

George winced. "Don't *ask*. Just do what you like."

Not getting a response, he glanced. Jack gawped at him.

"Look, I thought it would be all right because of what you told me —Jesus." Jack threw down his cloth napkin. "Get your fingernails out of your mouth."

George gripped his hands.

Jack shifted. "You're in dire need of a manicure. I'm taking you to one in London. They can paint something on your nails."

"I don't want painted nails."

"It's to keep you from biting them, you twit. My God. What a fool I am." The man wiped his reddened face. His eyes were sea-gray.

"I'm fine. We're fine here," he said to people noticing. "I need a refill of coffee. Where is that waitress?"

His gaze sought George. "Try not to hate me, would you? Do you want anything? You're not eating."

George gripped his tea. "I don't hate you. Easy now. Here comes the coffee."

TEN

"Dance at the Gym"

(LEONARD BERNSTEIN, 1957)

GIRLS WERE COMING FOR A DANCE. Some professors groused that their presence would spoil the discipline. Ninnies. It was about time as far as George was concerned.

A Mr. Bagley was brought in to teach basic steps in a cleared-away dining hall. Someone's titled mum, a Lady Caroline, was brought in for etiquette and manners. George tried to get out of the dance lessons, then volunteered to help teach them. Rebuffed, both counts. He endured the class by pretending to be awful, entertaining those around him. When the master's back was turned, he'd run through steps nimbly then feign clumsiness under the teacher's attention. Poor Mr. Bagley couldn't figure out why part of his line kept falling apart. He snapped at lads for laughing at Carveth's "inability."

Lady Caroline arrived to sort out the trouble and declared the young gentlemen would learn faster with a female partner. She was a green-eyed blonde in a smart wool suit, her hair lacquered into a bubble. She intoned darkly of poor posture, incorrect form, sweaty palms. Talc was shaken on hands, mints administered for breath.

George made the mistake of trying to impress her, even as clueless Bagley muttered, "Carveth may need extra help."

George approached, arms out. No faults to belittle here. Dry-palmed, he took her fingers.

She narrowed her eyes. "Your form is incorrect."

He broke away. "There's nothing wrong with my form."

Students gasped. Mr. Bagley said, "Mind yourself, lad."

Lady Caroline hardened her gaze. "You contradict me?"

"I know how to dance. My uncle teaches ballroom."

Now Mr. Bagley gasped. She said, "It seems he taught you incorrectly."

"My uncle runs the Fleet Feet studio in Clapham."

"How impressive. And they're nationally known, are they? Oh, yes, Mr. Bagley, this one needs extra help. I suspect we've found the cause of your troubles. The Fleet Studios in Clapham taught him. Well, Vernon and Irene Castle taught my parents, and I was schooled under the same high standards and won many a competition, so I assure you I know a little more than your uncle."

George pivoted away.

Which was how he came to be scrubbing the gymnasium floor hours before the dance. Around him, New Matron directed younger lads with decorations. Many a glance was thrown in his direction. Paraffin heaters had been brought in for the chill.

Between their oily scent and the washing soap in his bucket, George was feeling ill. Footsteps rapped down the center of the floor. With a sniff, Mr. Bagley stood over him.

"You are the lucky one. Lady Caroline took pity. Kindhearted as ever, she insisted you attend. Have you learned your lesson?"

"Yes, sir."

"I wonder. Very well, Carveth. Put this away so the floor can dry."

WITH CREPE PAPER, bouquets, and glowing heaters, the gymnasium was transformed. Lasses were herded along a far wall looking like Bavarian sweets in their colored frocks. Red-eared, soap-scented boys, plain and hearty as English tea, whispered excitedly. Thankfully, all had been allowed to wear long trousers. Some of the young misses sparkled with smiles. Others gawped. Two sneered.

Most wore puffy frocks, so George focused on the few in straight skirts, who might be racier. Then again, whirling a big skirt guaranteed a shot of leg. He stood slightly apart from his fellows, head chilled from all the hair cream. Even still, he felt the stuff separating, renegade curls tickling his forehead. *Don't touch it.*

He was Alain Delon as Tom Ripley as Philippe Greenleaf.

Donned in satin, her hair frothed large, Lady Caroline gassed into a microphone. "I know you'll conduct yourselves impeccably like fine young ladies and gentlemen of the Crown. Mind your distance when dancing. Rude behavior will not be tolerated. Enjoy yourselves, everyone."

Some idiot had chosen Edgely for DJ, who started with "Getting to Know You." Kids groaned on both sides. Lady Caroline said, "now, now" and waved her hands for movement. No one crossed the floor. Girls clustered to talk. Boys dug their hands in their pockets.

The few masters on duty were rapt to Lady Caroline, but for the tall lit master, who scanned the lasses with narrowed eyes. Mr. Wilburn's gaze jumped to the lads, nodding to one, calling to another.

George twitched with annoyance. He still felt wired to the man. Wilburn approached, urging fellows to make the crossing. From the front, Lady Caroline beckoned for action.

Winnie bumped George, startling him. "Are you going to dance?"

"Of course. Not to this."

"Oh, heavens, no. Wouldn't be caught dead with this."

Edgely indulged his flair for the dramatic with the "Theme from *Exodus*," a completely undanceable piece. Chaps booed.

Winnie smelled of hair tonic. "You don't think he'll put on 'High Hopes'? I'll scream if he does."

"I'll do my *dance* if he does."

Mr. Wilburn marched over to Edgely's table. "Oh good," George murmured, "He'll make it right." Mr. Wilburn sorted through disks then handed one out.

The swirling piano faded. Voices and trumpet started "Wonderland by Night." Sappy, popular, and good enough. George burst from his group, half aware that Lady Caroline said, "At last."

His step faltered. The row of girls rippled, alerted, all eyes on him. A poor colored lass was on the end. Her life couldn't be easy. But a blonde babydoll with hair like spun sugar glowed in the middle. She rocked and beamed as he approached, and accepted his hand. Why shouldn't he go for a tasty one? He whirled her to the center. She fell into him, breasts to chest. Lads whistled. Lady Caroline cleared her throat. George eased off his partner, creating proper distance, and made his form impeccable for the onlookers. His lovely partner was not terribly light on her feet. At a stumble, he counted her back in. Yet her hair smelled of flowers, a babydoll for sure.

Who kept stuttering her steps. Had she no rhythm? It couldn't be more basic. His fingers instructed—come forward, turn under, wait. The girl bumped him at song's end as if she meant to mash her tits on him. George held her off.

Could he abide a cutie with such disregard for the music? She'd probably be good for a snog later. He bowed and escorted her back.

She said, "Is that it? My name is June. Are you sixth form?"

"Upper fifth. Thanks for the dance."

He offered his hand to an attractive miss with a spray of freckles on her nose.

Lady Caroline loosened a cluster of lads who made it across, Winnie among them, who threw George a hopeful look. June was snatched up again. Amidst all the bodies, she knocked George and smirked, before his new partner stepped on his toe. Good looks did not mean nimble feet.

His third and fourth partners were somewhat better. The fifth hardly appealed at all, a bony sort who tucked her hair behind her ears, yet she'd clearly had lessons. When a waltz changed to a foxtrot, she made the transition. His toes were grateful. He kept her out longer until he noticed her pant between songs.

"Would you like punch?"

Mr. Wilburn was doling the punch. George iced up his face. The geezer broke into a smile. "Hallo, sport. I didn't think you'd ever take a break. Yes, he's real, young lady. You needn't gawk."

Pink-cheeked, the girl scooped hair behind her ear. George coolly took their cups. Mr. Wilburn's fingers brushed his.

His heart pumped. What on earth did *he* want, old fart, smiling and touching fingers?

The girl sipped punch and gazed around. "Very nice dance."

"Yes. Very."

If he thinks I'd do anything with him *now*, he's raving.

She said, "The grounds seem nice around here."

"We've a groundskeeper."

"Perhaps we should walk outside?"

"Oh. Ah, sorry, I'm—I think I'll keep dancing." He downed his punch, made a quick bow and fled across the room.

He meant to dance with every lass, which was easier than conversing. Some boys planned to escape later with dollies in tow. He scanned the remaining ones when Lady Caroline tapped his shoulder.

"Take me for a spin. I know you can do it."

He waltzed her. Her green-eyed gaze locked his.

"Relax, Carveth. I'm impressed," she said. "You've comported yourself as a gentleman with inferior partners. These girls are a sorry bunch as far as dancing skills go. I shall have to visit their school."

She smiled at song's end. Shadow George alerted. *She wants you.*

Lady Caroline patted him. "Your uncle taught you well, dear."

He let out his breath. What had she said about his uncle?

But Mr. Wilburn was chatting up MacIntyre. George sidled back toward the punch table and growled for the boy. The lad did a double take and rushed over.

"What was he saying to you?" He indicated the lit master.

MacIntyre's eyes were huge in their specs. "We were t-t-talking about m-m-moo—songs."

"That's it? He wasn't trying to...?" George huffed at the child's trusting face. "Be careful with him."

"W-why? I think he's n-n-nice."

"What do you know?"

George marched over and chose the colored girl for a dance. She said, "I was wondering if you'd get to me."

"Of course. I'm dancing with everyone."

"I suppose you were told to do it."

"No. I mean some of your lot can dance, but most— There shouldn't be such effort. I'd rather not think about it."

"You prefer to glide as we're doing now?"

He grinned. "Say. You're easy to dance with. That's a song in a Fred Astaire picture."

"Isn't he great? But so are the Nicholas Brothers. And Katherine Dunham. Do you know about Negro artists?"

"I know Chuck Berry and Little Richard. Sassy and Lady Day. Duke Ellington, Fats Waller…"

Her name was Christine, and he was happy to keep her as a partner. At the fussy departure of Lady Caroline, Christine smirked. "Good, the gorgon is leaving. Now we'll have some fun."

It was George's rock-n-roll mates who hijacked Edgely's gramophone. "Telstar" was played to a cheering crowd. Boys ditched their jackets, girls kicked off their heels. The few masters and mistresses couldn't quite maintain order through "Please Mr. Postman."

Mr. Wilburn grinned when George jived Christine to Eddie Cochran's "Summertime Blues." Kids circled to watch. Christine made George feel looser. He wheeled her over his head, her skirt flying out. She showed white knickers—at least, that's what he heard later.

The music ceased with a scratch of the needle. Barlow snapped, "Show some decency!"

Christine leapt behind George. A mistress from her school rushed out to claim her.

Barlow was red with ire. "I should have known *you'd* be making trouble," he spat at George. "At least you found your proper partner. And, Wilburn, my God, man. Why are you grinning at this ape display? Are we all Africans now? Rock-n-roll records are banned from this school. Rock-n-roll dancing is banned. And there will be more bans before I'm finished." He eyed George. "This mayhem is over." Barlow marched out the remaining masters. Mr. Wilburn's face was tight.

George panted, his body tingling from the assault of fear over the sheer fun of the dance. He felt resigned to punishment.

It was odd when it came. He was banned from the Christmas Talent Show, which stung, as he'd already prepared a dance and meant to win this time. More surprising still was the protest that followed. People wanted to see him, including some parents who remembered him from last year. The planning committee had even penciled him in as a highlight. So the punishment backfired. A compromise was reached with the headmaster. George could perform, but he was ineligible for competition. He would be the final performer. Even still, it was mortifying for George to explain his status to his parents.

Dad said, "You were dancing to rock-n-roll and what else? Did you have a smart mouth?"

"He was dancing with a colored girl, that's what else," Mum said.

Clueless Dad muttered, "Ah, no, that can't be it. I'm sure it's not."

In the end, George scratched his dance and opted to sing "Luck Be a Lady," his big number from *Guys and Dolls*. Jack had said singing would make him stronger, and so it did. Let the school see what a mistake it had made. Applause kept on after he left the stage. He didn't return. His days there were numbered. It was almost 1962. And come the fourth of March he'd be sixteen and master of his own fate.

JILL STUART SENT HIM LETTERS. She told of her life in London, of a shop called "Bazaar" on the Kings Road with radical threads and a talented designer. She wrote of almost getting a job at a coffee shop on that same road, only the owner hadn't liked her look; he'd dismissed her haughtily while wearing pajamas. Not that Jack wanted her to work. George probably wouldn't believe this, but she had studied anthropology at New York University. While she'd enjoyed the classes, she hadn't been keen on the idea of fieldwork. She apologized if her letters were boring.

But her letters were never boring. He was honored to get them. She sounded lonely, yet that couldn't be the case. She sent him novels even when he had more reading than he could handle. Though her books flashed with life. Using a torch, he read them at night under the covers.

Her husband also wrote. George delayed opening his "agent's" letter. But then Jack sounded like his old self, his tone jovial, plotting George's career, urging him to see certain films. George excitedly opened the next one only to be floored by sentiment: Jack hoped he hadn't upset him; he never wanted to hurt him; things were fine with Jill; he had some challenging clients, yet missed walking with George on the beach, clowning on the Royal Mile.

Whenever George thought of their odd night in Scarborough, he cycled through flattery, disgust, fear, arousal. Would it happen again? It mustn't happen again. They'd been men "horsing around."

Jack met a theater director from Blackpool, someone who might give George advice about the business and employ him for a summer production. Jack arranged a visit during the half-term break.

The Carveths invited the Stuarts for a Christmas supper. The couple arrived in a baby blue Peugeot, "Jill's Christmas present," Jack explained of the new car parked outside. "You mean *your* present," his wife chided him, smiling. (Americans certainly gave each other lavish gifts a day early.) On Boxing Day, Jack returned alone and told George's parents he didn't know how long they'd be in Blackpool, a few days or a week, depending on the director's schedule. Dad worried about George getting back for school.

George was thrilled to escape to the Peugeot. Even if it wasn't racy or Italian, he finally knew someone with a car. A carless neighbor stepped outside to gawk. He was keen to be taken to another resort town, a ballroom dancing Mecca, according to Uncle James, who'd attended the first Latin American tournament there last June.

Jack was full of chatter as they motored along and sped past other vehicles. George braced against the dash and the seat. How grand to see the world from roads instead of clattering train tracks. Jack turned a knob that made noises. George squawked. A radio, how fab! He settled with contentment as they drove beyond the sprawl of London. Smiling looks from the driver roused Shadow George. *What did Jill think of her husband riding off in her new gift?*

His eyes grew heavy and he dreamt of the sea. Waking brought the twilight surprise of Blackpool Tower edged with lights and looking like the Eiffel Tower. Jack pointed out the "Pleasure Beach" anchoring the far end. The stretch in between, called the "Golden Mile," was a lit-up wonderland. George bounced in his seat.

If St. Ives was a fair maid, Blackpool was her boisterous uncle.

Jack booked two rooms. George leapt like a rabbit when Jack entered his room through an unexpected door.

"We're connected," he announced. "Don't worry, I'll respect your privacy. It's just a kid's room—anyway, I'll meet you in the lobby."

They walked the promenade. George was hatless in the sharp night air, breath visible—young chaps often were, unlike the previous generation. He refused Jack's offer of his fedora.

The famous Blackpool illuminations were decked out for Christmas. A lit-up tram rattled past. Tourists were sparse. Despite the lights and music, the ping of the arcades, and the tang of onions frying in oil, many shops and stands were dark for the season. Signs promised exotic fare: the "Palace of Strange Girls"; the "Fattest Teenager you have ever seen"; Prince Eugene's Tattoo Parlour; the "Non-stop Strip-tease Theatre." George rather wanted to see the strip show but didn't dare ask. A hawker coaxed Jack to a curtained area called "What the Butler Saw." Jack dodged him and pushed George onward.

Jack bought fish-n-chips that were crispy hot. They walked the long central pier that jutted into blackness. The Irish Sea rustled with whitecaps. George inhaled its wet breath.

Jack said, "Tomorrow, I'm bringing the camera. Apparently, you get great views from the tower."

"I'd love to go to the top."

His ears burned with cold. The mucus was loose in his nose. Jack offered his handkerchief. Embarrassed, George used it and wished he were here with mates. He couldn't quite take the leisurely pace and rushed ahead to get proper looks at the displays. Women called him "love." Men called him "sonny." Jack lagged at a burlesque house, but was too slow to declare George eighteen. The ticket man said, "Sorry, my lad. No beard yet, no go."

"Sorry," Jack repeated. "I thought we'd get warm."

Jack plunked his hat on George's head. George masked his gratitude with some Fosse moves. But there was a poster for the upcoming Latin American Dance Tournament. He sprang ahead. "Look here. Should I do competitions?"

Jack caught up to him with a frown. "Ballroom dance is fine, but I see you as a solo artist. You should focus on tap or jazz this summer. I know your uncle means well, but he limits you."

George winced. All this time he'd fancied himself impressive. Not to someone like Jack. Why would the American even want a kid with a dribbling nose in a grownup's hat? Shadow George felt as jittery as a virgin when they reached the hotel, but ready.

Jack clapped his shoulder. "Get some rest. Goodnight, kid."

Well. What a thing.

The room pleased him. There was a hiss of gas heat. He could wank with abandon. Only he glared at the door adjoining the rooms, and crept oh-so-quietly to lock it, then leapt shivering into bed, aghast at his boldness.

THEY WENT to a theater inside the Blackpool Tower building, that also contained a ballroom they bypassed. The director seemed surprised to see Jack, almost bothered; people vied for his attention. Then he said, "Ah, Mr. Stuart, now I remember," and shook Jack's hand. He shook George's, too, saying, "This is your dancer?"

Jack clapped George's shoulder. "Dances and sings. He'll command your stage. We'd love to show you what he could do."

The director peered at George. "You've a smart look, sonny. No time now, I'm afraid. Midst of the Christmas pantomime, you see."

Jack said, "Of course. We're in town for a bit. We'll come by another time."

The director scratched his head. "Well, now, we've performances every day. I can't see him this week, and next week I'm away. If you come back in May, I'll try him out for the summer shows."

"Ah, jeez." Jack shifted. "He's still in school then."

"I'm sorry, but that's really the best time." The man turned away.

This was hardly the helpful chap Jack had described at home.

"I thought I'd be learning from him." George stood at the base of the tower outside. "Or performing. I could leave school early."

Jack stuck a cigarette in his mouth. "You can't do that. He was a lot friendlier in London. I assumed he'd make time to see you. Let's sit tight a few days. I'll see if I can't change his mind."

"But he's busy all week."

Jack clicked off the lighter. "We're not going away empty-handed."

Then Jack smiled as if the whole point of their trip hadn't just been dashed. "What do you want to do now?"

Or had there been another purpose? "I don't know." He felt itchy to flee. "I want to be by myself."

"Here, wait, take some money. I'll see you back at the—"

On the promenade, the Palace of Strange Girls was still deserted. The "fattest teenager" was there and quite fat, indeed; he glowered at George. The hawker readily took his coin for What the Butler Saw. He squinted into a peephole and saw a naked girl who sat very still. He was relieved to see the glow of a heater in the room with her. An urge slithered through him that felt rude to even think of, let alone act on. He backed off and noticed the stained wall before him. Disgusted, he exited. Awful to sit starkers in a room with anyone peering in.

A fish bar tempted. He doused whelks and cockles in malt vinegar and groaned with pleasure at the salty sweetness.

The sea sprayed the edge of the promenade. Having swallowed the entire beach, it boiled and sloshed the steps below. Gulls bobbed an air current. A man leaning against the rail tipped his black bowler hat. George's internal radar went off. He walked on.

Despite the cold, he bought an ice cream. Wind cut through his good trousers. If only he had on his warmer dungarees. Bowler Hat was going in the same direction. George increased his pace. Rides were running at the Pleasure Beach, still a ways off.

He had to try the roller coaster even though he was burning through Jack's money. Only a few people were riding. He slid into a seat by himself and grasped a rope. As the cars climbed the steep grade, he was awarded views of the surrounding park and the roiling, hungry sea at high tide. Cripes, was that Bowler Hat below? Dirty old sod came all this way. *He scented you. He knows what you are.*

George was much higher now, rounding the top, the wind stinging his ears. The cars rattled like they weren't going to hold together, then dropped so violently he almost tumbled out. He clung to the rope, expecting to fly out at every moment, shrieking—yes, he was shrieking. What else could one do on a speeding ride that wanted to buck him off? His meal shot to his throat, he noticed in the too-brief interim before the next plunge tested his stomach. And in the banking whoosh that followed in which he wasn't thrown, he felt exhilarated. His screams became laughter.

His legs were rubber climbing out. Yet he had to go again. It was still mad scary, and he should have puked first. Bowler Hat sauntered toward the exit gate. But as luck would have it, two young misses quarreled about whether to ride. Despite his wild hair, George smiled a greeting. It appeared to work, at least with one of them.

"Shall I ride with you ladies?"

They seemed to like the "ladies" part, and let him press into their car. Heavenly, when one climbed over him so he could be in the center, a better fit of hips and shoulders.

And far more frightening when all three nearly lifted out at the plunge. The girls screamed so loudly his ears rang.

After, they stayed together. Bowler Hat melted away. The Fun House lured them with its laughing clown outside and crazy rides within, including a huge spinning barrel that one could never get out of. One lass was in tears when George finally freed her. Of course, it hadn't helped that he and her mate had been laughing. He bought both girls candy floss. Then his money ran out.

The prettier one offered to treat him. "Me mum is always payin' for her bloke." He agreed to go on the wheel. There was a skirmish with her chum, barred from joining them. George waited until the top of the ride to kiss the girl's peachy lips. They snuggled through a windy plummet. The day waned. The sea surrendered the beach.

The threesome turned awkward on the ground, with outdoor lights coming on. When the pretty one stopped at a call box to ring home, George kissed the cold lips of her plainer friend. The lass tensed, then melted—what power he felt in that thawing. Racy now, to walk between them, grabbing waists, snagging fingers.

But on the north promenade, the girls turned for the train station rather than the Tower Ballroom, as he urged. They couldn't miss their tea what with grannies being in town.

George sat in the ornate, dreamlike ballroom, his sinuses running. His stomach rumbled with hunger. But he wouldn't go back to the hotel, not yet.

Couples practiced the tango. No teenagers here, and no ladies who weren't ancient. A few of the geezers could cut a rug.

JACK SAID, "I worry when we're in a new city and I don't hear from you all day. I'm responsible for you."

George heaped food on his plate from the morning buffet spread. "I was at the Pleasure Beach. I met some girls."

"Ah. Well, terrific. Are you seeing them again?"

George shrugged.

At the table, Jack sawed a banger. "I'll try our man today. I'll remind him of what he promised. I won't let him push us off."

An agent should do what he'd set out to do.

Jack said, "Do you want to get together later, maybe go see the Winter Gardens?"

George paused with the toast. "I don't know what I'm doing."

The large meal and the gas heat in his room proved too lethal a combination. George woke hours later. An envelope had been shoved under the still-locked, adjoining door. A few more pounds spending money. *Thank you, Jack.*

He skittered down the seawall. A man dragged a donkey from the beach. George ran to catch up. Icy water sloshed his shoes. When a stronger surge swamped him to the ankle, he stopped his journey and headed for the stairs. A human will never win against the sea. It had already shown a taste for him. He sat atop the seawall, bare feet tingling in the cold, wet socks wrung out, dungarees cuffed.

Why hadn't he made a plan with those lassies? They might well be searching for him. A whiff of seafood made him shove his bare feet into his clammy shoes.

He foraged a bag of winkles, pulling the meat from the shell with a pin. Perhaps he'd have a look from the tower, though he didn't want to run into Jack or that director. Bugger it, why shouldn't he go up if he wanted?

George rode the tower lift through red-painted girders. A biting wind rumbled at the top. The open fencing was enclosed by mesh. At least he had the whole freezing level to himself. Dizzying, the coastline laid out below, lapped by a lace-edged sea, unseen Ireland beyond the horizon, the city all around.

He put a coin in a telescope and scanned the promenade for the two misses or any interesting, big-haired dolly. How diverting to spy on people. There was a fair-haired figure who walked as Jack did. Someone trailed him. Or no, they strode together...with purpose. Irked, George stopped peering and drifted to the lift.

Likely it wasn't even Jack. Daft, to run all the way back to the buggery hotel, to stand outside the man's room. He heard nothing through the door. Was that a voice?

George slipped into his own room. Then quietly unlatched the adjoining door. Jack was on his knees before a teenager. Both parties jumped noticing him. Jack fell back, sputtered, "Go, just go."

The lad tucked himself into jeans. "Am oona needa get paid, eh?"

Jack said, "What?"

The room pitched. George grabbed a chair. "You need to pay him."

He doesn't want you anymore. Have you forgotten how it is?

Jack wanted him. He *knew* Jack wanted him. The man wouldn't block his entrance and say it was good he'd stayed away.

Cold tingles were coming on. With the boy out of the room, George shrugged off his coat. "Right. Let's do it."

Jack laughed. "Let's *do* it? I wouldn't do it with you if you were the last—"

George slammed the carpet with his knees, palms. The blood left his body, the floor a magnet. Jack was an agitated blur above.

"Oh, Jesus. George, talk to me."

He forced, "You don't want me."

An alarmed face loomed over him. "What? Of course, I…"

Relief, the attack of yearning, big arms scooping him close, kisses that missed his mouth and landed on his jaw, his neck. George dragged open buttons. Jack whispered, "Let me. Are you okay? You're pale."

It's only shagging. Nothing for you. A big deal for him.

HE BUZZED WITH BLOOD AGAIN, used and cozy on Jack's bed. How strange to have this surplus of love inside him, as if Jack had pumped it into him. His *agent*. He didn't know what to do with the love. He smoked a cigarette to keep it at bay.

Jack sang in the bathroom and came out grinning. "My ace, my Rocco, I bought you a Christmas present. I meant to give it to you earlier…"

George rolled to tamp the smoke. The gift was a necklace, a long chain with a coin.

"Like a lot of male stars wear these days. It's Florentine gold. Read the inscription." Jack gave him the coin.

"J.S. Oh"—George flipped it over—"Big Star." Tears pricked.

"Hey, you're not going to cry, are you?" Jack looped the necklace over George's head, then dragged him to the looking glass.

"We'll go to Paris and find Mr. Delon. I'll stand my big star next to Europe's big star and decide who's the most handsome. Wow. Look at you."

Had Jack gone barmy? It took all of George's will not to slither from his grasp. How could his naked self compare to the great Delon? The necklace gleamed. What if he yanked it off and threw it at the wall? He turned away.

"You're potty, J.S. No, don't take a picture."

Jack had grabbed the camera. "Come on, just a few."

"Wait." He hopped back into the dungarees.

A naked Jack fetched the tripod from its case and started setting up. "Nude shots are very artistic. Don't worry. I'm not sure I want others to see what I see. Leave your shirt off."

George felt exposed, even in his jeans. Flattered, too. He wanted to feel happy. Posing was fun. Would it spark ardor again? Funny, how Jack conjured this muddle inside him, even with being so different from Wilburn. Yet the love felt the same, his arse sore from it. What an odd place to feel love.

ELEVEN

"Happy Birthday, Sweet Sixteen"

(NEIL SEDAKA & HOWARD GREENFIELD, 1961)

IT WAS a Saturday night in March, 1962, the eve of his sixteenth birthday. George had come home to celebrate and officially decide about staying in school. He couldn't imagine not returning, what with being in the midst of lessons. But it was remarkable how his parents squirmed over it, Dad saying, "Of course it's your decision now. You're old enough to weigh it as an adult."

A fire snapped in the front room. They gathered at the dining room in back, Mum's usual sewing items put away for the set table. She served her spicy *cioppino*. The Stuarts joined them, confusing Jack, teasing Jill, both sitting across from George. He loved them both.

Jack was reporting on the business. "Oh, it's good, great, super—"

"A-okay, top-notch," George cut in with an American accent.

Jill grinned. Her foot bumped his. She looked sexy with her curtain of blonde hair, her eyes made-up.

Jack said, "Right you are, smartass. My clients show some promise. But this one will beat all of them. I tell you, when this kid of yours—"

"My kid will do well when he finishes his schooling and not until then," Dad said like a bore.

George slurped a clam and discarded the shell.

Dad continued, "I have a good friend who has done a lot for my family. One of the best things he did was get George into his school."

Mum added, "You must help him during the breaks—*Manners*, Georgie," she said in her ear-twisting voice. "The Stuarts are still our guests."

Jill erased a smile.

Jack looked from one parent to the other. "Though we are talking about his career. I thought that was the focus."

Dad frowned. "As a dancer? I don't know about that."

George nearly choked. "*Dad.*"

"Son. I'm not against your dancing. I just don't see it as a career for a young man."

Mum arched a brow. "It's not respectable, is it?"

George smacked down his spoon. "Rudolph Nureyev is not respectable? Fred Astaire is not respectable?"

Dad held up his hands. "Whoa, now. I didn't say that. They're very famous at it."

"Why shouldn't George be that famous?" Jack put in.

Mum raised her glass to him.

Dad said, "I'm just saying an education comes first. Then he can decide, then *you* decide, lad. With an education, the world is yours."

George huffed. "I am going to dance."

Everyone was silent.

Dad said, "Jill, you haven't shared your opinion."

She sat back. "Oh, no, I mean it's your decision to make as a family. It is not my, or my husband's, place to sway you."

Jack set down his fork. "Great. Thanks, Jill."

Her freckles blended rose.

THE STUARTS WERE GIVING George the best gift ever by taking him to a dance club that played American rock-n-roll. He vaulted to the arctic air of the upper level to choose an outfit. His brown trousers, of course, though they were tighter, hard to zip, and showed his fat bum.

Jack called it a sexy bum. George scraped them off, removed his bulky Y-fronts, then pulled them on again. He could clearly see the lump of his penis and stiffened looking at himself. Both Stuarts would want him. How on earth would he get by his parents? He would race to the hall and grab his coat off the hook.

Uncle James had given him a cool striped shirt. George sloughed it on over his vest and Jack's gold necklace against his skin. He left open the top buttons, flicked up the collar and rolled up the short sleeves. He looked a right tough now, sharp, but for his hair. Jack thought hair cream dated. "That Elvis look is over," he'd said. "You have great hair. Wear it naturally."

It seemed wild hair to George. He went to his parents' bedroom to find Dad's cologne. A distant train vibrated the bottles. He sprayed scent then hastened downstairs, and almost made it to the hallway when Mum cried, "Stop."

She hovered. "How did those trousers shrink so?"

Dad laughed. "Whatever you did to them, girl, don't do it again."

The Stuarts hid grins. George said, "I don't mind wearing them."

Dad said, "You're not wearing those. Go and change."

Mum shook her head. "How could I not have noticed?"

George cried, "But tight trousers are in."

"They're ridiculous," Dad snapped. "Change into something decent. Love of God, to wear trousers like that. I can see his parts."

George stomped up the stairs. Mum called, "Wear the new ones from your aunt, sweetie. Those are nice for the city."

They're balloons! Cousin Timmy must be getting fat. George secured the loose waist with a belt. A mate at school had given him a boxy Zoot Suit jacket. That would look sharp.

Dad said, "Oh no. You're a delinquent in that getup."

Mum said, "It's not nearly warm enough, baby."

George was allowed out in his shapeless cloth coat. Jill laughed and clapped his cheek. "They can't hide the face, kiddo."

Both Stuarts wore black leather coats. George got in the back seat of the Peugeot. Despite the cold, they rolled down their windows.

George said, "Hey, I'm getting a lot of air back here."

"Good," they said and laughed.

He adored his grownup friends. He could be mortified around Jill, considering what he and Jack had done. Yet attraction overrode the shame. Plus, he'd had a growth spurt and was taller than her now.

Jack parked close to the waterfront. George sprang out to the briny air. The couple lagged to light cigarettes.

The club stairs descended below street level. The interior was red-lit. Music jumped in volume, Elvis crooned "One Night." Jack knew the bouncer's name, and said, "This is the one I told you about."

"Ah, right, the Sunday birthday. Enjoy yourself, kid. No drinking 'til midnight."

Through the pall of smoke, the air dank with sweat, they found a corner table and shed coats. Jack ordered drinks all around.

Jill sputtered, "But he said—"

"He had to say that. George is a man now."

George liked the sound of that. Passing females caught his eye. Yet Jill was equally compelling. He shouted over the noise, "I want you to dance with me."

She shouted, "Remember the last time we danced, knocking things over in your house?"

He laughed. "And you flashed your knickers."

She gawped. He blushed, horrified to have mentioned that detail, let alone the instance of his clumsiness. Jack cleared his throat. Beers were placed down. Everyone drank.

She leaned. "What did they look like?"

She had fine blonde hairs on her forearm. George cocked his head for the dance floor. They edged past tables and the sweet smell of someone's homemade cigarette. She took his fingers, held his shoulder, her breasts wonderfully close. And stuttered off the beat.

He counted her back in. When she missed a second time, he shouted, "You're not paying attention." Then mouthed, "Are you sad?"

Her eyes gleamed. She blinked. "Ready."

He said in her ear, "They were lacy," and felt her smile.

Jill knew the opening lines of "Do You Love Me" by The Contours. George whooped at the fast part and Jack whistled from the table.

Couples danced apart nowadays, not even holding hands. But with a change to the bluesy "Please Please Please," George scooped her against him, thrust his leg between hers, and matched the song's loping rhythm. Jill was open-mouthed. Even he was impressed he'd done that. But her face lit with joy, especially as he stopped and started with the song, using it like a ride. And what an armful she was. Arousal surged below. Her soft groin bumped his thigh. Smoke and vanilla in her hair. James Brown begged his lover. *Don't go.* He pressed the small of her back. Oh, to squeeze her bum, to feel the cleft.

He said in her ear, "I think you're... when I'm back from school..."

She looked at him. "So, you are going back to school?"

A fast song started. He whipped her out. Her hair flew as she whirled, laughing. She smacked against him for another slow number. Her soft places were killing him. She must feel his aching interest. They ended apart, doing the twist. He stayed low until things settled, the balloon trousers good for something.

He said, "I don't care for twisting. You can't hold on to the girl."

"I don't think the girl should have to peel herself off you, though."

There was a smack-able swell in her skirt as she went ahead of him to the table.

Jack said, "Should we head to the Peppermint Lounge?"

Jill said, "George doesn't like to twist."

"Oh, I wouldn't mind going to the Peppermint Lounge. Have you been there?"

Jack said, "No, kiddo, it opened while we were here. But it's the happening place."

"It's the happening place, buddy-boy," George said in a Yank voice. "That's my Fred McMurray from 'The Apartment.'"

Jack swiped his hair. George ducked, shocked by the touch, and downed some beer.

Jack raised an amber drink in a tumbler. "Music, girls, new clothes.

Though I think he should've worn his birthday suit tonight, don't you, honey?"

George coughed.

Jill shouted, "He already has it on. What's with the hard stuff?"

Jack swallowed and smacked the table. "Hoo! Having a good time, too. What better way to express myself? I can't do it half the time."

"You're lit. George is smoking. You mustn't smoke yet."

George returned her cigarette. Only Jack stuck it back in his lips. "He's a man now."

George didn't feel mannish and parked the smoke.

Jill eyed her husband. "You're expressing yourself quite well, dearest."

"Smoke and mirrors, darling. I can't do what I...what I really want." He seemed to deflate.

She looked irked. "Do it then. Who cares what people think. Right, George? What's the matter?"

"Nothing." His voice came out high.

She grasped his arm. He said, "A twinge. I'm fine."

"You'd better not drink anymore. Are you sure?"

"As long as Jack doesn't do anything strange."

She massaged her husband's arm. "Troublemaker." She had each of their forearms.

Jack leered at George and snagged Jill's breast. She squawked.

George said, "I'll be back," and knocked a chair to get away.

He asked the first girl who looked at him to dance. She said, "I'm with..." A bloke glared. Another lass smiled and joined him. They had a vigorous romp. He also danced with her friend in specs.

A genuine ripe tomato brushed past, said, "Aren't you cute."

But when he offered his hand, she laughed. "I don't dance with boys."

Stung, he orbited the club, feeling cut off from everyone. A Negro man held out a cigarette. George accepted it though it was homemade, nearly falling apart—hoo, and sweet. The Negro seemed to want to take it back.

"It's all right," George mouthed, moving on. Though it wasn't.

Was Jack making a drunken confession? How could he have thought it safe to go out with those two? George gave up on the crumbling smoke. When he dared to return, Jack looked glum.

Jill rose. "Perhaps we should call it a night if you're ready."

Get out of our lives. We never want to see you again.

The fishy aroma outside breathed of the river's nearness. George felt surprisingly woozy from the beer and the dances. Jill nudged him. "Jack can't drive. Get his keys."

He embraced Jack, swiped the keys, and tossed them to her. Jack snagged his arm, whispered, "Cruel boy."

Jill unlocked the car. "I need to practice driving on the wrong side of the road. George, help me with the turns and roundabouts, okay?"

George scoffed. "It's not the *wrong side*."

Jack grinned getting in back. George plopped in front. "I wish I could drive."

Jack shifted forward. "We'll teach you to drive this summer."

"Really? Oh, that would be fab. Jill, drop me at Victoria. Or we could go to Chelsea. I'll bet it's happening now."

Jill glanced. "I can drive you home."

Jack grazed George's ear. "Let him come home with us."

George reclaimed his ear, scratching it.

Jill said, "Maybe we'll find someplace to eat."

Eating would be *heaven*. She nattered as the car drifted over. "In America we like the good old U-turn."

George tensed. "There's a roundabout—wrong lane!"

"I was getting there. Keep your pants on."

Maybe she shouldn't be driving. Thank God traffic was light.

She said, "You're right. All these cool, new places have opened on the Kings Road. We can swing by. But we can't keep you drinking. Your parents will kill us."

Jack said, "Let's go to our place. I'll make love to both of you."

George stared out the window, wishing to jump through it.

Jill's voice cracked, "Both of us?"

"Sure. A beautiful youth. A sexy wife. Why not?"

"Sounds like a French film." Her voice had gone hoarse.

Jack's voice was velvet. "I smelled Mary Jane at the club. Too bad we don't have any."

Who on *earth* was Mary Jane? Did she smell like Mrs. Althorp?

Jack shifted back. "Hey, don't take me seriously. I don't."

Laughter spilled in relief. Jill shook her head. Jack thumped George's seat. "Relax, sport. We'll continue our chaste evening."

Sport. They were quiet again. George's bum felt irritated as if he couldn't sit in the seat anymore. Did he want that love or not? Did he want to be plumbed and bitten?

Jill glanced at him. "Do you have to go to the toilet?"

He laughed. *Stop moving around. It's barmy.*

At a red light, Jill gazed in the rearview mirror, murmured, "Wild man."

Her husband answered softly. "Jilly."

He reached to sift her hair. She leaned into his hand. He said, "You don't drop me because of my faults, even when I have so many."

She caught George staring. George looked away.

She said, "Did you two fight in Blackpool? I'm sensing friction."

George blurted, "Hah! We talked of you in Blackpool. Jack would tell me your good qualities until it got boring. Then he talked about you to strangers in pubs. Talk, talk, talk."

The light changed green. Jill slipped the gearstick to neutral and kissed her husband. It was unbearable. George wanted to be kissed by her, by him. He was getting a monster boner. Vehicles beeped and swerved round them.

Jack murmured, "I don't deserve you, sweetie."

Jill whispered, "Hush. I'm lucky to have you."

"Jack's the lucky one."

Jack said, "Thanks, George. I could've told her that myself."

George mimicked, "You're the best, doll. You're aces in my book, sweetie p—"

Jack punched his seat. Jill popped the clutch and drove on.

George sat mute but for a frantic, "Left lane."

Jill seemed to have forgotten the idea of eating out and turned onto their street. It took her forever to find then maneuver into a parking space. George bolted from the car, dizzy with relief. Jill helped her husband up the steps of the maisonette. George supported his other side because he needed to hold on to something.

Jack looked amused. "Thank you, my good knights. The offer still stands."

Jill said, "Okay, Casanova," like she didn't believe him.

Inside, she switched on lights then went straight upstairs, saying, "Let me ditch these heels. George, I'll get you money for the train."

"No, I don't need…" She disappeared into the bedroom.

He was jerked back and kissed, and had to wrench free. "Not *here*."

His lover said, "Why must I hold back all the time? You torment me. Did he fuck you, your schoolmaster?"

"Shhh." Why bring *that* up?

Annoyingly strong, Jack kept George close. "Was he mad for you?"

"Mind your wife."

Jack pinned him to a wall and ate his throat. George squirmed away. But the American jumped on his back as if to wrestle.

Jill's voice cried, "Jack! Get off him."

George broke free and punched his schoolmaster, knuckles to bone. Jill screamed and flew down the stairs.

He froze, horrified. Big Jack Stuart lay sprawled on the black-and-white tiled floor.

Jill gawked at George as if she didn't know him anymore.

"Jill, I'm sorry. I would never hit Jack, honest. But I—he, he called me 'sport.' Why would he call me 'sport'?"

Her face flushed. "What are you talking about?"

Cripes, his hand throbbed. "He reminded me of…of someone."

She clearly thought him barking and knelt before her husband. George knelt, too. Her eyes on him were fierce.

"He was kidding before. You do realize that."

He held her gaze. "Was he?"

She frowned. "Your neck is red. Why is your neck...?"

George ran to the kitchen, fetched water in a glass, and doused Jack, who groaned. George and Jill sat him up, then carefully hefted the big, awkward man to his feet.

Jack staggered to shake them off and glared at George and pointed. "He hit me."

Jill stepped between, her look unreadable.

George said, "I'll go," and fled, glad to quit these mad Yanks. Glad for school on Monday.

TWELVE

"Can't Get Used to Losing You"

(JEROME "DOC" POMUS & MORT SHUMAN, 1963)

AT SCHOOL, George kept his gold necklace out of sight. At home, he got careless and returned from the bath one night only to find his dad in his bedroom, necklace in hand. "Who's 'J.S.'?"

His heart jumped at the sight. "No one. A girl, you don't know her."

Dad said, "A lass with money to spare to get you a nice piece and inscribe it with 'Big Star.' It's not Jack Stuart, is it?"

George smirked, took the necklace from his father's fingers, and looped it around his neck. Then he grabbed a magazine and flopped onto his bed, affecting a casual pose though his feet were bare and cold, his face warm. Dad sat on the end of the bed.

"You didn't tell your mother and me about this girl and the nice gift she gave you."

He could scarcely read the print before his eyes. "We broke up."

"Did you now? Perhaps you ought to return her gift."

"Perhaps I will." A flick of the page.

Dad grasped his ankle. George affected to be extremely interested in his magazine.

Dad spoke softly as if talking to himself. "You had that love bite coming home from Blackpool."

George balked. "I kissed a girl on the promenade, I *told* you." He raised the magazine to block out his parent.

"Aye." Dad cleared his throat. "It's just...you have your mother's beauty, and while I love seeing it on you, I fear you'll have trouble. There are some men who, who might..."

George's lips parted, his breath gave out. "Might what, Dad?"

"Who might, well, feel a certain urge like what a man feels towards a woman."

"You mean I'd have to cook and fetch things for him?"

"Er, no. More physical, like—ah, don't grin. It's hardly a laughin' matter."

George hooted. And recrossed his ankles so his dad would stop holding him there. "Don't worry. I'd pop him one."

"Good. You should all right. Don't let 'em—"

But George exploded in mirth.

"Oh, why do I even try?" His father got up and left.

George laughed until he cried, or maybe he just cried, the magazine on the floor, his bedroom door pushed shut. He crouched. That his father should worry how many years later? He sucked the coin of the necklace to calm himself, warm and metallic. Big Star.

He'd be so shocked to know how we truly are, he conveyed to Shadow George. *What happened with those boys? You haven't told me what you did.*

Shadow George said *I only know parts. I was only giving them a fright. A right pair of twits you never saw.*

But what did you do?

Shadow George said *I came to and something had happened.*

But we can't *both* have forgotten.

George rang up from the school one night and tormented his agent with the threat of telling just so he could hear the panic, the pleading, as if Wilburn was cornered at last, speared like an insect to velvet. Lost in his own storm, he didn't truly take in Jack's feelings. The American insisted they meet the coming weekend.

"Meet me at the arena in Battersea Park."

Had fear blinded him in the car?

There was an accident in Battersea Park. The Peugeot bashed a tree. There was blood on the dash, the seat, yet Jack had apparently walked away and out of everyone's life. Not Jill, nor any of them, had seen or heard from him since.

George had been reluctant doing the meeting. It would only be more muddle. He'd slipped out of the house and bicycled to the arena, even hearing a distant bang. The sirens and the lights made him crane for Jack, who likely wouldn't get through.

After the accident, his parents tended a grief-struck Jill. George had to return to school with everything unresolved. What if Jack turned up dead? The longer that didn't happen, the more he could almost breathe. Why would the man stay away from everyone? His own wife? George expected a letter, a phone call, a meet-up at the school. He couldn't believe the key to his future had vanished.

He didn't love you enough. He went off you like that other one.

George took his O-level exam and did well enough to enter the sixth form should he choose to resume in the fall. Uncle James hosted a party for him to start the summer break. There was no surprise appearance from Jack Stuart.

How was Jill faring? Was she suffering? The more time passed without contact, the more awkward it felt to initiate it.

Perhaps he'd go to Blackpool and find that director for summer work. But George was a Londoner now. The city was his home. He resumed assisting at his uncle's ballroom studio, glad for the bit of pay. Kids were aligning as "Mods" or "Rockers." Though he loved Rock-n-Roll, he enjoyed the current music and the fashion sense of the Mods, and bought clothes to suggest an affiliation—tight jeans, a polo shirt, and blazer. He stopped greasing his hair. Italian scooters were the coveted mode of transport, well out of his price range.

His parents kept sporadic contact with Jill. Mum worried. What did the lass do all day by herself other than her volunteer job at the Chelsea Library? Would she return to the States? The Home Office might force her out. Staying alone in that flat couldn't be healthy. Mum deemed George the one to find out more information.

Wending north, his bicycle hissed along wet streets. The river flowed brown and restless beneath the Chelsea suspension bridge, thundering with cars. Coming off that armpit-soaking structure, the sun broke through heavy clouds and shined up surfaces, making him squint and wish for a pair of sunglasses.

It was a relief in the quieter neighborhoods. The Stuart maisonette looked dormant. No one answered his knock.

He was dead knackered for going home. The door was unlatched. A reek of stale cigarettes hit. Sunny imprints blobbed before his eyes. He walked inside and saw Jill standing there.

"Oh, Lord, sorry."

But they stared like gunfighters, tense. *He's gone because of you* vibrated the air. Her freckled arms were thin in her loose, sleeveless blouse. Hair leaked from a ponytail. Her entire demeanor was wary.

Mum had said to ring when he got there. He dialed without asking. "Mum. Can you come? Just come," he said over her questions.

He darted to a window and cranked it open. Birdsong came in with the shock of new air. He picked up what looked to be Jack's robe and threw it on a chair.

Jill said, "Great. I needed maid service."

"It stinks in here." His footsteps crackled. "What's sticky?"

But he froze. Photos were strewn along the tiled floor, dented, shirtless photos and close-ups. The Blackpool pictures.

Jill came alongside. "What's the matter? Yeah, that's you. I couldn't believe it, either. You look good, cookie."

He shook his head.

"No, you do. I'm not sure you liked posing. It's funny. I thought you liked girls. You stare at my chest so much."

He winced. "I do like girls."

"Well, I don't know now."

He pled for her old self to appear. "I do like girls."

This Jill was icy. "I know it's shocking, not to mention illegal, but I have to ask. Did you…? You know what I mean."

He did a gasp like a laugh. Jack hadn't confessed?

"Of course not."

Her eyes shone like glass. Then she seemed to crumble. "I'm sorry. You don't belong in our problems. I walked on your photos."

"That's fine. Get rid of them."

She shook a cigarette from a pack. "No. They're quite good." Her hand shook lighting up. "I don't know what to think anymore. I don't know the man I married. We were fighting before he…"

He drew blood from a fingernail. "I'll make tea, right?"

A worrisome, half-empty bottle of Scotch was on the kitchen counter. Dirty plates crowded the washbasin. He filled a kettle and put it on the gas. Her fridge was nearly empty, the milk off. He considered making beans and toast, but her remaining bread was fit for the dustbin, and how could she not have beans? Weirdly, because his mum would've keeled over, he began washing the dirty plates.

She accepted a full teacup. "What do you have on your feet?"

He displayed his shiny, pointed shoes that had been hurting for a while now. "Winklepickers. They're the latest."

"They look it. And you've got blue jeans."

Good and tight, but for the waist. "I buy my own clothes now."

She smiled. Was she back, his grownup friend?

Her eyes filled, the cup clinked on the saucer. "He's not coming back. And I'm just so, so angry. It was wrong to take it out on you. I don't know what, what…"

He remembered the handkerchief in his pocket. She mopped tears and scooted over so he could sit beside her on the settee. But he was still sweaty from the ride over.

He sat, trying to make himself thin. They looked at each other. Loose strands of hair framed her raw face. There were dark circles beneath her eyes. She touched his cheek and he stopped breathing.

"Do you still think you're not part of this life? You get such a lost look sometimes in these pretty eyes."

He flinched. She moved her hand, frowned.

"Sorry. I drink too much—to sleep, I mean. I hardly sleep. You told me he was happy. Or he said nice things about me."

She pulled the band from her hair and reaffixed it. A musk hit him, like cooked onions. Gold hairs showed in her armpit. He nodded.

"You were his good friend."

"Yes, we were friends, at least, I thought we were. I don't know if I can be alone. I don't attract men that easily."

"But any man would be lucky to smell you."

Her eyes flashed alarm. "I smell bad?"

"No."

"The hot water, it hasn't been…." She bowed forward and shook with laughter. No, that was crying.

His eyes stung. He lightly touched her back. "See here, Jill. Come home with me. We'll take care of you. I'll look after you, I promise."

Mum had twice said "Jill ought to stay with us," and sounded quite firm about it.

Jill mopped her red, wet face. Her eyes were bloodshot, her scent like onions, her nearness giving him an erection.

"You guys are such good friends. The Home Office won't find me at your house. They want us to leave. Can you believe it?"

"You can't leave."

"I don't want to, that's the crazy thing. Britain was Jack's choice. And now *I* want to stay here. You're a doll, sweetie. Thank you."

He received her hot, musky weight and put an arm round her shoulder, her bare arm under his fingers. She sighed. "I'm so tired."

JILL WAS GIVEN HIS BEDROOM, and protested it, already changing her mind. Happily, Mum was adamant. Even Dad, who was surprised coming home, insisted Jill try a "spell of recovery with us."

George took over the sofa in the front room and agreed to hide the bedding daily. The thought of Jill in his bed made him sparky with lust, as did sounds of her in the bathtub. Wet-haired and powdered, she joined them for supper in the kitchen, where the family always ate. He already missed her onion smell.

When his parents turned in, he couldn't resist going up to his room one last time. Jill leapt in surprise. "I might have been naked."

As it was, she was soft-breasted in a tied dressing gown, her hair dry and shining. He forced a casual, "I just came by to say goodnight."

"You came by to say you weren't coming by anymore?"

He squawked as she dragged him inside and shut the door. A powder scent wafted, her breath pelted mint. "Listen, kid, here's the deal: I'll help you become famous, I swear to God. That's what *he* wanted. I'll just finish it for him, right?"

Nothing came out of his mouth.

She dislodged him. "Sleep on it, doll. Let me know what you think."

He crept downstairs, clicked off the remaining lamp, and eased onto the sofa Mum had already made up with bedding. A distant train rumbled. Streetlights filled the bay window like a sun. He had to get out to shut the heavier curtain then stubbed his toe in the dark.

It sounded mad was what he thought. It interfered with his wank session. He'd never heard of girl agents or managers. Boys promoted girls, not the other way around.

Yet there was excitement in her offer. Perhaps his future wasn't over. And who would have such a sexy agent? He drifted at the thought of her showing a thigh as she bargained.

He awoke to a closed kitchen door. Jill was imparting the same incredible news to his parents.

Dad said, "You've had a shock, lass."

"Yes, yes." She sounded impatient. "I understand it's not easy. But why shouldn't I try? Was Jack any more qualified?"

"Jack had connections."

"And I'll phone them, of course."

Mum's voice. "Jack knew the business world."

"He didn't know squat. He missed countless opportunities, some-times. But he really tried with George. And I ought to continue that, as he would want me to."

Who *was* this Jill? She sounded so bold.

"I meant it might be hard for you," Mum said. "You might find it more a man's domain."

"That doesn't deter me."

Dad said, "I suppose if you want to take a few weekends to try."

"Oh, this is not a weekend thing. Jack was wrong there. At that rate, George would have been discovered at, what, age thirty-five? This is a commitment."

"But George is in school."

"He just finished."

"But he's going on to A-levels. Don't you want him to get sent up somewhere, a university?"

"If that's what he wants."

Dad said, "Of course, that's what he wants."

How does he *know? I might want this.*

Jill spoke as if she knew he was listening. "If George wants an education, then I will defer to that. If he wants to act, then I will commit to him full time."

George leapt away as the door opened. Dad cut him a look.

"I'm off to work. Attend to your guest, son."

Their guest sat pensively at the table. With hardly a glance at him, she started the wash-up as Mum fetched his breakfast.

GEORGE SOUGHT his room out of habit and enjoyed the shock of her, this female sprawled on his bed, who snapped gum, deep in a newspaper, who startled easily. "You are the sneakiest kid."

"Socks." He sat beside her. "Can I have gum? I like your plan. Do you think it might flush him out?"

"I hope it gives him the metaphorical finger. What happened to your winkle-jobbers?"

"Oh. I'm giving them a rest."

"Pinch, huh? Have you talked to your parents?"

He rolled his eyes. "Dad's so fixated on school."

"That's not a bad thing. He's got your best interest at heart. I don't."

He smiled, not quite believing her. But this was a new Jill. Without makeup, her hair no longer curled. And she was looking at flats to let as if she didn't mean to stay here. Or go back to the maisonette.

AND STAY SHE DID, that summer of 1962. Mum giggled more and pulled Jill into her bedroom, the kitchen or sewing area. Sometimes, they both had tails of plaited hair. They drank afternoon cocktails.

Dad played the gramophone after work, its sound filtering through the open windows, competing with neighborhood tellies and the odd piano. He favored American West Coast Jazz, which set Mum swaying in the kitchen as she bopped cutlets with a meat mallet. Jill listened when Dad went on about Miles Davis, which made George listen. Both he and his dad were mad for Bossa Nova and played an album called *Jazz Samba*. When "Desafinado" started, George had to dance it like a snake to the charmer. The quieter stand-up bass enthralled, more than the sax or electric guitar. Jill watched him as if studying him.

He tried shaving to see if it induced beard hair. It made nicks and bloody flannels. "You have porcelain skin," Dad cried loud enough for certain people to hear. "It's no use moaning over it. You'll be damned sorry when it goes, believe me. The hair will come."

His body hair was sparse, his chest a blank. George slapped on aftershave that stung the nicks. He sniffed his clothes before putting them on. Instead of wearing his stink all day, he took baths. It was hard to relieve the tension with Jill so close. He could hear her movement across the hall. He'd die if she ever came in on him.

Afterward, he dipped into Mum's stash of scented oils. If Jill got too close, she'd find he smelled of oranges. Daringly clad in his robe, Shadow George thrust himself in her way. Jill pushed right past him.

Privately, Uncle James admitted suspicions about Jack Stuart. The man hadn't done enough for George. But he laughed outright when told of Jill's plans. "I have *got* to find you someone other than those loony Americans."

On Saturday nights, James hosted a "Lonely Hearts" dance at Fleet Feet. Dad hinted to Jill that James might want her to attend, Dad being convinced James would "shape up" with the right woman.

George and Mum exchanged looks. George only hoped his uncle would be pleasant to their new houseguest.

As the dance took a while getting started, George and Miss Kathy were sent on the floor to charge the energy. He kept Miss Kathy whirling, and ended the dance doing the splits. Ladies gasped; men winced. After, they mixed with the regulars to get everyone moving.

Mrs. Althorp wanted a turn, even with her husband there. George shot a nervous look at Mr. Althorp, who glowered. Then Myra flipped at the sight of Jill, becoming mulish with her steps.

George couldn't lead her. "She's just a family friend."

"Ooo, did you see the look she gave me? Your *friend.*"

He gave up on her. "I have to change. The Latins are starting."

He escaped to the sanctity of the men's locker room. He discarded jacket and tie for an open-necked shirt, and switched to Cuban-heeled boots, and a spritz of scent. He peeked out.

Happily, the two Althorps were rowing and heading for the door, Uncle James escorting them. George exited with relief.

Nearby ladies did a double take. He guided these safer partners through "Perfidia" and other sexy numbers. Jill wanted a spin.

"Wowee, the swivel is going tonight."

"Huh?" he said to her grin, and fumbled a step. How could she make him feel both excited and ridiculous?

"I must say I enjoyed your inappropriate friend being booted."

"You were the reason she was upset."

"Now you've made my night."

DAY CLASSES at the studio held a welcomed surprise. Delia, the tall, Caribbean beauty, had returned from wherever she'd been for a year.

"She followed a man," scoffed Mrs. Althorp, who didn't seem to like Delia either.

Delia went straight to George. "Well, well. So the dancin' boy still here. Let's see what you can do, baby."

Mrs. Althorp bristled. "He's a teacher now."

Why was Mrs. Althorp embarrassing him so much? Uncle James asked her to go show steps to other students.

Whenever Delia came to the studio, she lavished George with attention. How would it feel to make love to her? If only she didn't call him "boy" or "baby" so much. She was an amazing dancer who made him want to be better. He cycled to the studio early to do his ballet stretches, his sit-ups and push-ups. If Delia was limber enough to raise her foot to her face, then he would be, too.

Uncle James insisted they create a dance together. Delia stayed for sweaty afternoons as a floor fan whirred the air. The chosen song was jazzy with pounding drums. Delia's eyes sparked a challenge. George strove to impress her.

She grabbed his hips, stopping him. "I want you easy even when we go fast. Limp, loose. Pretend we on a hot beach."

Her touch was thrilling. "I'd love to be on a hot beach."

"You tell me with eyes now."

"I mean with you."

She covered his mouth. "Eyes. Dance is there. Weave a spell with partner, through partner, with audience. And when your back turned, you keep the dance going in this nice place here." She patted his bum.

His grin broadened. "You still want my bum to talk."

"Yah, right, you remember. And I don't mean farts."

When their dance debuted on another Saturday night, the crowd cheered well before it ended. Jill applauded as wildly as anyone. She bobbed over. "That was fantastic. Kiddo, you excite a crowd."

He beamed between his two fantasy women. "It wasn't just me."

Delia said, "It mostly you, child. Are you the agent? I t'ink this baby is going places."

~

AUGUST BROUGHT hints of fall and the dreary onset of school. Or would he sign on with Jill's mad plan? He'd missed auditions for the New Lights Players in Edinburgh. Yet it didn't feel right going up there without Jack.

His family lingered after supper, everyone talkative. Jill ticked off on her fingers, "He needs an updated portfolio, full-time dance lessons, a voice coach. I can cover the expenses."

Dad scoffed. "It's too much. You keep that money for yourself."

"Gerry, there's plenty for me. Wherever he is, my missing husband isn't touching it. I've been checking the statements. George needs to start on the strongest foot possible."

"Save the funds, lass. George will be back in school."

"Dad—"

"Son, this affects your life. Lucy, tell him."

George said, "I think I'd rather work with Jill." Oh, to never see Wilburn again. Or Baldy Barlow. No more hauntings from Wells and MacIntyre.

Mum set down a full teapot. "Your father is right, sweetie."

But she turned to Dad. "Remember, we felt lucky he lasted in school until sixteen. We weren't going to push."

"But stopping at O-levels is ordinary. Our Jory is not ordinary. Didn't we know that from the moment he came into the world?"

Both parents seared him with love.

Mum turned. "But it is his future, love. How many of your favorite performers went to university?"

"And how many performers never make it at all?"

Dad looked distraught at Jill, who hunched like she wanted to slide out of her chair.

Mum said, "He'll make it, Gere-bear. I have a feeling."

George reached across the table. "One year, Dad. Let me try one year with Jill. If we don't make it, I'll go to school, I promise."

Dad signaled him to the back garden. George could've predicted his words: *La-la-la, the school; your future; a risk. She has no experience.*

You'll end up with nothing. But he already saw his new life—dancing at auditions, doing plays.

Dad squinted and looked off. "Oh God. One year."

Jill found a bed-sit in Islington, near the Angel tube stop. It was shockingly small after the Chelsea maisonette. George envied it, even if it was just a room with a kitchen. Heavily bombed in the war, the area was crowded with new apartment blocks. Jill said it suited her mood of starting over. And the cheap rents didn't hurt.

She partially redeemed herself with Dad by proposing the Royal Academy of Dramatic Arts. George wouldn't be eligible until he turned eighteen. But she reasoned she would use the time remaining to help him break into show business. If it didn't work out, he'd attend the school. Professional work would disqualify him for admission. She saw both options as win-win.

How odd to be home when the autumn term started. Not that he was home much. George wended his way north to Islington in his new role of a potentially famous dancer with a girl agent. He wore his mod gear, a striped blazer over a polo shirt, and Levis, and sucked a grape lollipop. Though it felt good to finally get the candy out of his mouth after the much-longer ride.

"You don't think anyone's going to nick my bike, do you? You didn't come to the dance on Saturday. Twice as many people showed up—for *me*, Uncle James said."

He pirouetted with joy and knocked a pile of books.

She picked them up. "Yes, they are coming for you. Listen, a theater in Battersea is auditioning for *Gypsy*—"

"You look so serious, like an office girl. You're just missing specs."

She seemed a bit mannish in her button-down shirt tucked into trousers. Why hide that curvy body? Her waist looked grab-able.

"As I was saying, a theater in Battersea is doing *Gypsy*. It could be popular, what with the movie—"

He sang "Small World." Jill spoke over him. "So I'd like you to try out for the lead boy in the chorus. Jack was right about needing to dance and sing. You have a nice voice. You'll please your father. We have to please your father."

George faltered. "I wish he hadn't said that. It will be unforgivable if I fail."

One evening, Dad had confessed to Jill that George was his favorite singer after George had claimed it was Judy Garland, though Sarah Vaughn had been a recent favorite.

Jill eyed him. "Then don't fail. Singing lessons would help, right?"

"Yes. Please." His "please" was muffled by the jammed-in lolly.

She sat at a table and wrote, "Singing lessons for DF—that's you, doll-face."

"Why do you call me 'doll'? I'm a man."

She cut her eyes to the sucker. He blushed and tossed it.

She lit a cigarette. "You need to be a local star before we try London. It's like Manhattan. The next step up is huge. And before you dance again at Fleet Feet, I want a sign advertising it and an increased fee. No one should see you for free anymore."

She sounded like such an agent. He slid out one of her smokes.

"Speaking of your uncle, we should talk about your name. 'Carveth' is awfully Cornish-sounding. Why not 'George Hartley?' Keep it in the family, your mom's side."

He blanched. "Dad."

She flashed worry. "I know. I feel I'm on his bad side."

"Let's change my first name. How about 'Trent?' Or 'Rick?' 'Blaze.'"

"How about forget it? 'George Hartley' is a compromise."

Staring at wash lines outside her window, he imagined George Hartley. *Blaze Hartley.* Her cigarettes were awfully strong. He picked a fleck of tobacco from his tongue.

"You have a grape tongue."

For a moment, her smile was the kind, teasing one.

"About your look, no gum or lollipops. You should look older, but not too old. No cigarettes. More like an art student. I liked the black roll-neck and brown trousers you wore for one of your dances."

She was mad with this nonsense, and wrote furiously. "Here is the address for the photographer I want you to see. We need updated photos. Bring that outfit, a suit, and tie. Winklepickers stay home. Cuban heels are good. Cu…ban…heels….”

Fear seized him the morning of the photo shoot, only it turned out to be a real studio with spotlights, backdrops, and a screened area to change behind. The photographer said, “Give me more of that terrific smile,” and didn’t come off like a player angling for a date.

Meanwhile, the singing coach told George to stop smoking or he would ruin his throat. She considered him as rusty as he knew himself to be.

The *Gypsy* audition had a queue of boys for the casting of the male chorus, featuring the coveted role of “Tulsa.” George had done stretching exercises all morning to make himself limber. He would wow them with his extension.

When at last he took the stage, someone in the seats asked if he was British, then pressed “Originally?”

George maintained his smile, though his heart sank.

The voice said, “Carry on.”

He read the lines with defiance, flew through the dance, and managed to warble on key. He was Mowgli entertaining the blue-bloods again.

The group in the seats had a chinwag. Why drag out his dismissal? He deserved a new 45-rpm for putting up with this humiliation. A man kept glancing at him as if gearing for insults.

Someone said, “Smooth out with practice.”

The woman balked. “I mean, really?”

The pensive man looked up. “All right, son. You’ve got the part.”

Bloody…hell…? George shook various hands and was given forms, a script. Had he heard correctly?

An assistant told the queue of boys the role of Tulsa was filled.

A rotter smirked. “Did *he* get it? I knew it. I knew it as soon as I saw him.”

George sprang for the lout, but a shouted *“Mr. Carveth”* stalled the mania in his limbs, the surging need to pummel someone.

The assistant's eyes were steely. "We're not going to have trouble, are we? You see plenty of others ready to take your place."

George backed away in horror. "No, sir. Sorry, sir."

He wobbled on the walk home, heart throbbing as if he'd been the one set upon. He would quit the play at once.

He told Jill and his parents there had been no decision. Fear of being booted marred his sleep. Surely that assistant had told the others about him. No one would want a dark troublemaker.

The casting soon closed. Then he was, incredibly, invited to rehearsals.

The joy of the play overwhelmed him. All members were a family working towards a shared goal. The chaps didn't seem to want to push his face in the dirt, but for the assistant, who kept a wary eye on him. The lasses smiled at him. George vowed to be saintly. He would absorb all he could. He loved watching the actress playing Louise go from dowdy to sexy, which was rather the opposite of his beloved Jill.

Uncle James lauded him for the role, until he realized he'd lost his dance star of Saturday nights.

Jill said, "You could always put up a sign advertising that he'll be back in four weeks, and a sign for 'Gypsy' to whet their appetite. Then charge more for the night he appears and pay George the additional amount."

Uncle James narrowed his gaze. "So now you're his agent?"

She said, "You're catching on."

Jill was a constant surprise, much nervier than her husband. Yet he saw her courage falter for the name-change talk. Mum brightened at the idea of using her family name. Dad looked sorry Jill was back in their house. She argued that George shouldn't have to face any regional prejudice that, sadly, was out there, that had dogged him throughout his schooling, or so he'd told her. He nodded vigorously.

Dad stood up. "You decide my kid's future. Now you want him to give up his name?"

George and Mum rose from their chairs.

Jill said, "Not give it up. Keep it in the family."

"Not *my* family. Not the family of his Cornish birth. And, yes, we're damned proud of that fact."

She nodded. "You should be proud. But it's not relevant—"

"Not *relevant?*"

"To the decision that his name shouldn't get in the way of any job prospects, so people won't know if he's a city boy or a country lad so that he can play whatever role he wants." Jill rushed the last sentence with eyes shut as if anticipating outrage. She opened them.

Mum hovered. "Gere-bear, let's think about this."

Dad whirled. "You take her side again?"

"Sweetie, she may have a point. I think Jill is trying to be professional."

Dad's eyes gleamed, "To hell with all of you," and marched upstairs.

Guilty, George sat, blinking. Jill slumped as if shot.

Mum took Jill's hand. "I'll talk to him. It is a good idea. I don't mean because it's my name. He needs to get used to it. He's thrilled about the play."

Gypsy sold out every night of its run. Despite feeling sick, once George started his scene, the song came naturally enough. He strove to better himself each night and even earned a mention in a local review as "a lad who bears watching."

His comeback at Fleet Feet merited another local article that Mum clipped and saved. Those were the last times he would appear as "George Carveth." Dad yielded to "whatever works for the boy." But it seemed his spirit had shut down.

George bonded to "Hartley," the clean, English-sounding name of his tawny mother, a moniker he could be new in. *Was he British, indeed!* Dad would have to get used to it. Dad hadn't minded George erasing his Cornish accent. His father attended all the *Gypsy* performances.

Teenaged roles were popping up everywhere. Jill sent him on several auditions, with just as many rejections, and sometimes "callbacks," a good sign. Somehow, he never made the final cut. Jill vowed to chase down the decision-makers. She later reported the fit wasn't right or he was almost selected.

He heard her tell Mum someone claimed he'd draw in the wrong element. What on earth was the wrong element? Some adults thought all teenagers were trouble.

"And someone always asks if my husband approves of what I'm doing." Jill sounded incensed.

Mum said, "Ridiculous," as if she agreed.

THE RUSSIANS and the Americans were having a standoff in Cuba, a tiny country across an ocean. Nuclear war loomed. Everyone at his new dance studio was riled, the instructor too upset to teach. Students queued at pay phones, so George pulled out his own 6p coin.

Mum said, "Come home."

Instead, he intercepted Jill in front of her block on White Lion. She said a surprised, "DF?" as he took her hand, and jerked free at the news, eyes flinty. "I don't believe it."

"My parents want me home," he said softly. "I'm not leaving without you."

He gave up on her hand and took her elbow to guide her towards the tube station. She lagged, murmured, "Jack," then "we should get drunk." He pushed her on. All around was an unnatural quiet as workers headed home. On the rocking train, newspapers with "World War" headlines obscured faces. Some fool held a transistor radio to his ear as if it would work underground. A woman dabbed her face.

Would all this life be wiped out in a flash? Or was the slow poison of radiation wafting from Berlin to be their lot? Jill swallowed what sounded like a sob. He clasped her hand.

George caught his parents' surprise at seeing Jill though they feigned gladness. Dad thought they should all go to Cornwall; he was sure Jill would be accommodated. Jill said she'd tough it out.

Perhaps George would wait, too. Dad dragged him into the kitchen. "Son, she's a grown woman. She's not our family, and she's an American. No one's terribly happy with America right now."

"*You're* not happy with her, Dad."

"All right. I'm not."

"But she's alone here. I said I'd look after her and I mean to."

George held his gaze. Dad blinked and said they'd discuss it in the morning. He sensed his father didn't really dislike Jill.

That evening, the telly broadcasted a three-minute warning so everyone would know the alarm when the missiles launched. They sat in horror.

Jill balked. "I don't want to know I have three minutes to live."

George shivered. Dad turned off the telly and fetched whiskey. Jill rose, eager for it. Mum muttered, "I prefer my wits about me."

Dad gave George a watered-down version. It made a fire in his throat. Dad and Jill refilled their tumblers.

Weirdly, Dad said, "Go on, son, play one of your Rock-n-Roll records. I don't know why you like it. But I might hear it differently."

Dad agreeing to Rock-n-Roll was absurd. George couldn't decide which record to select, then played Elvis.

"He's got a good voice," Dad said.

George nodded, embarrassed. Mum announced she was baking a cake and banged about the kitchen. She came out to say, "I can't take another world war. I really can't."

Elvis stuttered the word "baby." The cake smell filled the room.

Jill paced. "Kennedy won't let it happen. He won't."

"Aye, he seems a reasonable sort," Dad said with worried eyes.

Mum marched out with a spatula. "Communists are a fact of life. The Americans will just have to live with that. They antagonized Castro. I know we're allies. I'm not anti-American, Jill, you know that. But there has been hysteria. McCarthy."

Jill raised her hands. "On the brink of war, I'd say that's a fair charge."

Dad pounced when Elvis finished and dropped on Miles Davis.

Jill insisted she'd sleep on the sofa downstairs. Mum brought down bedclothes. George lingered after his parents went up. Jill had gone tipsy, a faraway look in her eyes, and confessed, "I miss my parents. I should've phoned them. I need to in a few hours."

They nestled on either end of the sofa, feet almost touching. He said, "What are they like?"

She smiled to tell him. Parts of her life spilled out, all of it prior to the singular moment of showing up here. She railed about Jack's secrecy and selfish ways, a dangerous topic. George braced for an attack that didn't come. She confessed about men not taking her seriously and a director who'd tried to pull her.

He smirked. "I've had that, as well."

She held her head as if it was the worst thing ever. "I didn't realize. I hope you told them where to go. Don't sacrifice your integrity."

He didn't dare mention how that slut Shadow George liked to exploit people's interest.

Tell her about me. She's tanked. You never let me out when she's here.

Because she'll think I'm batty, and don't try to come out anyway.

Jill looked awfully cute as she snuggled down to sleep. Her loose jumper obscured her shape, as if she meant to hide it.

When her breathing turned to snoring, George looked up the word "integrity." It meant wholeness, soundness, uprightness, honesty. Fancy Jill thinking he had any of those qualities. Of course, she was unaware of his past. It touched him that she assumed his integrity. He placed a blanket over her before going upstairs.

Morning dawned gentle and familiar. Clapham Junction ran its trains. His pajama bottoms were wet. A urine whiff hit. He clamored from the bed, horrified. He couldn't have done this at his age.

He recalled last night's horrors. Bombs might well drop today. What did it matter if his sheets and pajamas were wet? What did *anything* matter? It was the older generation's fault. How could they create a world like this?

He tore off the evidence. Mum would notice missing sheets. He shoved his wet things to the bottom of the laundry bin. After a rinse in the tub, he padded downstairs.

All the adults looked haggard as they listened to the news on the BBC. His dad figured they might as well wait one more day. Jill asked to take a bath and reminded George he had an audition. When she went upstairs, Mum sprang, wild-eyed.

"I don't want you going out. I heard places are canceling events."

"Mum. I have a jazz lesson as well. I'll need the warm-up for the audition."

Dad stepped in. "We have to go on with our lives, flower. We're waiting on Moscow now. They'll be sleeping at the White House."

"I doubt anyone's sleeping. First Nazis tried to kill us. Must we live through Russians now? If they run those sirens…"

She shuddered. Dad touched her head. "Finish your tea, love."

What had his parents endured in the years before he was alive when bombs fell on this very neighborhood?

Mum hugged Dad. "You were the best thing to happen to me, Gerren Carveth. That war brought me you."

He held her. "It did indeed."

George blinked. "Mum. I'll stay home if you like."

Her look softened, and she drew him into their embrace. "Daddy is right. Do what you must. Then come home."

In the West End, a sign was taped on the stage door: "Auditions are ON for today." George had half prayed for a cancelation. Other young men stood in a queue, most looking furtive, likely all dance-trained since childhood. His inexperience would be glaring. How dare he try to look like Gene Kelly.

A woman checked a list. "George Hartley? You're on, love."

He padded out in his soft, black jazz shoes, handed off his photos and CV. No one asked if he was British.

He returned to the wings. Cue it! The piano started.

Out he danced, a big smile for the seated watchers. The first few steps were rote until he could get his nerves under control and move more fully into the sound. At least if the bomb hit now, he'd be dancing away, fried mid-twirl, like those victims in Pompeii.

It was partly thanks to Mr. Wilburn for this ability to lose himself, to block out distraction. When his timing was dead on, it happened. He became the interpreter of marvelous sound, the dancing note, the bouncing ball. *Look* at what you're listening to. And they would look, and he knew he had them, those professionals, and that was thanks to Shadow George. *See what my body can do?* It was a fantastic power.

But then he thought he sensed… heads were shaking… they were laughing. George whirled to a stop.

A man said, "Son, you're not dancing the girl's part, that's already filled. Appreciate the enthusiasm, but you need to bring it way down. This is a male role."

His face heated. "I know that. I wanted to show you what I could do."

"You've shown us plenty. Thank you."

That was it? The woman in the wings waved for him to get off.

Can a girl do this? He ran into a front flip, sprang the second with no hands and whirled a sequence across the stage. One of the men hooted. Another said, "We don't need acrobats either, sunshine. Next!"

George stalked off the stage, past the louts in the queue. He felt like stalking straight for a beer. *Dance like a girl.* Were males never to do anything fun? Throwing his body around was the joy of being male. If he looked graceful doing it, all the better.

Jill startled him at the stage door, eyes bright, tits amazing in a snug jersey, and said, "Uh oh," at his face. She pushed the door with her backside.

He said, "Did you phone your parents?"

"I did. And I don't care how badly your audition went. The Soviets will dismantle. You don't have to go to Cornwall, and I don't have to find a bunker."

THIRTEEN

"Night Train"

(JAMES BROWN ADAPTATION, 1962)

THE AFTERNOON SKY was a rosy gold between the massive buildings of Piccadilly Circus. With the fountains turned off for winter, George saw his chance. He took a running leap at the Eros statue, hoisted over the jutting middle, then clamored up icy cold bronze, pulling to the base of the winged figure that balanced on the ball of one graceful foot. Claps sounded below. He glanced at those smiling up. Triumph washed through him. Though it was dizzying above the tops of double-decker buses. But now he could scan for the defector from the Kirov and new star of the Royal Ballet. Rudolph Nureyev had been spotted in this area. George felt bold enough to approach the artist and offer friendship.

The structure vibrated; another lad tried to climb. As if sensing ill will, the kid slid back. George eased up his coat collar, one-handed, against a sharp wind. This was his conquest.

He'd spent his week feeling like a garden flower amidst the bees. He'd sparked the interest of females, and ended up bedding one with sad eyes, a large nose, and weak chin. She'd seemed surprised as he followed her to her attic room. But he wondered about the bodies of lots of girls, not just the pretty ones. He wanted to fall in love, which was supposed to happen at his age. His gaze caught on a fair-haired man below.

How could he not look for Jack? The bastard, loving him and dropping him. Like that other one. Nowadays, George could think of the big man without almost losing his breath, yet resented him even taking over his thoughts. Jack hadn't been too bad off if he'd walked away. Was he recovering somewhere? Was he quietly dead?

He couldn't get rid of the old letters and kept them stashed in a drawer of private things and still wore the necklace against his skin.

Sometimes, Shadow George wanted trouble. The staring men. Would they inject him with love in that tender place? It always hurt, with fleeting arousal, mostly fear. Yet there was comfort in walking with soreness. Like walking with love.

He confessed about the men to Mrs. Althorp, who called him a "pervert" and threw him out of her house.

The wind lanced his ears and neck. Getting down looked utterly precarious. Who did these mad things? A photo was snapped below, no one offering help. He didn't dare move his slippery-soled shoes.

It killed him that Jill had all but guessed about him and Jack. Those damned photos. He still marveled how she'd dozed in his arms the day he fetched her out of the Chelsea flat. He used that memory to call up deep feelings in his acting class.

Jill kept bettering his life. She discovered some RADA prep classes for youngsters shy of eighteen held near the school and taught by former faculty. Now he was gaining poise and reciting Shakespeare. He called her "boss." Dad called her "Slim," in a teasing way. She was still sexy, though not in the way of before, not so curvy and padded. The laughter was gone from her eyes.

Police! George shinnied down the statue and nearly fell on his arse and darted on rubbery legs through milling pedestrians. The two coppers bobbed in the crowd.

He stayed amidst tourists and tore down a side street, keeping a rapid pace, and nearly crashed into a shop owner, who shouted, "Oi!" He must look a thief! George fled around a corner, then slowed.

It was dangerous on Fridays without a class to attend. He thought he'd enjoy roving the city, mapping it with his feet. The thing was not to look suspicious. Coppers were wary of teenaged blokes. He eased his pace and recited lines from his theater class.

The theater prof had called him, "our leading man," and privately told George, "You will go far, my dear." The acting teacher was immune to his charm, admitting he moved well, was a keen mimic, but she stressed the difficulty of his getting into the Academy. The theater prof said the Academy would "scoop him up."

Lasses were back in his life, lively, fun ones, like Fran, with her dimples and infectious laugh. Some were serious and full of themselves, like gorgeous Philippa, a student at the RADA, lunching at the Italian café, cutting her spaghetti so as not to spatter her exquisite front.

Since his father gave him pocket money, George ventured to have a few dates, though not to pubs where he was asked to prove his age—where Philippa had balked, "I thought you were older." One wasn't expected to go very far on dates, sexually-speaking. (Timid Laurie, not on the acting track, content to be a stagehand.) He was expected to be the initiator, and his date would stop him at some point. Fancy drawing an urge out over weeks. Who needed Mrs. Althorp?

Mum had tried to sniff out his business yesterday, entering his bedroom with an armload of clothes. "Your uncle tells me how popular you are with the ladies. You know they're married, some of them. You don't want trouble."

He flinched at her reference. "Don't worry."

"They're pretty old, yah, love? I know how it is, getting a lot of attention." She filled bureau drawers. "You don't have to do what you don't want."

This advice was rather late. Incredibly, she blushed, and added, "You might even get it from men. Remember you're a good boy..."

He couldn't decipher a line of the script before him.

"You can always tell your father if someone troubles you. Or your uncle. He might be able to help."

If she didn't shut it, he would scream! He dodged her reaching hand. How could Uncle James know about the men? He'd certainly spend less time around that big-mouthed gossip.

A "good boy." Hah.

The coin of the necklace was in his mouth. George hadn't remembered getting it out of his shirt. He tucked it inside and glanced around. No sign of the police anymore. Though he was by the entrance to a certain pinball arcade. He'd make quick money in here, if he wanted to be worshiped, to be hurt.

She thinks you have integrity.

He didn't want to lose Jill's respect, no matter how unwarranted it seemed. And though there was a part of him that longed to shock, horrify and punish his parents, another part couldn't bear to disappoint them.

ALL THE BOYS wanted to date Philippa. Even the bouncer perusing IDs at the club barely looked at his and gawked at the girl with Veronica Lake hair. George appreciated his rare fortune. What girl dated a man two years younger, even if he was nearly seventeen? She'd yet to see him dance, but said she liked how he walked. She said he didn't leer or swagger, which made him wonder if he *ought* to be leering and swaggering. He kept his hand on her shoulder or deliciously around her waist when other louts passed close.

They joined a line dance to the sexy pulse of "Night Train." George watched the sway of her backside and couldn't wait to get her alone. She smiled to see him dance, mouthed, "You are good," even though it was nothing what he did, just keeping time.

A chap with a beard, a real beatnik, muscled close to them and bought a round of drinks. "You're the handsomest pair in here. Is this your brother?"

Philippa laughed, and George said "no." He said "date" as she said "friend." The beatnik raised his eyebrows with a laugh.

George glared, worried. The beatnik tossed him some coin. "Do us a favor. A pack of Players, mate. You mind?"

Philippa didn't protest. Why did being younger mean he had to do someone else's bidding? He'd keep a few smokes for himself.

When he returned, the pair had gone. *Hell.* That conniving bastard took his date! And off she went, glad to be rid of him, no doubt. How could he think he'd make it with a girl like that? He was merely a "friend," a loser, a bumboy— He whirled at fingers on his shoulders.

Philippa said, "Where did you run off to?"

"I was buying fags. Where's your bloke?"

"Not *my* bloke. He's at the bar. He wants to take me home."

George stiffened. "I'm not stopping you, if that's what you want."

"I'm with you."

"But you'd prefer him, is that it? He's worldly and older."

"Stop." She palmed his cheek.

He was shaking with rejection. And yet she was trying to tell him she hadn't rejected him. Would that happen later?

She flinched. "Oh no, here he comes."

The beatnik scanned the room. Both ducked. George snaked back to their chairs and grabbed coats. They raced laughing out of the club into the sharp night air. He felt better outside, less barmy. The jitters waned.

Philippa shivered. He pulled her close. She swiped his hair. The unoiled curls on his forehead went nearly to his eyes. Girls seemed to like that look.

On the train, they deep kissed in a near empty car. She murmured that he smelled nice. Would he finally have her tonight? He imagined her thighs in suspenders and relieving her of her bra.

They grappled in the alcove of her basement flat. Her roommates were supposedly asleep, yet she wouldn't let him come inside and continue the bliss. He tried to cup her bum. She kept moving his hand. He rather hoped she'd squeeze his bum, or better. But girls didn't seem to go for his body as the grownups did. They looked and smiled, but, Lord, they just never touched.

She finally hiked up her bra. Her breasts popped, dim globes in the darkness. Such sweetness! Once he started fondling breasts, that was it, he was lost. He put a hot kiss on each nipple then kissed her hard on the mouth, sucking in her little tongue, then back to silk heaven, then her mouth—

She pushed him back. "That's enough, didn't you hear me?" She tugged her bra over the softness.

"Why, what's the…? Let me come in, Phil, please. I'm mad for you."

"No. I thought you were sweet, not a, a grubby-handed boy."

"What? Phil, wait—"

She shut the door on him. Bollocky hell. Now what was he supposed to do? Had he come on too strong? She seemed to enjoy it, but for all that squirming. How do girls walk around with those lovely things and not be always touching themselves? He couldn't have a wank anywhere. But she wasn't the only tall, curvy dolly in the city.

He sprinted toward the underground and caught the last train to Islington. It was quarter past one at the Angel tube stop. Snowflakes glittered in the air. At Jill's block, he counted the windows. Her light was on.

She wasn't surprised to see him. "Hey, DF. Cold out? Your cheeks look bitten."

Bitten. Her flat smelled of tobacco and something fried. How great to have one's own place and eat whatever one wanted for supper. He offered her a smoke from his new pack. She swayed as he lit her. Her cool-eyed gaze assessed him through a veil of smoke, her hair loose, no makeup, clothes baggy. Was that one of Jack's shirts? Were those *nipples* popping beneath the fabric? She turned away. But there were knickers pegged on a wash line over the basin. Black ones, beige ones—

"Stop looking at my underwear."

"What?"

"Turn your head. Turn it. Thank you."

He bunched his coat over his front and heard her taking the knickers down.

Lights glowed on a hi-fi unit, still warm. He tuned the dial to Radio Luxembourg. The Watusi was playing. "Not loud," she warned.

He sloughed off his coat and slinked to the song by the Orlons, singing the "wah, wah's" in falsetto. The tune made him feel loose and sexy.

She grinned. "Aren't you the hot ticket?"

Shadow George danced with his eyes as Delia had taught him.

But Jill reached for an open bottle of Scotch and poured. An older chap would join her. George worried like a mother hen. The song ended and she brushed past him.

"That was all very cute. How about some grownup music?"

He winced at the needle coming down hard. The record on the gramophone was Julie London's "Cry Me a River," a smoky, sultry tune. She swayed in her blue jeans and Jack's oversized shirt. Longing came off her like steam. Or was that just his frustration that a girl danced alone to a fabulous song when he was right there.

Just take her.

I can't.

She wants it.

Not from me.

Was she remembering another man? (The wrong man.) This music made him weak like a lover at his neck.

He checked the teakettle for water and banged it on the gas ring harder than he meant.

She stopped. "Didn't you have a date?"

Mum was always nattering about him. "She's home."

"Which one of your girls?"

"Philippa."

"Is she the giggly one or the one that's 'stacked'?"

His face went warm. "Fran is the giggly one."

"Shouldn't you ring your parents, DF, and tell them you're here?"

"They know I check on you, boss. I wish I lived on my own."

Her burning cigarette glowed in the low light. "You look good tonight. The crimson shirt. Plays off your hair and eyes."

He stared with surprise. "Thanks."

He'd prepped with care for this date, even using one of his mum's scented oils, so he smelled like almonds. He'd made himself appealing for a night of frustration.

She finished one smoke and started another. "Are you gaining weight?"

The teakettle whistled. "I am. Do you approve of my body?" *Don't say that.*

She assessed him. "It's not up to me but your future employers. I think you have a body like a cat. You're still young."

He searched for milk then busied himself with cups and spoons. Shadow George reminded *we're not her type*. Now he was a cat.

She said, "You're sensitive. That's just your age."

"I'm not sensitive. What does my age have to do with it? Don't you like being around me?"

No. He couldn't pour and stared at the empty cups. "My date almost ran off with another bloke tonight. He tried to take her right from under me."

Jill spoke softly, "What a rat. She didn't go, did she?"

"She...wanted to stay with me."

"You sound surprised."

"I-I don't know if girls want me, really want me. Men want me."

She blanched. Then flashed concern and stubbed the cigarette. "I bet a lot of girls want you. They're probably as scared as you."

I'm not scared. Would they talk about the men? It hung in the air.

He gave her a cup mixed the way she liked.

She shook out another smoke. "I should never have bought a carton of these. My throat is raw. Feed Shylock, would you? There are coins in the dish."

He fed the meter for heat, now knowing why she called it "Shylock." Out the window was amazing.

"Wow. It's really snowing."

She seemed lost in thought, not lighting up.

He ventured, "Were you thinking about him?"

A sharp look. "You shouldn't be around me so much. I'll kick you, and you don't deserve it. I'm sorry, DF. Having a weird night."

He spoke barely above a whisper. "It's all right. You can talk about him."

Water gleamed in her eyes. "I don't want to talk about him."

"I'm sure he's not dead."

"I wish he was dead."

You couldn't have helped him. You're wonderful. I miss the old Jill.

He said, "I wish you weren't so sad."

She wrapped herself in a lap rug. "Go home, kiddo."

It wasn't until he was halfway down the stairwell that he remembered the trains had stopped for the night. But he didn't have the heart to knock again, not after that "kiddo."

IT WAS shocking how much snow was coming down. The world seemed softer, the sky with a lavender hue behind the lace. Every so often, a car swished past. He walked south even though it would be an awfully long walk. He buttoned his coat as high as it would go and stuck his hands deep in his pockets. If only he had a hat.

Buildings formed dark walls, the odd window still lit. A few souls of the night scuttled past, a hand raised in greeting. George cut to the right. It was slippery going, the pavement lined with sugared trees, former green places blanketed in white. He strode past the darkened Sadler Wells Theatre, its participants long gone.

Moisture ran down his neck and stung inside his shoes. His hair must be getting wet. He checked his coin again; not enough for a cab. Not that there were cabs about. He couldn't go back to Jill. And he wouldn't go to Philippa, who'd shut the door in his face. His heart leapt at a bus…that was empty of passengers, abandoned.

He made it to the southbound Farringdon Road, wishing for a bus, a cab, a friendly face, but it, too, was nearly deserted. Had the world come to a stop? Snow caught on his lashes. His ears burned, his nose ran. His feet were planks of pain. He would let himself get picked up, only who would be searching this time of night? And was that even a good idea? *Fuck good ideas, he was freezing.*

A miraculous cab crawled in the distance. He frantically waved it down. It put on a blinker and fishtailed.

The driver smiled for a fare. "Lovely morning we're having."

George got in, raining snow onto the floorboard, before admitting to his seventy pence.

The driver turned cold. "How far?"

George offered a weak "Clapham?"

"Get out."

"Please. How far will it get me?"

"I shouldn't even be driving in this weather."

"I'll take however far it goes."

It was a slippery ride, the pace not much faster than his feet had gone. The wipers swished frantically. George held his ears and tapped his ice block toes. Water dripped from his hair and nose.

The driver wanted to dump him at a light well north of the river. "Please," he begged, "to Blackfriars."

"That's a good deal farther. And I'm not going over a bridge."

"My dad will pay you. I'm sure he will."

"You think I haven't heard that, lad? Out, I mean it."

"I…" He swallowed. "I'll put it in my mouth."

The driver twisted round. "Christ. So now I've got a pansy in the back? Piss off before I have you arrested."

George hastened out. The cab snaked before finding traction. He watched the hateful thing turn.

Have me arrested! With what coppers? Perhaps he should sleep in a tube station. He set off for one, his wet head sizzling.

A whine of tires swished close. The cab had circled. The driver beckoned through the window. Relieved, George got in with his best smile. "Thanks heaps."

"Yeah, yeah. You going to make it nice for me, princess?"

Bile rose. The man parked in a loading area and joined him in back.

After, the driver was much friendlier and invited him to sit up front. George would've ridden atop the cab if he could. Nausea welded him to the back seat. He scarcely realized they'd gone west of Blackfriars, parallel to the restless, choppy river, following trails made by other cars. He only knew they were going very slowly and it was going to take a long time. When they finally tried a bridge, some vehicles had stopped. This driver had a nerve at least. They fishtailed, and George's stomach spiked. But the cab pressed on.

"I'll never get out of here, I'll tell you what," the man said, as they crawled streets south of the river. Was it snowing harder? Yet George felt he was nearly home. He could taste it. He'd run if he had to.

The cab spun into a snowbank along the common. They got out by creaking doors and checked tires white and slick.

"Ah, Christ. Give us a push then, eh?"

George gamely pushed. But then he wondered why and bolted over the snowy expanse of the common.

"Hey," the driver cried. "Come back!"

His shoes slipped wildly. Water flew from his eyes. The park was a glorious world with the old trees caked with snow. At some other hour, on some other day, he would savor the view.

When he made it into his house, his parents thundered downstairs, Mum wild-eyed, Dad behind her. "Thank God! Where have you been?"

"What do you mean coming home at this hour?"

They embraced him. Dad pulled back. "You're wet."

"You're freezing," Mum said.

They dragged him to the boiler in the kitchen. Mum struck a match to light the cooker. "Gerry, his clothes."

Dad turned him to get off his coat. "We'll talk about this later."

George shivered from one parent to the next. He'd never felt so loved.

FOURTEEN

"From Me to You"

(JOHN LENNON & PAUL MCCARTNEY, 1963

CLAPHAM JUNCTION WAS EERILY QUIET. But the bomb that silenced it was snow. So far, in this new winter of 1963, temperatures had not gone above freezing. Snow packed the ground. Frost rimed windows, leaching inside during the dark days without power. The Carveths stayed bundled, nursing their socks and underwear longer than they should. A few nights they slept by the fire downstairs when going upstairs felt like being outside. George and his dad ventured out to shovel paths. Then Dad decided they should help others on the street, the widows and elderly neighbors. George was joined by Thomas, the large lad from two doors down, who had the same type of father.

After days of clearing, another blizzard came. Worried residents queued for fuel. George and Thomas queued for the shut-ins. The clothes Mum washed were stiff as planks and arranged near the fire to dry. According to the BBC, the countryside had it worse. Livestock were buried.

George worried about Cloud and her sister sheep. They'd not heard from anyone in St. Ives, a place usually safe from the perils of winter. Mum rang Jill, who claimed to be all right.

On a sunny day, with roads and pavements mostly cleared, Mum baked an extra fish pie and loaded George and his dad with provisions. They took the tube to Islington.

Jill's eyes glistened at the sight of them, which made George blink.

Dad said, "Now, now. This one means to look out for you."

Jill hugged them. George warmed as if her Shylock meter was pumping heat, though that couldn't be. She wore a bulky sweater and fingerless gloves, a scarf tied around her head, to perhaps hide unwashed hair. (Did her body smell of onions?) She looked thin, her freckles more noticeable. Airmail stationery was rolled into the carriage of the typewriter. *Dear Mom and Dad.* He didn't read on.

She chattered and made tea. The pipes in her building had only recently thawed; did they know her Chelsea flat had had central heating? A luxury.

She turned away when Dad fed her meter with coin. He said, "If I'd known you were living this way, I'd have never let you spend that money."

THE PREP CLASSES resumed with meager power restored to the building. It was good to see his fellows again, everyone with stories about the weather. Dance lessons resumed. Still, the thermometer would not climb. A locker room sign said pipes were frozen. George wore his stink as a layer, and trousers over tights, then leg-warmers over the trousers. His sweaty hair chilled his head. He longed for a woolly Russian hat but bought a saucy leather cap instead. It was better to look smart than warm, as he still had the odd audition. He always bathed for auditions. At least Jack had got him parts. Jill produced callbacks, dashed hopes and no jobs since *Gypsy*. Perhaps she was aiming too high.

Shadow George worried. George seemed ready to piss away the time until he got into the Academy. Shadow George wanted to dazzle an audience or win over a leading lady. He wanted something impressive on his CV.

An audition with Reginald Burns, a known director, appeared to work in Shadow George's favor. The man greeted him with "You're rather a stunner, aren't you."

A Nancy, what luck. He played it coy until the director deemed him "not quite right for the part, I'm afraid."

Shadow George made a suggestion.

Reginald Burns ordered him from the room, thankfully too old to get violent about it.

Sometimes normal men leered at him and were far less predictable in behavior. It could have stayed an unfortunate gamble.

George arrived at Jill's bedsit, dropped books on the table, unwound a scarf and removed his leather cap. There was no relief of warmth here. She seemed preoccupied. He blew a bubble of gum but popped it at a fierce look from her.

"What's the matter, boss? It's freezing in here."

She flapped her arms. "I just heard you solicited Reginald Burns."

He couldn't suppress a flinch.

She paced. "He said I can't handle you. And I guess I can't. Because I never imagined you were— He even wondered if I was a *madam,* so we'd better call it quits right now." She pulled off her fingerless gloves and wrestled from an oversized sweater.

"I-I can't believe he would say such things."

"Oh," she held out her hand, "don't even try that."

She was furious, the kind of fury formerly thrown at Jack. George didn't fancy being the new target.

He affected nonchalance. "I thought he, you know, wanted it. They do, sometimes."

She came so close he stepped back. "You are a kid, not a hustler."

"Some hustlers are kids." At least he was taller than her. "You don't know anything about me."

Her freckled cheeks were blooms of color. She gave off a yeasty whiff. The fight dimmed in her eyes.

She sank to a chair and held her head, her voice coming out tired. "Do you feel, by any chance, a 'certain kind of love'?"

What on earth was she talking about?

She opened her arms. "You can tell me, I won't be shocked. I already know something you don't know I know. George, do you prefer men?"

He squawked. What did she know?

"Jack told me—"

"He *told* you?"

"Don't be upset. He was concerned. He confided in me about you."

"That I prefer *men?*"

"Not that, exactly. More about what happened. Honey, it's okay." She almost touched him. "I think it's despicable what he did."

"But you *forgive* him?"

"Forgive him? No. That pervert? Well, *you* know."

He braced a chair. Something wasn't right.

She rose. "I assumed you didn't like it. You were twelve, right?"

He nearly blurted "fifteen," then realized: "My schoolmaster. He told you about my schoolmaster. I was eleven."

There was a dry click in her throat. "Eleven? Was it just one time?"

He hooted. And nearly choked on the wad of gum that sent him running for the sink where he spat.

"Bloody hell. Two and a half years more like."

His laughter bordered on weeping. Of all the things Jack should tell, he blabs about Wilburn? The pink blob of the gum sat on a dirty plate. He wiped his eyes.

"Oh, lord. You met him once. The talent show at school, backstage. Black suit."

"That tall, awful man? I *knew* there was something wrong with him."

He scoffed. "How could you know? He wasn't so bad."

"I don't believe your words. They're lying words."

He whirled on her. "How would *you* know? He was nice, we did things together, like hearing the '1812 Overture' with real cannons. He even brought me to London for a weekend to hear 'Beethoven's Ninth.' It was…"

But how was it, really? Though the music was… "Sublime. During the 'Ode to Joy,' we had tears pouring down. As we had for the bells and the cannon of 1812. I'll never forget those experiences. He felt the music as I did."

How gratifying to have known someone else odd and fanciful, equally transported by sound. And Mr. Wilburn had been gentle after. George mopped his eyes with the sleeve of his sweater.

"So he rewarded you."

Leave it to her to make it ugly. Her face had gone shiny. He banged her meter. "*Ow*, shit. This doesn't work, does it? You are funny. I believe you're sweating."

She jammed her hands in her hair. "It might be out of coin. It's hot in here. What do you mean I'm funny?"

He flapped an arm. "Your concern. I'm hardly innocent."

"Of course, you were innocent."

He shook his head. "You sound sure, but you don't know."

"What don't I know?"

"*Jesus*, don't make me— I was his lover!"

She winced. "Why would you say that?"

Was she thick? He wheeled away from her. "I tempted him, right? He wanted to see me dance. He said, 'we're both males,' I was an artist, I should take off my…"

What a load of bollocks *that* sounded.

She said, "Eleven-year-olds are not tempting."

He kicked over a chair. "Stop being funny! If you had any idea what happens— You guessed about Mrs. Althorp, she had me at fourteen. People come on to me. People you know."

She danced back. "Oh, God. If Jack hurt you, I apologize."

He nearly laughed. "Jack, Christ. Jack fucking loved me. He loved me. But I-I didn't love him back and now he's…"

She was flat to the wall, eyes round with shock.

He kicked the chair again. "You shouldn't have asked me. Why did you *fucking* ask? I'm filth. You shouldn't care about me. Jill, please."

She cowered from him.

Someone rapped the floor. "Quiet up there!"

Shadow George broke through, the atmosphere charged. He knew at once he had to run.

It's the end of Jill. He's shocked her. She'll have nothing to do with us now.

Shadow George hardly realized the snow-cleared pavement, the many people dodged, streets crossed, until he slowed at a pinball arcade and staggered into it, breathless. Men turned his way. The regular lads sneered. He knocked into a rough sort, a sailor.

"Easy, mate. You looking for trouble?"

Heart pulsing in his throat, Shadow George shook his head.

The sailor caught his sleeve. "Hang on. You want company?"

He pulled free, he wasn't a rent boy!

The sailor cornered him between machines. Shadow George scanned for an exit. Yet here came the dark pull—caught by searching eyes, a grizzled face. Tobacco fingers reached.

"Easy, laddie, relax. We're good. I've a room across the way."

Machines rattled and pinged. Cousin Timmy had shown himself to a Norwegian sailor.

The sailor guided him like a friend out to the grazing cold. Shadow George lagged. He could make a break for it and be home for supper. Jill had *cowered* from him.

George reminded—*She'd been saying those awful things.*

But were they awful?

His ears burned, his head was bare. "My cap, I had a cap."

"Nah, you're fine. You didn't come in with one. This way." The sailor bumped him along.

So, this was it. Shadow George strode over the threshold of the block, slower on the stairs. The sailor's hands got inside his coat and pushed him by the buttocks up the last few steps.

He loathed the flare of arousal, and the sickening things he knew he'd let happen. The sailor tussled him in the spartan flat, pushing him to a wall. A miasma so close! Hard to breathe. It only happened through a hiccup. He would be loved and devoured. Forced and cared for. It was only the resistance that was so, so terrifying.

Shadow George said, *if you don't leave, I can't do this.*

Smoky breath pelted him. "I ain't never had one looked like you before. I'll be buying you a new cap soon enough. Look at me, brown eyes. Tell me what you want."

WITH POUND NOTES in his pocket, he escaped to the singeing night and staggered to a call box. The old man shakes befuddled his fingers, especially for getting a coin in. He did somewhat better on the dial-up. A story poured out:

"Mum. I've been to see Jill. She's feeling poorly. I'm off to the chemist. Don't know when I'll be home."

Mum believed that voice. Why shouldn't she? She instructed him to buy soup and ring her if Jill grew worse.

Soup. He didn't need soup. A crowded restaurant beckoned. He pushed straight back to the gents' toilet. Empty, thank God. The glass showed a mark on his neck, blotches near his collarbone. The bloke had been a biter.

He ducked into a stall to check inside his pants then froze as someone came in, and scarcely breathed through the piddle sound, not moving until the closed door signaled safety again.

Out in the restaurant was high fun and drinking, the smells of a savory roast. All these people enjoying their lives. A hostess caught his eye. He tried a smile. She came over, not fooled.

He pleaded soup for an ill friend. Her gaze fell to his neck. He shut the coat.

She said, "We've beef barley, but the kitchen is about to close. Have you money?"

Had he, indeed! Shadow George had nerve when it came to payment. But he needn't stand here waiting for soup. Though the longer he waited, the hungrier he became. Beef barley might be just the ticket. He dug his hands in his pocket and slunk to the side as diners went past. The hostess returned with soup and wrapped bread.

"Thanks awfully." His stupid fingers couldn't sort the right coin.

The hostess squeezed his hands. "Never mind, love. Take care of yourself. Stay out of the cold."

The night air grazed him. Had he lost his scarf, as well? The soup carton warmed his hands and midsection, his feet heading north. But whatever for? He couldn't go to Jill. He'd stabbed her with his hateful words.

Her light was on. Amazingly, she answered the door.

"I brought soup."

She turned away, her shirt looking blotched, and sat on the bed in the corner. "You left your books."

He placed the soup on her worktable. There was his cap.

He deflated. "I know you hate me. Jill, I'm sorry, it was nonsense. Jack didn't love me."

Her lack of response made him check her. "Are you all right?"

She was flushed. "My head."

He dared to feel her forehead. "Golly." And pulled back his hand. "Lie down, yeah? You should undress."

She slumped.

Oh, lord. She was burning up. He wet a cloth and laid it on her forehead. He hated removing her socks in a cold room. Her bare feet were warm.

Her trousers were snug at the hip. "Oh, gosh. You must stay in bed. Let's try and remove these, right? I'll look the other way."

She wasn't much help. He glimpsed sweaty, white panties hugging her parts. His groin woke and stung. (That damned sailor.)

Her dear legs were soft. He threw a blanket over them so he wouldn't caress them. She whined about the woolen nightdress he found, calling it hot. The other was only cotton. He unbuttoned her shirt but left it closed. "You finish."

Soup in a saucepan. Gas on. Coins in the meter.

She hadn't removed her shirt. "Boss. You have to help."

He lifted her shoulders to ease off the shirt. Her bra was white and sweaty, her skin hot to the touch.

With the cotton gown on her, he rewet the flannel and dabbed her chest and arms. A bubbling sound made him leap to switch off the cooker. She mustn't have scalding soup. He poured a glass of milk.

But she was shivering! He threw the damp flannels on the floor, grabbed the woolen nightdress and dragged it over her clammy, shuddering body. Her teeth were clicking. The wet panties were probably chilling her. He foraged underneath for elastic, dragged off the pants and threw them across the room, and tucked the bedclothes around her. Her bra was probably damp, but he dare not go for that.

He didn't like her unfocused gaze. He shrugged off his coat, put it over her. Then got on the bed. "I used to warm my cousin on cold nights." Was it awful to love her nutty smell? *Don't get hard.*

As her quaking eased, he placed a towel between her damp head and the pillow. The beef barley was tepid. She managed a few spoonfuls. He settled on the carpet, after, with his coat and a fallen pillow.

HE AWOKE WITH A KICK. St. Clair was attacking him. But it was Jill stumbling and staring. "I didn't know you were here."

Daylight filled the bedsit flat. "How are you?"

She held her throat. "Sore. I need to…" She grabbed her dressing gown and went out to use the facilities down the hall.

He got up and collected towels, put the kettle on the heat and a coin in the meter.

Jill slipped back in, her look wary, as if she remembered the awful things he'd said yesterday. She wavered before him.

"I'm wearing two nightgowns."

He laughed, then stopped. "You put on one over the other."

Across the room were the discarded knickers she'd yet to see. He added, "You were feverish. I turned away, of course."

Her gaze sharpened as if he'd said he'd gawked at her.

She clutched her dressing gown, grabbed her cigarettes on the table, then released them at his look. "What happened to your neck?"

He clamped his neck and turned away. The ugly memory revived in his mind, that sailor. The money burned in his pocket. He had no scarf to cover the shame. *You should have left by now.*

The kettle whistled. He readied the tea as Jill climbed in bed.

She muttered, "Weird. I dreamt Jack was taking care of me. But it must've been you."

He wilted over the basin. "I'm sorry. I said ugly things yesterday, made-up things. They weren't true. Please believe me." If he could've said Jack had come over last night, he would have.

"You were so angry with me."

He shook his head. "You think I'm better than I am. I was good, once, as a child. He tainted me. I'll detest him forever."

He brought over her cup. His shoulder hitched wanting to cover the bruise on his neck. "Thanks," she said softly. "Will you have some?"

He sat at the table with a cup, his hand on his neck. She watched him from the bed.

"George. I won't be your agent if you're going to solicit people. I don't represent that. I barely know what I'm doing as it is."

Mortification burned anew. "I won't. It makes me sick."

"Don't ever cheapen yourself, sweetie. Promise me?"

LATE AUGUST IN HYDE PARK, Jill and George were stalled on a bench, looking like a pair of movie stars behind sunglasses, facing the placid, glittering Serpentine. Its water reflected a cobalt sky and a wedge of trees. Not that George saw any of it.

His mind, so often caught on the divine figure of Philippa, was troubled by what he'd learned. Philippa was having an affair with an older man. Her flatmate had intercepted George and his flowers and got him to come into her room as she filled him in. He and Phil had been doing so well, though she'd yet to give in to him. Why should she prefer an old sod who was nearly forty?

"She must be blind," the roommate had said.

Jill muttered, "You should've been Bernardo."

He added, "I can Mambo. Didn't that count?"

Jill was obviously stuck on the *West Side Story* role he hadn't got. He didn't like thinking of all the roles he hadn't got, the excuse this time being "not oily enough" for the Shark leader. He would've been fine in the Shark chorus. But the "oily" comment made Jill potty for that lead. Then her rowing with the director squashed all chance.

In just over six months, he'd be eighteen and ready for the RADA. He was keen to try that school. His time might overlap with Philippa. Or, possibly, she'd be gone and trying the real world. Or would she marry her old man?

Passing blokes cut a look at Jill. Sunny in yellow gingham, Jill's figure had filled out more, legs tanned, her toenails painted pink on sandal-shod feet. She claimed to hate stockings and never wore them in the summer. He didn't like a vest in summer and preferred his cotton shirts against his skin. He undid another top button for air.

"Going to the chemist he said. What was at Battersea Park?"

"Why are you mumbling about that old guff?"

She sighed, leaned back. "I was thinking about Chelsea."

"You've been very distant, boss."

"You know me too well, DF. You should be with classmates."

"And miss you?"

She grinned. "What am I, 'The Jill Show'?"

"The Jill Show!" He leapt up. "Starring that sexy, smoldering doll from—what part of New Jersey, sweetheart?"

He held an invisible microphone, interviewing her as they wandered past the Achilles statue. Girls noticed and smiled.

She halted. "It appears Jack dipped into the checking account."

"He's *alive?*"

"It has to be him. No one else has that information. I never found his checkbook. Amazing that its taken him this long to need money. Someone has been supporting him."

How incredible! Would Jack reappear? The thought brought up a tangle of odd feelings. "Perhaps he's been working."

She scoffed, her hands on her hips. "It's hard to imagine Jack Stuart working for anyone."

He dared to confess, "It was me, boss, on that day. He was meeting me in Battersea Park. He didn't say why."

She shoved him. "Why haven't you told me this before? No more secrets or we are done, you and I."

"That's it, I swear."

"You must have an inkling why Jack wanted to meet—Oh, forget it. I can guess." She stalked to a newsstand on the corner.

Odd, her caring about someone who *deserted* her.

Various newspapers held dregs of the Profumo scandal. George had never bothered with that business. Jill was a devout follower of it. She snatched up a tabloid and angrily flipped pages.

The newsagent said, "You can buy it and read at home, love."

She said, "That Dr. Ward should've gone to prison."

"Right you are, love. A real piece of work, that one."

She glared at George. "Not unlike somebody's schoolteacher."

He pretended not to know her.

But there was the new *Beatles Monthly Book* featuring the "moptops" in their collarless jackets. They were the most exciting band on the radio. They made girls scream.

He pushed back his sunglasses for better perusing. Until he realized Jill was breathing on him.

She said, "I've got an idea. Come on."

Barely giving him time to buy the magazine, she hailed a taxi, instructing "New Bond Street." He wouldn't ask about her idea. He only kept secrets to spare her feelings.

She directed the driver to stop at Vidal Sassoon, which looked to be a salon, and explained, "You're getting a hairstyle."

He hooted. But she was serious.

He pointed out, "There are ladies in there."

"They also do men. Haven't you read about that?"

Men and women together?

She pushed him inside. The waiting area was filled with women.

No, wait, there was one sheepish fellow. The receptionist had kohl-rimmed eyes and a short, mannish hairdo. She looked bored and amazing, all pouting lips and silky skin as she dealt with the hens. Jill seemed almost dowdy. She stepped forward as the women dispersed.

"I need an appointment for my friend here. Does Mr. Sassoon do Beatle haircuts?"

George sputtered in shock. "Dad will hate that."

The girl cut eyes at him, then resumed her boredom. "We can do the style, but Mr. Sassoon is booked in advance. When would you like the appointment?"

"Well, I'd really like it now. I'd like it with Mr. Sassoon."

Jill could be so embarrassingly American.

The kohl eyes flashed disapproval. "That's impossible, there's a waiting list. We have other stylists, but I doubt if anyone can see him now."

"Oh, I'll take him," piped a male voice.

A chap with a brushed-forward fringe, comb in his hand, scanned George head-to-foot. "Yes, men do come in. Pop stars, mainly. You're not a pop star, are you, love? Won't be a tick."

What mad business had Jill got him into? He was in a beauty shop!

The salon was decorated in black and white. An article on the wall touted *This Year's New Hairdo – "The Bob Cut."* The model in the photo had the same do as the bored minx in reception. Classical music played low from somewhere.

He murmured, "Tchaikovsky, 'Serenade in C.'"

Jill said, "You never hear music in a barber, I bet. Cool, huh?"

It was. Sort of new and exciting. Teenagers didn't have to look like their parents anymore. The Beatle magazine was still in his hand. He read it with interest. Jill nudged him when a young bloke emerged from the back with a brushed-forward cut.

Sometime later, his name was called. George had to look like a Beatle now or die. But how could he with his wild hair?

The hairdresser whisked a smock around him. "I hope you're ready, handsome. Kiss these curls goodbye."

Jill hovered, grinning. He snapped, "Go away," and she slunk off.

Now he felt bad. But he couldn't bear a witness.

Something strong-smelling was glopped in his hair. What if his hair fell out? Surely this was a giant mistake. What if Philippa was turned off? She thought the Beatles strange. He couldn't watch anymore. The hair washing was pleasant. Scissors snipped. Wet, black locks danced over his eyes. The stylist reached into a tub of gel. Then he waved a blowgun of air and roughly pulled and brushed. More snips. He smiled. "You've just left the fifties. Welcome to the new decade." He whirled George to the glass.

How shocking!

George leaned closer and touched his chestnut mop, that was long-looking, mostly straight. A fringe covered his forehead.

The hairdresser winked. "You're a pop star now, love."

He *was* a pop star. His hair looked amazing.

Jill had thankfully paid. She wasn't anywhere in the shop. He stepped outside, blinking in the sun, then unrolled the magazine in his palm. All he needed was a collarless jacket to squat down and pose with these four on the cover. A voice cried out. Jill just dodged a braking vehicle as she skittered across the street.

"Oh, my God, look at you! He covered your ears, that's good."

"You made me get straight hair. I've never had straight hair."

"I can't get over the difference." She turned his chin. "Your sexy eyebrows are gone. But you look sweeter, less catlike, the way the fringe skims your eyes."

"You never told me I had sexy eyebrows."

She shook her head at his clothes. "These jeans and plimsolls. You should look like a Beatle."

He showed her his magazine. She said, "I can't decide if they're cute or ugly."

"Oh, Jill. They're cute, especially Paul."

She elbowed him. "So, it's my birthday today. And, lucky you, I'm going to buy you presents. There are some new men's shops I've read about. It's time you went fully mod."

How fab! They headed to Regent Street. She kept grinning at him. He tried to catch his reflection in windows. They cut between the rows of department stores to the back alley of Carnaby Street.

He surprised her with a grab around the waist and a dance leap over the verge. She giggled to be swung round—Ginger to his Fred.

He launched into a tune. "Strange how a dreary world can suddenly change to a world as bright as the evening star…"

Her freckles turned pink. She glanced around. He sang louder as people noticed. It didn't matter. She tried to sidle away, but he wouldn't let her. Crooning the great old Irving Berlin tune, "I Used to be Color-Blind," he corralled her in a dance. Her embarrassment only made him ham it up even more. What did he care if people peered from doorways? Maybe it was the new hair, the sunny day, or her rosy freckles and teasing eyes. He took her hand and knelt for the finish.

Claps and whistles broke out along the street.

"That's my birthday present to you, Jill Stuart."

Her eyes glistened as she nodded.

MUM GASPED at the new hair. Dad shook his head. "Well, I've a daughter at last. Just as I get used to things, she throws me a surprise."

"Who, Dad?"

"Your Yank girl, who else? I see her fingerprints on this mop."

George bristled. He wouldn't tolerate any more putdowns of Jill, no matter who said them.

Anyway, he felt quite taken with himself. Would Jack have liked the look? He couldn't wait for his prep classes to resume.

He showed his hair to Philippa, who blanched, even as her roommate beamed, and said, "Wild."

Philippa crossed her arms. "Now no one will take you seriously. You've succumbed to a trend, an absurd one."

His heart sank. The roommate made faces behind Philippa. Yet he felt a kid now.

What would Uncle James and the gang at Fleet Feet say? Worried, he wore one of his new mod jackets to the studio.

Uncle James deemed his style "a transformation," and said he looked like "an Italian film actor."

George repeated the compliment to Philippa's roommate, who leaned close. "It's true. The style shows off your pretty face."

He winced. "Men aren't pretty."

"You are. I bet you're smiled at all the time."

How absurd. Or did he get a lot of smiles? Too bad he didn't fancy the roommate, who couldn't help living with a goddess. He drifted closer to her, weakening for a snub nose and berry lips.

She flushed. "Forget the schoolmarm. She chose an old man."

But that killed his mood. Why should Phil go for a daddy? He had qualities, he could be a good lover.

The roommate sighed. "I bet you get hired now. Any auditions coming up?"

"Auditions? I don't go to auditions."

"She told me you go. Who's that school to dictate what you do in your spare time? They just want to get their hands on you first. If only I could."

But then Jill did have an audition for him, only not for a stage show but a shoe commercial handled by an ad agency. The agency liked his mod look and dance training. He was called back, so they could test him on camera. "George Hartley. Take one." As opposed to George Carveth, who'd applied to the RADA.

He met Mr. Sullivan from Sullivan's Shoes, who seemed pleased with the takes. The agency stressed they must review all options first before announcing their client's decision.

Jill didn't seem worried. She claimed inspiration from Brian Epstein, the Beatles' manager. If he could make it with his pop group on little or no experience, then she could as well. She started a fiercer barrage of telephoning and tapping out letters on her typewriter, its carriage bumping and pinging. She said changing his appearance had been the right thing to do.

At school, his new look awed the kids. Until another loon came in with the same hairdo. Philippa winced when she saw him. George still turned up at her flat, though that was partly in hopes of checking out his rival. Would it be awful to bed her roommate in the interim?

One day, Phil arrived with the bloke in tow, a swanky sort, who went sneery towards George, one eyebrow cocked at the hair.

She chided George, after, for not being nicer to her man, then encouraged him to date her roommate! George pledged his love to Phil alone. Not that he loved her, though he must on some level. He wasn't bonking anyone else—not even Mrs. Althorp—yet unspent semen was backed up to his eyeballs. Philippa declared them over.

George felt kicked in the head. He came home, and there were both his parents *and* Jill gawking as if they'd come to jeer. He waved his arms. "Right, she broke up with me. Now everyone knows."

He trudged to his room, and then paused on the stairs. Why were they all here?

Mum tempered a smile. "Sorry, baby. Jill has news."

Jill beamed. "That girl will be the sorry one, DF. The agency wants you for the commercial. You're going to be on telly."

He missed a day of classes to do the filming. With a bit of rehearsal and easy steps, he became the dancing teenager for "Sully puts a swing in your step." Jill was there for the filming, in a smart frock and up-do, nodding to the agency chap. In the end, George was handed a check with a fat sum. He'd forgotten the getting-paid aspect. What easy money. Jill was given a check with her percentage.

They joined his parents at a restaurant, a rare treat. Jill raved, "They called George a natural. Apparently, he's great on camera. I can't believe it took me so long to realize that. Their client liked your smile, DF. They said they might use you again."

Her words made him dizzy. Everyone chattered at once. Jill cautioned, "It's only a first step, but it gives him exposure."

Dad was all smiles for Jill now. He was a handsome man in the golden light of the restaurant. People always focused on Mum, the dazzler. But George felt a heart tug toward his proud papa.

Of course, no one mentioned the fate of his schooling. It was easy to keep a low profile when one was rejected. But an advert on the telly was professional work.

HIS JAZZ CLASS was set to give a performance at the Academy. In rehearsals, the instructor switched him from the back to a front position, George assumed because he was a potential RADA student. The dancer forced to move griped about George's inexperience, while the instructor praised his enthusiasm. It was all a bit embarrassing. He hated irking his fellows.

Everyone was jittery backstage. There were to be faculty present. Maybe Phil would be out there. Nerves whizzing, George got into position, vulnerable in the front spot. The curtains opened to lights. Blinded, he beamed. The first number was a group dance to Dizzy Gillespie's "Manteca," his sole duty to show what a great song it was.

Audience faces became clear yet too fuzzy to see reactions. By the applause, some people smiled right at him. He returned with a partner for a fun Nina Simone number. Buoyed by the song, it was easy to flirt. His energy jumped to the audience. They seemed excited when he hit his points; their energy shot back to him. Applause for this dance went on longer than the first one. It would have been a perfect moment but for a groin pull on a high kick. The pain didn't hit him until he hobbled off the stage. He was struck from the final dance.

Jill, Mum, and Uncle James joined the clamor backstage. (Dad had to work.) A fellow from the RADA admissions office stopped by to clap George on the back. "You're an impressive chap. I understand you're a candidate for admission. You'll learn a lot here."

Did that mean he'd been accepted? He flashed excitement at Mum.

Philippa and her roommate appeared. Phil said, "You were incredible, I had no idea. You should come over."

The look on her face! Did she want him now? Not that he could shag her with groin pain. He said, "There's a dancers' party after, sorry. I'm expected."

Phil pouted, but kissed him before leaving.

Jill sidled up. "So was that her?"

Mum wiped lipstick from his mouth. "Good to play it cool, baby."

"I don't care. Did it look like she wanted me?"

Jill squeezed his arm. "Oh, she wanted you. But you have better things to do."

"I do?"

Uncle James snapped, "You can't walk."

The Sullivan's Shoes commercial ran for consecutive afternoons. The ad agency tipped off Jill so they could catch it. Surely no one at the school would watch afternoon telly. Dad came home early from work. They sat raptly, with Mum stifling a scream.

Dad leapt up and paced. "That was so—that was *you.*" He promptly rang Jill. "Did you see my son? ... It's amazing... What else have you got lined up?"

How odd to have seen himself on the box. The bits of that filming day had come together in a short, lively dance. He'd almost seemed another person. Like George Hartley.

After weeks of missing each other, Philippa charged him at the Italian café, breasts a-bob in a polka dot blouse. She pulled him aside. "How could you take such a risk? You're spoiling your chances for a fine education."

"Weren't you the tiniest bit impressed?"

"Hopeless." She scoffed. "All right, yes. But I know what you're throwing away. With your charisma you could go into theater."

"What charisma?"

Her green eyes flared. "Don't try to pull compliments out of it. I'm disappointed."

"Scold me tonight, darling, at a dance, perhaps?"

Her gaze froze that idea. *Buggery hell.*

At home, both Mum and Jill were giddy about a job prospect with a Friday audition. Some contact Jill knew had slipped her a favor.

Jill explained, "A television series called 'Harrington's on the

Heath' about a Lake Country B&B. They want four sons, like the Beatles. They're casting the last son."

"A Lake Country B&B doesn't sound too exciting."

"Maybe they'll have wacky guests. The point is we're getting an early audition, a first crack. Everyone else goes on Saturday. You need to make a good impression. This is big time, George."

Wow. She called you 'George' instead of 'DF.' Shadow George gave her his best smile.

THEN A LETTER CAME from the Academy. They were no longer considering his application since he'd taken professional work and wished him luck with his career. His heart sank.

Someone had told them (not Phil, surely). He couldn't tell his parents. He thrust the letter in a drawer. His scalp itched. There were bumps on his neck and hairline.

Dad checked. "Ach, you're breaking out. Looks like pimples."

"I can't get them *now*. I've an audition tomorrow."

"It's that long hair."

"What if it's the hair gel?"

"Don't use it then."

"I can't *not* use it. I have to have straight hair."

Dad shook his head. "You're as fussy as a woman."

It was pouring rain for the Friday audition. Jill came early. She clacked around him in heels and fumigated him with hairspray until his hair felt like a helmet. She smelled nice and looked tall and posh in a jacket and skirt, tresses tucked into a bun, lashes black with mascara. She smoothed his John Stephen suit from Carnaby Street and approved the Cuban-heeled boots. "My Beatle boy."

In the cab, she went on about the audition as if she were doing it. Gusts of rain pelted the windows and slowed their progress.

He interrupted. "The Academy knows about my commercial."

The eagerness died on her face. "Oh. I'm sorry."

"I couldn't wait to go there, I mean, I thought they'd want me anyway." He blinked the sting from his eyes.

Jill sat quietly. Then said, "Don't chew your nails. Someone might notice them."

She took an emery board from her bag and nabbed his hand. He jerked his hand away and put both between his thighs.

She snapped open her compact. "Just a spot. May I?"

He said, "I'm breaking out under my hairline. It has to be the gel."

"They're not going to see under your hairline."

He let her peer closely at him, even look up his nose. He noticed she'd muted her freckles with makeup. "Smile." He showed his teeth. Blushing, she said, "You're good. Sorry to do that."

Appalling these camera auditions. He gave her his hand.

She filed a nail. "You need a proper manicure next time you get your hair done."

He jerked his hand away. "You're as bad as Jack."

"How am I as bad as Jack?"

"He was always on about manicures. It was tiresome."

Shadow George cackled inside his head. *It's falling apart. No one will hire you. Jack's bumboy. His wife doesn't know what she's doing. She's only getting back at her husband.*

City workers hustled by with black umbrellas. A girl stopped under an awning. The taxi pulled over. Jill said, "Christ, we're here." She paid and tied on her rain scarf. He wrestled to get the brolly open.

They shook themselves off in the lobby. He snapped, "I don't get my hair done."

"It was just a figure of speech."

"I want a *fucking* cigarette. Fucking, fuck. Fuck Jack, fuck Philippa! What do we need them for, eh?" He pounded the wall, "Ow," and shook his sore hand.

"Feel better?"

"You think I'm off my head?"

She flapped her arms. "I'm not even thinking. Let's get this over with."

The lift ride was silent. Priscilla, the phone contact, greeted them and led the way to a smoke-filled studio. "Wait," Jill stopped him, "for luck," and kissed his cheek.

Warmth flooded through him. He realized all the work she'd done on his behalf.

Too many people were introduced. George smiled, not catching a single name. He was directed to stand on a marked line at the front of the room. The director peered through one of those big, rolling cameras. "Right. Turn, please. Good."

He was given a script. The part was for a Yorkshire lad, explained a writer, "who helps out at the B&B, possibly still in school, the youngest. We're not entirely how he will develop yet."

The Beatle suit was wrong. He shed jacket and tie, and rolled up his sleeves, though Jill shook her head at him.

He read his lines opposite an assistant doing the other part and bungled it. "Sorry. May I start again?"

The groundskeeper at school had been a Yorkshire man. George channeled his accent. Jill flashed daggers—he'd gone to a voice coach to perfect his speech! The director smiled. George downed water.

What was left should've been easy, a song and dance. But his sheet music of the pop hit "How Do You Do It" seemed wrong. New togs and a hairdo did not make him a pop star. Luckily, he'd kept other sheet music for sentimental reasons.

"That's an old one," the accompanist said with surprise.

Would Jill remember the song? It felt natural feigning Fred Astaire, painting the world of his childhood. Jill looked stunned. The whole room looked stunned. George sang beyond them all, conjuring the bluffs of St. Ives when he used to dance alone.

There was delayed applause. The director said, "Charming."

Everyone chattered and lit up smokes. Jill hung near with a strained smile. George re-suited and gave effusive thanks. Priscilla walked them to the lift. A man burst out of it before they could get on; he smiled right at Jill. *Randy bugger.* Then noticed George.

"Priscilla? What's going on, love? You know I have a stable of boys for you."

Jill hit the lift button and urged George through its opening doors as the man said, "What about Andy—" The doors shut. She muttered, "Jerk," and George said, "Arse."

It was another quiet lift ride.

At the front door, Jill snapped the umbrella into bloom. He charged out, but was promptly doused, and turned in surprise.

She stared with upset eyes.

"I'm so angry with you, George. That was our big chance. What happened to your song? You were carrying different sheet music."

"It didn't feel right. I had to do something easier."

She stalked off with the brolly before he could get under it. She said, "You thought Fred Astaire was right? In this modern age?"

His fringe wilted heavy on his forehead. "They're both catchy melodies, but I'm better at Irving Berlin."

"You jeopardized an opportunity." She stopped. "That was, that was *my* song. Your gift."

Hard to meet her wounded gaze. "I—yes. I thought with you there, it might be a better option."

He shivered getting soaked. She stepped close, the brolly over him, not that it mattered now.

She said, "Do you blame me for not getting into that school? I'm sorry to be cross. I'm sorry about this whole nutty endeavor."

Or was he trembling like the old days? Of course. It was bloody lunchtime. "I could do with a Cornish pastie, boss. I know a place."

"I don't know how many more opportunities I can provide, sweetie. One commercial is not success. You may have to get a job."

He made a face. "What can *I* do?"

"No, no. You're a bright boy. What *can't* you do?"

"I can't do this," and he kissed her mouth.

She pushed. "Don't do that!"

He sprinted streets to get away.

~

HE COULDN'T TAKE Mum's eager face. "It was fine," he mumbled, then shut himself in his room. When she knocked, he spoke through the door. "We had a row. I didn't do it the way she wanted."

"Why not? You know she means to help you."

"I've a headache, Mum. Let me rest."

Feigning illness made him ill. He spent most of the weekend in bed. Jill never rang. His parents must've phoned her. He overheard them speculating about the audition. They wondered if he'd sabotaged his chances.

Dad said, "He wants to go to that school. His girlfriend is there. Already his style had matured from the prep classes. It could be just the place for him."

Dad. George clasped the pillow around his head.

On Monday, he wondered why bother with his prep classes if he wasn't academy-bound anymore. Why go to dance if he couldn't get hired anywhere?

How mortifying to have forced a kiss on Jill. Of all the times to try to kiss her. He couldn't have made a worst move.

Mum poked her head in. "Shall I ring for the doctor, baby? It's not like you to miss lessons."

"No. I'm fighting it off."

He grew bored lying around, but didn't trust Shadow George going out and possibly getting him in a muddle with some bloke. Shadow George suggested Phil. *I'd rather be in a muddle with her.*

How can I? She may have stabbed me in the back. Piss on her.

Mum shouted up that Jill was on the phone. He shuffled from his bed, thumped downstairs, and took the receiver.

She sounded stilted. "You're being called back. They want to see you this Friday. The director, he, ah, he liked your Fred Astaire. Apparently, everyone else was trying to be a Beatle—"

His heart thudded.

"He said you had an innocent quality. He liked the Yorkshire accent. I thought you were reverting to Cornish. DF, I owe you an apology. You had the right instincts."

Mum hovered, waiting. Jill said, "That's not all. The ad agency wants you for another televised segment, a 'Britain Youth' campaign for ITV that will run between shows, with kids dancing—"

At the noise coming out of his mouth, Mum pounced on him. "You're hired?"

He shook his head. Jill was still talking.

"I can hear her. Tell her it's a bigger budget this time, so a bigger check. They said once you learned the dances, they'd film in a couple of days. It would run during prime viewing—"

Mum pounded him. "What's going on? What is she saying?"

Ringing off, he fell back in a chair. "She apologized."

"You were making that sound because she apologized?"

"The show wants me back on Friday. The ad agency wants me for another commercial. Mum, I can't go to the RADA. They saw my ad. I'm letting you down, and Dad."

She gripped him. "Darling. You're doing what you want to do, yes? Don't worry about Daddy. I bet he's going to be quite okay with it." She mashed him close.

And on Friday, he officially signed to play "Jamie Harrington," the youngest son on the new ITV series *Harrington's on the Heath*.

PART III
Part Three

OLD TIES

1964-1966

FIFTEEN

"Always Something There to Remind Me"

(BURT BACHARACH & HAL DAVID, 1964)

INSIDE THE ACOUSTICALLY PERFECT Royal Albert Hall the full chorus of the "Ode to Joy" rushed George in a wave of jubilation. The hair rose on his skin. Tears pulsed in his eyes. A male hand gripped his thigh. "Mr. Wilburn, it's grand."

The hand let go.

A frisson shot down his back. "I mean Dad, sorry," he added as his father stared.

He gazed ahead but saw nothing, heard nothing, and had to calm his breathing. If only he could stop the fire in his skin. He could feel his dad's questions being held by the music. The drawn-out fourth movement nearly diminished the faux pas.

Applause was extended with much cheering. When the lights came on, Dad said, "Mr. Wilburn?"

"Oh, hah. We saw a performance together. He loved the work."

"He took you off school grounds?"

George cleared his throat. "Wait, what? No, a group came to us— an orchestra and a chorus, not a large one, but—we went to hear it together, or just sat together really." He turned away.

In the private box with him and his parents were Leo, his director for *Harrington's on the Heath*, their newly popular television series, and Leo's wife, Marie. George felt he was out with two sets of parents. But Leo and Marie were the cool ones—worldly, rich, steeped in theater and television. It was an honor to be out with Leo. He supposedly wasn't that sociable with his actors.

Leo smiled at him. "It delights me how you love this music. You haven't lost your head to pop nonsense like many of the young ones."

"Well, I do like the pop nonsense, too, I'm afraid."

Black hair piled in a crown, earrings swaying, Mum beamed at Leo. George saw the man blink. "My son has eclectic taste, like his father. Of course, a public-school education helped round him out."

Marie said, "Yes. I'm impressed George went to—"

George plunged his fingers into his hair worrying the new bumps on his scalp. Dad still appraised him.

Leo said, "Not an easy place, I heard." Mum nodded as if she'd barely survived the school.

A guide from the theater popped in. "If you'll sit tight one more minute, we're getting out Mr. Nureyev's party then we'll fetch yours."

"He's *here?*"

George pushed out of the box and down a carpeted hall. The obsequious guide directed him to where the great Russian dancer was leaving by a back exit. A few patrons watched curiously. Nureyev never turned, but one leg extended gracefully as he waited for the lady in front of him to slide into a limousine. A photographer's flashbulb went off.

Mum breezed alongside with a whiff of perfume. "How exciting."

"He gave me a card for you," the guide said, "but the lady snatched it right away."

Leo said, "I saw him perusing our box with opera glasses."

George turned. "Then he must've meant the card for you."

Leo laughed as they followed the guide out the same back exit into the cool night air.

Had Nureyev seen his show? George didn't dance on it, probably for the best. What if the ballet star thought him a bumbler?

Leo leaned. "Careful, lad. Rumor is he's a sodomite."

Mum clicked her tongue. "Never mind. You could do worse."

"Lucy," Dad said low behind them.

She turned. "To have so famous and handsome an admirer, a great artist, the toast of London? Our lovely son is bound to be popular with both sexes."

Dad sputtered, "He doesn't need to be popular with—Lest we forget, eighteen is not yet a man's age."

"Oh, at eighteen I was beset with admirers."

George gawked at them. Must they row in front of his director?

The photographer approached their group. George gathered his parents on either side. All smiled for the flash.

Leo said, "Marvelous." Another limo glided up. The two couples climbed in. Mum reached. "When will we see you, baby? On the weekend? You'll ring up, at least?"

George waved them off and put a cigarette to his lips. He pawed for his lighter. A silver-haired gent had a match at the ready. George smiled his thanks.

The gent said, "Lovely evening."

George said, "Isn't it?"

Inner radar going off, he hastened onward, which he hated doing on a crisp September night. The magic of the great hall lingered. He now resided in Kensington, sharing a flat with Nigel, another of the Harrington actors who was single.

Rudolf Nureyev meant to give me a card. Incredible. He could be part of Rudi's set now, joining a late-night supper, discussing ballets. He would rise in the world, beyond mere television, and meet the top performers of stage and screen.

Yet if the dancer hadn't known who he was, perhaps it was best *not* to have received a card. That "sodomite" jarred. Leo usually seemed liberal-minded. Not that George engaged in that behavior anymore.

A passing couple smiled at him. Strangers smiled more now that he was on telly. Or stared more openly. Perhaps he cut a fine figure in his evening wear.

The flat seemed deserted. On the front table was a large wrapped package addressed to him. He eagerly ripped it open.

Aunt Tiffany had written: *Jory, love, I was remiss not sending you a net for school. Forgive the delay and accept this one for your first home.*

The fisherman's net was new and white, with shells, sand dollars and sea glass, a silver ball and a wooden Saint Ia. It was awful and wonderful, an icon of childhood happiness. Though the night was young, not even midnight, perhaps he'd stay in and hang his prize in his bedroom. Yet when he flipped on the lights, another prize waited.

"I didn't know you'd be here."

Philippa blinked at him from his bed, looking gorgeously naked, the thoughtful girl. "We broke up early. Problems with the script."

He exposed her back and tapering waist, her lush, spank-able bum —God, this bum! He'd burst his trousers because of it. He turned her to get at her glorious front side.

She said, "You're in a tuxedo, how lovely. How was the…"

But that could wait. It was still amazing that Philippa let him do whatever he wanted now.

Some time later, she pointed with her cigarette. "What's that gruesome thing on the floor?"

He retrieved his net and draped it on a desk. "Not gruesome. My aunt made it."

"Ah, right, the provincial relatives."

"Don't be a snob. Help me out of this monkey suit."

She emerged from the bed, her nudity reviving his interest.

He said, "I suppose Nigel wasn't here to pester you with lust."

"I wouldn't have stayed if he was. He doesn't mind flirting behind your back." She collected his trousers from the floor. "This is a fine suit. You must take care."

"Sorry, Mum." He opened studs and hastened out of his shirt.

"Again?" She gawked downward.

"No thanks to you."

Her severity cracked to a smile. He snagged her in his arms, glad to be fully skin-to-skin with her.

"All this youthful vigor," she panted between kisses.

"You're young, too."

"Not so much, really. That's why Todd and I got on."

"No Todd." (Her former, older lover.)

She squirmed from his arms and into his dressing gown, enhancing it, of course. "I'm going to need tea before we continue."

"What am I going to wear?"

She cocked an eyebrow. "Why wear anything, lovely boy?"

Fine with him, he preferred not being trussed. He couldn't help preening a bit under her smiling gaze. Until he saw a gawker in the adjacent flat. Phil hooted, and he leapt to pull the shade.

"I hope he's not a *Harrington* watcher. I must say it cramps my style. I should be free to gad about in the altogether in my own home."

She grinned. "Will you celebrate your first car that way?"

"There's a thought."

"Daft boy." She scooped the Earl Grey. "What does Nigel think of your starkery?"

"He peels, as well. He doesn't like me doing it when he brings home a bird." He started a cigarette from her lit one. "Say, whatever happened to your roommate? She was a laugh."

"Swiss Cottage, I believe? We didn't part on the best of terms. She fancied you. I told her you were out of her league."

He winced. She added, "Better to face reality."

Her statement pricked him like a pin in a shirt. "Are we in the same league?"

She laughed. "Darling. Of course."

"But...I'm on telly and you're not."

A clack of cup on saucer. "You know I prefer the theater."

"And you know I'll introduce you around. It's awful, though, classing people."

She huffed. "Everyone does it."

She'd severed her fling with old Todd soon after George debuted on the series, which had pleased him at the time, but now he realized "We're temporary, aren't we? I'm a steppingstone."

She gawked. "You *are* in a mood."

Had she always been this superficial? "Why did you look at me the first time? I was a kid to you."

"Why did you want me? We're a handsome pair, as you know. And we can have a nice go of it if you accept that fact and stop being tiresome." The disapproval was back on her face.

He pushed off from the counter. "No tea for me. I'm off to hang my gruesome net."

He was hammering when she left.

DAD RANG THE NEXT MORNING. "Son, I'm still having a think about what you said at the concert. Were you saying Mr. Wilburn took just you out or other boys, as well?"

George had forgotten that awful slip. "I don't know what he did with other boys. Must run, I'm late meeting Sam. We're off to Carnaby Street."

"It's just that, when I asked you years earlier…" The voice softened. "If anyone hurt you at school, it never occurred to me— Should I have asked about an adult? …Son? Are you there?"

George's heart pushed like a fist. He forced a "yes," a metallic taste filling his mouth. His voice came out flat.

"Why ask now? I have to meet Sam."

Dad was slow to answer. "Are ye sayin' that—pardon?" Mum murmured low. "Your mother says to ring Jill. She's not doing so well."

"What do you mean?"

"Ach, she's low being back from the States, living in Chelsea again. Your mother says she needs a man. I say she needs to start a business, she was good at that."

"I agree with you. I'll ring her later."

"Will you ring me later? It might be easier."

Easier! Memories flooded in. A schoolmaster forced his head.

George nearly gagged and had to control his voice. "Dad, don't worry. I love you."

"I love you, too, son, very much."

He dropped the phone. Mr. Wilburn was having his way again.

SHADOW GEORGE FLED the phantom Wilburn. He was done with that lout, real or imaginary. He'd rather *this* life, George's new life.

Here, in a West End men's shop, he was a great blooming rose to a hovering bee of a salesman: "Edwardian collars are all the rage. No more the plunging collar. I say, you're one of those 'New Faces of Britain' chaps, aren't you, the dancers on telly? The bird said you and your mate were on some program, but you're the dancer."

"I do both, guv."

The jacket Shadow George wore was cut close to the body, no doubt absurdly priced, not that he was entirely clear on what jackets should cost. How fun to peruse the latest outfits, free at last from mum Lucy's taste or Cousin Tim's hand-me-downs. A pirate radio station blared in the background (Radio Caroline South was literally beaming in from a boat in Essex). Between the recorded jingles, Georgie Fame sang about getting off work and going to his girl's flat to listen to records. The salesman buzzed close.

"Looks super on you. Keep the jersey, our treat."

Shadow George winked. This was not the first time Hartley, the telly actor, had been given free merchandise. He joined Sam Owen, another actor from the show, who was trying on caps and flirting with the cashier, a tasty thing with big eyes and pert tits.

Shadow George winked at her, too. "Sir Ginger, are we done?"

Sam said, "Ah, my dear. Have you met Lord Legs, of the famous Legs clan?" (As his flatmate Nigel called him "Hartley the hoofer" or "Hoof," Sam called him "Lord Legs" for the same reason.)

Shadow George beamed at the girl, but Sam dragged him away.

"Sorry, darling. He's dishy but a bore." From the radio, the shouting disc jockey trampled the end of the song.

Outside was a bright, cloudy Saturday. The back alley of Carnaby was gay with birds and loons perusing its rows of boutiques. Patrons passed them, recognition in their glance. Though Shadow George had an eye out for shoppers more known than he.

Sam lit cigarettes. "Why do you never have your own pack?"

"My dance instructor says we shouldn't smoke."

"And you listen to him? Legs, have I taught you nothing?"

Shadow George blew a ring. "Legs is in a muddle about his past."

"What about the past?"

"It's a bore. I've told him to forget it."

Sam halted. "'Him?' And you are?"

"His bolder half."

Sam hooted. "Hartley, you are a scream."

"George is the funny one. I'm the sexy one."

Sam slapped him on the back, hard. "Don't I know it, and I'd say that about damned few chaps. You might want to dial it down. Hang on, not yet. A comely wench, fair of hair, is sizing you up."

Two girls in front of the Lady Jane shop window looked their way. Lightheaded, George surfaced with a worried sense of Shadow George stealing chunks of his time. He recognized one of the girls.

"That blonde. She's in my dance class."

"She was at the studio trying out for the new part. I bet she gets it, too. Charlie fancies her."

"But Charlie's married." He raised fingers at the lass, who waved back.

Sam nudged. "Let's approach."

"I don't know. She's dotty and stares at me."

"Everyone stares at us. It's nice when sweeties like her do it."

"I don't want to encourage her."

"You're resisting a can't-miss after wolfing over my dolly at the shop?"

Ah, he felt they'd been in a shop. "I didn't realize, in the shop."

Sam gawped in a way that told him his shadow-self *had* caused trouble. He elbowed Sam. "Anyway, you're married to a grand girl."

Sam's hair went fiery in a bath of rare sunlight, face in a squint. "Are you 'the funny one' now? I know I have a wife. You're the damnedest fellow, Hartley. Maybe you'll turn out to be one of those great, mad actors, but hell if I can sort you out." His mate strode off ahead of him.

George staggered to follow. Having come from Mr. Wilburn, the shaking would start soon—no—he'd come from a shop.

Dad and Mr. Wilburn.

How could one father know about the other?

BEING RECOGNIZED and having fans had taken some getting used to. George had been flattered, of course, when people first noticed him on the streets, and when the few bystanders outside the studio's entrance greeted him by name. After several episodes, and especially after ITV aired their "New Faces" promos—in which he danced with other teenagers, the girls in black and white, the boys in black—the feeling changed to vertigo. Friends and crew members turned deferential. The fans at the entrance tripled. Girls squealed at the sight of him, which was alarming, he was hardly a Beatle.

Charlie, the show's hip young producer, told him, "You'd better get used to it. There's nothing like it in the world."

In those first heady weeks George slept little and coasted on adrenaline. Mornings were for dance lessons and learning the promo routines, that were filmed over a few weekends, where he was taught to woo the cameras. Barmy, that anyone should have noticed him amidst the other kids. One noticed the girls in adverts, never the blokes. Viewing the ads later, he saw how much he was featured.

For the show, he learned to ignore its cameras while staying within a certain radius of their spying presence. Initially, *Harrington's on the Heath* was broadcast before a live studio audience every Tuesday. It had been terrifying at the time. He was not to get a line wrong *ever* or his part would be docked. At least, that's what they told the newer actors. He'd seen the older ones flub lines, yet push through as if nothing had happened. This next season was employing the new medium of tape giving them the ability to retake bungled bits. And he had far more lines to memorize now.

The show was about a widowed mother with her four troublesome yet goodhearted sons, and her lay-about brother-in-law, running a bed & breakfast in Yorkshire. Various guests were featured each week. The large house of the show was merely a painting shown during opening credits. Recently, the crew filmed an actual house, someone's relative's estate, nestled in a scenic valley, and inserted the footage on the show as if they lived there.

Fatherly Leo, the show's director, said, "We're all a family now." The older actors, like Cyril Hernshaw, the brother-in-law, were known, the younger ones new like George. The young ones were there to provide mod trendiness. Not content to be mowing, plowing country boys, these lads wore shaggy haircuts and hip clothes, a boon to the plot. The elders were always complaining, especially if a lad who should be milking bopped by with a radio at his ear.

George felt dead lucky playing Jamie Harrington, the youngest of the sons. The youngest and the eldest, played by Sam, got more attention from the writers (who all wore specs and smoked like chimneys). Jamie's character was hardly a stretch. At first, no one knew what to do with him. He was a good sort, mad about sports. He admired his eldest brother, felt slightly competitive with the handsome second oldest, played by conceited Russ, and got on best with the third brother, played by his flatmate Nigel.

For some mad reason, Jamie idolized his annoying uncle. Which meant he got to work with comic veteran Cyril. The writers created scenes for the two of them. Director Leo said "they clicked." It started by accident. George had forgotten his lines during rehearsals and stalled by repeating Cyril's lines, making Cyril get testier and funnier. Apparently, George had looked "as if butter wouldn't melt in his mouth," though he only remembered his panic. But everyone in the studio had laughed as if the botched scene was intentional.

A former music hall performer, Cyril was a physical comedian, his plump body agile. George wanted to learn what Cyril knew. Under the man's tutelage, he took to pratfalls as easily as dance moves and learned to trip, flail, fall from a hit, and slam into things without hurting himself, sound effects being key. He cringed, winced and Jamie grew dimmer, naïve.

Cyril told him to "use that innocent expression, bat those girlie eyelashes, and watch me. Time yourself to me."

Cyril would call out, "Lad!" and George would run up with a "Yes, Uncle?" and start their routine: the scheming elder and innocent dupe. Cyril played his scenes fearlessly. George had to turn back and forth with a spade over his shoulder while Cyril ducked in the nick of time. After, Cyril said, "Good work, Hartley, nicely done," even though George had had the easy part.

Cyril owned reels of Laurel & Hardy and had George over to watch them. Laurel & Hardy turned out to be almost as big a treat as Fred Astaire. But Cyril didn't want an imitation of Stan Laurel.

"Laurel's expression worked on Laurel's face. It don't work on your face, kid. Use what you've got. Eyes are key for you. And you've got a smile to light a room. Hold it back. At the right beat—you'll get to know when—let it go."

George did a wordless scene with Cyril that was almost a dance, the audience quick to chuckle. Jamie in a cap and overalls, Beatle fringe to his eyes, it was just looks and touching his cap during Cyril's antics, plus the occasional flinch and one well-timed bubble from gum.

The show debuted in the spring of 1964 with most of the actors' families in the audience. Now, in September, the second season had just started with its taped bells and whistles, its filmed "house." They were becoming a cross-generational hit—the older actors beloved and impressive, the four youngsters, hip and attractive. George loved the hoots and cackles from the audience, even grins from the crew. What a high to be deemed funny again, as he once had for halcyon moments at school.

It was still an effort not to sign "Carveth" for autographs. George Hartley with his straightened hair, the famous loon who winked at birds, was another part to play.

Carveth thought everyone had gone mad. Carveth knew he hadn't sprouted wings or a tail, so why should everyone gawp at him? Sometimes he swore he saw *MacIntyre* in the crowd of fans, or at least a tall, skinny version of him. But that was bats. Surely little MacIntyre was still in school. He wouldn't dare start preying on him here.

FRIDAY NIGHT, end of the week, their final performance had taped before the studio audience. A buoyant Cyril nabbed George and gave him shots of whisky and invited him for supper. But George had plans to go "disco hopping" with the lads.

"So gorgeous women await? I'll not stop you then. Conquer away." Cyril clapped him on the back.

Nicely addled from the whisky, George had an urge to cat around. He'd lately become aware of certain cast and crew members having trysts with one another. A script girl passed with promise in her eyes.

Desperation flared from her after only a few kisses. Sometimes, it was best to halt at once. Lasses gave in way too easily. He extricated himself, ladling politeness, and hastened to the sanctity of his dressing room. A large bouquet of powdery-scented flowers was parked in its midst. The card read:

Warmest congratulations! I knew you could do it. A friend.

Well, that was annoying. It seemed too matey for a girl.

He sorted through the fan letters, mostly from teens or housewives expressing enjoyment on behalf of their families. A thought of Mrs.

Althorp snaked down his spine. He sometimes received the odd cheesecake photo. One letter read:

Dear George "Hartley,"

How the hell did <u>you</u> end up on my telly, you fucking poofter? Couldn't they find any worthier actors? Makes me wonder what you did to get the part.

He dropped that one. Hate mail was always a shock. And why the quotes on his surname?

He stashed the letters and grabbed his bag of dance gear. The door of his small, beloved space closed with a thunk. The dressing rooms were a new honor, a Season Two honor. Being the youngest, George had the smallest. Prior, all the lads had shared a room, a right lark.

The lead cameraman brushed by reeking of peppermint. George faltered. Reg turned. "All right, mate?"

It was only a bald man in shirtsleeves sucking a common candy. Heart thudding, George noticed the quiet dressing rooms.

Reg confirmed, "They left."

"But I was supposed to go with them."

"Well..." Reg sidled close. George stepped back. Reg looked surprised. George smiled. Feeling jittery now, he shouldered his dance bag and shoved hands into pockets.

Reg leaned close. "It sounded like they didn't want the competition. I bet you're the one who attracts the birds, eh?"

George did another back step.

Reg said, "Relax. I'm not going to pounce."

"I know." George stuffed his hands under his arms. The bag fell down his arm.

Reg replaced it. "Our Russ claimed to be unthreatened by your presence. He doesn't know, but the camera sees he's really a smug bastard. Not me, mind you, I don't care. But the camera sees what comes across, as Leo sees. You're the pearly ingénue, my lad. Heart on your face. There may be jealousy but stick with Cyril. There's your meal ticket."

Was there jealousy? "I suppose 'ingénue' means 'young'?"

Reg laughed. "You'll be old and jaded soon enough." With a squeeze of the shoulder, the cameraman moved on.

George wiped off his shoulder and shuddered. Why was he still being plagued with this absurd shaking? Nice what Reg had said.

Christ, he'd been ditched! On a Friday night by his so-called mates. Was he colored again, the person who didn't deserve this job?

They're jealous, whispered Shadow George.

No, it's you *causing trouble. It's time for you to pack off forever.*

You need a loving penetration, the mauling of someone stronger.

The need softened his body. Reg was big.

Bollocks! We don't *do* that anymore.

George darted to a hallway telephone and hooked fingers into the holes, but replaced the receiver after endless rings of Jill's telephone. Curious, he tried Mrs. Althorp. A gruff male voice answered. He rang off.

He longed to phone his parents. He'd never followed up with his dad. But why ask now? They would only get hurt. He was done with those awful years. A few more paces around the hall and he spun through the familiar numbers.

"Hello, Mum?"

"Swee-tee!" she chimed. "How perfect that you phoned. Jill's here. We're discussing the new PM and whether Mr. Goldwater has a shot at the presidency. There's curry on the cooker. You couldn't possibly join your old parents, could you?"

"Is that the star?" Dad called in the distance.

George fought to contain his joy. "Er, yes, I suppose I could come by."

How grand. And the shaking was gone, how marvelous. He would go bearing gifts. Now that he was on television, he felt more worldly than his parents, and worldly people were generous. The studio was stocked with food. He took a wrapped loaf of almond cake.

And he dropped it at the house, at the sight of a strange man rising in the front room with Jill. Mum said, "This is Jill's friend, Leonard," giving George a look that meant "date" and, *whump,* the dense cake hit the floor.

The man—trimmed mustache, thinning brown hair, thick, powerful build, yet George could probably take him—extended his paw. "Wow. The famous son. You look just like yourself." His firm grip said he could take George.

"Thanks, I guess. Boss."

Jill smiled fetchingly, her foam-blonde hair past her shoulders, curves evident in a tight frock.

Dad approached, warm-eyed. "Glad you came by, son." George kissed him and held on to him.

Leonard blurted, "Hoo, you still kiss your father?"

Everyone turned to the guest, who stuttered, "Well, I mean, I stopped doing that when I was ten, maybe sooner."

Jill said, "I think it's sweet."

Mum said, "Let's adjourn to the table, shall we? Supper is ready."

"I mean that's your business, of course," Leonard added.

"True enough," Dad said in his end-of-discussion voice and ushered the guest to the sewing room now in its dining room state.

George had to sit opposite this non-father-kissing interloper. The man's eyes flashed warily at him and followed Jill bringing in the dishes. The blighter clearly thought he was lucky—indeed, he was! George could almost see the plans for later hatching behind beady eyes. He managed to paste a smile on.

Jill flashed a plea at him and sat. "Lucy, it smells delicious."

Leonard eyed his food. "I've never had curry before."

George said, "Mum's curries are the best."

"Darling." Mum squeezed his arm. George was glad he'd come.

"I've heard about foreign spices." Leonard had yet to pick up his fork. "I've a sensitive stomach."

The word "foreign" grated. George arched a brow. "Mum's curries are devilish."

"But not this one," Mum put in at Leonard's worried face.

"You might need this." George pushed forward the yogurt.

"Is that cream?" said Leonard.

The fool didn't recognize yogurt? Dad got up. "Lucy, we forgot the toast and beans. No, don't bother. I'll fetch it."

George blurted, "Toast and be—" but Jill kicked him. "Mum, how could you forget?"

His mother flashed soulful eyes at their guest. "So sorry, Leonard. How did you two meet?"

Jill said, "We live in the same building."

Leonard sampled a forkful. George couldn't tell if he liked it or not. His foot was bumped, so he stopped staring.

Leonard dabbed his mustache. "I couldn't believe this sexy lady was on her own."

George coughed and reached for water.

"Then I find out she's a talent agent. Of course, she couldn't get her tap to stop dripping or the toilet to shut off."

Mum beamed. "And you were the rescuing knight."

"Or the block maintenance man," George muttered.

"No," Leonard said to him. "I work at the power station, an executive, recently promoted. I know how things work. Jill seemed grateful for my help."

Mum cut George a look. "I'm sure she was."

He was going to be ill. Jill wouldn't meet his eye. Her freckles had darkened on her cheeks.

Dad brought in the beans and toast. Leonard helped himself to a hearty portion. The front doorbell rang.

Mum left to answer it. George thought he heard her say "Myra."

Then Mrs. Althorp charged in and stopped in the doorway of the back room. George clanked his spoon in surprise.

Dad echoed, "Myra."

Mrs. Althorp wrung her hands. "Dearie me, I'm interrupting your supper. Smells nice, whatever it is. I won't stay. Just wanted to say 'ello to the big star here. I never see him no more. Don't be a stranger, love. What a sweet home, Lucy. Wish I had time to fix mine up like this. I'm alone now—I mean just for the night. My husband's gone off with his mates. Fishing in the Fens. Worrying to be a woman alone in a house all night. Isn't that right, Lucy?"

"I don't believe I'd mind."

"Well, of course. Even if you didn't have 'andsome Gerry for a night, you'd still have your lovely son—" Myra flinched at Jill giving her a pointed look.

George couldn't quite form a smile, as if he'd forgotten how to do one. Mum said, "Won't you sit down?"

"Don't mind if I—" But Myra did a little dance at his glare. "No, I'd best push off. Sorry to intrude. Cheerio, all."

The frontdoor shut to silence. Mum resumed her seat.

George stared at his half-eaten food, cheeks tingling. He felt a push on his toe and moved his feet.

Leonard said, "What a pleasant woman. Nice when neighbors pop over."

George waited an interval after the meal, that he hadn't enjoyed nearly enough, before excusing himself and ringing Mrs. Althorp from his parents' bedroom. He quaked with the need for sex and rang for a cab.

Mum clung to him in the hallway by the frontdoor. "Darling, you're not looking in on that silly woman, are you?"

Dad stepped in. "I think that youthful nonsense is over. Right, son?"

"What nonsense? I'm just going home."

"Must you leave so soon then?" Now Dad sounded hurt.

Mum said, "It's not that I mind you being with someone older—"

"Ach, Lucy, he doesn't need to be with—"

"But I find her small-minded. You're too good for her."

George huffed. "Right, Mum, and how do you find Mr. Fix-It back there?"

Mum shushed him. "We can't talk about that now. Jill will come to her senses. Pity. I do wish she'd find someone more suited."

"'Sexy lady,'" he angry-whispered, flapping his arms. "He called her a sexy lady right in front of her."

Dad creased his brow. "Well, Jill is attractive."

"I know how she is. I hate her dating, is all."

Both parents looked as if he'd said something potty.

He amended, "You should pick out the right man for her, Mum, and that will be that. No more of these apes with mustaches. Ah, there's my cab. Cheerio."

He fled down the walk as it pulled up and slid next to Myra, who looked as smug as a cat with the cream, her overnight case on the floor. He was already hard.

HE WANTED HER GONE. Luckily, he had an 8AM class. He rolled from the sliver of mattress Myra had left him and snapped on a fresh dance belt. He'd had to wash his dance gear last night after she'd fallen asleep. The tights were still slightly damp.

Roommate Nigel had pointed out early in their relationship how *not* masculine it was having tights drying in one's bathroom, until George caught Nigel darkening his pale lashes with mascara. They soon laughed and agreed they were a fine pair of lassies.

His weight on the bed made Myra come to life. She said, "What are you doing up, lover? It's only six o' bloody clock."

"I told you I have dance today."

The tights felt clammy on his legs. She smacked his bare bum that he quickly covered. He slid from her grasp to pack his kit for the day.

The exciting woman who'd once matched him in size had grown smaller over the years. Less exciting. She rolled from the bed, breasts a-wag (vastly different from the splendid Philippa).

"You were on fire last night, lovey-boy. Mr. Hot Poker. Whatever got you going, may it happen again."

He blushed at all he'd imagined doing to poor Jill.

Mrs. Althorp used the loo with the door open then walked naked into the front room. George half feared she wanted Nigel to wake up and padded after her with a dressing gown. "Missus—Myra..."

She rifled through her handbag on the sofa. "You worried about your friend? Don't you think he'd like the view?"

She walked away from the garment, stood by the window, and lit a smoke. "Speaking of views, you're lucky having one of the park. Must have cost a pretty penny, that. Just a couple of lads with this nice flat and nice… Oh, all right." She donned the robe. "I was going to suggest a quick one, but John Thomas is all hidden in them tights. Funny seeing a man in tights."

A bubbling in the kitchen made him hasten to lower the heat on the coffee—that he'd recently decided was his drink, though he preferred it with lots of cream and sugar.

"Coffee. How continental." Her cold hand invaded the back of his tights.

He couldn't prepare a cup with her fiddling. "Isn't your mister home this morning?"

"You trying to rush me out when you have such a lovely, warm bottie? Don't forget who taught you what you know. When you're out with fancy girls, remember it's Myra who's got your handle."

Why did arousal feel like a weakness? Yet a shag might get her out the door.

MOURNING doves cooed from the lush trees that bordered the park. With Myra's departing cab, it felt as if a weight had stopped pressing. In the chill autumn air, with few people about, he decided to walk to the dance studio. What a precious thing, the freedom to walk unobserved. He must escape this stickiness.

Surely his mother's dismissal and Jill's obvious scorn gave him permission to drop Mrs. Althorp. She would always be twenty or more years older. She'd never said exactly.

He limbered up quickly in the top-floor studio and worked the woman out of his body, stretched away from her, leapt away from her, and kicked her back to hubby. It wasn't his problem if she was bored in her marriage. A grueling class followed, he was glad, and thrilled at the challenge of keeping up with the better students, who acted as if he was one of the best, but that wasn't true. The instructor, Mr. Olivetti, said George had "a keen sense of musical timing" and that was true. He could hit movement to notes better than anyone. Mr. Olivetti had no rigid ideas about what men should or shouldn't do and wanted all his dancers to be remarkable.

The studio air was muggy by the time class broke up. George remained to finesse a new promo dance with Mr. Olivetti coaching. Both were startled by a clatter of applause. Mr. O shooed away the lingering students. Then the instructor left to take a phone call.

Woozy with exhaustion, his odor an atmosphere, George conjured breezes, a cool, rushing sea. And found movement to match. The crash and sluice of water… a gull bobbing… His arms reached, his shoes squeaked across the floor as he marked steps.

"There may be an artist in you yet." Mr. O smiled at him.

George had been called an "artist" once before. "No, no. Just a bit of nonsense."

He sped to the showers and washed quickly, not wanting to be caught naked. His leg muscles quaked from overactivity. His stomach yawped with hunger.

Bypassing the curled-edge bacon and congealed beans in the first-level canteen, George opted for newly fried eggs, kippers, and a pile of toast, selecting jam over marmite. The young cashier blushed to see him, grinned. His actor self winked at her automatically.

His tired self perused the tables. There was the blonde who stared at him in class, her wheat-gold hair a bun on her head. Seeing him, she bloomed with rose. Now he must play the actor again when he preferred a table on his own. Shadow George noted, *Willowy bird there.*

The girl often placed herself behind him in practice. What if she was a follower like MacIntyre? Her teeth were rabbity, her bust small.

A little tit can still be nice.

He forced some pep in his step. "May I sit down?"

She was holding a chocolate bar that she slammed inside a *Beatles Monthly* magazine. "Yes!"

His legs weakened at the chance to sit, he landed heavily in the chair opposite. "I like the Beatles, too. They're tops."

"Oh, they are. What songs do you like?"

"'I Saw Her Standing There.' It swings."

"Yes, it does. Have you heard the new album?"

"Who hasn't?"

Well, she was lively. Probably had that burst of after-class energy. Slate eyes. Lips frosted pink. Her pinned-up hair looked damp. It must be a bother to wash such long hair. Some girls used entire evenings to do their hair, or at least Philippa did. He wolfed his eggs before realizing her gaze.

"I've heard you're called 'Lord Legs.' Do you like to run?"

He swallowed hard. "Sam Owen calls me that because I dance. I call him 'Sir Ginger' because of his hair. Just a joke. It's 'Toni,' isn't it?"

"Yes, Toni Banks. I know I shouldn't have been eating chocolate. Please don't tell Mr. Olivetti."

"Bugger him. I mean, I've half a mind to get a chocolate for myself."

A flash of front teeth, an alluring dimple.

He sliced the kippers. "What else are you keen on, besides the Fab Four?"

"Lots of things. Fashion. Art. I'm mad about art, although I draw terribly. Once I went to Italy, to Florence, and saw all the great works. I longed to climb the Donatello David."

"To *climb* it?"

She blushed. "Of course, Papa stopped me. But the figure was, I couldn't help it." She looked down. "I-I fell in love with it."

How extraordinary. Was it a nude statue? He confessed, "I fall in love with pieces of music."

"Really?" Relief showed on her face. "How lovely."

He swirled jam on toast that crackled horribly when bitten into.

She said, "I've auditioned for your show. I'm on callback."

He gestured his "congrats" and could have told her more, that the producer fancied her, that she had a good shot, but why give hope?

Did he even want her on the set every day in addition to dance? Not that he would have any say.

She said, "It must be exciting to work on a program. You're awfully funny in your scenes with Cyril Hernshaw."

"Thanks." That pleased him. "I don't get to dance."

"You dance so well." She reached for his cheek. "A bit of jam, sorry. You, you have marvelous skin. Have you Mediterranean blood?"

"Farther east…"

What a mad, fetching girl. She had marvelous pale skin. "Ah, look, you wouldn't want to go to the cinema or—?"

"Oh! Oh, I'd love to."

How will you stand a date with her? She'll be bubbling like suds.

I thought you wanted it. She has that cute overbite.

Adorable.

I ought to take her out anyway, if only to stop that silly staring.

SHADOW GEORGE WOULD *NOT* BE GOING on this date. *You'll need me for sex*, he reminded. But George hardly thought so and worried more about the film. Would she like to see *Darling* or *Goldfinger?* Surely, she'd seen *A Hard Day's Night.* Damn it, no. He'd take her to something different that he found appealing. If she didn't care for it, then that would settle that.

He went through his assortment of jackets, the velvet and gabardine, and chose mod stripes to wear with his butterscotch tab-collar shirt, black tie, snug black trousers, and boots with elastic sides. Cheeks, hair, and armpits were patted with cologne.

He had to fetch her in a taxi. His next purchase would definitely be a car, but he was, belatedly, still learning to drive. He'd recently failed his driving test and forced to a doctor and given a case of very unbecoming, black-rimmed specs. What a shock when the world got clearer. Only now he was a "Four-Eyes," a Clark Kent, his glamorous image shattered. Not that his vision was bad, other than squinting to read road signs. Girls used to remark on his "cool squint." His parents were gobsmacked that he'd needed specs.

The specs stayed in an inside pocket as he enjoyed a soft-focus evening. The cab meandered through St. John's Wood. Toni lived with her parents. He was spared meeting them when she darted out of the house and slid into the seat, wafting a strawberry scent. The scoop neck of her close-fitting frock showed the smooth plate of her breastbone and a little gold heart on a chain at her throat. He thrilled at the exposure of her knees in shiny tights. Her hands were hidden inside the sweater bunched in her lap.

They went to the Classic Cinema to see *Swingtime* with Fred Astaire and Ginger Rogers, Toni looking surprised but not displeased by his choice. Jack had mentioned the picture as one to see, and of course, Jack was right. Fred was young again and Ginger Rogers adorably sexy. And George could see well enough. He'd never had a problem with films before. He was curious at how much better it would be but didn't dare pull out the specs on a date.

They assessed the dance numbers with excited whispers and stayed for the next showing, through to the "Pick Yourself Up" dance, before hustling out of the theater. He hailed a cab and instructed it to go back to her home. Her face fell, but he said, "Your tap shoes." She flew into the house, then out.

The cab went on to Clapham, which surprised her, too, and George had a pang of embarrassment. But it shouldn't matter. If he'd survived a school full of snobs, one girl shouldn't matter.

No one was at Fleet Feet. He flicked on lights. Sure enough, his old locker still held tap shoes, that pinched now. Yet tapping remembered steps distracted him from the squeeze.

"Wasn't this a nifty bit?" He went from tapping into a smooth arm-in-arm walk, then into another transition.

Toni demonstrated. "I liked how she held her hand out and not on his shoulder."

They sailed across the floor, each responding to the slightest touch of the other when a movement changed. We're *equals*. We could be partners! Catching glimpses in the mirrored wall, he saw the oddity of their dancing this old-fashioned way when their peers were likely grooving at the Ad Lib discotheque.

Giddiness evaporated. Both collapsed to the wood floor. The shoes clacked coming off, toes grateful. George smiled at his "Ginger."

She panted beside him, cheeks a-bloom. He kissed her, sparking a note of surprise from her.

At that, he couldn't stop kissing her. He fought to loosen the back of her dress to get at her pale flesh. She didn't protest as he wrenched down her garment. Her brassiere was mostly padding over sweet mounds; he tongued the nipples awake. She didn't stop him as he dragged her frock right off, snapped open the suspenders, slow with the stockings, then—incredibly—drew down her blue-flowered pants so that she was a lovely, naked girl (but for a gold heart necklace). There wasn't the shock of brown that many "blondes" had when their knickers were off, her tuft was a duskier wheat color. He kissed the muscled leg she raised for him, descending. She flinched at his mouth on her, alternately writhing away and pressing close. Wasn't she enjoying it? Mrs. Althorp had schooled him in the act often enough.

She tugged his hair. "Stop, join me. Take off your clothes."

He scooted out. She sprawled like a conquest. How easy to become a ramming-bull monster. *What?* The thought made him back away. Two big-eyed youngsters watched him, rapt. *No.*

No, his charming date waited. And he was confident about his body. Shedding irksome garments, the mirror showed not a young man but a bullish satyr. He shook his head to clear it.

Would his lad-self appear next, the one standing shocked in Wilburn's loo all those years ago?

But there was innocent Toni gazing at him in the glass. "Shift your weight to one hip."

He did so. She smiled. "*Contrapposto.* I love that stance."

She had a dotty way about her. Endearing.

A sweet, peppery scent in the air. The big man whispered *You've enchanted a new lover. Here she comes.*

She went for his buttocks.

Thick fingers jammed, arse hurting. Lights blazed overhead. Teeth on his throat... can't get away.

"Oh dear, I've startled you. Are you all right?"

Wilburn wasn't here... only a lass... who crouched beside him. "Please tell me you're all right."

But he was splayed on the floor. "Ah, lightheaded."

"Of course. One feels lightheaded sometimes."

He could've wept. And wished the floor would swallow him up.

She stayed kneeling until he rose. He staggered from her help and wiped his eyes. He would *never* see her again, not after being a pathetic, fainting twat.

Shadow George flooded in, summoning strength. He saw there was no revulsion on the girl's face. More a fascination. He cracked a smile. "Were you going to climb me?"

SIXTEEN

"The In Crowd"

(BILLY PAGE, 1964)

IN 1965, Philippa halted relations with George since she claimed he'd already dropped her by not paying her enough attention. He protested, then caught himself. She was right. He had little time to spare, as well as a much greater social life.

He and Cyril had become favorites of the show with their comedic spars. The writers not only concocted more situations for the two of them, they focused on Jamie's character, and thought it a laugh to have harmless animals show an aversion to him. Trained dogs growled, cats hissed. He and Cyril doused each other with flour in a pantry scene; sprawled in mud in a pigpen scene; sprayed each other with hoses or cow's milk, and received that old comic standby, cream pies in the face. No matter how predictable the absurdities, the audience loved it. "Uncle" was a master of the slow burn, and Jamie forever running from him, or some angry goose. George argued that Jamie running from small creatures was getting preposterous.

They put him in a pen with a bull, as the script directed:

Jamie sleeps in a pasture blissfully unaware of the bull nudging his face. He awakens horrified and runs for the fence, diving over it. (Onto unseen mattress.)

George loved working with trained animals but the bull terrified him, docile though it was. Fans seemed to enjoy his scared face and run. Even members of the crew laughed. He loved when the crew laughed.

It was a relief to film at outdoor locations, away from the studio fans and MacIntyre. Yes, that tall apparition waiting at the exit *had* been MacIntyre. One stuttered "Carveth" sealed it. Now George pretended not to hear as he wormed through fans, his autograph sloppy.

Dances swirled in his head, creations he longed to choreograph. His tight schedule kept such ideas on hold. The Harrington producers weren't even keen on his dancing. He might get hurt! Never mind the flexibility it gave him to do batty routines.

Now in a swank West End office with a secretary, Jill boldly vetoed adverts, even ones that promised him high payment. She declared him "above that now" and selected guest appearances with or without Cyril.

George was invited to do sketches on the *Morecomb and Wise Show* and appeared on the teen hit *Ready Steady Go!* What a treat to see the surprise on people's faces when he snapped into a flashy dance. Was this clumsy Jamie grooving to "I Want Candy"? (In a striped jersey and white cords, shaking his straight-ish hair.) And who was the blonde bird joining him? He wasn't quite done with Toni Banks, who was a savvy dance partner, a good looker at the end of his grasp. He was happy to show her off on camera, if reluctant in a social setting, no matter how the chaps gazed longingly at her. George preferred to enter a party solo or with his mates.

There were more parties in his life, more discotheques to visit. It was almost part of his job to attend, or so claimed "PR Pru," the show's agent on Public Relations. Why be a middling celebrity when he could do the town with the Smart Set, dip into a photo with pop stars, or be seen with a mini-skirted dolly.

George was tickled in the presence of famous people and always seemed to miss "Rudi." ("He was just here!") He was still nervous about meeting the great dancer. He lucked into seats for the Nureyev-Fonteyn opening of "Romeo and Juliet" at Covent Garden. (PR Pru did not approve of ballets, declaring them "not young.") He wavered over a backstage visit, then backed out. Of course, Nureyev would not remember seeing him.

At another party, he heard Nureyev wanted to meet him. Surely such an artist didn't watch *Harrington's on the Heath!* Party chatter was nonsense. Starlets approached George having no idea who he was. "Didn't I see you in the Positano Room?" They never watched telly. How about coming to bed? It was hard not to be shocked by these forward ladies. Lately, he'd been refusing the she-lions, and once got a drink in the face. Why should he provide service-on-demand? He was having enough activity of that sort.

Though his mood plummeted when someone said "I don't fancy you" or "You're not my type," or an overheard "I don't get his appeal. He doesn't do it for me at all."

They're out there, those who know the truth. You need to be overpowered. You're getting too successful.

He phoned his mother after famous encounters, leaving out the sex parts. Mum listened, delighted, shocked, not surprised, and declared it all his due. He promised to sneak her into a party.

She said, "Your father would hate it. But I would love it. Come steal me some evening."

Dad was unimpressed by all the craziness, and said, "Keep your head." Dad knew something was amiss in his son's background. George slid away from attempts to bring up the past.

It was more fun to gossip with Mum. She could make herself chic enough to attend one of his parties.

Shadow George balked. *One does not do the town with one's mother.* (PR Pru would surely agree.)

George had boasted to her of a photo session with a prestigious photographer who was shooting the hot names for a series called "London Now." However, when the event finally occurred months later in a lit-up, busy room, The Mamas and Papas playing in stereo, the photographer leaned close with a suggestion. "Of course, it would be private; everyone would be sent away."

George fled at the tea break. Hadn't posing shirtless in an overcoat been undressed enough? Now the rotter wanted more.

He phoned Jill to complain since she'd been the one setting it up. Only the photographer had already rung her about his desertion. George was nearly apoplectic explaining why.

Jill said, "I wish I'd known. What nerve."

Shadow George wondered what the harm was in a few photos.

Posing nude in *my* career? Let him bother some new lad.

Avedon shot Rudi in the nude. He could've been the one, you know. He could've overpowered you, taken you down, shut you up.

AS IF STARTING A DANCE, George swayed in his dressing room. The character of Jamie came to him through movement. But there was a damned knock on the door.

Charlie, the producer, poked his head in, frowned. "This won't do."

George whipped off his specs. He wasn't allowed to wear them for a taping; he parked them on his head. Charlie opened other dressing room doors. "Won't do at all... Leo!"

Charlie reappeared in George's doorway. "Why does 'Jamie' have the smallest dressing room?"

"It's no bother, Charlie. I like it."

Charlie went to Sam's room. "Why is this room so much larger?"

The actors collected at their doorways. The director strode up with annoyance. "Why the ruckus, Charlie? It shook out that way, nothing intentional."

"George should move in here."

Sam sputtered, "I'm not moving into his room."

Charlie's gaze hardened. "You're jolly well moving somewhere, my friend. Or one of these other chaps will have to do it."

Leo said, "Surely we can sort this later."

George said, "I don't mind my dressing room."

Charlie drifted about, hands on hips. "Which one of you lads? Russ? Nigel?"

Russ bristled. "I'm popular with the ladies."

Sam added, "I've been acting longer than he has. Why should I get a cupboard?"

Charlie zeroed in on Nigel. Nigel flashed a heated look at George.

George shrugged, it wasn't his doing.

Perhaps it was flattering being moved to a larger room, only now everyone was riled before a taping.

Charlie snapped, "Sam, take Nigel's room, go on." He smiled at George, clapped his shoulder. "Get your gear, lad. You've earned better digs."

Russ, who didn't have to move, guarded his doorway.

Sam and Nigel swept back and forth with black looks. George grabbed his outfit, his rucksack, makeup kit, transistor radio, family pictures, his script, and a dog-eared paperback. His specs fell back on his nose. His gold necklace swung free of his shirt: jewelry was another taping no-no. He filled his arms but couldn't manage the piles of fan mail that littered his route.

Charlie scooped up the post and hissed to Leo. "His agent has my balls in a vice. We can't have our popular actors holed in cupboards." Leo ushered the man away.

Was *Jill* responsible? She was supposed to be raising his salary.

George dumped his gear in Sam's room as Sam hoisted out a comfy chair, leaving an old stool. "Sam—"

Nigel marched in. "Well done, mate. Worked out peachy for you."

"Nige. I didn't know he was going to do that, honest."

Sam bolted in. "Oh, don't pretend you didn't know. And don't think you look sympathetic in glasses. Things have been going your way for a while now. You probably make more than the rest of us."

George straightened. "I don't know or care what anyone makes."

Nigel glowered. "Must be nice to smile and get whatever little thing you want."

George flapped an arm. "I don't!"

"Getting your agent to phone, kissing up to Cyril. Getting the best tables in restaurants and all the cute birds, even one of *my* birds." Nigel turned to Sam. "He walked around starkers in front of a bird I brought home."

George explained yet again, "I didn't know she was there."

Sam smirked. "He flirts with my wife."

Innocent encounters. George waved them both away.

But Sam bumped him as if to say *I'd like to push your face in the dirt.* "Leading a charmed life and trampling a few mates. Ah, but where's the harm in that, eh? Only the price of fame."

Nigel crowded. "Yeah, the price of being Mr. Adorable Twit."

Sam got in his face. "Always the darling, right, chéri, with the gold necklace? You do know what it says, Nige? 'Big Star.'"

"Big Star? Big Arse."

George rescued his necklace. "Sod off."

He spun away from them, but they nabbed his sleeve, forcing him onto the stool. Sam said, "You need to mind your manners, son."

"Piss off! I'm not sucking either of you."

The two gawped. Then came peals of laughter. George realized his gaffe and flushed.

The men staggered. "'You had to perform the service, love? Oh, that's a good one."

"Too many willies in the kisser?"

"Did you hear George? He said—"

Leo shouted from the hall, "Enough! We've a show to do. Focus!"

George slammed the door. *That was bad. They hate you in the post. Now they hate you here.*

Tingly... a faint coming... Was it? Or—

WHAT WAS THAT? Shadow George sprawled on the floor. The door behind him thumped. Leo called, "George? You all right?"

Shadow George forced, "Yes. Right."

"Open up."

"Out soon."

Woozy, he reached for the runaway specs. *My head feels so weird.* Had that been a moan before? Had it been him?

It was that other. That weird, panting self.

That one tried to take over, but not for long, only seconds. Shadow George remembered his panic—George's panic. Those rotters still laughed in the distance. Shadow George staggered up.

"I pushed in, so he wouldn't stay. You need to come back. You've a show to do."

No one there.

Here I am talking to myself. Wacko weird bugger, what am I supposed to do now? He's the actor, not me. I don't know lines. Wacko weird bugger.

Shadow George donned the specs and hunched on the stool. Wilburn pressed close, all peppermint and piss. That sod was in his mind too often. Hadn't he ruined them enough? How could memories be so incessantly like the real thing?

Noting the clock, Shadow George changed into Jamie togs, returned to the stool, and sucked the coin of the necklace. Big Star.

I want to die.

Shadow George breathed with relief. *There you are.*

I want to die.

You're just embarrassed. You've a show to do.

Let me die.

Viewers are waiting. Don't worry about those gits. Show them how good you are. You're better than me, you're the talented one.

George returned to do what he was paid for, though he felt black inside. Would he finish his year in a loony bin?

He removed his specs, the necklace, and quietly ran through scenes. He avoided the others on emergence, yet caught Leo's eye.

Leo's gaze asked readiness. George nodded.

Charlie popped in front of him, rubbing hands together. "Well, now, happy in the new space?"

In the distance, a laughing Russ jiggled a sausage at him from the buffet table.

Charlie said, "Be sure to tell Jill I'm looking out for you, all right, lad? Lad?"

~

GEORGE DECKED Russell at the buffet table. Russ needed makeup to cover the mark. A furious Leo vowed repercussions after the taping.

Everyone got through the show, with Russ's eye puffing beneath the pancake. Oddly, the audience seemed fine with the minimal effort.

Jamie remembered he was really "George" and cupped the knuckles of his right hand. His gaze flit anywhere but on his glaring director, who'd dragged him to his office like a misbehaving pupil.

"Fighting is just not done, you *know* that. No doubt Russ provoked. Don't 'yes, sir' like a schoolboy. How are you feeling, lad? Fame can be hard to navigate. And I don't care for all that gadding about Pru wants you to do." Leo softened his tone. "Perhaps you might like to talk about it with, with a professional, say, a doctor of… They're quite discreet."

Blood burned in his cheeks. "I'm quite fine, Leo."

"I can't have another episode like that."

"No, sir." He shuddered.

At least the others had a scolding, as well.

Days later, he was still seething at his parents' house. Dad told him, "We're human, we stumble. We're absurd creatures. Try to treat people well and laugh at yourself."

George sputtered, "Laugh at myself. When others are laughing? Certain people aren't treating me well at all."

"Then for God's sake be especially kind. They may not think well of themselves. No one is above another. Give credit to others. Take the loss upon yourself."

"I don't believe you. You want me to be utterly weak."

Dad's eyes flashed. "No, son. You misunderstand. I'm asking you to be strong. Being right doesn't make you big. Let it go. These are squabbles among children."

George decided to act the role of a good sort, an oblivious sort, pretending not to hear when Sam or the others made sour remarks. Not that a biting response didn't spring to mind.

But Dad would not have reacted. Odd. An old soldier set on being peaceful.

George sensed insecurity in one of Nigel's barbs, his flatmate not meeting his eye. Did cocky Nigel not think well of himself?

Give credit to others. Take the loss upon yourself.

Buggery hell.

Meanwhile, Toni Banks was hired to appear in a certain number of Harrington episodes. Her first day on the set, she said, "Do you ever want to get married? Not to me," she stammered to his shock, "I meant in general."

"Oh. I suppose. Although, if I do, I'd likely marry a musician."

She turned away. Good lord. Why ask that?

Toni asked if the script called for her character to be paired with Jamie. The writers said, no, they were pairing her with Russ, the "ladies' man." George masked his relief. She wouldn't be on for long.

If only Shadow George hadn't taken her virginity the night of their date. If he'd known she was a virgin! She'd told him, "I'm glad it was you."

Now she let him have her anytime they were together. He was careful, a plonker at the ready. He wasn't getting trapped into fatherhood. Honestly, he preferred older lovers as randy as he was. When things went off, stiffies less stiff, older women didn't cry and blame themselves. If Wilburn flashed in, George quickened the pace. Until his lovers complained.

As if we can stay ahead of memories? Just stop. Stop the sex.

Stop the—? But that's all we're good for!

A wincing thought. And was it even true, now?

Funny thing was, the celibacy that followed felt like getting his breath back. George swam at a pool near the studio that opened at special times for the actors. He tooled around in his own car now, a bronze E-type Jaguar with a leather interior.

The government helped itself to huge chunks of his salary. According to his accountant (Dad), he needed to invest, perhaps in real estate. He tantalized his parents with promises of a new home.

Of course, Dad protested the idea, saying he hardly needed a house bigger than the rattletrap in Clapham, and even declared the trains helped him sleep. George should buy his own home.

But he was mostly happy in the digs with Nigel. Why should his dad feel in debt to that war chum, Lord Kettering? The schooling was finished. George had paid the bloody dues. He could offer his dad independence.

In the end, he assumed care of the big house in St. Ives and had indoor plumbing installed, with lovely bathrooms and toilets. His relatives didn't mind accepting money from him.

He and Dad had shouted, unusual for them, the air full of unsaid things, his voice with a warning: *Don't push about the past. You don't want to know.*

Yet didn't he love his dad for pushing?

Dad hadn't pushed back then.

SEVENTEEN

"Downtown"

(TONY HATCH, 1964)

AFTER DRAMATIC LANDSCAPES AND OCEAN, the view out oval airplane windows showed endless blue sky. George put away his specs. Perhaps he'd wear them openly in the U.S. People wouldn't know him there at all.

Jill had struck a major deal for Charlie. A cousin of Jack's who worked for CBS in New York had expressed interest in a possible season's worth of *Harrington* episodes after she'd sent him tapes of the show. Jill and Charlie were meeting with him in New York City. Happily, PR Pru suggested the four boys ought to tag along as it was January, a downtime for the show. Then she arranged for a photographer to record their experience for a magazine. Charlie had a mate in sunny Florida, so that jaunt was added to the itinerary. A lot was riding on the American deal. Jill's initiative got George his raise.

She and Charlie conferred a few rows up. Attractive women in uniforms tended passengers. George was ecstatic going to the land of Elvis, Motown, and cheeseburgers, if somewhat alarmed by the novel experience of flying in this great silver tube of a vehicle. He and Nigel were the only two with a pallor on. He'd refused a drink earlier, yet perhaps alcohol might be a help.

Married Sam and single Russ were chatting up two stewardesses. His shadow self sparked at the thought of a conquest. The celibacy could end in America.

However, he felt more tickled to be going somewhere with Jill. Just a glancing smile from her encouraged him to make the tentative walk to her aisle seat. (As long as the plane didn't lurch.)

She wore the black feathers of false eyelashes, her lips glistened pink, her freckles barely visible. "Why the paint?" he asked.

Her smile died. "We're not all fortunate. I look undercooked in photographs. See the leprechaun up there?"

Their hired photographer did resemble a leprechaun. "The chap who likes you?"

"He doesn't like me. Why do you say that?"

"Men know that sort of thing."

She flashed skepticism. The photographer threw them a look.

He caught a whiff of floral amidst the cigarette smoke. Lavender, was it? Most birds spackled on makeup and looked sexy. Why shouldn't Jill wear makeup and smell of perfume?

Oddly, he didn't know what to say to her anymore as he braced Charlie's vacated seat. She rifled her handbag. He guessed her search and offered a cigarette. A camera shutter clicked as he lit her. The leprechaun ducked low. *Crafty bugger.*

He pocketed the lighter. "Remember Jack used to tell me I'd come to the States? Don't you wonder if he went home? We should ask his family. Will I meet the Stuarts?"

Her eyes were a startled blue. "We won't have time. You'll meet Franklin. He's the important one." She picked up a magazine and flipped through it.

George flattened to let someone pass. Strands of her hair were stiffened with spray. "What's wrong?"

She waved a hand in dismissal.

Sam called, "Legs, you're missing all the fun." A stewardess giggled.

.   .   .

"AMERICA LOOKS LIKE HERE, MAINLY," neighbor Thomas had once said. And while that was true, especially around Idlewild Airport, New York City proved to be emerald, or at least silver and gleaming, a modern vista against a clear winter sky. Surely there was a wizard at its heart. Deep in Manhattan, the famous skyscrapers loomed like a shaded forest as they wended uptown in a jam of vehicles and car horns. A lady in furs sashayed behind a toy poodle. Men marched with briefcases, not umbrellas. Children were herded to a park.

Jill squeezed his arm. "I got in this car to see your face." Her fingers laced through his and for moments that was all he noticed. "Isn't this a fabulous city?" she reminded, and the view snared him again.

At the hotel everyone was too excited to rest. Charlie had a supper planned at the famous 21 Club. One moment, Jill hovered with them, the next, she was gone.

Charlie said all lads were sharing a double room. "No complaints," he warned. "You're lucky I let you all of you come."

Of course, he took his own key and went off with Miss Blount, his secretary. The lads snickered and speculated.

It was fun being in a room together. George and Nigel lounged on one double bed; Sam and Russ took the other. Cool Sam popped a rolled cigarette from his case and ignited a marijuana fragrance.

He sucked in and spoke through smoke. "Why shouldn't we… have some fun… on this trip?"

With the joint shared to a nub, they barely changed their suits in time and staggered with giggles down to the lobby. The leprechaun blocked them, a flash bulb going off. Charlie frowned.

Miss Blount waited in a sparkly frock and stole, her sexuality jarring, as opposed to her usually modest safety. She swanned out with Charlie to a waiting cab as he played the gracious host.

Wouldn't his wife like to know about her. Where on earth was Jill?

Jill arrived later. The leprechaun rose as she sat. *Randy bugger.* She winked at George, the black feathers still on her eyelids, her lips silvery. She looked puzzled. George forced a smile. She answered it, barely.

George glimpsed himself in a mirror. *Good Lord.* He still wore his Buddy Holly specs. He slipped them off to a soft-focus world. No wonder he'd seen Jill so clearly. Luckily, the more she ate and drank, the more the lip paint wore off, and the flush returned to her cheeks. The food was plentiful and better than English food. George cleaned his plate with every course. He was smiling so much his face hurt. (He was in America!)

Exhaustion hit like a stupor over the pudding, or "dessert," as they said here. It was after two in the morning. George squinted at a local clock. That couldn't be the right time.

Everyone drifted out to yellow cabs. The freezing night air woke him up again. He was dragged into a car with the lads.

Sam said, "We're not going back yet. Right, mates?"

The boys cackled as the taxi gunned past Charlie's. What a look on their producer's face.

Only Nigel had dollars. They couldn't understand the driver, who seemed agitated and promptly dropped them at a money exchange. Yanks gawked at the four English actors. Why weren't there more lads with fringe to their eyes? Could America be backward to London? Passing girls noticed them—a pull looked promising. Russ caught his eye, clearly thinking the same thing. But with dollars in hand, Sam and Nigel urged them back in the cab.

George donned his specs. What heaven just to ride and watch nightlife. *Jack, I'm finally here. Are you here?* A younger Jack had wooed his Jill in this very city. How did she feel about this trip? And what was wrong with meeting Jack's family?

Sam was going spastic. There was the famous Apollo Theater!

They yelled for a stop and battled to emerge, a wad of money thrown at the driver. More girls stared, colored girls now, with wary boyfriends. The four lads scanned for seats in the filling theater and drifted to a side section. Someone asked, "Are you a pop group?"

"We're actors," Russ said.

"We're the new thing," Nigel added.

The acts were fantastic, the crowd even better. No one sat. It was the only way to enjoy this music, these "Pips" as the group was called. They sounded like Motown. Was New York at all close to the Motor City? One couldn't be in America and *not* go to these places.

A bloke next to them shouted, "Are you from Liverpool?"

The boys responded with their best Beatle-ese until the bloke convulsed. "Tell the truth, you're them? Oh, my God!"

"Don't tell anyone," Sam shouted, as news traveled down the row. Sam nudged George to remove his specs.

Two girls squeezed over and declared in delicious accents: "Those aren't the Beatles."

"You're, like, Gerry and the Pacemakers or something, right?"

The lads knocked each other with laughter. Their friendly neighbor now seemed irked. George appreciated a curvy dolly in front of him. Until he felt her boyfriend's searing glare. But he had to catch her eye again. He wanted an American girl, a gum-snapping, wide-hipped one with a thick accent, a nasty girl.

The curvy doll glanced back, mouthed, "You're cute."

He loosened for seduction and gave a penetrating look. He could sway his body to impress. (Did someone say, "knock it off"?) He'd lure this dark lady to a dark corner. But he was assaulted!

Yanked by the lapels and forced from the row— "Bloody—what? Hey!" He fought to pivot. Hands slammed him to the aisle wall. A big man blocked the way.

"Don't come back and I'll let you keep your teeth."

George covered his mouth. As the bloke retreated, he shouted, "It's a free country. But, hah, the British have returned."

People stared as if he were daft. He felt daft. Bloody hell. What time was it? A million o'clock? A short woman got in his way.

"Time to leave, mister."

George looked around. "Sorry? No, I'm a paying customer. I'm watching—"

"You're trouble. Get out of here."

"I *beg* your pardon? My mates are there. I'm a Beatle. How dare you speak this way to a Beatle."

"Your mates are leaving, too."

Russ, Nigel, and Sam were being ejected from their row by the same hulking thug. George fumed, "Just wait until I tell Brian. He won't like this one—" His mates knocked into him and all were escorted down the aisle and out of the theater.

Back in the cold night air, under the bright, empty marquee, breath freezing, the four stared in a daze.

Sam glared daggers at George. "I can't believe we were tossed out of the Apollo Theater."

But Nigel said, "We got tossed out of the Apollo Theater!"

Then all were laughing insanely, bending and trying not to piss. It took a ridiculous amount of time to get another cab. No one would drive four giggling nutters.

GEORGE WAS SO tired as he brushed his teeth, and barely made it through his bath in a surprisingly shallow tub for a posh hotel. There was still chatter going on. He opened the door to a pall of smoke.

"Oh, Hartley, Jesus."

"Whoa. Don't wave your dangly bits in our face."

"You mean like this?"

Sam grabbed his hips. "Turn around, son. The rump is better."

He was smacked as he bent to take a drag. Nigel said, "You see what I deal with at home? You're not getting into my bed naked."

Why was Nigel upset? "You know I sleep nude."

"I'm not having your bits touch me."

George bristled. "My bits will be quite shrunken around you."

Sam said, "Oh, shut up, all of you. I'll sleep with him, for God's sake. We're tired and bloody high again. Jesus. This has been the longest fucking day."

George flew under the covers, stung by his flatmate's words. Many were the nights Nigel had peeled. Was he just complaining to show off? Or had Nigel always hated him?

They all hate you. Remember when they ditched you? Remember when...?
George froze as Sam crawled into the bed. The lights clicked off.

CHARLIE WAS THERE at an ungodly hour, raving about a "stink" and "running off," the room absurdly bright. *Where am I?*

Charlie nattered about a business meeting. (A body was in bed with him!) Some wanker lit a cigarette.

Russell's voice snapped, "Put that out!"

MUCH, much later, befogged but re-oriented, the boys gathered in the lobby. George felt guilty going without exercise, not that a fortnight without a dance belt and tights wasn't heaven. He'd have to stretch later.

A cross, perky Yank strode over, a tour guide Charlie had retained. He alerted at the man's accent. The guide shifted with energy, his gaze darting.

"It would have been *better* to have started *early*. Of course, jet lag happens; it's *okay*. But we'd better *run* if we're going to make the Empire State Building."

Russ said, "We're not into that tourist scene, man. Where else can you take us?"

"But I'm *here* to take you to tourist sites and museums. Your manager said—"

"He's not our manager. Can you take us to the Factory?"

The man looked flummoxed. "Andy Warhol," Russ added with annoyance.

The Yank said, "The soup can weirdo? If you want real art—"

"You're released," Sam said. "Cheery bye, shove off and all that."

"See ya later," George added, as they swept past the stunned bloke and out to waiting cabs. He wore his specs because who cared.

They went with the cabbie who said, "Yeah, dat's midtown, come on," in a stellar accent.

The traffic was appalling. They could have walked faster. At least, if they'd kept the guide, they would've known what was around them. Yet it was all New York City. He wouldn't have minded seeing the Empire State Building. Suspiciously, they were dropped in front of an old building, the driver saying, "Yeah, yeah. Fifth floor."

Inside, they rode a lift with silver walls. Doors opened to the warehouse of the Factory. A vision! The boys sailed in, gawking. It was like a future land—silver everywhere, walls and pillars wrapped in foil, flashing, mirrored pieces, metal art boxes. "Andy isn't here," said a heavily made-up woman, who may have been a man.

Russ huffed with disappointment. The woman smiled at him.

The place reeked of fresh ink and turpentine, and beneath, the scent of marijuana. Working artists pegged prints on paper like clothes on a line. Longhaired kids lounged on a crimson sofa. A bird drifted by twisting her hair.

Sam nudged George. "She'd be easy."

"She seems touched."

There was a huge canvas propped against a wall with multiple Elvis Presleys. Sam leapt to it. "Fab. How much?"

The woman said, "Sorry, darling, it's already sold."

The pot-smoker, a rough looking sort, offered his pipe to Nigel, who took a drag and passed it to his mates. The woman said, "So foul. We also have pills."

George melted inside. Stoned again. What a dreamscape they'd crashed. No one seemed to mind their presence. Their accents were praised—*their* accents!

"Who are you guys?" said someone with a movie camera, clearly transfixed by Russ. "You're beauteous. Do you mind if we shoot you?"

George smirked, offended and glad not to be noticed. He watched Sam buzz over to the dotty girl, the lech.

Russ's discomfort was a laugh. Until the filmmaker noticed George. "And you. Stand with him. I want both of you guys."

Russ muttered, "He wants us. Sounds like Bogart, doesn't he? If poofs can sound like Bogart."

An odd word, "poof." Just because a bloke liked a bloke.

"You know," Russ announced, "we're going to have a show on American television."

"Yeah? What do you do?" The little camera whirred.

"We're actors. It's a comedy."

The filmmaker said, "We dig that pop TV junk. Can you take off your glasses, man?"

George gave his best smile. "No. And we're not taking anything else off either."

"Shut *up*" Russ said, as the filmmaker grinned behind his lens, and said, "You know you can strip if you want to."

George demurred. "We're awfully shy."

The filmmaker said, "People get naked here a lot."

Russ cringed. "Christ, Hartley, you've nerve."

The filmmaker said, "Do you want to see our naked pictures?"

Russ said, "Only if they're girls."

George hooted at his mate's worried tone. The filmmaker said, "Spoilsport."

Russ winced. "This place is loony. Where's Sam?"

"He went after that bird."

Russ strode off. Nigel was admiring art! As if he knew anything about it. The film camera shadowed George like a hovering eye.

He turned to the lens, "Well, you scared him now. Lost your chance with Dreamboat."

"You want to jack me off?"

Shadow George gasped. "We don't jack. We're *jacked*."

The filmmaker laughed. George darted from him. Shadow George ranted in his head: *We're not seconds. We're not runners-up.*

Someone snagged his jacket. "Where did you get your threads, man?" Another said, "Where in London are you from? I know London. Where in London?"

With even greater fervor than they had on arriving, Russ hastened them out of the silver world. The "woman" trailed them to the lift. "Stay, you yummy British lads. Don't go yet."

Outside, the pavement was busy with Americans marching to-and-fro. Were they going to work? Or was it afternoon? Sam wore a smug grin. George said, "You shagged that bird, didn't you?"

"Easy as pie."

"She was touched."

"Great arse, though."

He bolted ahead. Sam called, "Sorry, vicar. Have I offended?"

George whirled back. "You don't take advantage of weaker people. You don't shag their arse."

"I didn't shag her in the arse. I just said—"

But Russ got in the way, stopping George's fury. Sam cowered, alarmed. "*You're* the one who's touched."

George lowered his arm, surprised, and loosened his fingers. Energy pulsed with nowhere to go. Matron had shouted, "You dare accuse a master? A kindly man?"

Face heating as if he were in front of her, he shook his arms.

Up ahead, Nigel waved. "Look at this. I've always wanted to try a submarine sandwich."

IT TOOK a while to straighten up, even after the huge, sloppy sandwich with its oily meats—that was kind of good, admittedly. Back at the hotel, Jill had left George a message wondering would he join her tomorrow for a trip to New Jersey, that might be tedious, but would he be a sport and meet her family.

He was ecstatic. What could be better than going to New Jersey and meeting her family, away from his batty, so-called mates? He rang her room with no answer, then resolved to wait in the lobby.

People came through the revolving doors, never the right one. After a while, he purchased postcards and wrote to his parents, then to Toni Banks, his sometime-girlfriend, *if* he had a girlfriend. He had half a mind to write to Philippa knowing how envious she would be. *Phil, darling. Finally in New York. Miss you.*

The hotel bar was dark and crowded. He saw the leprechaun bring a drink to Miss Blount in a corner. Charlie's secretary was tarted up and smoking.

"A business supper," she said to his query, a sour tone evident. "I thought—*we* thought—he'd be back by now."

"She's out, too," the leprechaun added.

Miss Blount ground out her ciggie. "Oh, yes, Mrs. Stuart is with him. Well, they are her in-laws, or one of them is. I really should've gone along, don't you think? I can talk to Americans."

George smiled his way out of that one.

But why hadn't *he* been included in a supper with the Stuarts? How irritating the turn of events today... the Factory... Sam. The need for sex shot through him. Only the bar felt intimidating.

He opted for the cold outdoors, surprised anew by the sounds, the lights, the jabbering Yanks and vehicles going in the wrong direction. Specs on, he smiled at the absolute right thing to visit across the way: a bookstore.

GEORGE RESOLVED to catch Jill early. He lathered and turned under the shower spray, finally realizing Americans took showers, not baths. He squawked at Sam in the room, in pajamas, hair awry.

Sam threw down a towel. "You're making a puddle, son. You're supposed to shut that door."

"It was just me." George closed the pocket door. Sam was watery through the mottled glass. The need to apologize ran down his spine. *He was the one in the wrong. Slimy bugger.*

Sam said, "You're making it hard for me to piss."

Of course, he did almost hit a costar, which he wasn't supposed to do anymore. Sam wouldn't go to Leo about it, would he?

Sam slid open the door with a leer. "As you were, darling."

Was he getting an eyeful? "Do you want to join me?"

Sam sneered, "Fuck off," and banged the door shut.

That was odd. Back in the darkened bedroom the others were still asleep. Sam was under covers, facing away. George dressed quickly. He crept out to the hall and fluffed his wet hair, then donned his specs to better read room numbers. He rounded a corner. Charlie!

He leapt back, unseen. Charlie had gone livid about the ditched tour guide. He peeked. His producer rounded a far corner.

After an interval, he walked again. But that was odd: Charlie's door was… *Go back, just go back now.* His arm sprang up, knuckles rapped the door. It opened at once. Jill clutched a dressing gown over bare skin. She blanched at him.

"Oh! Uh, hi. Can you come back in a few—?"

He pushed into her room. "Or come in," she added, "I guess you got my message."

The bed was in disarray, the smells intimate. Evidence everywhere. It turned his stomach. "What are you doing with a man like that?"

"Excuse me?"

"Now he's cheating on his wife *and* Miss Blount."

Her eyes flashed, her color high. "That's not your business."

"You're better than that. You used to tell me not to cheapen myself."

"I—look—you have no right butting into my love life. I don't have all the options you do."

He balked. "Why wouldn't you have options? You're a beautiful woman."

Her eyes gleamed. Her breasts were loose in the silk. He averted his gaze. "I'd rather have seen the leprechaun come out of here."

She flapped an arm. "He's your boss."

"Well, he's not *your* boss. You don't need a favor from him unless he's thanking you."

"Oh, Jesus. Get out!"

She pulled on him to move. He stalled. "I do want to meet your family." She pushed him out the door.

He stalked back to his room, but paced outside the door, fidgety for a smoke.

Sam emerged wearing a jacket over his pajamas. George pivoted. Sam called, "Wait a minute, hold on," and jerked him backwards.

"What kind of bloke do you think I am? You don't say 'join me' unless you mean it, you don't say things like that."

George freed his arm. "Leave off!"

"You don't say 'join me.' I'll smash you."

"Do it then. It doesn't matter to me."

Sam waved. "Shhh. Keep your voice down."

George marched over and pounded the lift button. Sam started in with him, but George said, "No," and got on the lift alone.

Somehow, he eluded his mates for the day. He waited until well past noon before ringing Jill's room, then phoned the desk clerk, who informed him Mrs. Stuart had hired a car and wouldn't be back until late.

EIGHTEEN

"The Warmth of the Sun"

(BRIAN WILSON & MIKE LOVE, 1964)

THEY LEFT the cold skies of New York for the warm state of Florida. George sat well away from Jill in the plane's cabin. She oughtn't to have left him for the day in that hotel. It was a terrible thing to do. But catching her eye made her look away. Why should she be cold? It was hard not to be disgusted with her, and with Charlie. He couldn't look at the man. Only his producer kept twisting around to scold.

"I can't have expensive actors getting lost in a foreign city."

Sam said, "What expensive actors? You brought expensive actors?" Someone coughed "George."

Charlie said, "Didn't I see to you? Yet you behave like naughty children."

"We behaved like naughty adults," Sam said, "but for George."

George sat with Russell and tried to focus on a magazine. He was nearly twenty, no child. Sam could go to the devil!

Charlie scoffed. "Well, you're not quite setting a good example then, are you, as elder and no-doubt leader?"

Russ put in, "Sam doesn't lead me."

Charlie interrupted, "We have important meetings in Miami. And we're on the beach, for God's sake. That should be enough."

Sam said, "Can you get us some girls?"

Charlie said, "And how *is* the lovely Mrs. Owen?"

"Living it up with *your* wife," Sam answered in the same tone.

Sam did have a nerve. George brightened at the thought of a beach. But it was raining in Miami, which made for a scary landing. After that, he felt he'd had quite enough of airplanes.

It was still pouring when they got to the hotel. George went straight to the back window to view a gray and restless ocean.

Charlie called him over and stepped too close. "Listen, lad, don't let those others lead you around. Do you want your own room?"

"Why should I get special treatment?"

Charlie held out his arms as if it were obvious. "How about I split you in two? Who do you want? Don't pick Sam—"

"Nigel, I suppose."

"Good lad." Charlie slapped him on the back.

The hotel gift shop was selling the same loudly patterned shirts Elvis wore in *Blue Hawaii*. The boys had to buy one each. Jill leaned in, dubious, "Are you sure?" and was shouted down.

In the room, George and Nigel donned their shirts and agreed they looked splendid. George was ready to head down, but Nigel said, "Don't forget your specs. They go, somehow."

"I can certainly see better." He faced the mirror. "Oh, Lord. I look *awful*. All I need is a camera around my neck."

"I'm sure Donal will loan you his."

"Is that his name?"

George lingered in the lobby and wondered if he looked like a Yank tourist. The leprechaun said, "Gear shirt."

"We're all wearing them. The others will be down in theirs."

Donal photographed George without specs for the fan pictures. George was surprised to see Nigel stroll down in a roll-neck jersey.

Donal called, "Where's the shirt?" but Nigel headed into the bar. "Bugger. There goes our photo."

Worried, George re-donned his specs. Sam and Russ also came down in regular clothes. Donal shouted, "Hey!"

Russ glanced back with a telltale laugh.

George leapt up. "I'm going for a walk."

His face heated as he strode away. He'd get his own bloody room, all right, he'd ask Charlie for a switch.

Music tantalized down a hallway—Latin music—that started an itch in his body. He traced the sound to a ballroom. A sign proclaimed "Bossa Nova classes in session." A young lady manned a table at the door and gave that American "Hi."

"Hello. Do you need any men for the class?" Then added to her raised eyebrows, "I'm not from around here."

"I know. Only tourists wear shirts like that." She rose. "I'll ask the señora, Mrs. Lopez."

Señora Lopez was a curvy number, who nodded as the girl conferred, and waved him in, saying, "You want to try? The class has been going for a while."

"Perhaps I could help. I know how to dance."

She gawked—again at the shirt. He said, "It looks ridiculous."

"No, no, it's just, with the hair…" She waved her hands. "Why don't you watch then join in when you're ready."

George nearly walked out. It was only Eydie Gormé Bossa Nova. A new song started. He caught the teacher's gesturing hand and snapped her into a dance. Her eyes were shocked, and a very intense brown.

She followed his steps, body responding before the mind, easy to move, this señora with the heated gaze. Her class watched. He gave staccato steps for those spiky heels. How sexy to guide this sinuous female, and good to move his body, what with ignoring it for a week. She grew breathless, or maybe he did. He went double-time through a section and caught her annoyance. But rhythmic rules were made to be broken; why shouldn't dance be play? Students often missed that aspect. Her anger cracked, eyes misty. Surely heat rose between them. He would have her tonight in his solo bedroom.

There was applause and whistling at the end. Señora Lopez broke away from him. "That was showy, disrespectful to the dance. The intent, the subtlety."

He said, "I push to the brink. I play with possibilities."

People gathered round; he barely caught her words. "...move like a cat, so sure. Who are you? All right, class. Just a show."

He pivoted from the ballroom. He respected music more than anything. Who was *she*, this hotel dance teacher? He glanced out a window and didn't care anymore that it rained.

When he crossed the wet expanse of sand in his swim trunks, the rain had stopped. Sunlight pierced through clouds. Waves from the storm smashed warm, a surprise, foam fizzing his legs. Here was the place to cauterize the hurt in his heart.

The setting sun spattered the sea in shards—gold winked into silver and bronze, magenta to violet. He swam through treasures, until the dark sky was pinpricked with stars.

AFTER THAT FIRST DAY, George sought the ocean as much as possible. His evening bathe had put Charlie in a panic, who chastised the boys for "losing George." Now his mates lingered near him or they tried to horse around with him. Momentarily flattered, he gave in—as Donal the photographer snapped them in their play—then dove under creating distance.

The Atlantic lapped Miami Beach and pounded Cornwall. George was diagonally opposite his home. The landscape here was utterly flat. Surely Calypso lived in tropical waters, with Rio but a skip farther down. All right, quite a skip farther down. He still wanted to go to the hot home of Bossa Nova, Ipanema, so he could dance in that wild, free manner. Perhaps one day he and his dad would share a beer with Jobim. Chagrinned about the señora, he couldn't decide whether to seek her out again. It could've been her words weren't all bad.

Charlie went to a meeting with the high-heeled Mrs. Stuart and Miss Blount clattering behind him. He sought out the boys in the afternoon and promised the Jackie Gleason studios on Friday.

"Lark about now. Enjoy your freedom. The next time you come to these shores, you'll be known, I guarantee it."

CBS television had agreed to run their show in the summer. Charlie booked them a ride on a yacht courtesy of his friend, a rich bloke who liked to drink. Miss Blount came, but Jill did not.

Her absence stung him. It was a thrill to cruise emerald waters in such a fine rig. Why would she miss the opportunity? Was she avoiding him? He'd been too hard on her. Who was he to scold?

"She bowed out, said she had things to take care of," Charlie said briefly, with scarcely a look to explain. He convulsed in his lunatic laugh and poured the bubbly with his old, fat chum. Miss Blount lounged in her one-piece, straps daringly lowered, breasts seeping out, legs fish-belly white.

George almost didn't want to look at her. Yet it was better than his gaze snagging on their fat host's browned tub of a midriff. He wandered from everyone else, squinting for skin on other craft. Women waved from a passing speedboat.

His open shirt billowed. There was a flush on his smooth chest with its sparse black hairs. His old trunks and matching shirt weren't fitting well anymore. The front package needed adjusting; he had to pluck the fabric from his rear.

Someone smacked his bum. Sam, of course, who murmured, "Nice suit, Hartley. A bit small. You trying to turn us into homos?"

"Don't you like girls?"

"I thought I did. Quit distracting me."

"If I'd known I'd outgrown this suit I'd never have packed it."

He wrapped himself in a beach towel but Sam had an edge of it. George wouldn't let him take it, until Sam said, "Forget it. I'm being a shit, okay? Why didn't Jill come along?"

He let go of the towel. "I'm not her keeper."

"We haven't seen much of her."

Sam caught up with him. "All right, I confess I'm glad you have insecurities and don't go around like a prima donna."

"You think I'm insecure?"

"Hartley, please. You just answered your own question. You ought to shave off those hairs. I'm not saying I'm any better, only that no one is peering at me, secretly or otherwise." He swiped the reddish mat on his pale skin.

A smile pushed against his will. "You're a pain, Sir Ginger. I guess I'm sorry I tried to hit you."

"Ah, yeah. Don't do that. You were odd that day."

An understatement. "My insecurities."

The yacht stopped, motor off, and lolled far from land. The two young men went to the rails and gazed on jewel-like water.

"I bet you can't swim under to the other side."

Unable to resist a swimming challenge, George almost didn't make it. He had to kick quite low to get under the beam, and surfaced at the end of his breath, floundering for something to grab. Someone plunged in and propelled him to a ladder. He held onto it, coughing until his lungs burned. The others hauled him up and over.

Everyone talked at once. Charlie cried, "Are you utterly mad?" Miss Blount dabbed his shoulder blade. "He's bleeding."

George winced at her touch. "I scraped going under. I feared I wouldn't make it."

"You went under from the other side?" Nigel looked impressed.

Charlie flapped his arms. "I need you insured! I should fine you for that tomfoolery."

A wet Sam stood beside George. "Fine me. I dared him to do it."

Charlie said, "Why is *that* not a surprise?"

Miss Blount said, "George, we must disinfect this wound."

"Oh," he realized, "I can do that."

He broke free and dove overboard. Had Charlie just screamed?

He surfaced quickly to explain to gawking faces: "Don't worry. The sea cleans the wound. The sea heals anything."

THE SPARSE CHEST hairs were ridiculous. George shaved them off the next morning. He wasn't going to feel sad about it, he did look better smooth. His color had deepened from the day on the yacht. A tan made his brown eyes gold. Jack's necklace gleamed on his skin.

Yet Charlie had said to him yesterday, "Good heavens, you tan dark. Are you sure you're English?"

The mantle of Mowgli so easily diminished him.

Missing the rigor of the dance studio, he opted for laps at the hotel pool. A few guests lounged in the mid-morning. A waiter served Bloody Marys to two ladies in large hats. Their legs suggested age, their cackling laughter, earlier drinks. George went to a chaise, sloughed his things onto it, and stepped out of his shoes.

The ladies ceased their chatter. Aware of their attention, he smiled, couldn't resist a "good morning" as he passed, and dove in.

He hoisted out much later, muscles quivering, glad he'd pushed himself. The hats were still there. He mustn't show exhaustion.

Their attention pleased him, even electrified a little. Would a member of the viewing party oil his back? This celibacy must end! He flattened the chaise and laid on his stomach.

There was a snatch of laughter, their voices muted. The sun seared his back and dried his suit. A waiter stopped by.

"Orange juice," George answered. He was mad for Florida orange juice. It came iced in a glass with a straw.

Sensing a shadow, he twisted to see sunlight flare around a female form. "Hullo," he said.

"You might want to cover yourself. The sun is very strong."

Jill! He glanced and caught a two-piece suit, her hair in pigtails. He'd preened in front of her. Could he slither off the chair back into the pool? She said, "You didn't lotion your back."

"I know."

A chair scraped. But *she* wasn't going to…

She grabbed the bottle before he could reach it. Warm liquid streamed. Her hands rubbed vigorously, too hard. "You're stiff."

"Sorry?"

"Relax."

Her palms made long strokes on his back. His body gave way beneath them like something breaking. An erection bloomed in his tight shorts; he had to shift to give it room.

"What's this?" She lightly touched his scrape.

"Boat hull, yesterday. Stupid."

Why didn't you join us? Who was I to make you feel bad?

He meant to say those things. Only her hands—so often gesturing with a cigarette or typing letters—furrowed his spine, spanned his waist, then surged to his shoulders, thumbs digging in. "Unh," came out of his mouth. He was liquefied.

She stopped. "Got a smoke, DF? Can I have some of your orange juice?" She sipped loudly through the straw. "Don't look now, but those two cows in hats have been leering at you."

He realized "You've been here awhile."

Her leg jiggled against his chair. "I didn't know it was you doing laps, then you emerged like, like some kind of… Do you have ciggies?"

Some kind of what? "Don't say 'ciggies.' Your Yank accent is finally coming back."

"Bugger. I thought I'd banished New Jersey."

"Never banish New Jersey."

"Okay, doll-face."

He heard the smile in her voice. A tickle of liquid and her hands smoothed again. Just as his nether region had calmed, it re-inflated. Hadn't she oiled him enough? She murmured to herself. He caught "Your dad… lucky skin… Scotch eyes."

What on earth? "What about Scottish eyes?"

Her touch slowed. "What are you talking about?"

He barked a laugh. "I don't know. What are you talking about?"

Why was she going on about his dad? He pushed his face in the slats, feeling foolish.

"I meant they're potent. One needs a sure… head."

His bum was smacked. She jerked up. Was she angry?

She half turned at his call. "I'm just, I'll be right…."

Her wrap belled to a glimpse of gingham bottom. She strode towards the hotel. Out came Russ, Nigel, and Sam in trunks and towels, surrounding her, eyes leering. They wouldn't let her pass. But then they did. They waved at George as if things were ducky.

JILL NEVER CAME BACK. She never showed at the poolside café. George scarcely paid attention to his mates. That massage had been so surprising. And did she have a thing for his dad? She'd meant his dad, hadn't she? He thought about searching for her, yet, equally, didn't want to stumble on anything unpleasant, like a certain person leaving another person's room.

In the afternoon everyone moved to the beach. A voice said, "There you are. I've been looking for you."

It was the señora in sunglasses and a bikini, rising and smiling. "My dancer. I kept seeing boys who looked like you but weren't you. These here," she realized with a blush. "Are you all dancers?"

Russ said, "Do we look like dancers?"

George tensed at his mates closing in. She bravely said, "You all look nice. But he has the physique."

"Lord Legs strikes again," muttered Sam. They dispersed. Nigel said, "Coming, George?" as Sam said, "He's not coming."

"No. I am."

George backed off from the señora, surprised to let her go. She seemed surprised, as well.

Charlie wasn't with Jill but splayed on the sand in dark glasses. The leprechaun waved from a beach umbrella, camera bag near.

Russ had bought one of those odd American footballs. George ran out of the waves to catch Russ's wobbling pass. His return throw was equally crazed. There must be a secret to throwing the thing.

His mates clustered away from him, the usual grouping. Too bad Cyril hadn't come on the trip. Cyril was an inclusive sort.

From a distance the señora watched him. He stretched his shoulders. *Why resist that one?* He ought to have his head examined.

"Tinker Bell!" Russ called as the bullet ball came rocketing.

George stopped it from hitting his head. *Wanker.* In the distance, Russ shrugged. Slippery pigskin wasn't easy to retrieve in the surf. He felt like his bumbling character. And so he laughed.

Yes, he was popular on telly. He worked hard to maintain that role. And, yes, he was paid well. Perhaps he might buy his own house by the sea. He lobbed the ball with intent, the pass high and straight.

Russ leapt for it. The others piled him in a tackle. George whooped at a wave sloshing them.

A transistor radio played the tummy theme from Alka Seltzer. Then the Fortunes started up about their troubles. She cut across the sand, his American agent, passing Charlie without a look. Her hair was platinum in the sun, still in those pigtails.

George feigned to ignore her approach, heart pattering. *How silly.* "Hey, gorgeous," came out of his mouth.

She gawped in response.

His face warmed. "Want to play?"

Her cover-up gapped enticingly. Freckles like cinnamon on her chest, stopping at her cleavage, her tummy pale. She removed her sunglasses, her eyes a lighter blue. Wary.

"You're angry," he said.

In the distance, Russ mimed a throw then stopped. George flinched at her nearness. She spoke softly.

"Sweetheart. I just rang home. Your, ah, dad…"

His blood froze.

"…had a heart att—"

"*No.*"

NINETEEN

"Baby, I'm Yours"

(VAN MCCOY, 1965)

"DON'T!"

His hands stayed her, yet she kept on, eyes brimming: "I'm sorry—"

"That's the *worst*, the very *worst thing* you could say to me."

"We should go. Your mother awaits your call."

Blood roared in his ears. The world pitched. He banged ground, gagged in saltwater. Hands tugged him up. He wrenched from Jill and staggered out to the hard, damp sand, spat salt, and wiped his mouth. There was a sting on his knee, a blotch of red. People gawped nearby. Jill turned for the hotel.

He followed her. Someone approached in his vision. *Keep away.* But Dad was what, forty-eight? The absurdity fumbled his footing. One had to be at least fifty to have heart attacks.

How batty to walk on soft sand. Shifting grains ate his progress. Jill forged ahead. He blinked to see. Stupid to be without sunglasses. Someone braced his arm and gave a push. Short Donal, with his clunking camera bag, who said, "It's hell walking on sand." The man guided him for the long traverse. Neither spoke.

In his freezing cold room, Jill dialed a series of numbers, spoke to an overseas operator, then handed the phone to him.

A tinny voice urged Mrs. Carveth to speak. She cried faintly, "Georgie, I need you."

He shouted into the receiver, "How could this happen?"

Donal left, but Nigel burst in. His chatter with Jill interfered. George shushed them both, and told his mother, "Of course, but we're in Florida, in the south."

There was a crackle on the line. (Nigel was packing? Good. If he can't shut up, then he can bloody-well leave.)

Mum said, "…a funeral in St. Ives."

He erupted, "But he's too young, this *can't* be true." Mum's wail stung his ear. "All right," he murmured, a headache coming on.

"George." Uncle James was on the line. "Come at once." George slammed down the phone.

Jill stared at him.

"'Come at once' he says. I'm on the other side of a fucking ocean!"

Her eyes glistened. "Nigel is, is bunking with the others."

She was showing so much skin. They were both nearly nude. He'd gotten browner. Perhaps he'd bathe.

She followed him to the bathroom. "I'll book flights—"

He shut the door on her.

Lord, Lord, Lord. No good snapping at Jill, at Mum. They'd done nothing wrong. He had to blink clear his vision. Had the sun burned his eyes? Why was he in here?

There were palm trees on a plastic curtain, a shallow tub within. He peeled off his trunks, removed his necklace, and sat shivering in the tub. Ah, right. He turned on the taps. Water boiled around his legs.

Bugger, one showers in America. He eventually turned off the taps and laid back. Pain throbbed in his skull. Nausea threatened. A voice moaned in his head. Dad wouldn't disappear forever with his son so far away. It must be a mistake.

Jill's voice: "Sweetie? I'm leaving to change clothes. I'll be back."

Could smells hurt? A brine smell intruded. He opened his eyes. The room seemed blurrier than usual. A bar of soap exuded faint vanilla. He momentarily forgot its purpose, then rubbed it over his brown legs, his cut knee. His penis bobbed like a plant, while his skin showed the ghost of his swimsuit. He slid wincingly back until the position was tolerable. Eons later, a knock startled.

"Come on out, George, please."

Mum? The bathwater let go. His dripping head felt thick, but there seemed to be less pressure. Though now he was freezing. A terry robe hung on a hook. He wrapped himself in it to stop the shivers.

There was a dreadful noise in the flowery bedroom. That bloody air unit whirred in the window. What did he care if the air was conditioned? He turned a knob to blessed silence.

Jill stared again, in clothing, the pigtails gone from her hair.

That Charlie had had her! Too sickening. The Charlie-thought made him miss the edge of the bed and plop to the carpet in front of it. She made a sound. His suitcase was open.

"I'll do that," he said.

She crouched near him. "Oh, I don't mind packing."

"You can go if you like."

She repeated, "I don't mind" in an artificial voice.

She wants to go, just like Nigel. Some friend, frantic to get away.

But she inched closer and sniffed him. "You smell like the ocean."

Good lord. He could almost count the freckles on her face, it was so near. Her startled eyes were morning blue. She shifted against the bed with a whiff of talc, her arms bare.

"Ah, what I mean is— Sweetie, I'm here if you need me. I'm sorry Nigel wouldn't—"

"What if it's hospital error, they have the wrong man?"

Her gaze shone. She frowned, looked down. "I rather think it wasn't. Your mother would have made sure, plus your uncle was with her. They would have verified before phoning. We'll know the details soon enough. We've a flight midmorning."

A possibility too horrific to bear—the torture of never seeing his father again—made his body spasm. (Had Dad been alone when the attack happened? Had he been frightened?) "Oh" fell from his mouth. Tears ran.

He tried to speak to Jill, to warn her, but had no breath—until a wail blasted out of him, like that helpless time on Wilburn's lap when he could only endure the wretchedness. She tried to hold him. He pushed from her grip and scrambled across the carpet to muffle the howls.

WHEN THE SEIZURE ABATED, he propped, weak as a lamb. Snagged down his arms, the robe gapped indecently, though Jill was behind him. He whispered an apology. She reassured him with tears in her voice. Awful coming apart in front of her, yet better her than those others. And there was a truth he needn't face with his dad anymore.

"I think he may have guessed about Wilburn," he croaked. "I knew it was eating him. I kept wanting to, to punish… as if it was his fault." He winced. *The very idea.*

Her caress felt like silk on his shoulder, his neck, he arched like a cat to it. But she ceased and gripped her hand.

"Surely he bears responsibility."

He stopped himself from collapsing into her. "No. He never deserved such pain."

"Did you?"

He flinched. "There you go again. I won't blame him."

"Not blame him, only you may be angry with him."

"I'm not! Leave off." George re-donned the robe, though it felt an encumbrance. He wanted to bash something.

He said, "You always think I'm innocent. I've told you I have a dark side. I could go away now, and he would come right out."

"I'm sorry, but you always think you're guilty. I can't blame a kid for what a grown man— Who would come out?"

Pain speared his head. *Now you've done it.* He leaned against the bed, eyes shut. Could this day get any worse?

"No one. I meant just a shadow… self. Who causes trouble. Does bad things. Braver than me."

Jill was silent to this lunacy. Oh, to dunk his head in cool water.

She said, "We all have sides like that."

He opened his eyes. "You couldn't possibly."

"Well, I'm not going to tell you about it. But that's the point. I wrestle internally. I've done things I'm not proud of."

Charlie.

"I'm human," she said softly. "I make mistakes, have dark thoughts."

Her eyes were red-rimmed. Yet true and kind. Had she been weeping with him? How pretty she was without makeup, showing her natural self.

She said, "You put me on a pedestal sometimes. You shouldn't."

Did he? "I'm sorry. I shouldn't have scolded you before, about him."

"You were right."

Yes, he had been that. They sat quietly. He was warm in the robe. His legs were brown and thick next to her slim ones stretched out in peach trousers. Her feet were not small, despite the sandals and the pink nail polish. He had an urge to grab her foot.

She nudged him. "I'm proud of you, you know. You went from a sweaty kid dancing in a living room to a skilled comic actor. Believe it or not, I never miss your show."

"Wow." Her words pinged inside him.

He said, "Here I thought you were a discerning viewer. You would remember me being sweaty. I'm horrified I let you slip."

"Yeah, that hurt. I think I hit a table."

"I saw your knickers." *Idiot.*

But she grinned. He smelled the talc again. A lovesick fool might want to count every one of her beach sand freckles.

She grazed his cheek with the back of her hand. "Your eyes…"

It warmed him below. *No, your eyes.* "Did you mean Dad or me? You were angry. I thought you were."

"No."

"You said I emerged from the pool like a… like a what?"

She blushed. "I think I'd rather not say."

"Is it bad?"

She shook her head. Such a dearest, wet-eyed look she gave him. He brushed away strands of hair and scarcely realized kissing her lips until she squeaked, and said, "It's hot in here."

"Isn't it? I'm roasting." He sloughed off the robe.

Her focus dropped. He hooted. "I'm not wearing anything!"

Put the robe back on. He didn't want to put the robe back on.

She said, "Look at your tan," and let out a loopy laugh that made him laugh, too. Yet her appraisal seared him.

Both moaned through a mouth-bumping, badly-needed second kiss. They kissed as if starved for each other. What lunacy!

Needing a moment, he mashed her close. Their hearts beat like trapped things. Her fingertips danced with electricity down his back, his waist. Then Poolside Jill took over. He rose on his knees. What heaven, being naked for her, letting her hands roam him (torturously) everywhere. "You're beautiful," she murmured. "Your skin... Love your smell."

It was maddening hard not to detonate under her ardency. (This was *Jill!*) A hiccup shot out of him. She laughed and cooled his face with kisses. He popped again. She caressed his throat, whispered, "What's happening to us? Are you all right?"

Another had done this. Memories boiled black inside him. Yet her lifeboat kisses rescued him to the present. Aching for connection with her, he realized what was in the way.

"I didn't wear the best bra," she protested, "I didn't know—" Arms up, faint onion whiff, and the damned thing was gone.

Half undressed, gorgeously transformed, she arched as he dragged off remaining garments. Freckles scattered and faded on the exposed beach of her, all warm skin and sea wetness, places to dive and explore. Her body was flushed and glistening. For him.

FELLED by another bombshell in so short a period, they lay flattened and apart. Ecstasy shut his eyes. He wanted to tell her he loved her.

He reached, and bumped her reaching hand. Both smiled. And gazed. Slowly, what had been done in haste was reverently repeated. Until the light in the room grew dim. Hours slipped by without words.

Fronds flickered on the palm trees below. White edges traced black surf. His voice cracked to speak in the darkness.

"Nice to see palm trees. They remind me of home."

She hugged his waist. "There are palm trees in St. Ives?"

How had she never been to St. Ives? The press of her body distracted.

WITH LAMPS on for a room service supper, Jill came naked from the loo. "This is a nice piece. When did you—?"

George knocked a glass of water at the sight of his necklace, blurted, "Jack gave it to me."

"I don't remember him buying it. Only a spill, honey, leave it. I don't care, you know."

She settled with a lovely wobble onto his lap. He managed to say, "But you might care. It was an early birthday present. He gave it to me in Blackpool."

She thumbed the coin, her brow furrowed. "Did he love you?"

He felt pinned beneath her. "It's boggling to talk about him. I doubt it."

She palmed his cheek. "Don't. It's okay. It's boggling that I married him. No wonder we weren't great in bed. I was so naive."

"I never knew why he wanted me when he had the most marvelous girl."

Her smile sparked his heart. He looped the necklace over her head. "I claim you with this."

THE REALITY of loss cut him anew. George sat up on the bed to ease the pressure in his sinuses and shut his burning eyes, a soggy handkerchief crushed in his fist. Jill didn't know his young dad had once been a frail target in the sky.

"A paratrooper? I heard about those landings before all the ships. He was lucky to have survived."

"He was a fit Cornish lad with all our swimming and cliffs. There were dicey hours in France. He helped a chap with a broken leg. Turned out the man was a peer. Those sorts are usually officers, unless he was a jumping officer." *Buggery Lord Kettering.*

George honked in the rag. "Anyway, he never forgot Dad and got him the job in London. Got me into his sodding school. Dad told me the story and said anyone would have done what he did out there."

"Oh, I doubt that. I had a bit of a crush on him that summer I stayed with you."

"Of course you did. Dad's a hero. I'm more a court jester."

He felt the metal of the necklace as she sat warmly against him. "I wasn't talking about your dad at the pool, by the way. It was you. Getting to me." She nipped his earlobe. "Had he met Lucy then?"

He leaned into her, loving her words. "Met her at a dance in London. Courted during the Blitz, can you imagine? Married her and got her to Cornwall for safekeeping. Not that she was happy there. But they were mad for each other."

Jill nuzzled his neck, her hand on his scalp. He grasped the silk of her inner thigh. They clicked off the lamp.

MORNING LIGHT PERVADED. George moved. An ache lanced his groin. "Ach! Pain."

Jill squeezed his shoulder. "I know."

"No, my nuts. Oh, oh, Lord." He rolled on his back, wincing. "They feel huge. Nothing can touch them." He kicked off the covers.

"Really?"

"Yes, really, delectable girl. Though it was worth every minute."

She looked sweetly mussed. He sought her again. Though trying to have her in the daylight proved a mistake. "I'm sore," she protested.

"This is killing," he agreed.

More intimacy in the shower, she put her soapy finger inside him, which caused a surge of emotion. Even he was surprised.

She blinked in the spray. "I've crossed a line."

He held her seal-slick body. "But you can touch me anywhere. I want you to. You're not him."

After, she left for her room to pack.

Lightheaded, he grabbed items for the journey ahead. How odd to don clothing again. As if he were covering an enchantment. Was her smell gone from his fingers? Why had they been so ruthless with the soap?

Yet he'd made love and Wilburn hadn't intruded. Or maybe because it *was* love, Wilburn didn't belong. The old man couldn't claim him. Not with this one. She'd dared to take back his body, even that intimate place. He belonged to her now.

He got to the lobby first. Donal rose to greet him. George blinked at the man's condolences. How awful to have to hear *that* now. The sight of Jill dragging suitcases claimed his attention. A porter rushed to help. George had to force his feet to move. How hard not to take her in his arms. Her body was covered, her face naked and amazing. Donal hung near them with an odd look.

In the dining room, Charlie signaled. Jill stalled, resistant. The man mimed concern, his paws on George's arm, and nodded to Jill. George told his boss, "We don't have much time." *She's not yours any longer.*

Charlie launched into plans about their American debut, things they ought to "think about on the plane." Jill clasped his fingers under the table. Pleasure flushed his cheek. How could Charlie not notice? A waiter brought coffee and Florida grapefruits.

Jill slid alongside him in the cab, thigh-to-thigh, placing his nuts on high alert again. He massaged her knuckles to keep from mauling the rest of her. Or he sniffed her fine, long hair that blew on his face.

Then they were mounting stairs to the door of a rumbling airplane. The Buddy Holly specs stayed in his jacket pocket. The only thing he needed to see was right beside him. Their seats thrummed. He caught her with an open-lipped kiss. Even here, the feelings surged —and she, sweetly receptive, until the acceleration of taxiing jolted them apart. Nervous laughter. She thumbed the lipstick from his mouth. A fellow passenger smiled.

∾

"GIRLS ARE STARING," she said in the Newark airport. "They think you're a Beatle. I've noticed people are more robust on this side of the pond. You are unnaturally healthy for a Brit."

He made a rueful sound. "I'm a fit Cornish lad."

Her heels clicked alongside as he steered her through the crowd, then stopped to buy her coffee, as any bloke would for his girl. Plus, Yanks weren't terribly good at tea.

He said, "I wish we weren't leaving yet."

She squeezed his arm. "There's so much I would show you."

Her eyes promised more than sightseeing. He nudged her to an alcove. "Oh," she sighed. It was heaven to steal a moment, even with the barrier of fabric, the return of coats. Did they look like lovers bracing for a separation?

A stewardess at the flight desk flashed interest in him. Eons ago, pulling a bird like that would've been a kick.

"Women look at you," she said again. "I mean, understandable. I need a cigarette. You made me forget about smoking."

"We ought to quit."

"Speak for yourself."

Both lit up when the cabin scented with tobacco. Jill ordered a Scotch. George declined a drink and gazed at fading light through the porthole of a window and tamped his cigarette at the halfway point. Was it wrong to be so happy? What horrors would he find at home? Grief raced to the forefront. Jill left her seat.

He was glad for a spate of privacy, and gave in to unraveled weeping. He'd packed away his snot rag of a hankie and had to use the cocktail napkin from her drink until it was almost in shreds.

The window showed a reflection. The sky was dark. She came back to her seat and ordered a refill. He reined in his tumult of emotion. She startled when he nudged her.

She mouthed, "How are you?"

"Not good, I'm afraid."

He squeezed her hand, glad not to be embarrassed about it. She would be with him for the bumps ahead. The stewardess brought her drink. He said, "I'd love a rum and Coke."

Luckily, the woman didn't ask for an ID. He swiped off his tie and opened the buttons at his neck. Jill downed more of her drink.

His arrived with peanuts. He dipped his napkin in it to cool his eyes. He should've asked for a dampened cloth. The Coke was fizzy, the rum a hot swallow.

Jill cleared her throat. "So. You're not going to like this, but, anyway, I think we should leave this here."

"I'm far too muddled to like much of anything."

Her look of distress made him straighten. "Sorry. What are we leaving?"

Her eyes were blue chips. "This. Us. It ends with this trip."

It was a kick to the windpipe. He gasped.

She said, "It was wonderful, love, but I've done a great wrong. It can't go home. Are you okay?"

His breath caught in his throat. "How… wrong?"

"Your dad would kill me. I should have resisted you."

Dad? He shut his eyes. "Don't be absurd. We're in love."

"I'm not being absurd. Don't assume I'm in love. I… reacted to you."

He gawked at her. She looked away from him.

He stared at the seat-back in front of him, not seeing it. "You wanted me. I felt how you kissed me."

"You're very compelling."

Blood shot to his face. "You're lying. I don't know why."

"You're nineteen!" she snapped.

A passenger turned to stare. She slumped down, whispered, "I'm thirty. Can you imagine how it looks? Pathetic. We have a professional relationship. Now I've broken that trust. I can't tie you down when your career is taking off."

"Why are you doing this?" His heart would jump from his throat.

"You deserve a full life."

"So you toss us away?"

She straightened. "It's what grownups do."

The statement made him tremble with rage. "I should've known you wouldn't—I *hate* you!"

She shrank from him. Then grabbed her bag and rose. "Don't worry. I hate me, too. There's an empty… I'll just go."

TWENTY

"You've Got to Hide Your Love Away"

(JOHN LENNON & PAUL MCCARTNEY, 1965)

THE THUNDER WAS BACK in his head. He caught surprised stares, a double take in Heathrow Airport. He ought to have been wearing his specs only he hadn't wanted to see. After Customs, he signed two autographs with a rictus smile and waited for Jill, who was rowing with an official. He felt exposed standing there like a bloody advert, his headache going fierce.

She joined him, muttering, "He had to see my work permit, never mind all the money I make for this country."

He said nothing.

He'd resisted her weeping on the plane when she was a few rows down, because it was *her* doing, this dagger to their hearts.

A familiar blur ahead—Uncle James. Good Lord. Toni Banks stood with him in a belted vinyl raincoat and white go-go boots, a silk scarf tied over her head. She said, "I'm so sorry," her slate eyes shining.

He embraced her and caught the whiff of strawberry. "How sweet of you to come."

Uncle James winked. "I didn't think you'd mind seeing your dance partner, lad." Then he mugged a serious look, with a shoulder pat. What presumption in the smoothly tanned face, Mr. "Come-at-Once."

For a moment Uncle James looked rattled. Then he recovered a smile. "I see you got some sun in Florida. Hello, Mrs. Stuart."

George unclenched his jaw and spoke to Toni. "You haven't met my agent."

But Jill looked so startled he nearly laughed. Toni had to introduce herself as he grappled for a chair, swamped by another wave of grief. He was back on his homeland with its low dark clouds, its cold rain. Unbearable after America. Someone rubbed his back.

It wasn't Toni. Her two boots shimmered before him. He took her in through beaten eyes.

She looked distressed. "What can I do? May I go to the funeral?"

"Would you?" he managed. "It's in Cornwall."

"That's what Leo said. He's going to go. I'd like to go with you, if I may."

The hand ceased on his back. Uncle James warned, "You're being noticed. Let's move."

∽

GEORGE PAID the expense of a hearse driving from London to St. Ives. He would've driven his shell-shocked mother, but with Toni along in the Jag, Uncle James took Mum and Jill in his car.

Joining the family in St. Ives was a relief, despite the jovial force clearly missing. Dad's history filled the old home, his visage etched in the faces of relatives. George hugged his way through damp-eyed condolences. "Look at 'ee, all tanned," Cousin Margie said, because of course he hadn't been home with his dad.

Grandy Morwen was slow to rise. He scooped her in his arms, her body lighter. She patted him. "He left us too soon, like his father. I put 'ee in the old room, love."

George dumped his things in the bedroom he'd once shared with Cousin Timmy, who now lived in town with a wife. The bunks had been replaced by a double bed. The fishing net looked ragged and gray on the wall, its shells and trinkets dimmed of their luster. Toy mountaineers still climbed the bottom edge.

Thank God for the view outside, a window-pelting West Country storm that had come up during the last hour of their drive. It smudged the landscape and darkened the sea.

Toni bumped in behind him. "Shall I be here with you? Otherwise, I'm to go to a hotel."

"Oh. No. Grandy would never approve. Sorry."

He turned back to the window.

GEORGE SET up his portable reel-to-reel tape recorder alongside Timmy's old gramophone and hauled in piles of records fingerprinted by clumsy cousins. His dad had always held records reverently by their edges. There were so many pieces to go through, and some were hard to listen to, but now selections were caught on a reel of tape. Aunt Sally would also play Dad's favorites on the piano, "On the Sunny Side of the Street" and "Skylark." Dad had passed along his fondness for Bossa Nova music to her, so she had sheet music for Jobim. Uncle Arthur was bringing his band of local musicians.

There were taps on the door. Yes, he was fine. No, he wasn't hungry. Could he have a beer? All right, he'd eat the bloody sandwich (he never did). He tamped out a forgotten cigarette. He beckoned in Toni to hear the dance-ability of certain songs, but she fretted about the weather. Then Timmy, Margie, and Irene crowded in, everyone too large for the room now. He sent them back out and shut the door.

A mistake to have played Barber's "Adagio for Strings." He felt a wreck on the bed, his specs pushed back on his head.

"George." Jill's voice. "How are you doing in there?"

He leapt up and stood sock-footed at the door. "All right."

His absurd heart pattered as he leaned in, body electrified by the nearness of a lover. She was close, yet said nothing more. Memories made him swoon. "You're wonderful," she'd poured in his ear long before her hateful words on the plane.

He clicked open the door. The hall was empty but for the hum of the wind and the sound of a distant radio.

THEY BURIED his father on a grassy moor overlooking the sea. The ground was sodden after the storm. Most put on wellies for the trek. A cold sun broke through the clouds, a patch of sea sparkled.

George braced his tottering mother, holding her close. Both of them wore dark glasses. He'd started the day with another bad head. Timmy had given him prescription pills that dulled the pain but made him a bit high. As the casket lowered, his heart leapt to his throat.

Mum nattered, "He was our pillar. He held us up. What are we but a pair of colorful awnings? What will we do?"

This is real, this is real. The last of Dad goes into the ground.

His mother gripped his jacket. "Gerry!" she shrieked. Relatives pulled her from his arms. He shivered because she was right. A three-legged stool could hardly stand on two. He swayed by the open grave.

Grandy nabbed his arm, said, "I've got him, Mrs. Stuart. Help with Lucy," and dragged him from a reaching Jill.

Grandy commanded him to look at the sea and rubbed his arms as if he were cold. His teeth were chattering though the weather was mild. "Margie," she cried. Cousin Margie rubbed his other side.

Something tugged deep inside of him. With a woozy tingle, he felt he might just... *No.* He pulled himself erect, a knife of pain in his skull.

Margie braced him, a place to lean. "Easy, lovey."

Grandy broke free to bend and weep, breaking his heart. Presently, she raised a tear-streaked face. "I'm off to get things started. Take your time, loves."

THE AREA around the bar was jammed. Uncle Arthur and his fellow musicians warbled a ballad. George swallowed another pill to help him through the socializing. His gait felt pillowed. Older ladies pressed food on him. He smiled, took a bite, moved on. If anything, he could do with a drink, though maybe not a *drink* drink. Had Jill just downed a shot?

Faces from long ago, old playmates gave a sock to his shoulder or thumped him in an awkward hug. Did they want to reminisce? No, they wanted to talk about the show. What was it like being famous?

"Completely and utterly barking," he said, which didn't seem to satisfy. His sheep farmer neighbor wondered what Cyril Hernshaw was like. George considered giving the same response.

"Shame he couldn't come." Farmer Hale threatened a pout.

George gave him a "buck-up" squeeze to his arm. Toni had come! What a dear girl. Oh, that's right, she'd ridden down with him.

The music switched to Pet Clark on the hi-fi while the musicians strode to the bar. "England Swings." *Really? At a wake?*

"Does that seem appropriate to you?" he said to no one. What had happened to his reel of tape?

Blessed Uncle Dan brought him a pint. He dipped into the frothy head and sucked it down. Then stifled a belch in view of his mum. Unsteady from her lie-down, black makeup ringed her eyes. Female relations ushered her along the buffet like an invalid.

He felt Jill's gaze. She turned away from him.

Bollocks on her. Making him famous so people thought him important. For what? Playing the fool? Surely, he'd done his part being social. He'd flee outside to wind and weather.

Aunt Sally blocked his exit and handed him sheet music, her eyes agitated. "We'd best do the Jobim now, lovey, right? Will you sing?"

"*Sing?*"

He was his dad's favorite singer, what a joke! Yet, bolstered by the pint, he scanned the Jobim songs and drifted to the mike stand. Aunt Sally settled at the grand. Pet Clark ceased. The crowd hushed. The Big Star was about to open his gob. He let go a laugh.

Plus, he was roasting. He used the piano intro to "Once I Loved" to loosen his collar, came in late on the song, then stopped.

Aunt Sally quit playing. Faces stared with concern. He shut them out. *Don't sing badly, not for Dad.*

He would ape Sinatra. Be the balladeer. He nodded to his aunt. She whirled through another intro. Uncle Arthur's band picked out a rhythm.

It turned out Jobim was hard to sing, notes that started high cascaded to very low. It was horrifying. Yet, somehow, he was on it, his voice elastic. He was almost swayingly stoned and able to soar or pull in softly. In the crowd, Jill gawped. A cousin knuckled tears. He closed his eyes. The lyrics flew from memory. Aunt Sally continued through the scattered applause, followed with "Meditation," a song about missing a loved one, an ache of a melody. Each word spoke of Dad. George hardly cared that tears bathed his face. His aunt played like an angel and his looseness held. Why did the applause sound like an effort? Aunt Sally pressed him for another. This singing felt like a badly needed workout.

He had nothing left after the third song. People crowded him as he tried to leave. Two local lasses vied to sleep with him! That toff, Lord Kettering, elbowed the girls, his eyes shining.

"Son, tonight you became a star."

Disgusted, George fled down a back stairway. Inside the kitchen pantry was his old hiding place, tight now. People went in and out and didn't see him crouched beneath a shelf. In the distance, the band resumed playing. His skin flamed with itching. No smokes in any pocket. How potty that he'd managed to sing like that. It seemed as if someone else had done it. Clattering steps and women's voices:

"Well, I'm a basket case now."

"Too right on that. I always sensed the child was different."

"Our Jory was special even as a wee one."

Toni's voice: "Sorry—have you seen George?"

Aunt Tiffany's voice: "No, love. But he can't have gone far."

Toni apparently left, because he heard his aunt say, "I s'pose she's a pretty thing, but she's got no meat on her bones."

"Aye. Those London girls don't eat," said his aunt's friend, Mrs. Sawle. "They go to finishing school. They shop and look smart. But can they cook a meal, I ask ye?"

"Jory can hire a cook. He'll marry a girl like that. Mark my words."

I won't. George scratched his ankles inside his socks.

"Have you talked to the director yet? A nice man and him comin' all this way."

Yes, it was nice. If George had any manners, he'd be out talking to Leo and Marie. A bouquet had come from everyone in Florida. How far away that seemed now, like a dream place. And what happened there a dream.

Mrs. Sawle said, "Come on, girl, let's have a little."

Glasses clinked. "The hair of the dog," Aunt Tiff said in a mannish voice that made him smile.

He was saddened when the ensuing quiet told him they'd gone off. He peered out the door. Jill!

He kicked a broom that fell forward with a crack. She cried out. Then darkened the pantry doorway. "There you are. Everyone's been asking for you."

He hiccuped and covered his mouth.

She knelt, black stockings strained at the knee, concern on her face.

He backed from her as if allergic. "It's barmy up there. I know everyone means well. But they want to talk about the *(hic!)* show."

Oh, this buggery business. He glared at a mousetrap on the dusty floor.

"You're hiding," she said softly.

Stray hairs floated from her up-do, her lashes sooty with mascara, freckles muted with makeup. "Am I giving you hiccups?"

"Did you like shagging me? Was I a good ride?"

She blinked at that, her color up. "I loved making love with you."

"Was that what it was? Well, it was for me. I don't know about— *(hic)* I could be a bastard to you."

"I understand."

His eyes stung. "Don't understand!"

"George. I'm sorry. There's so much we should talk about. Your singing was incredible."

"Scant applause. Lord Kettering said I became a star as if I wasn't one."

"People were crying, love, that's why you didn't hear much applause. You were an artist up there. You didn't just use your talent, you scorched us with your heart."

Odd to hear the word "artist" again. He said, "It actually felt good to sing, in a barmy sort of way."

He grimaced. "Let's not talk about me. What about you? What goes on in your head? I still see you sassy in the front room on the day we first met, fresh and, and like a new energy. I fell straightaway. I guess you'd call it 'love at first sight.'" The hiccups had stopped.

Her eyes shone with surprise. "I didn't know."

Their foreheads touched, mouths kissing-close. She reeked of Scotch and lavender. A tear spilled down her cheek.

She said, "You saw me as better than I was, than I am."

"I see you, boss. That's enough for me. Even though I don't think well of you now, not at all."

She laughed-cried. He stroked her downy cheek, busked her salty lips. "We mustn't," she mouthed against his lips.

It was hopeless. Sparks caught anew. They were out of the cupboard, through the kitchen, past startled guests, and down narrow steps to the sub-level and the washroom, that luckily had a door.

He resumed kissing her against her moans, backed her to the laundry table. She hitched her skirt. He dragged down her sheer black tights, fell to his knees and washed his face in her flesh, her ocean scent.

She cried out—a lovely sound—then muffled herself. He felt the quakes within her. She tugged his hair.

He rose and fitted himself, pushed through the hot ring of her—oh! Here was the place, the one place, to burrow—hide—run—die—oh—God. (She was off the ground, her leg going around.)

Yet amidst his thrusts broke thoughts of Dad, petals of Dad. *Why didn't I tell him the truth? Did he think I was angry?*

"Oh... no."

She said, "Don't stop."

Revulsion coursed through him. He deflated, pulled out.

That spicy scent… How could it be here? He affixed his trousers and glared around, even at the shadows.

"What's wrong?" she said behind him.

"I—what?" He raised an arm. "I'm losing my head."

He opened the door, flew up the narrow steps into the smoky hall, reversed direction from the rabble in the kitchen, and ran smack into Margie, who held him fast. "Where are you going?"

He surrendered to the raisin smell of her curls. Here was a pure place, a pre-Wilburn place.

She jerked him back. "You reek of fanny."

"Shhh." He let her go, but she snagged him again.

"Dousing yourself in snatch perfume? Who with, your dolly-bird, Miss Carnaby?"

He wrenched away. "Leave off! Don't talk like a slag."

She pushed him to the wall. "You're the slag. I guess you don't need my comfort then, eh?"

"Margaret!" snapped an aunt. Margie stalked to the kitchen.

TWENTY-ONE

"Visions of Johanna"

(BOB DYLAN, 1966)

Darling G, I'm going back to London. I'll care for you always. I'll stay your agent if you'd like. But you need time to grieve. I want you to have a full life. It may be there around you, but you don't see it because of me. I blame myself. Don't hate me. One day you may even be relieved. J.

HE SAT on the bed rereading the note as if he were missing something. Then he crushed it and threw it. Cousins burst in at his howl.

"Go away!" he shouted at their gawking faces. How would he get through the days, the hours? He writhed on the bed, bunching the quilt.

Presently, the room grew frigid. He rolled from the bed and twisted the knob on the radiator. It gave a feeble knock. Who dared to not fill the boiler? Crappy old heating in a crappy old house! Hadn't he poured enough money into it? Already Ethan had hit him up for cash. When would the others start asking? He'd be writing checks soon enough, the good old Bank of George.

He retrieved her note and smoothed it out.

What did you expect? You went barmy in the washroom, bollixed a great shag. She's the one relieved.

He ought never to have taken those pain pills. Last night, he'd fallen asleep when he should've sought her out. Yet he'd caught her gaze before retiring, her smile across a room like a promise. He'd woken with grief and hope, and let her sleep in as he went with his cousins to see Tim's house. And all the while, she'd been packing, planning her escape.

He thundered to the basement and blackened his hands filling the boiler. Why should he, a celebrity, be filling a boiler?

On the main level, his oblivious cousins were pouring at the bar, the lads flirting with Toni. Of course, they'd only lost an uncle. A welcoming fire roared in the hearth. Margie looked askance at him.

Timmy noticed him. "What's the matter?"

George said, "Nothing" as Margie said, "Don't ask."

"What's it to you?" he spat at Margie, who'd called him a slag.

"It's nothing to me. Have a drink."

She slid him a pint like the experienced barmaid she was. A pint was just what he needed.

Toni gaped at him. He roared, "Does no one tend the boiler round here? It was well low."

Timmy stopped Ethan from answering.

George took his ale to the hearth, with Dad speaking in his head, *What sort of behavior is this?* He blinked at the fire, dimly aware that people talked around him.

Drinks later, he had the grand idea of killing himself. It would serve Jill right. He shuffled upstairs, unable to decide on a method and ended up ringing her flat in Chelsea. No answer.

He hugged his sad, sweet grandy in the hallway, though she pushed, "Laddie, you smell of drink." Guiltily, he went back to the main level, considered eating, and passed out on a sofa.

He woke on the same sofa with a pounding head, the fleeting urge to be sick. It appeared to be morning. How had yesterday got away?

Margie eyed him as she picked up in the room. "What are ye gonna do about her? She's waiting."

"I don't know. Do you really think she's waiting?"

Margie smacked his bum. "Not *her*. The other one, Miss Carnaby. Ethan's been gawking and followin' her about."

"Miss who?" But he realized as he sat up, head throbbing. "Ethan's seventeen." He straightened his twisted sweater and vest.

Toni joined them looking like a girl on holiday and donned a look of sympathy. "How are you?"

"Beastly head."

She sat. "Perhaps we could go away together, later or sometime?"

He couldn't summon an answer. Sure enough, Ethan sidled in and threw them a glance. The lovesick dog.

In the kitchen, George downed aspirin and drank a badly needed tea since no one had coffee. Arrayed on a platter were various rolls from the bakery. He wolfed three. Toni chatted with Timmy's wife, then joined her for a walk on the ridge as if they'd become mates.

Upstairs, in one of the expensive bathrooms he'd had installed, he assessed his miserable state. His shaggy hair twisted with curls. A dusting of bristles lined his jaw. He only had a will to brush the foul taste from his mouth.

The bed in the old room creaked with his weight. But lying down called up a crueler pain. Why wasn't Dad here? How was he supposed to live not seeing his precious parent again, never hearing his wisdom nor seeing the pride in his gaze? A hand clasped his shoulder.

George froze, whispered, "Dad?"

He rose quietly, hyper-aware. And knew it happened.

The house was a series of creaks, scarcely any human sounds at all as if everyone had melted away. In the scullery, he tugged on wellies, a jacket, and stole a cigarette from someone's abandoned packet. He'd quit smoking later.

The sea was a haze, only the curling surf visible. *Are you here?* He kept absolutely still. Until the fag end burned his fingers. He dropped the cigarette and crushed it.

A manure scent drew him to the neighboring sheep pen, where he clucked to the animals nosing under his hand. Moisture sparkled on wool ready for shearing. No telling which one was Cloud.

A female voice called him. The sheep scuttled. Toni climbed the hill in her flat London shoes, too slippery for this ground. He offered his hand, but Ethan shouted from the house.

His younger cousin looked spooked. "You've a telephone call. It's someone from *The Harry Black Show*."

Relatives clustered by the wall phone in the kitchen with expectant faces. George wrestled off his boots then picked up. "Yes?"

"Mr. Hartley—George—so sorry to ring you at your home."

It was an annoying chap he remembered meeting, who went on, "Do accept our condolences from Mr. Black and all of us here. Your agent thought it might be good to ring with happy news."

The pause was a little too long. "That it would be," he said, sounding like Dad.

"I'm sure you can guess. We want you to dance on the program. Mr. Black was delighted about the prospect."

He felt a beat of pleasure, though really, he expected this. "I'm going to dance," he mouthed to his relatives.

Toni stepped close with a hopeful look. "Super," he said. "So I'll be doing the 'Taste of Honey' number with Miss Banks?"

"Er, no. Just you. We thought the Cozy Cole number was more the ticket."

"Miss Banks has danced on telly before," he pressed because of the girl's worried face. She detailed her other appearances at him, as if he didn't know.

The voice in his ear said, "Yee-esss. She's not really known. Mr. Black didn't want her."

He shook his head. Grandy and Aunt Sally patted his crestfallen partner, though he had to agree. The jazzy Cozy Cole dance was the better option.

"It will all be terribly modern. We see you in black, surrounded by young chaps in contrasting patterns—"

He snapped, "No! No men. Too many people think I'm queer. I want girls."

"Ah, right. Girls it is, no problem."

"And I want to come in first and view the set."

"Of course, Mr. Hartley. We can arrange that."

George rather liked the man's shift in attitude, but Toni and his female relatives appeared indignant.

After ringing off, and after Toni was guided away with sisterly sympathy, his grandy blocked his path.

"So that's how ye talk to the man from *The Harry Black Show*, is it?"

"Grandy. This is how it's done, you don't know."

"So you forget yourself with *me* now? Did we raise ye to speak that way to your elders, and people offering you a fine opportunity, and shouting you want girls in front of the poor miss who's soft on you and won't get to dance on telly?"

He flapped his arms. "I'm sorry but—"

"Heed me, boy. Don't go high and mighty in this house. You have manners to those tryin' to help you. Are ye hearin' me?"

Mortifying, to be spoken to like this!

"You're not a telly star in this house. You're still a Carveth, though you go changing your name… and you'll be…" her voice choked, eyes glistening, "remembering that."

"Yes, ma'am," he said, shaken.

She waved him off and started the tea.

He felt horrible. Margie took his hand and coaxed him upstairs to her corner bedroom. His ridiculous photo was hung here as it was in other rooms. He put it face down.

She said, "Hey, what're you doing? Ah, come here now." She lay on her bed, arms open.

She was full-bodied, soft and motherly in a loose-weave jumper, her hair a tangle of dark curls. He finally had a couple inches on her in height. Her face was dear and familiar. She wanted to kiss as they had when they were younger. He felt a slight repugnance and broke off.

She said, "So you're not going to kiss me now?"

"Don't *you* start."

"Ach. You've forgot what it feels like with 'er. She did lose a son."

Grandy's pain felt too much to bear. He noticed a burn spot on the ceiling. Margie's kisses on his cheek were ticklish. "Don't." He turned away from her. Then rolled back. "Thank you for loving me, Marge."

A huff. "It seems there are plenty who do that."

He faced her. "You're the very most important one of all."

"Don't butter me up, Butterfly Boy."

He grinned. Her mouth twitched in a smile. She tickled where his sweater gapped from his hip-hugger cords. He warned, "Don't."

She said, "So your agent's right fond of you."

He looked at the burn on the ceiling.

"Couldn't take her eyes off you. Miss Perfume coming from the washroom and tugging her skirt—"

He rolled off the bed, then whirled. "Don't speak ill of her, don't you dare! You've no idea."

"Easy, boyo. We're worried about you."

"Well, don't be. I look after myself."

"Don't attack me, tiger. I'm defenseless, I swear."

"You? I'd hate to see a tiger in a ring with you. It'd be the one needing a chair."

She looked so offended he had to laugh.

He joined her again, and closed his eyes, happy to drift in afternoon blindness. Safe in her room above the sea. Her breath beat warm. She stroked his cheek. "Someone needs a shave."

Her touch sparked the memory of other fingers and fierce desire. *Don't think about it.* He felt her head on his shoulder.

"So you don't fancy the dolly-bird."

"Her name is Toni."

"As I was saying, you don't fancy Miss Carnaby, the dolly-bird."

He opened his eyes. "She's a nice girl."

"Then why aren't you with her?"

"Because I don't fancy her. It was sweet of her to come. But I wish she'd go."

Though he sensed a gulf had opened with his family as if too much had happened in the ten years since he'd left. As if Toni was more his speed. He put his arm round his cousin. "I'll break her heart."

"You will," she answered breathlessly as he lifted her hair from her neck. He flinched at her hand beneath his sweater.

She said, "I suppose you've had lots of lovers."

He grew warm down below. "Perhaps."

"'Perhaps,' he says. How long ye been doing the deed?"

"Since fourteen with females." He belatedly heard the slip.

"Go on, fourteen? Who with? Some chippy at your school?"

He seized her wandering hand. "There were no lasses at my school. Why do you care? Do you have lovers?"

"I'm no virgin, if that's what you mean."

He raised his eyebrows. She said, "I can enjoy a pint and a dance at the pub, and who knows what after."

"Margaret Susan."

"I can if I like. I'm older'n you. You didn't answer the question."

He wasn't sure he liked Margie giving herself to local pub-goers. "A housewife in Clapham."

"A married lady? Dirty old thing, going after you at fourteen. What d' you mean 'with females'?"

His mouth went dry as he considered responses.

She propped. "What happened?"

"Nothing. I mean… I had an affair with one of my schoolmasters. I'm not a poof or anything. It was just an experience. No one liked me," he said to her look, his face warming. "He was nice to me. He loved music and, after a while, you know, things happened."

It sounded like a natural buildup. But she gawped as Jill had.

He said, "Honestly! You should see your face."

"He molested you?"

"Oh, bugger, it wasn't like that. I mean I let him."

She frowned. "But what did he do, exactly?"

"What do you think? We had sex, exactly. It went on for a while. It was an experience." He picked at a loose thread on the counterpane.

"Did he hurt you?"

"Yes! No. I'm fine. It ended. I was too far into puberty, not so attractive." He smirked. Margie looked horrified.

He said, "Oh Lord. I shouldn't have told you."

"Do your parents know?"

"Of course not. Don't you say anything. Mum doesn't need to know."

"But you should tell somebody."

"I'm telling you."

"You, poorest poor lamb."

"For God's sake. Don't worry about me *now*. No one worried about me then. I was 'ungrateful' then. I didn't appreciate such a fine school."

"We thought you'd become grand and standoffish."

He huffed in remembrance and pulled at the loose thread. "Anyway, it's history, water under the bridge and all that."

HE FELT IRKED LEAVING Margie's bedroom, as if he hadn't explained things properly at all. Toni loitered with suitcases in the hall.

"I think it's best I go. Could you give me a lift to the station?"

"Where are you going?"

"Home. I just wanted to say goodbye to your—" He took her wrist. "Why? Where do you want to go?"

"Someplace far. I really can't stay here another minute."

"My parents have a cottage in Windermere. It's vacant now."

"Could we? Let me pack."

What relief at the thought of driving away. They found Mum and Grandy in the kitchen. Mum hugged Toni, and told him she'd see him in London. He felt awkward with his grandy, jarred by the age in her.

"You're in specs."

He lagged at Toni's surprise, then loaded suitcases into the boot of the Jag. She smiled. "They make you distinguished."

She beamed as he sped along the motorway. Maybe her mood would infect him, as well. He admired her profile, her teacup breasts in a pale pink sweater. They wended northeast, ultimately for the Cumbrian Mountains and the Lake District, quite a trek. He didn't care if he drove all night. Perhaps he'd make love to her. Jill no longer had a claim on him. She'd thrust him out for the world. And Toni was a tasty morsel for any man.

Still in Devon, they stopped at a farmer's cottage that advertised a room and pretended to be married. Toni was sure the proprietor would recognize him. He whispered, "He's too busy for telly."

Despite his yawns, Toni donned a negligee. Making love felt impossible, especially in someone else's house. Or was that what she slept in? What kind of man was he not to make love to a sexy girl?

He undressed but left on his underwear. Then put his socks and sweater back on until she asked what he was doing. He stalled, unsure, removed his specs, and sloughed back to his underwear. He peeled her slowly. Her slim, neat body sparked a response. *This was the way sex used to be.* Though he fantasized Jill to sustain his erection until Toni came, or seemed to come, and then worked on himself as she washed in the loo. Not that he was interested anymore.

She wanted to snuggle. Thankfully, her quiet snores came soon enough. His mind seemed to grow more awake. What was he doing in this stranger's house, in a strange bed, with the wrong lover? That sort of lovemaking would never do. It was substandard.

Damn you, boss. If Jill wouldn't love him, then he had to release her from his mind, shed her, shake her off. It was ridiculous to shudder over perfectly sexy women. He may as well go queer again.

He wished for a pair of pajamas now, thick, woolen ones, so that no part of Toni could touch his skin. He eased away from her as best he could. And now he'd blathered all his muck to Margie. At least he'd left that depressing old house.

He felt for the coin of his necklace, then remembered where it was. Let it torment her! He felt weirdly disconnected. No home. No dad. No Jill.

∽

THE BANKS FAMILY cottage looked out on an inlet of the enormous lake. It was a stone house with a wood-planked floor. There were crocheted grandmotherly effects here and there for quaintness, plus a ratty looking piece of carpet in the sitting room, that contained worn furniture from the 1940s, as well as a large blank area where a television was normally kept. Toni's dad didn't like to keep a telly in an empty cottage where prowling, northern "rockers" could break in and pinch it. In the large bedroom, the bed was a brass four-poster, soft and squeaky. The smaller bedroom with its narrow twin beds had been for the two Banks girls.

George masked his disappointment. For Toni's family, this little house was a prize and worth the long drive to the end of the world. He had to staunch the bleeding in his soul that it was a mistake to have come here, that he wouldn't make it. *Don't lose it. Be a man now.*

He said in a controlled voice, "I think I'll have a walk outside."

"I'll go with you."

"No. Please. I-I need some time."

He caught a flash of hurt before she said, "Of course. I'll unpack."

He charged off, keeping lakeside, wanting cigarettes. They'd passed a house coming in. Maybe there was a woman there to share a smoke and stir his blood. She'd be a fan of the show and beg to suck his cock. The husband would want to fuck him. He'd have one on each side. A dog would sniff their sweaty arses. It would end with a pie in the face and a spray of seltzer.

George bent to laugh or cry—who could tell anymore? He crouched on the chilly grass. Wind combed the lake and sliced through his jacket. At least they were by water. He must always live by water. The Banks cottage seemed to lie across a chasm. What if he slept outside? Toni would wonder, of course.

Light flared in a back window. Somewhere inside, she hung clothes and brought out blankets. It even looked a comforting place in this northern valley penned by mountains. All it lacked was a trail of wood smoke from the chimney. The least he could do was light a fire for the evening and try to sleep with her. *Don't start shaking.* He wasn't about to be trapped in a hotel room with a huge, bony man, for God's sake. Though the thought of being pinned and fucked held a perverse comfort.

THE LOVEMAKING WAS ANOTHER STRUGGLE. He bucked on the squeaky bed as if he could shake off the phantom Wilburn, then rolled over and let Toni be on top, which made him feel less exposed. She soon wanted to switch again. He had an orgasm on her tummy, not inside her, despite her Dutch cap. After her scrupulous cleanup, he dropped off to sleep in a cocoon of covers.

And made love at dawn. Jill's fullness was beneath him, his face in the silk of warm breasts, prick buried to the hilt, snug in the grip of her, her voice soft as a breath. "You're wonderful."

Realizing the unreality, the cruelty, he moved against the mattress. His erection slid into nothing. Desire hung in a warm rush of blood.

It really happened. She's not here. Dad is dead.

A morning storm rattled the windows. The scuffing sound of slippers brought him back to reality. Water drummed in a teakettle. He lay beneath a heavy pile of quilts and slid his naked arm and shoulder back underneath and feigned sleep when the girl approached.

His heavy layer was thrown off. Freezing air claimed him. Then the petal touch of her lips. He masked his recoil with a twitch and looked back at her. "You like my bum, eh?"

"All untanned, it looks like a peach."

He twitched his arse and she cupped him. She climbed on the bed in her silk dressing gown, already smelling of her toilette. He stayed uncovered, wanting more. "You like how I look?"

"Very much. You're like a big cat."

"Ooo, will you whip me into submission?"

She looked thrown, so he snared her and loosened her gown, exposing one little poached egg breast then the other. She arched the more he kissed and softly bit. Was it a tiger she wanted? He made growling noises and nuzzled downward, her scent getting worriedly more floral. The teakettle whistled. She edged out.

"Don't wear the robe." He wrenched it off of her.

She stood surprised and exposed. He stuffed the garment beneath him and donned his specs. "Go on. Get my tea."

She left defiant, slippers scuffing, her own bum looking tasty.

Shivering, he pulled up the bedclothes. And relished the view of her coming in with the tea tray.

She set it down, then lunged for the robe. "It's chilly!"

"I see that."

She was easy to fight off. The tussle excited him. He nearly said she should learn to enjoy her body more, as a certain person had once said to him. Her cold, hard nipple grazed his arm. He gave her the robe. "I'm sorry."

"Beast. Try me in warmer weather."

She covered her sweet form, not joining him in bed but taking a chair nearby, not that he blamed her.

They supped their tea. This was cozy. *I'm scum.* These moments took the edge off. *Just pretend.*

"It hasn't stopped raining since I've been back on British soil. It's like a reminder of…" He swallowed.

She sat forward. "We can talk if you need to."

"But I don't need to. It's monstrous, and I don't…" He blinked back the danger of tears. "Anyway, it's nice here."

"Yes," she said, "it's lovely. I'm sorry for you, but I'm happy."

He did a gasp like a laugh. "One of us ought to be."

"You will be again. I know it."

He mopped his face with the sheet. The glasses bumped, heavy on his nose. Wetness smeared the lenses. The damn things were always bending his eyelashes.

He said, "You shouldn't want me, love. You're a good girl. I'm a shit who's done bad things."

She radiated concerned. "No one's a saint. Your grandmother seems to think you're pretty wonderful."

"Does she? No, but I've, ah, fiddled about with the lads, you know, in school. Sexually."

Her teacup clinked. "I've heard about that sort of thing occurring. I don't think it's terrible. As long as you don't still do it."

He gave a surprised smile. "I'm quite off boys, I can assure you."

"Did you beat little boys for burning your toast?"

"Certainly not. I hated that business."

"There you are."

Indeed, there he was. Not all *that* bad. What an understanding girl. Perhaps he'd landed a gem. Could he be that lucky?

Later, after building a fire in the hearth, he found a book, *Oliver Twist*, and began reading. At least there was no shortage of books. His grief sat huge in the room like a great, hungry bear. But he needn't pay it attention. It was cozy here with his graceful girl.

Who'd put on a cropped sweater with ski pants and short boots as if they were on holiday in a chalet. The ski pants clung to her bum. Perhaps he might have another go at being the lover.

She tried baking biscuits from the few ingredients they had in the larder, but the biscuits came out hard, even after a dunk in tea. They found a block of cheese and cut away the mold. There were leeks and potatoes for soup.

George was fully absorbed in the Dickens but hated how the adults were treating Oliver and had to stop reading. In the afternoon, she napped on the bed as the soup simmered low. Everything was quiet but for the wash of rain. A glowing log collapsed in the fire. There wasn't even a radio. *I'm trapped.* (The bear saw its opening.)

Nonsense, he could flee if he wanted. He could leave her the car and walk to London, like Oliver. It made him smile: *Jamie Harrington hitchhikes to London in the back of a lorry with menacing goats.* His grief was not so easily distracted. But he was used to distracting predators. He practiced his dance for "The Harry Black Show" light-footed to not wake her. *You've gotten so good,* the man had said. A pipe was puffed. Memories fumbled his feet. He was forgetting steps! He restarted the song in his mind. It was better when the music dictated the steps rather than matching steps to music. Sometimes he felt a move should be different than what Mr. Olivetti had choreographed.

The picture window looked out on their finger of the lake. If only he could swim. He'd sort the dance in a swim. He leaned into the cold pane of glass.

Darling dear, I need you. Please help me.

How could he hate someone he loved so much? But he could phone her. She'd be at work now. An operator made the connection. The number rang distantly.

"Good afternoon. Stuart-Johnson Agency."

He spoke quietly. "Hello, Vera? It's George."

"Oh, hiya. Aw, how are you doing down there, love? I'm so awfully sorry about your dad."

"Thanks. Is she in?"

"Yeah, sure. Hang on."

His heart thudded. But that was okay. They'd have it out, as they should. A momentous change had occurred between them. A discussion was in order. He'd leave at once for London. He'd inform Toni, it was only fair.

Vera said, "Er, I'm sorry, love. I'm afraid she's not available."

A lie. A sucker's punch, like that of an angry youth in a courtyard. "I see," he forced. "When should I ring again?"

"Ah, not sure. She's heading out for an appointment… that could run long." Vera sounded uncomfortable. "I'll tell her you phoned?"

He rang off, lightheaded.

Shadow George awoke on the floor, always on the floor. He scrambled up. His other self raged, ready to tear out his hair—she wouldn't even *talk*, leaving a coward's note, right when you thought you knew a person and had given your heart—!

He convulsed from the blow of it, and staggered.

A rhythmic snore sounded in the other room. The girl Toni was deep in slumber. Shadow George groped his way through the cottage and fought not to lose himself—this pulling inside, this tingling. But George must need him for something.

The view out the window blurred. Then sharpened. The lake seemed mild, pitted with rain. He had no swimming costume, not that that had ever stopped him before. Sod it! Off came the woolen jumper, his trousers, his socks, and pants.

Shadow George ran naked through the purifying rain, and with a whoop, he plunged off a pier into the sizzling lake. It was a shock, so cold it burned. He thrashed to warm up, grunting with the effort. Nothing like a jolt of life. Trouble was there'd been far too many jolts of late. His blood wasn't heating. *Keep moving.* His limbs ached. *Too cold.* Looking back, the cottage was a dark blur on the landscape, the nearest jut of land a rain-flattened bank of yellow grass. He couldn't decide which way to go. While a girl slept, he would sink in a northern lake, one frenzied moment before slipping into blackness.

"Move."

He jerked and looked about. The downpour pelted the surface with a spray that went up his nose. *Too much. Can't breathe.* The bank of grass wasn't far. With a whip-like action, he propelled forward. Only a little way. He stroked, but a shiver of pain went from his fingers up his arm, sluggish, a nagging ache in his feet. Shadow George could no longer help his other self.

Oh, to let go.

Muck and heartbreak curtained. The roar of rain muted. *Down.* He was under the water. *Down.* Last bubble trail. Skin flayed, burning. Limitless space. I always thought I might drown in St. Ives Bay. *I am the same sea. I tried to take you as a lad. I claim you now.*

Dad brushed near. Who knew he dwelled in water?

But that made a blowtorch of fear. Shadow George was up like a shot breaking the surface, gasping in a shower of pellets, and plodding with leaden limbs. Everything hurt, it was hard to breathe, but not impossible. Keep moving. Curtains of rain blinded. His knee bumped a rock, a lovely pain. His feet found a muddy, gravelly, shifting bottom. Fingers clawed at mud, pebbles, a grassy bank. He would've collapsed on it gratefully, but cold air gave him all-over tingles. His legs and joints were stiff, with needles in his feet.

Yet he moved, a freed thing. Sharp objects jabbed him underfoot. Stalks of high grass swiped his flank. His hair felt like icicles. The cottage was close. He tried to run. His feet were like stumps.

Toni whipped open the front door and cried out. She disappeared for a moment then met him with a towel, pulling him in with surprising strength. "You were in the lake! Your lips are blue."

He fell forward onto the ratty carpet. His teeth chattered. "Are there icicles in my hair?"

"No, it's wet."

She threw towels at him though he was too stiff to use them. Her face was fraught with concern as she rubbed down his legs, his feet. He was safe, dear God, the fool was safe. Rain drummed the roof, unable to penetrate. Kiss me. He thought he'd said it aloud. His lips were numb.

She placed a towel beneath his head and tucked the heavy bed quilt over him. After a while, he felt the roar of the banked fire in the hearth. Then she got under the quilt and laid herself on him, instant heat at last. A blank nothingness fuzzed his mind as if he might go under the water. "Help me," he gasped.

Her cheek pressed his. "You're all right. You're safe now, honey."

"I'm not… please."

"You are, I'm here for you. Take my warmth. You won't believe this, but I woke up with a feeling of something wrong."

"You care." She was a gem. "You should… marry us."

"Oh!" She lifted her face. "Yes, I will marry you and take care of you. You need someone, my angel."

She kissed him fiercely, taking his breath, then laid her cheek to his. With services rendered, Shadow George faded out.

TONI DROVE them from the Lake District to her home. Then George slid to the driver's seat and headed to Clapham to check on his mother. Only he was so exhausted on arrival he nearly toppled inside the front hall. Mum helped him up to his old bedroom. A doctor was summoned, a beef tea made. He was diagnosed with the flu.

"Sorry, Mum," he croaked when the doctor left. "I meant to take care of you."

"Nonsense. I must say, you've grown rather large for this bed."

Rain spattered the window. Clapham Junction rumbled with activity. The sound of trains sounded like home. He was glad to be here instead of in his lonely flat in Kensington.

His beautiful mother sat on the bed. Gray tufts showed in the black hair. Her deep-set eyes looked sunken. Yet her skin was fine and fondness lit her gaze.

"Your birthday is coming. My bit of spring in the winter. When you were a child, you danced all the time. Daddy would stop me from whatever I was doing, and we'd spy on you through the window. You'd be doing your butterfly dance."

"It wasn't to *do* with butterflies."

"You liked them when you were small. Dad called you 'our sprite.' It almost seemed you were a gift from another world."

"I felt a freak later, like I wasn't supposed to dance."

Her brow pleated. "He told off your uncles. He said 'don't break that marvelous spirit. You let him enjoy his childhood.'"

What would his strong dad have said to the schoolmaster? He would have taken him down. Though Wilburn would've fought, he would've said what George had done.

"Now I'm a big fright," he quipped, meaning it as a joke, though she didn't take it that way. "Have I disappointed you? You sent me away. I didn't like the school. Or this house. I didn't go to university."

Her eyes gleamed. "That wasn't your fault. It was ours, your ignorant parents. You've pleased us immensely. Yours is the dearest face your dad and I could look upon."

"I wish I could be with him. Don't you? I tried. I went under the water at Windermere, but got scared."

Her face leached of color. "Your father would not want you with him, I can assure you."

"I felt him under the water."

She leapt off. "Don't do that, do you hear? Don't make me worry!"

"No, Mum."

She paced the room. He oughtn't to have told her. Now he felt hot, his headache returning.

HE WOKE IN THE NIGHT, achy, desperately low. He escaped the clutches of his childhood bed, crept downstairs, and perused titles on the bookshelves. There were soft, worn books about far-off Tibet, part of his bloodline, after all. It might be worth a read.

But the books were fantastical—yellowed pages about shamans and obscure rites, recorded by a skeptical French woman who, in a later volume, made it to the sacred city of Lhasa disguised as a native. He found her companion book on Buddhism, taking it for context, still in the grip of her amazing stories. These ancestors came from a place more bats than India. At least they were only a small part of his blood.

Yet they lived in his dream, religious men who glowed, these "lamas" speaking in a strange tongue. George sat naked and sweating in the snow while lamas danced in pointy hats. He came to in damp sheets. A plug-in fire glowed in his bedroom.

Hadn't he read somewhere of a Tibetan lama in Scotland? Why Scotland? Because it was cold and mountainous. It would be daft to go there.

Activity sounded below. George gathered the books from the floor, stowing them on the nightstand, his thoughts still whirling. The Buddha had actually admitted life was suffering.

Female voices sounded, a fruity scent wafted. Toni appeared. "Your boyhood room, I love it. Hello, invalid."

Mum came behind her. "Toni, might I impose on you to look after him? I must run some errands."

"Of course, Mrs. C. Take your time. Though I may *steal* him for a while." Toni beamed.

In her short skirt and patterned tights, could the girl be any cuter? Mum glanced at the books on his table.

"I'm not sure he should be out. Take his temperature first."

"He'll be in good hands, don't worry." Toni winked.

Her energy grounded him to the known world. She dawdled through the sounds of his mother leaving the house as if waiting to kiss him. He rose expectantly.

But she hissed, "You're still in bed. Didn't you get my note? Mummy and Daddy are expecting us at five. They're keen to meet their future son-in-law."

"Oh! Right."

The mention of marriage. Was that her unopened envelope beneath the books?

He felt odd about that business. Shadow George had been the one proposing. After botching the suicide. Not that George was against marriage. It could be viewed as something shocking, victorious, a respite from loss.

Toni perused his room. "I kept ringing your flat, then rang here. Speaking of, you haven't bought a ring yet, have you?"

"I've been ill in bed."

He recalled urgency, his birthdate a target.

She said, "No matter. It would be better if I chose it with you since I'll be wearing it for the rest of my life. We won't stay out long. We'll make an appearance, probably drink champers. Have you a suit here?"

"The garment bag." He hauled himself up. "Do you *really* think I should meet your— Be ready in a jiffy," he said to the look on her face.

He went to the bath for a quick scrub and toweled off, shivering, despite being in the warmest upstairs room. Dad's robe hung on a peg. Toni startled in the doorway, saying, "You will shave" as a half question, half command. He shaved. Then sat on the toilet seat as she swiped his hair with straightening gel, declaring his hair too long.

When he was properly trussed in a suit, she asked him to wear his glasses then changed her mind. He fetched the car keys, but she said, "Darling, you oughtn't to drive. I have the Morris."

"We should talk about this," he said in her Mini car. "You know, perhaps a longer engagement?"

"Two weeks will be hard enough to bear. I long to care for you, dance with you, love you." She snared him at a stoplight.

He detached her. "No snogging. You'll catch my illness."

If only he had a clearer memory of the intent of this proposal. Especially if Shadow George was merely another part of his own self, as Jill had claimed: "We all have sides like that."

Another part of his *own self*?

That did things he didn't like. All that sex.

At the family home in St. John's Wood, Toni's cool, elegant mother gave George the once-over.

"Well done, Antoinette," she declared, eyes alight, blonde-haired like her daughter, the sort of handsome older woman he would have happily—his sexual radar was going off. Here was someone he'd shag but not want to shag.

Mrs. Banks said, "Isn't this one the star?"

"Mummy, I *told* you he was Jamie Harrington."

"Oh, who remembers names? But the face…"

Dr. Banks peered over his specs at George's hair, his own head closely shorn, and led him to an office.

"You're the hairy dancer my daughter intends to marry."

"Sorry?" George felt perspiration seep under his arms.

"Her dance partner? I presume you like women? One can never be sure. Do you think that's enough of an income?"

"Well, I don't actually dance, I mean, sometimes I do. But I act on the program, sir."

"Ah, you've a part on the show?"

Rather a large part. Hadn't he heard his wife?

The man rose and poured a drink. George rose, too, wanting the burn on his throat. The doctor gazed out the window. "My daughter is a lovely girl. She could have her pick of men."

George sat, drink-less. "Yes. She is a lovely girl, indeed." *He hates me.* Sweat trickled from his hairline.

"I hope you love her. I don't want to ever hear of you hurting her."

George withdrew his handkerchief and dabbed. Lamas danced in his vision. "No, sir."

Dr. Banks hovered close. "Young man, you're flushed." George flinched at a hand on his forehead. "You ought to be in bed. You'll infect us all." The interview was at a close.

They rejoined the women. Mrs. Banks dove in for a hug. "So happy for you."

"Suzette! The boy has a fever."

She sniffed him. George could smell his rising perspiration. Fingers grazed his bottom! He blurted out, "Toni-love, we should tootle off now."

Dr. Banks concurred. "Put this boy in bed and you come back."

Toni said, "Oh, Daddy, that's no fun."

"It won't be any fun catching his infection. Off you go, cricket."

Father kissed daughter. George bolted for the door.

BLOODY SHADOW GEORGE getting him into fixes. Yet he felt so real at times. Surely there were others with two personalities.

No one he knew, though. Jill had fled their involvement. Leo had wanted to send him to a headshrinker.

He would've escaped into sleep, but happy Toni was determined to make him hot tea with lemon. She lingered in the Clapham kitchen that she called "perfectly adorable," but really looked small and shabby after the Banks home. He said, "Left cupboard... your other left."

Her skirt rode close to the bum whenever she reached. Toni squirmed from his grasp. "Don't distract me."

The front door opened, his mother just getting home. He saw her eyes were swollen. She'd had a cry somewhere.

She took in his suit, not pleased. "You went out."

Toni came from the kitchen. "My fault. I brought him to my parents for a visit. In fact, we have news." Toni shot him a look.

George forced a gay, "We've decided to marry."

Mum plopped to a chair. Then gawked at Toni. "You're not…?"

Toni laughed. "Oh no."

Not what? Surely Mum would tell them not to do this potty thing.

Toni said, "We thought we might wed on George's birthday at the Registry—a small wedding, with family, no need for anything large." Her voice softened. "I know this is a difficult time. I do love him, Mrs. C. I only want to take care of him."

He looked at the girl. He needed care, lots of it. She gazed on him, a loving nurse.

Mum's shock melted to a smile. "I should like him to be cared for. I would feel better. A wedding would be joyful, something to take the mind off—"

Toni leapt to hug her, flashing more thigh. Taking the mind off was absolutely necessary, carving it out even better.

Rosy-faced, Mum said, "I suppose you'd better start calling me 'Mum.' Have you told Jill?"

Now his legs gave out, bum smacked to cushion.

Toni said, "Oh yes, do ring her."

"No! I mean she may not approve, bad for my image. Mum, would you tell her? I would, but there's so much to do. Would you phone her later, not now?"

"Of course. Two weeks. You've no time at all. We ought to plan a luncheon or supper. Toni, we'd best make a list."

"I've already started one. It's in my handbag."

George shivered, his tea with lemon forgotten. So much for being cared for. He took himself upstairs. The bedroom was frigid, the linens clammy. Perhaps he'd phone for a cab and ride to Jill's. She'd throw her arms around him. Or shut the door in his face.

She'd pushed him to have a full life, and so he would. Why not marry, buy a house, and have procreative sex? He hadn't envisioned such a future. Now it was here, why not claim it? It was either that or run off to Scotland to find that lama.

THE ILLNESS WAS LEAVING his body. It felt better to be up and clean than glued to a bed and a book, though he might hang onto the book on Buddhism, just to finish it. He broke the news of going back to his flat over tea in the kitchen.

Did panic flash on his mother's face? She worried about the fever returning. And her bedside clock no longer worked, perhaps he could take it apart for a cleaning. "Your father could always figure things out. I'm sure you can as well."

She wasn't ready to be alone. It was mildly diverting to look at and clean connections within the clock. The phone rang.

"Hello, dearie," Mum sang out in recognition. "You've heard our news? … No, he's right here. Hold on." She passed him the phone.

Fear of Jill prickled his skin. But it was only Margie.

"Tell me I didn't hear properly. You're not marrying the dolly-bird you don't fancy."

"Yes," he said, as Mum smiled expectantly at him.

"But you don't fancy her, twit! Why on earth would 'ee marry her?"

"I care for her, of course." He got up for privacy. Mum scuttled from the kitchen.

Margie said, "You didn't a week ago. You went flying right out of 'ere. Anyway, it's fine if you care, but whuy marreee?"

"It's safe. Mum's happy about it."

"Oh, no, no, no—"

"Look, it's all set," he whispered. "She's going to take care of me."

"Are you an old man now? You don't love—"

He rang off. The receiver clattered to the floor, emitting beeps, and took repeated attempts to cradle, the bell giving a loud ping.

Mum looked in worriedly. "She's not pleased? Margie was always sweet on you, baby. That happens with our looks, and you being famous."

He glared at clock parts on the kitchen table. How was he supposed to figure out the old broken thing?

Toni "yoo-hooed," entering the house and the front room with an older woman. Mum rushed to the girl, besotted. George waved but opted to leave the females to their wedding chatter.

Toni called, "Wait, I need you. There's a house we must see."

The woman, an estate agent, reached for his hand. "*Mister* Hartley. A pleasure, young sir."

Off they went in the agent's car, hurtling towards Surrey County, Toni in the front seat while he shared the back with an overstuffed handbag. Housing folders threatened a tumble to the floor. No need to look handsome, he put on his specs and thrust a hand under his hair to feel a pustule coming in.

The Buddha said everything in life was impermanent yet people lived in denial of that fact, treating themselves (loved ones, homes) as lasting, and suffering through inevitable endings.

But how else was one supposed to feel? Of course, he knew Dad wouldn't live forever, yet he hadn't regarded him as temporary. He hadn't seen the reality.

The Buddha warned about seeing thoughts as reality. Absurd, that something so ephemeral, the chatter of a mind, should drive one's entire life.

Like Shadow George being real. George gnawed his thumbnail. Where was he now, the troublemaker? Why didn't he speak? Who thinks they've got two personalities?

From the city to a rural, gentrified setting, church towers flagged from the low-lying areas; large homes appeared on hillsides. He really couldn't imagine living in some posh banker's neighborhood and preferred the city if he wasn't near the sea. Not that he was attached to any sort of house at all.

They wended up a hill through trees and occasionally glimpsed a sprawling home. The agent slowed, then parked along a wall of hedge. A small sign simply read "Jingles."

Toni clapped her hands. "It has a name, how lovely."

There was a hidden gate in the hedge. He and Toni followed the chattering agent up a flagstone path to the sudden view of a vine-covered cottage with leaded widows.

Toni gripped his hand. "Oh, George."

But what a charming place. Not so terribly large. Could he live in a gingerbread home?

The agent said, "Those are wisteria by the window. I'm told it looks fabulous in the summer. Blossoms everywhere."

Toni pressed her heart. "I love it already."

The interior was equally charming with its wooden beams, maple floors, and discreet wallpaper, and more rooms than they could possibly fill. Best of all, the previous owner had modernized the heating and plumbing.

George could see himself living a life here. Cousins would come for visits. A back garden intrigued him through the windows.

"There's a surprise out back," egged the agent.

Down stone steps through a gantlet of rosebushes, he cried out. Toni giggled. The agent reeled him in.

"Your fiancé said you were keen on swimming. You don't find this every day—a dream house *and* a pool."

Toni said, "Oh, it's California! Everyone has a pool there."

"You'll need a pool man, of course. The previous owner had a local chap take care of it. He'll give us his name."

He murmured, "I can swim."

Toni squeezed his arm. The agent beamed a witchy smile and handed him a sheet of numbers with a startling price.

Toni nudged him. "This won't be a problem, right, darling?"

He cleared his throat. "Of course. I'll run this by my... my..." he gasped, "my accountant died."

"Oh no, drat," said the agent. "Bad luck. Ah—you were close?"

Toni rubbed his back. "We'll talk to your mum, love. She'll find us a new accountant. Or talk to Jill. Really, that's her job."

She pulled away. "Darling, you're much too soft on her. I think you're afraid of her. My agent does whatever I ask."

Leave it to her to ruin things.

He marched back to the car with her "What did I say?" echoing behind him. He felt too restless to wait inside the vehicle.

Why hadn't Jill rung him? She knew his plans now, she must have an opinion… or she hated him… or was relieved.

"She'd gone quiet," Mum had said. "She sounded shocked."

IN THE AFTERNOON, he drove to the television studio to collect his post. The words of fans would make him feel better. *Harrington* wasn't filming, but other programs were. He exchanged hugs with the staff. Condolence cards were evident in the the bundled pile. One envelope was addressed to "George Hartley (Carveth)." He ripped it open.

> *Carveth – if you're really reading this,*
>
> *What a nuisance I must've been. I shan't bother you anymore. I've developed the courage to take matters into my own hands.*
>
> *You had a profound influence on me—you'll never know how much. I don't know why I'm writing you at all. You are so ~~beautifully~~ heartless at times. But I don't care. I'm happy! Be happy for me. Then forget me, if you haven't already.*
>
> *–Your MacIntyre*

My MacIntyre. Be happy? Was this a joke?

His heart thudded. So, the creature dared to write. He reread the letter. No postmark or stamp on the envelope.

He bolted to find the studio deliveryman, who said, "Sorry, Mr. Hartley. Fans are always slipping letters in. Can't say when it came."

He sidled past a soundstage. Mustn't catch the eye of these other actors or he'd be claimed for a chinwag. Surely MacIntyre lived nearby, not that he would drive about asking people if they'd seen a lanky blond lad with specs.

He hastened to the building entrance. Fans gawped to see him. He stopped the request for autographs. Most shook their heads at his description of MacIntyre. One said, "I've seen him. Used to come by bus. Hasn't been here in a long time. I could ask round."

"No, it's urgent, never mind. Thanks." He wheeled back to scribble autographs, his signature worse than ever.

This was madness! Why must he run about like a headless chicken? MacIntyre obviously didn't want to be stopped or he'd have left an address. It was probably too late. If only his heart would quit pounding.

In a deserted lounge, he shut the door and snatched up the telephone directory. Too many MacIntyres listed. *Think.* He rifled more pages and found the listing for the school.

No, he would not talk to that child-molesting gang of Nazis ever again. A female voice answered the line.

He stammered, "Right, yes, hello. Trying to reach a former pupil. Need contact information. The name is MacIntyre, if you'd be so kind."

"I'm sorry, sir. We don't give out that information unless you are family."

"Oh, yes. Yes, I am family, a cousin. It's urgent that I reach him."

A pause. "His full name, sir?"

"Ah...I..." *Balls.* "All right, I'm not family. But this is terribly important. He was there some years back, 1960 to 64, something like that."

"I'm sorry, but I can't—"

"Bother! I mean what does it matter if you look up one name?"

Silence.

Oh, bugger this bloody place. He ought never to have tried.

The woman said, "Are *you* a former pupil, sir? You sound like one of our alumni of whom we're all quite proud."

"Well, that wouldn't be me, I'm afraid."

"You sound like George Hartley."

He hesitated. "It could be I am."

She squawked. "I knew it! I'm such a fan. I knew we'd hear from you one day. Wait until I tell the headmaster. He's very proud, sir, we all are. We boast about you at assembly."

"Am I talking to the right school?"

"We have cut-outs posted and your picture in the front hall."

How surreal. "Doesn't a bald sadist named Barlow reign there?"

She laughed. "Oh, Mr. Barlow is still here, yes. He remembers you and tells stories."

I'll bet he does. George swallowed. "Is schoolmaster Wilburn there?"

"No. I'm sorry. Mr. Wilburn had to—he took retirement last year."

He felt a pang. Then relief.

She said, "I suppose I could bend the rules for you, sir. If you would hold the line—"

"Miss," he urged, and poured it on when she gave her name, "if you could please not tell anyone I phoned, I'd be so grateful. You do understand, yes?"

Why on earth had he asked about that pedophile? He curled directory pages as he waited. She found numbers for Sir Percival James MacIntyre and a Randolph McIntyre. George rang the first one.

A wireless announcer answered. No, the younger MacIntyre wasn't there. The voice seemed reluctant to fetch MacIntyre Senior. After more pleading, Sir Percy came on the line.

"I didn't think my son had any mates from school. He used to natter about one who became a famous actor. Who is speaking?"

In a rush of relief, George said, "Just a school fellow. I was a few years ahead of— Look, I must get in contact with your son."

"Why? Has he done something wrong?"

"No. I mean I don't— Why would you—? If you could give him a message or give me a phone number."

"My dear fellow, I'm not a secretary."

"Right, sorry, I didn't mean—is he all right? That's the main thing."

Yes, it was the main thing. And high time to talk to the lad after all these years. Stupid to have avoided him. Now he wanted to talk to MacIntyre more than anything.

But the man said, "All right? I neither know nor care. My son moved out some time ago to become a longhaired hoodlum in the city. His education was not important nor was his place in the family. Whether he is all right, I can hardly ascertain. I am too 'backward' or 'square,' or whatever slang you people use. Frankly, he is and always was a disappointment."

George was dumbstruck. "What kind of a father are you?"

"I *beg* your pardon?"

"Your son's a disappointment? Of course, he leaves home. Yet you don't know or care where he is, what sort of danger he might be in, whether he's even alive?"

"See here," Sir Percy started, "who do you think—"

"I'm the famous, bloody actor. More than that, a concerned schoolmate. And, apparently, a very lucky son with a father who always cared when I was in trouble, who wanted to help me no matter how... no mat—"

George slammed down the phone, unable to continue.

TWENTY-TWO

"Keep on Running"

(JACKIE EDWARDS, 1965)

WOULD these seizures of grief never end? And now MacIntyre was gone, who might have no one weeping for him, who didn't deserve to die alone amidst coldness. Yet people died that way all the time. It felt unbearable that anyone should.

And here he was, brought up with love, his early years a paradise, like a prince with riches. He even panged for his schoolmaster booted into retirement, *if* he'd been booted, not that the old sod deserved a crumb of sympathy.

George plucked facial tissues and slunk from the lounge, leaving his mail for later. He had no stomach for further surprises. In fact, he had an urge for the Buddha book. At least the Buddha addressed the hunger of a heart, if mistakenly fed with possessions and other people. Never quite sated.

He couldn't see changing his life to meditate in Scotland or levitate in the Himalayas. Everyone would think he'd gone off his head. Yet there was something promising about finding a new kind of teacher.

He drove back to Clapham picturing MacIntyre as a child, the poor mite with a stammer. Interest was up in the neighborhood. Kids clustered in front of his house and hovered round the Jag. He made his smiling way to the front door, honored and floored by their excitement. Perhaps his mother would finally consent to move now.

She told him she'd had to unplug the phone, and added quietly, "You're leaving then?"

With shades drawn, he gave her one more night and read by the fire in his dad's chair. She knelt on the Indian carpet cutting patterns for a frock, and admitted she was glad he'd found the books by Alexandra David-Neel.

"It's good to explore religions. Growing up, I only wanted to be Church of England. Now I find it dry. And no one seems to believe in God. They call our background 'Oriental,' as if we're exotic or less civilized. Embrace your eastern side, darling. Go to the tea slopes. See where your grandmother lived, where the Tibetan traders came. Immerse yourself in the lore. Talk about it with your girlfriend."

But he couldn't see talking to Toni about that, let alone drawing her attention to his mixed-blood heritage. The marriage plan was starting to feel absurd.

BACK HOME IN the Kensington flat, Toni visited him, her mood playful, and bent to show stocking tops and bare thighs where usually there were tights. He got a hand in, then was biting her through silk knickers, his need for a serious talk shelved. How could girls go around wearing so little under their skirts?

Maybe she knew what he meant to say. Was it so crucial to say? A randy, kittenish wife would be all right. He asked about extending their engagement. Topless, she pelted him with details already set—a luncheon, flowers—and sat on his chest, adorably determined.

As his birthday neared, Grandy Morwen, along with Uncle Arthur and Aunt Sally, arrived in London by train. No cousins came, thanks to Margie, no doubt. The relations were packed in the house with Mum, even though George offered a nice hotel. Grandy said, "No need to waste money." As his E-Jag was now like a lit sign, he was dropped off by hired car.

It was a strained supper in the back dining room, despite Aunt Sally gushing how his father would be pleased. For some reason, Grandy wasn't meeting his eye. Everyone seemed to be play-acting for Mum as if she were the one invested. Perhaps the relatives thought the wedding barmy but were too polite to mention it.

As the women washed up, George poured a whiskey for his uncle in the front room and winced one down himself, needing the buzz.

Uncle Arthur cleared his throat. "I s'pose you have some experience, bein' in your line of work with all them lovely girls. I went to my wedding night a virgin."

George coughed his surprise. Arthur added, "Weren't so uncommon. Sal was my sweetheart, my first and only. Not that I don't have an eye for the fillies. And I do wonder. Mighta been good to 'ave some experience." He scowled into his glass.

As the ladies came in, George escaped to the kitchen.

Mum followed him. "You okay, lamb? You seem off."

He hugged her. "The wedding makes you happy, doesn't it?"

"It does. I do like her." She pulled back and palmed his cheek, loving eyes agleam. "You're missing him, I know. He thought you and Toni a smart couple."

Again, his dead father approved of Toni!

Mum assembled a cheese plate. "Don't laugh at this. He once thought you and Jill might end up together—I know!" she said to his shock. "Highly inappropriate, I told him, and with a ten-year age difference." She shook her head, as he braced the counter.

Mum gave up her bedroom to Arthur and Sally, insisting she would sleep on the sofa downstairs. Grandy was in George's old bedroom. As he was saying his goodbyes, the hired car waiting outside, Grandy beckoned him in and had him shut the door. She gazed out the window.

"I weren't going to say nothing, what with all your trouble and now this hasty decision you've made. God knows, if you're happy, that's fine, that part's not for me to say. But I can't keep this inside."

He could've kissed her with relief. "Go ahead, Grandy. Say it."

She turned blazing eyes. "Wicked boy, to tell such lies to your cousin!"

"I...? What?"

"Oh I got it out of her. You've *always* been mazed about that school, and to say such a—such an *outrageous*—and with your pa just—well, it's beyond me. You've upset your cousin. And I'll not repeat any of it to your poor mother. We'll go on as we have to. But I'm ashamed of 'ee, to do something like that."

HE WENT through his days in a black mood, not wishing to see anyone, only seeing Toni long enough to break up with her. He told his mother the wedding was off and refused to elaborate or see the relatives.

It helped to dance until his sweat streamed, until Mr. Olivetti barked, "Good! Again."

His March birthday dawned cold and rainy, with a ringing telephone (that he ignored). He stayed at the dance studio until late, part of his time coinciding with Toni, who didn't speak to him, and almost got through the day. Then some fool came in with a cake and candles, a "20" drawn in blue icing. The group sang.

Mr. O piped, "Small pieces, everyone."

George had to explain that he wasn't doing anything tonight and it was quite all right. Such astonished faces!

What if he'd told them he was going home to meditate? The night before he'd sat cross-legged on the floor trying to clear a mind wild with thoughts, determined to realize the "path out of suffering." Wouldn't it shock everyone if he went to India? With its blue god, its monkey god, and those great umbrella trees to sit beneath, perhaps that was the setting for battling demons.

An excited Nigel cornered him at home. "Since you're clearing out, I'm moving in with my girl, what the hell. It's time I settled. I bought her adjacent flat."

"I'm not clearing out. I'm not getting married. It's not what I want."

Nigel's expression dimmed. "I already gave notice for this place. I just bought a flat," he said to George's protest. "I don't want to retract. I'm looking ahead now. I thought you were moving on."

"I *am* moving on, maybe to another country. Eventually. Today was," his voice cracked, "supposed to be my wedding day."

Nigel said kindly, "Share a blow?"

They lit a joint in Nigel's bedroom and were soon giggling like the old days. Until Nigel's bird phoned. George left him and peeled off his warm-up trousers and sweaty tights. Too stoned to meditate or read, he felt a sinkhole of loneliness. Someone was at the door!

He saw through the peephole it was Toni, and stood in turmoil before opening. He still wore a shirt and dance belt.

She gasped, her eyes darting low. "I wanted to, to wish you happy birthday." Her smile collapsed.

He'd best bring her in. When he faced her, she erased a grin. It was too annoying.

"You leer at me, yet I'm not even sure you like my body."

She looked surprised. "I think you're beautiful."

He'd shag her good and hard if she wanted it so badly, if she wanted to take it the way Mrs. Althorp used to.

He said, "Why are you here? I'm not going to change my mind."

She glanced down. "I-I knew you weren't ready for marriage, I mean, I wasn't surprised by your decision."

She met his gaze. "What were you doing in the lake?"

Blood shot to his face. "What does that matter now?"

"It does. I worry."

"You don't have to."

"But I do. Also, well, I want the house. I was wondering if you wanted it with me. I'd put money in."

He'd almost forgotten the gingerbread cottage with the pool. "We'd live together?"

"Why not? Everyone's shacking up. Marriage is so awfully square. Don't know why we were being so conventional."

He admitted, "I need a place, as it turns out. Nigel is giving up the flat."

She couldn't hide her gladness. *Don't be glad*, he wanted to tell her. Although, as long he as he stayed in the U.K.—he had a plum job, after all—perhaps, he, too, wanted that house. It was high time he made an investment for himself.

IN THE SUMMER OF 1966, his solo dance—with sexy girls backing him —was well received on *The Harry Black Show*. The bouquet in his dressing room was from Jill, fond but distant in her note, who now communicated all messages by note or secretary or via the new bloke she'd hired.

Harrington's resumed taping in the studio, with some filming on location. In his role as "Jamie," George steered a wobbly bike into a pond on location, then had to do his studio scene wet. Filmed in a farm pen, he ran from angry geese. In a pub scene, he spattered Cyril with brown sauce, that started a food fight. Silvered with sardines, a defeated Jamie faced an aroused cat.

Toni was a regular on the show as Russ's long-suffering girlfriend. Her new popularity made she and George a celebrity couple written about in magazines, who now lived in a house befitting a celebrity couple, though they scarcely filled it with their few possessions.

His mum took the new arrangement in stride, Toni's parents, less so. He could well imagine the vitriol whenever he left their presence, not that he cared. He signed checks to his grandy for the upkeep of the house in St. Ives, no card or letter posted with it.

Celebrity spotters called their names as he and Toni sidled past a waiting queue for easy entrance into a happening club. All was dark in its thumping depths. Until kerosene green exploded on a wall and the thumping became a song, "Keep on Running" by the Spencer Davis Group. The room was full of revelers. Peter Sellers swept past with a dolly in tow; John Lennon laughed at the bar. Female dancers needing work performed as Go-Go Girls on raised platforms.

Toni hailed a friend, so George squeezed through the crowd to get to its joyous center on the dance floor. The gang of loons he often saw made space for him. All bounced to the harmonica riff of "I'm a Man" by the Yardbirds. No longer strangers, a shared love of music and dance made these club-goers a family.

On the edge of the group was a moon of a face, a bearded man trying to catch his eye, as men sometimes did. George didn't know him or care; he never wore his specs in public. He feigned playing the guitar and grinned at other chaps doing it. This was definitely a chaps' song. The tempo changed, a dual of guitar and harmonica, the dance turning awkward. The bearded man edged closer. The song's acceleration was faint at first, then coursing through its rhythm, the guitar wailed higher, so high! the band revving now. Jeff Beck's guitar pick was skating over the strings, scratching, flying, buzzing, his hand surely a blur. Everyone was possessed by the trance of the Bacchanal. George shook his head wildly. The bearded man gazed exultantly. The dance floor was one churning, frenetic organism until the bang-bang ending. People laughed and let go, the bearded man swallowed. Couples broke away to sit even with heartbeats of bass guitar, followed by a surge of lead. "Eight Miles High" arrived triumphant, another fab song to sear his skin.

Familiar, that man, like Jack, he was …

George flew off the dance floor and wormed through the crowd, ignoring those who greeted him. The fair-haired, bearded man leaned at the bar. George whirled him around. The gray eyes filled instantly.

George laughed embracing him. Jack pulled him off his feet and stroked his hair. They must have privacy! Impossible here. Colored lights splashed over them.

He dragged his prize down the long hall to the exit and pushed Jack away from the waiting queue of scenesters, Jack saying, "I never meant for you to find me. But after I read about the clubs you frequented, I started going. I just wanted to see you from afar." (How English he sounded.)

"You're seeing me close. Oh, Jack."

George hugged the familiar body. And remembered himself—still famous, still visible. He had to brush the whiskers. "You've hidden your handsome face."

"Do I look distinguished?"

"You look older."

The gray eyes clouded. "So much has happened."

He laughed. "Well, you must tell all. Bastard!"

He shoved Jack harder than he meant. Jack looked startled.

George said, "Do you have any idea how much you hurt your wife? I mean *really* hurt her. She became an agent because of you."

"I set her free."

"Is that how you see it? Christ." He shook with anger.

"Jill was always bright, a strong girl. It's what I liked about her." Jack looked worried. "Maybe this wasn't a good idea."

George winced. "No, wait."

Such violence in his arms! He'd nearly thrown himself on Sam once. Now he wanted to rage at Jack, at Wilburn. At Dad. He wheeled away, horrified, conscious of being in public view.

He stepped close to this person who'd once been so important to him. "I'm sorry. Come home with me. I've a fabulous house—or we—I live with Toni, my dance partner."

"Is he here?"

George blinked. "Don't be absurd. Toni is a she."

Jack glanced down. "Of course. Silly of me. "

"You sound so English."

An old grin flashed. "What did you expect? I've been here a while. Should I still be calling you 'kid'?"

George couldn't answer. Love and anger stopped his throat.

The gray eyes gleamed. "What a marvel you've become. I knew you'd be heartbreak handsome. I knew you'd command an audience. But being on television." Jack shook his head. "How did I miss that? You got the right agent. I can't see anyone just yet. I've only come back to the city recently. I'm glad I've seen you." He reached out.

George captured his wrist, squeezed it.

Jack seemed to realize the situation. "You can always find me at the all-night pub. I've become a night owl."

"Wait. I'll just get Toni, we'll go somewhere else. We've so much to catch up on."

"George—"

"Stay here. I'll be right back."

But when he finally pulled Toni from her clot of admirers in the club and squeezed back to the damp outdoors, Jack was nowhere to be found.

THREE IN THE MORNING. When Toni suggested they go, he obeyed. The dance coursed in his limbs, unquenched, like the yearning for Jack. Jack's desertion infuriated him. He'd shouted himself hoarse calling, until Toni begged him to stop; people were watching. Now the encounter felt imaginary.

Clearly, the man had changed his mind. George had failed to live up to some dream. He couldn't bear it if Jack didn't love him anymore. People always seemed to go off him. Wilburn. Jill. When would Toni?

The air was full of misting rain. He'd parked the E-Jag too damned far away. Toni cradled a fuzzy bundle, her hair gilded in lamplight.

"Peter O'Toole gave it to me, I couldn't say no. Someone brought the kittens. He was handing them out. He kissed me."

George took in the orange tabby she held, its fragile head. He had to scratch a furry cheek. And realized: "You do see the absurdity—Jamie with a pet cat?"

She let out a cackle. "I hadn't."

How he'd love having a pet in his life. He put his finger beneath gripping toes, needle claws. The kitten's blue eyes seemed shocked.

He said, "Mad bringing kittens to a club. The sound must have been hard on their ears. Did he give them all away?"

"I saw a few running along the floor."

"But that's awful. We should go back and fetch them."

"I'm sure they hid. I wouldn't worry."

With all the loons and drunks stomping and kicking? He'd been completely unmindful of his feet.

She giggled. "He was like Father Christmas."

"Who's this?"

"Peter O'Toole. Aren't you listening to me? I hope we have some milk. Under the circumstances, I might call this little one 'O'Toole.'"

George tap-danced ahead of her in case he had blood on his feet, and spun round a lamp pole to keep back the thought of kittens, one minute warm in a litter, the next, running in panic, battered by sound and pounding feet. But life was suffering, was it not? Sometimes it happened straightaway. *Boom!* Welcome to the world, you useless, kill-able creature. Your life is nothing. Watch you don't get trampled here in London's hottest nightclub.

She called, "Don't you care that I was kissed?"

"Who kissed you?"

She stopped and flapped an arm. "Peter! Honestly, George. I thought you'd be impressed. He's quite a charming devil. Might be married. Though some people have open marriages. It's all the rage."

"Good thing we're open."

"Are we?"

"But of course we are, you know we are."

How annoying of her to snog someone else. Why should he be impressed? A black cab trolled past, looking for a fare. He waved it on. "We have no ties. You're free to sleep with anyone."

She cut him a look. "Are you cross with me?"

"Who'd be the lucky chap besides Peter?"

She was slow to answer. "I-I suppose I'd do a Beatle."

"Aiming high. Good for you."

He danced on. How barmy this night had become. The city was sopped in moisture, its earlier gaiety drained away. He halted at the sound of running steps. That also halted. An echo?

Ahead was Leicester Square, lit for no one like a tart past her prime. He skidded forward on wet pavement.

Toni called, "What about you?"

"I'd ball the dwarfs and cripples. They don't get it much."

"Are you trying to shock me?"

He gamboled atop the Shakespeare statue and the slick edge of its fountain. Lord—there was his own face, stories tall and grinning like a devil. Toni cried out seeing it.

He gave a sharp laugh. "What a fright. Pru said there'd be a giant advert. Mr. Barlow, you, old sadist, here's your dark lad. He thought me ugly, you know."

"Who?"

He jumped down possibly needing to be sick. Droplets clung to his lashes. The kitten mewed, round-eyed, its fur spiked by moisture, dependent on the kindness of larger beings. Were its ears ringing? He said, "Can I hold it?" and took its featherweight from her hands. Claws punctured his trendy jacket. "There, beastie. You're all right."

He crossed to St. Martin's Street, shielding the animal. "We must get the kitten out of the rain. Cats don't like rain or high volume, I should imagine. We were talking about your lovers."

Her steps rapped behind him. "But I have no lovers."

Fear shot up his spine. That echo again. He squinted at a figure under a streetlight who paused before darting into the shadows.

Toni stalked up. "You're being very bloody tonight. Now what?"

"My ghost..."

She looked around. Then dubiously at him. "I don't know what you mean."

But there was his shining, bronzed vehicle at last. He darted for it. She scurried after him. "You want to see others, is that it?"

The kitten crawled up his shoulder. For some reason, Toni looked ready to cry, her hair frazzled. "Don't we love each other just a little?"

"*What?* What are you on about?"

A madwoman's cry lanced his nervous system, piercing the night. Toni charged in an opposite direction. "Taxi!"

What on earth? Claws stuck his shoulder. He followed her. "Where are you going?"

He snared her arm but she yanked her arm free, eyes steely. "Do what you like! I'm going home." She snatched the mewling creature from his shoulder.

The black vehicle veered close, spraying him. He jerked back, but Toni got in it quickly. The cab accelerated with a reek of exhaust. Tail-lights blurred in the distance. She didn't even look back.

Well. That's her off the plate.

Loathing raged inside him. It bucked him in a storm that could only be tamed with a loving kiss on the neck and a ripping cock up the arse. He gripped the Jag and looked about wildly.

"MacIntyre? MacIntyre!"

TWENTY-THREE

"Once I Loved"

(ANTONIO CARLOS JOBIM, 1965)

HIS VOICE NEARLY GONE, George felt he was luring a wild thing. The figure emerged from the shadows, damp and real, hair plastered dark, glasses speckled. *You're alive.*

Heart thudding, George said, "You followed me."

"I c-can't believe you're t-talking to me."

The voice was mannish. "I was at the cu—" The youth blinked, frowned. "I didn't know you were there. I c-couldn't sleep."

There were spots on his chin, with bristly side-whiskers, fair hair straggling long.

"You're taller than me," George realized.

MacIntyre took the measure of him just as closely, eyes storm-green, darting back and forth. "You rang my father."

"I thought you were *dead.*"

MacIntyre winced. "I'm sorry. I should not have sent— He, he said you were worried about me."

"Get in the car." George went to the driver's side.

Mac hesitated. "Why should I g-go anywhere with you?"

"You shouldn't. Get in the car or tell me to fuck off."

Mac got in the car but stared at him. "I don't trust you."

"At last, MacIntyre!"

"You s-s-s-scare me."

George heated. "You scare me, too. My hands are shaking." He dug them into his lap. The car reeked of wet clothing.

"I guess you saw me get ditched by my girl."

Mac said nothing. His hair dripped over the collar of a cheap coat. He must live without the family money. George started to squeeze the locks, but Mac flinched at the contact.

George held up his hands. "Sorry. You're safe."

A whisper, "What if I don't want to be?"

Buggery hell.

"We're going out. To a pub." He started the powerful engine, then nabbed his spectacles from the glove box, knowing they killed his allure. Mac's surprise was obvious.

"Disappointed?"

Mac said, "No. Delighted."

George almost smiled. The Jag leapt onto the road. Mac braced.

"Relax. I love driving this late, or this early. Not even a copper about."

"They're probably m-mucking in Soho."

Where the queer lads were. "Well then. We can do this."

George slipped the gearstick to neutral at a light, turned towards his passenger, and kissed his live, startled mouth, making it a good one, feeling the youth react though he, himself, felt little more than the power of it—though, truth be told, that had its own stir.

"Oh God," MacIntyre gasped. George glanced for the bulge and drove on. Mac sprawled, ready to be taken.

Leave the boy alone.

"Fine," he said aloud. Anyway, Jack waited. Hadn't he given himself years ago to the American couple? One partner had turned away. Perhaps the other might love him again.

The trip was short. He dove for a spot, backed up with a screech, parked, removed his specs, and finger-combed his damp hair.

He strode to a bar with etched glass windows where the "names" liked to gather. Outdoor smokers ceased their chatter as he passed. Inside, the place was crowded, smoky, most patrons well into their cups, likely shagged-out or back for a second or third go.

He tried not to squint. His old lover didn't look to be anywhere. He noted fluffed hair, glossy hair, tits and bums of various allure. *Look at the men.*

One wore sunglasses, no one he recognized. There was Burton, often seen with his American starlet. Didn't that long nose belong to Townsend? A man who seemed familiar openly stared at George.

A distinctive laugh sliced the mayhem. There, in the corner, in a smoky haze, was a very famous pop star, a sheep in wolf's clothing, a supposed lover of ladies who had leered at George on several occasions, who'd love it if George glided up to him and whispered, "Fuck me" in his ear. Arousal surged just thinking about it.

Mac bobbed up, rain-damp and pink-cheeked. "Whoa, look who's in here. Incredible. There's n-no table."

"We won't need one."

He started forward, but a large-haired woman got in the way, exhaling booze and tits onto his person. "Hello, baby. Don't I know you?" He removed her, "Excuse me," onto Mac, who went, "Ahh-augh."

"Pansy," snapped the woman.

Dead ahead, the pop star saw him with a narrowed gaze. George smiled. But the staring man intervened, and said, "What do we have here?" in a strongly accented voice.

George gaped. The pop star startled him and claimed his arm. "George-love. Join me. I'm so bored by my crew always hanging around like cheap necklaces."

"I saw him first," said the staring man.

"The hell you did."

The pop star steered George to his full table, even as George tried to look back. "But isn't that—was that Rudi?"

"That was trouble. Make room, slags. Let him sit. Who the hell are *you?*"

MacIntyre said, "I'm with him."

"I doubt very much you *are*, love."

George hated that superior tone. "Wait." He pushed Mac's lanky body to a corner. "Mac, I release you. Go, if you want."

"But I want to stay with you."

"Do you see who's here? They want me, too."

The green eyes hardened. "Right. And I'm no one. I've never been anyone to you, have I? Why did you even talk to me? You told me everything would be all right."

"I lied."

Mac looked struck, eyes shining.

The pop star butted in. "Sticky fan problem, George? Run along, mate. You don't belong."

Irked, George said, "Don't talk to him like that, he's a human being," and added, "Maybe I want him here."

The pop star balked. "Have him then, darling. And sod off."

The Russian appeared, two vodkas in hand. "Is there problem?"

MacIntyre bolted through the crowd towards the front doors.

George faced the splendid-looking Nureyev at last, said, "I'm afraid there is, sorry," and tore after MacIntyre.

The light was murky in the chilly outdoors, the rain stopped. MacIntyre was a dim figure staggering down the pavement. George called out. The youth ran. Mac was surprisingly fast and barely noticeable as he veered down steps to lower ground. George slowed on the steps, hardly able to see them, and wishing for his glasses. When the pavement flattened, he was hit by colder air, the tang of dead fish and lapping nearness. He stalled, blinking.

"Mac! I can't see you."

Somewhere, the running patter of feet halted. He was winded from his slight exertion. Why was his heart going so? Before him, the Thames sloshed black and alive. The sound of footsteps increased.

Mac emerged to his right. George smiled with relief.

Mac shouted, "Just who in hell do you think you are? What gives you the right to treat me as rubbish? Because you're famous? Or good-looking? Are you that daft?"

"You're right, MacIntyre. Good for you."

"Don't cheer me on, you fucker!"

George was banged in the face, sent stumbling, and snagged a granite post before pitching over. A scum of debris slapped below.

MacIntyre moaned, "Christ, my hand," then came at him.

George shrank. "Don't throw me in. I'm a good swimmer. I've survived cold water before."

"Carveth—ah, George." The lad threw up his arms. "I love you."

"You were doing better before, MacIntyre. Now I know you're mad. I've read all your letters."

"Letters? I wrote you once."

"The hate letters. Aren't they yours?"

Mac paced in the clearer light. "They may be from Wells. I saw him a while back. He despises you. I only wanted your friendship."

George winced. "You don't want to be friends with—you don't *love* your abuser, MacIntyre. You think I loved Wilburn?"

Mac gawked. "It was true then, you and Wilburn?"

Though he had loved him, in a way.

Mac leapt, wrenching him from the granite post—this was it! But he was hauled him to a bench farther in and fell onto the seat.

Not even worth a toss in the Thames. He laughed. Tears poured. His left eye throbbed. Mac collapsed beside him.

He flinched, fearing more violence. Better to take charge.

"MacIntyre. Of course, this will sound like absolute crap, but I don't—don't remember what hap—" Shame crumpled him up. "I hurt you. It was done to me."

A hand warmed his back. Mac spoke. "There was talk you'd had an affair. Chaps built you up back then."

"I was frightened of him. I feared you all knew and despised me."

MacIntyre drew him close. Shivering, George was glad for the bit of warmth, and a neck in which to hide his shame. "Thing is, it keeps happening in my mind. I can hardly live with it."

Mac tightened his hold. "You know what I tried to do. What you don't know is you stopped me. Your show did. It preempted another program, not the usual time at all. Was that a fucking message? It was a repeat, Jamie-the-newsboy episode, one of your sillier ones. I couldn't exactly hang myself after that."

George touched the whiskered cheek. "You were going to hang—?" Both of them had muddled their attempts.

Mac said, "I had it all rigged up. The moral of the story is don't off yourself with the telly on. I was low about not pulling it off. But I'm glad now. Otherwise, I wouldn't be here helping you. Am I helping, Carveth?"

He smiled. "Your stutter is gone."

"Only comes when I'm nervous. There's my fist on your hard cheekbone. Hope I don't close your eye." Mac lightly stroked him.

The whole area tingled. He stopped Mac's hand. "I'm sorry."

"But you didn't hurt me. You say 'abuse.' I thought you were trying to take my virginity. Which, technically, you didn't finish. You reached out when no one else did. Yeah, you got sort of rough and demanding. I guess I was a bit scared." The youth went quiet, remembering.

George hoped he looked too pitiful to hit again.

Mac said, "You were making my naughtiest dreams come true."

"For God's sake." George sat away. "I meant to hurt you. Then I felt so guilty after. I feared you wanted to rub it in my face or report me. I ran from you."

Mac said, "Is that why?"

"Didn't you hate me?"

"I thought you hated me."

He winced for their younger selves. How ridiculous and sad. "I hurt Wells."

Mac pressed him to his shoulder again. "Yeah. You put your finger in Wells. You wanted me to suck you off. You got a bit forceful and weird, breathing funny. That *was* scary, actually."

He shuddered. "I've been told that before. I think I... black out." Mac's fingers strayed in his hair. It felt lovely.

Mac said, "Perhaps you did black out. You shouted at us as if you were surprised to see us."

"I'm fucking bats, MacIntyre. I thought I had two personalities. I should be committed."

This horror was exhausting. He closed his eyes with the need to sleep. Fingers stroked his chin.

A mouth muffled his! But the kiss was bold, somewhat erotic. An answer to the kiss in the Jag? George slithered out. "Mac. We're too barmy a pair. If you'd any sense—"

"I've a flat."

"I think I'm liking you too much to just have a bonk and split."

"You'd consider a bonk with me?"

He laughed and squinted. The sun blasted the horizon, sprinkling the river with shards of light. Blinded, both young men rose in awe. How grand to catch a sunrise. Relief opened inside him. He fished for his handkerchief to blot tears. Cripes, his cheek throbbed.

Mac was still amorous, a needy kisser. George stayed his clutches. "All right, love, that's enough. I'll give you a lift home."

He couldn't seem to open his eye or see well, even with his specs on. Mac went flustered at his block, thanking him, offering the bonk again, swearing to leave him alone.

George took Mac's hand and wrote his phone number in ballpoint pen. "I hope you don't have sweaty palms. I live in Surrey now."

Mac looked ecstatic. "And I live here."

What a loon. But a good one, perhaps a mate?

Alone, the exhaustion hit. George debated even driving home when he was due at the dance studio in a few hours, then the television studio. Squinting at the sun, he meandered through the city, parts of his route lost to thought or worse, a barely-awake stupor. Here was Chelsea, the happening neighborhood, cafés and boutiques locked up, discotheques silent. What was the name of that street? But it appeared in throbbing vision—Flood Street (how miraculous he even saw it), a turn towards the river. He even remembered the number for the building to which she'd moved. There was enough space between cars to wedge the Jag. Lights flared in a couple windows. Still awfully early. He'd wait an interval.

He jerked awake, head off of the steering wheel, glasses pressed into his face. Some kids passed in school uniforms. He got out of the car and walked unsteadily to the front door. His vision was worse; it was hard to see the numbers on the intercom.

"Cripes! Sorry," he said to the first, botched attempt, then "It's me," to her voice.

"Downstairs?" She sounded shocked. Then buzzed him through.

Jill leaned over the banister of the staircase, saying, "You're really here" as if she still cared for him, then "What happened?"

She pulled him up the last few steps and into her flat. Dazed with happiness to be in her kitchen with its inviting coffee scent, he started an embrace. But she backed him into a chair.

"Who did this to you?"

"A bloke hit me. I deserved it."

Her brow furrowed. "Are you sure you deserved it?"

He smiled at that. "Positively. You look beautiful."

Her freckles went pink. She darted to the icebox and handed him a bag of frozen peas for some reason, and removed his glasses. Then she moved his hand so the bag touched his face. It stung!

She said, "Have you told the studio yet? They won't be pleased."

"They won't," he realized. Bugger, he was in trouble.

She sat. "I can't believe you're here. Gosh, I've missed you."

"I've missed you, too. I'm not far away, you know."

She brushed crumbs off the table, rose. A rag came out. "So much has happened in your life. Your mother showed me pictures of your home. It's lovely."

"Toni wonders why you haven't been by."

"I should. I will come, if you invite me."

Had he never invited her?

She shook out the rag and sat, brows still knit. "I'm glad you didn't marry. It was too hasty a decision so soon after your dad."

"I didn't marry her because I don't love her."

"Don't you?" Her eyes caressed. "Oh, DF."

He grasped her warm, freckled arm. "Boss. What are we doing?"

"We're doing our damnedest to let things be as they were."

"Why?"

"I don't want to hurt you again."

"Why hurt me at all? Don't you think about me?"

She popped from the chair as if looking for a new activity. He said, "I think you love me."

"I do love you."

"Ah, well, you don't have to say it like that."

She rolled her eyes. And withdrew the gold necklace from inside her collar.

He beamed, though it hurt the side of his face.

She said, "I don't always wear it, but put it on this morning. The pull of you is strong." That last part was said so softly he almost missed it.

"Then why aren't we together?"

She jerked as if shocked. "Because of *this*. You've obviously been out all night. You show up on a workday morning having been in some fight, yet you have a job where you need to be on camera. You live with another woman, and yet you're here, wanting me. You look like you haven't slept. I can't entirely blame you—you're twenty years old. As your friend, I'll say 'take care.' But as your agent, I don't want you to get careless. The press won't ignore a celebrity behaving badly. And, honey, you're at the top of your game. You're with a group that challenges you, shows you in your best light, *and* they pay well. These are not things to take lightly. You mustn't be seen with a black eye. Keep those peas on it!"

He moved up the bag to cool his mortified face.

She wilted against the counter and held her forehead. "I'm hurting you again. And I've done hugely stupid things. Like sleep with two men on the same publicity trip. One was a big mistake. The other was an amazing mistake."

He flinched. "You ruined sex for me. First, *he* made it a muddle. Then you go and show me how incred—" He couldn't continue and was glad for the wet bag of peas.

She spoke softly. "I'm sorry for those terrible things I said on the plane. Darling. You made me feel like a girl in love. Wondrous. Charlie was nothing to me, an embarrassment. And you were too important." She turned away.

Then faced him. "So I don't know what to do. I can't be careless, I must be a better person. Honestly, you'd find me boring. I'm wrapped up in my business. I'm not flashy and sexy like the girls around you— What did you say?"

"I wouldn't mind being bored."

She turned away.

Was he forever the lad to her? Someone to handle? How many more rejections must a person take? How fleeting, this adulthood. One moment, a firm part of his life, the next, not there at all. He scuffed back the chair. "You were right, what you said earlier. This doesn't look good. I hadn't realized."

He left the peas. "And you don't have to be a better person. You're one of the best people I know."

Mascara streaked her face. She reached out. "Don't go yet. Let me do my job."

She rang the studio and told them he'd bumped into a cabinet. He made a face; she shrugged.

"Very 'Jamie,'" she added with a fake laugh. "A noticeable bruise. He came straight to me in concern about… No, I sent him home with an ice pack." She turned and spoke less audibly before ringing off.

How fitting: blame it on the fool. He gripped the chair to keep from toppling over. "Did they buy it?"

She waggled her hand. "They wondered if you could come in later. Makeup will assess how it looks."

"Oh Lord. Thanks, boss. You're a good boss. I'd wink, but I'm already winking."

He collided with her wall thinking there was a wider opening.

"How can you see to drive? You'd better rest here."

She steered him through her front room past a large picture

window and potted plants. He lagged. It all looked so different from the flat with Jack, cozier.

"I love what you've done here." She nudged him to a floral sofa. He said, "I warn you, if I go horizontal, I'll be out in two shakes."

"That might be best."

She clacked to the kitchen. He breathed in the faint lavender of her perfume and sank to the decorative pillows. How lovely to lie down— *Don't fall asleep! Tell her about Jack.* He opened stubborn eyelids.

She stood over him in a blur. "Coffee is ready to start whenever you wake up. I-I wish I didn't have to go to work."

He forced himself from a dizzying pull. "Jill."

She knelt close. "Yes, love?"

"What if you come home tonight, and I'm in your bed?"

She cupped his good cheek. "I'd love it. You know I'd love it. But that's not playing fair. It's complicated between us."

How was he supposed to read those gorgeous baby-blues?

She said, "Do the right thing. Your dad was a great one for that. So are you."

Oh God, it was too much, this "right thing." Too important. Better to chase dreams already starting. He barely felt her kiss.

Acknowledgments

It's far easier these days to research the past since one can mine nuggets of memory on the internet. I have always been fascinated by Britain in the 1960s, literally since childhood when I became a Beatles fan. I think I've read most Beatles books, until I had to stop, as well as books on "Swinging London," such as, *Ready, Steady, Go! The Smashing Rise and Giddy Fall of Swinging London* by Shawn Levy, just to name one of way too many. I never thought to log down all those books that merely fed my nerdy obsession.

I devoured movies from the 1950s and 60s. Thank you for existing, TCM, and for showing obscure films from the U.K., at least to this Yank. [Check out two fascinating films, *The Entertainer* and *Room at the Top*. From the other end of the spectrum, there is *Having a Wild Weekend* or *Mrs. Brown You've Got a Lovely Daughter*, though, honestly, I never made it to the end of those stinkers.]

I have been in three helpful writing groups over the decades. One member, the long-suffering Bob, has been exposed to my work from the beginning. The man deserves a medal. Three ladies who are deceased, Carol, Ann and Bunny, were standouts from my second group. They corralled my abilities and challenged me. Thanks to the current (and past) "Holey Road Writers Group," specifically Alice, Bob, Catherine, David, Frank, Ginny, Harley, Joye, Kathy, Linda, Paul, Phil, Solveig, Susan, and Wayland. You guys gave me some tough love.

Thanks to Rogena for a thorough editing. Thanks to Denny for signing me up to various author groups. Edie, Nancy, and others provided moral support—I am rich in friendships. Kisses to Ted wherever you are. My brother and his family are a lifeline.

Of course, none of my stories would have flowered into anything without my girlhood writing pals, Julie Preston and, earlier, Patricia Ton. We were just kids amusing ourselves, filling the hours, easing difficult times. We thought ourselves hilarious and brilliant. That's where it starts.

About the Author

Despite a useless Fine Arts degree, Leslie M. Rollins has spent much of her career in the world of direct marketing and graphic design. Her writing was done on the side, in the car, in bathrooms, when she should have been working, progressing from pen and paper, to type-writer, to keyboard, using big floppy disks to compact discs and those thumb drive thingies. With the help of sadistic writing groups, she honed her craft. A great procrastinator, yet she completed two novels, *Good-Time Girl* and *The Man Dance*, and is currently working on a sequel to *The Man Dance*. Rollins has also managed her own business, traveled, and attended several Buddhist retreats. She has survived marriage and widowhood, and the loss of some lovely dogs, and currently resides with cats in Virginia.

For more information, visit: lesliemrollins.com

Also by Leslie M Rollins

GOOD-TIME GIRL

An excerpt from **Good-Time Girl**

Chapter 1

I HAD MY FIRST ever "Law & Order" moment. You know…the arrest at the bottom of the hour?

Yeah.

Cuffs. Miranda rights. My usually docile Labradors turned into Cerberus behind my hastily closed kitchen door, their confinement being "an order" from a pair of nervous, threatened cops, who are not unlike nervous, threatened dogs.

Outside, the neighborhood comes alive! Imagine the diversion of a cop car pulling in. Officers badged and holstered pound the door of an end-unit townhouse. Even better, they drag out the short, snarly white bitch who lives there—me.

Upon my departure, neighbors swarm like hens to feed: *Was that Leah Mason? What was* she *into? We've never liked her. We heard she was part of some* [unsolved, fill-in-the-blank local crime]. I imagine my dogs howling over the clucking, their true hearts wounded by the abduction of a pack member—not merely because I'm the food source.

And what crime caused this intrusion in a quiet dell located within the sprawl of our nation's capital? I'd like to say I was a successful madam running a high-class whore house—a *male* whore house. That's right, with working *boys*, hot and sexy, but with manners, my goldmine of a clientele being older females who don't have a hope in hell of getting laid again (not me, mind you, but some of us). My hos would get it up with Viagra, I mean, right? Is that not the best use of that drug? Older guys, don't answer.

Anyway, I'd like to say that was my crime. But it's more embarrassing than that.

I do regret my actions, mostly for involving the boy. Why did I buy that gun?

AFTER BOGUS Y2K and shocking 9-11, those of us in the DC area were treated to an anthrax scare through the mail followed by random sniper shootings—I mean, *jeez*, I'd never felt so jittery just going about my daily life. Now we're in a damned war with color-coded fear. We have another Bush in the White House, and he wants us to keep shopping.

So I did.

I bought my gun on Valentine's Day, 2003. Not the sort of holiday that brings to mind automatic weapons...unless you've been single a long time. At forty-eight, I'm like a fine wine or an overripe cheese, still fertile, technically. But my body seems to be hosting a keg party for the hormones. As they are nearing retirement, their work ethic has gone to hell. Whatever accord we'd had over the years has disintegrated. I wouldn't be surprised if those hellions influenced my decision-making.

Or did I buy the gun because my day was bad? I work in a marketing firm. It was a rough morning. Let me back up...

A FIERCE RAIN turns the morning rush into a sea of brake lights. An early meeting is scheduled with one of our nonprofits, the gun control client, a favored cause of the company president. We have to keep this client happy and help them battle the bullish NRA—no easy task.

As an art director, I manage the graphic designers, a bunch of snarky, under-valued introverts. The girls look worried as they hand over the mockups and presentation boards. The boys joke as if a weight is off their shoulders. I am in a power suit and heels.

Arms full, I clack down the hall and elbow on the conference room lights. The "Partner Pride Committee," a party-planning, balloon-buying group of employee volunteers, has turned our professional offices into a high school with so much Valentine hooey. The snow-spray from Christmas even got some use on the windows.

My creative director boss, the evil prince Damien® (not the name he goes by in public), sails in behind me with pastries.

"Are we ready?" he says.

"Of course, Evil One," I say, or at least the first part.

The client is close behind, ushered in by the president who's all grins and backslaps. The "client" is actually three people: Racquet Ball Guy, an alpha who once mentioned the sport—I know he must bang the hell out of those balls; Bearded Guy, a nice, nerdy Liberal, along with Little Sister, a serious young woman always trying to get a word in and usually ignored. After the ass-kissing bonhomie, and a pointed look at us, the prez ducks out. I get in my own schmooze. Damien hovers, thrusting in comments, exalting the pastries. He and Racquet joke about weight even though Damien is as thin as a whippet. He offers a plated apple fritter to me. I refuse and go to the front of the room. Racquet gives me a wink. Bearded Guy smiles. Little Sister gazes seriously.

Right as I start, Damien blurts, "Happy Valentine's Day," as if that point hadn't been hammered home already. He and Racquet whine about gifts for their wives. Bearded Guy shows annoyance. Little Sister stuffs her face.

I'd like to shove an apple fritter in a certain someone's pie hole. But the married men settle. I don my client face.

"So, gun violence, wow. Your latest report was frightening, especially how someone with an arrest record can still buy a—"

"Disgusting," Damien adds, "yet incisive reporting. It made our creative juices turn. Right, Leah?"

Do you believe this guy handles copy?

"We were inspired," I say and unveil the first board. "Here are some ideas for a 'Take Back Our Schools' campaign."

I'm barely into the explanation before Damien jumps in.

"For next year, of course. We need to raise money *before* the school year and the time to do that is right now."

"No, you're right," lobs Racquet Ball Guy. "It takes a while to get things in play."

Damien smacks it. "Bingo. Here is a program for teachers and counselors telling them what signs to look for in troubled youths."

Racquet bristles. "You don't expect us to visit a bunch of schools!"

Damien is smug. "You won't have to. They'll come to you. Leah, show them."

Jesus Christ! I grab the handouts, my rhythm thrown. Even though the D-Man had been too busy all week to vet our ideas until late yesterday when I gave him a mock presentation, that he rearranged, I will not seethe.

I say, "Here are outlines for a course you can have on the internet or presented as a seminar."

Beard puts in, "Is this really our niche?"

Sis adds, "We're into legislation."

"It's a great idea," Racquet declares.

"It is a good idea," echoes Sis.

"But you're putting us out on a limb, Leah. I don't like being on a limb," Racquet concludes.

My boss glares at me. "You're putting them on a limb, Leah."

I rip open my chest so he can see my exposed, beating heart. Not really.

I smile. "I'm glad you mentioned that. It's all part of your new Community Outreach Program. Remember, you wanted us to produce ideas for that? This wouldn't come out of your legislation budget."

"We weren't going to touch that," Damien confirms.

Racquet shifts. "Ah, well, that's different then. I wish you showed us the legislation stuff first."

Which was what I had planned.

Beard signals with a question. Damien gets to him before me, ready to decipher any nonsense. Sis catches my annoyance. I smile at her. Her mouth widens slightly. Racquet thumps the table for her attention.

I guess I needed running shoes to stay on top of this meeting. Has Damien had too much coffee? I ready the next board. *Whoa.* My uterus contracts.

After ducking out last month, my period blunders in from its vacation. Dear God, if men had to deal with menstruation during a meeting, they'd snap like twigs. I am not entirely unprepared, though the timing *is* incredible.

The three-headed client talks at once as Damien flits round, the obliging elf. I wait for a lull, fighting not to glower, hands clenched... Medusa hair pinned...beauty faded...womb no longer empty as my cycle bangs around.

Before Damien, I had free rein in a room like this. Creative meetings were my forte. But the company has grown. Damien was brought in from the outside, the hotshot ten years my junior, landing a position I had presumed for myself. I fear upper management has me on watch, as if my job security is ticking—nothing overt, mind you. That would be ageism. Yet most employees here are under forty.

I get tired of all the backing down. I should have walked when they hired Damien. But they pay me awfully well.

I drop my pointer so I can bend through a searing cramp.

Damien says, "Leah?" All eyes are on me. I straighten. Client face.

"You must know about the gun show in town." I pause for their grumbles of disapproval.

Damien says, "Are any of you going? You could do undercover work."

Racquet says, "We should, but no one has the time," and throws a pointed look at Beard, who hunches and writes.

Lil' Sis says, "I'll go, boss."

But he snaps, "You have too much on your plate. Sorry, Leah. Go ahead."

Damien glides to the back of the room to check his Blackberry, so I get through the next part without interruption.

The meeting crawls. More sugar consumed, tangents explored. With all the pastry gone and design boards unveiled, the client rises, resigned, at last, to continue their day in their own offices. I edge door-ward, fighting my urge to sprint to the ladies' lounge.

Damien says, "We'll send Leah after work. I'm sure she's not rushing off to do a Valentine's dinner like we are."

Racquet says, "Nah, man. I bet Leah has dates galore tonight."

Damien smiles. "Of course. We'll send her this afternoon then."

I gawk as amiably as I can. "Send Leah where?"

"To the gun show. You're game, right, girl?"

"I'm…busy."

"Let me see what I can work out." Damien winks.

Which is enough to send anyone running. I fly to the ladies' room. Despite a full stall, I bitch like a crazy person.

"Calling me 'girl!' Sending me off wherever he wants like *he's* the damn president."

"Who, Damien?" says the other stall.

"I had to do my whole presentation on the rag!"

"That sucks. Men are so lucky."

Her voice is familiar, one of the youngsters in production, though her name eludes me. The turnover *is* high there.

My stall mate asks, "Hey, Leah, do you have a thong mini-pad?"

I shudder. Is there a more idiotic piece of apparel than the thong?

Oh yeah, I was suckered into the women's movement at a young age. And let me tell you, we've gone nowhere, baby. I thought thongs were a joke. My gender wouldn't be conned into wearing *G-strings as underwear.*

Now we're saddled with places like Victoria's-hush, don't tell, that promotes hooker gear for teenagers. Their president must be Humbert Humbert. It even looks like a bordello. I expect to see men planted in various corners of the store masturbating.

My irritation flies out of my mouth.

"Who cares about panty lines? Is it better to look like you're *not* wearing underwear? I've got news for you: men are having a fuck-fantasy about you regardless—"

"Whoa."

"And if someone with a big trunk is wearing stretch pants and bikini underwear, I hardly think a G-string is going to solve *that* problem."

"Okaaay. I'm guessing you don't have one then."

"Oh, ah, no. Sorry, kid."

I hasten out so I don't have to face her. No visits to the production department today.

I'M UNABLE TO talk the Evil One out of his loony gun show idea, where I'm saddled with the opaque task of "gathering info."

"Now they expect it," he hisses.

Although, I distinctly remember Racquet's touch of chivalry: "Are you sure you should send Leah there?" with its implied "Shouldn't you go yourself?" I do have a soft spot for macho guys. But Damien practically shoves me out the door.

"I've already relieved some of your schedule. Go!"

I laugh inside my car. And scare myself. I've seen enough movies where spinsters laugh crazily before losing it.

The windshield wipers barely flash a view in the downpour. I stop home to change and take solace in Juice and Coffy, my yellow and black Labs. Ah, the canine greeting—wet snouts and wiggling bodies.

My black girl pushes between my legs. She seems to enjoy the hug. I think she can't get over my whole two-legged lifestyle. Their fishy tongues and dense, finger-sticking fur are heaven, a respite from the day.

But they *still* won't pee in the rain, damned defective water dogs. I could stay home, pop an Aleve and some corn and watch Turner Classic Movies, and work up a story about going to the gun show. But guilt—and, I must admit, a fair bit of curiosity—kicks in.

Bejeaned, I navigate a treacherous drive to the expo center with its massive parking lot that is mostly full, despite the weather. Which means I must park a mile away, which means I'm fairly wet and lacking in NRA cheer by the time I pay the fee. I snarl for a receipt and enter the Dark Side.

Click. That's the sound of swallowing with no saliva.

Rows of firearms crowd tables, display cases, booths draped in camouflage, and machine guns are propped for use. The place is crawling with hunters and mercenaries, dads and despots. I quake for the birds and hapless citizenry. All these devices of death in one convenient location. Don't want guns? How about a collection of disemboweling knives? I would be backing out now and running as fast as my chickenshit feet could carry me if they weren't rooted like gum to the floor. As it is, my stomach is madly pressing the up button.

There are NO females. Wait—spoke too soon. A chick in an ATF shirt walks by checking out the merchandise. Of course, people who wield firearms must be able to shop for them. Children tail some of the dads. How isolated I've been in my little world of art, novels, and gamboling wildlife.

I'd better move before a "Bleeding Heart" sign drops and alarm bells go off. Be cool. I'm on a mission. My cell phone can supposedly take pictures. (At the price it cost, it should do my taxes.) I fish it out and open its clamshell. *I can't figure this thing out here.*

I stuff it back and feign interest at a Glock table. Why, there's a pink rifle for the ladies! And a sign: Wife won't carry a gun? Get her Pepper Spray!

Blood: return to the face.

Here is a table of swords, how quaint. Ah, the case of semiautomatics, their sole purpose being to kill people.

Like creative directors?

Nobody notices me. That's how good the middle-aged camouflage is. I am kind of on the short side, which is nice in some situations. I flick my hair over my shoulder. It is an asset, or a pain, long and wavy when it behaves, enjoying life today as zippy auburn snakes—which, apparently, looks dramatic with my gray eyes, according to my ass-kissing, over-charging hairdresser. *Seriously, can you imagine Medusa at the hairdresser?* "I'd like an up-do this time. Oh, don't mind *them*."

Am I attractive? I've been told so. I don't always see it. Then sometimes I do. It's frustrating and merciful that we don't know how we appear to others.

I swipe open my raincoat and undo the top button of my shirt. I know—the Liberal in me just keeled over. But another part is glad to be Miss Cleavage in middle age—fat padding when you need it, nipples wide awake and buzzed with estrogen as I stand over the brightly lit case. A man slides near.

"See something you like there, honey?"

Tit-snared, he reeks of a cigarette. A salesman joins him, jovial. "Hello, little lady. What can I do for you?"

I smile at the accommodating men and go back to being perplexed.

Smoker says, "Looking for protection? Something to make you feel safe?"

I've already got some tampons, thanks. No, I don't say that. I say, "Oh, I've got two big dogs. I want puh—"

My lips start the "p" for "power," but I swallow the word and feel embarrassed for wanting it. The wily salesman seems to understand.

"You want that little something extra?"

He offers a flash of chrome.

Lucille. The name comes immediately. She seems to float in my palm, a ladies' gun, sleek and low-cal, the mere weight of a cell phone. Being a P32 semiautomatic, she can get off eight rounds before the bother of a reload. Just holding her gives me a surge that melts the beached-whale heaviness inside my body. I point, and she makes me taller. She makes me stronger.

"Looks good," affirms Smoker.

It would be so easy to take out these horn-dogs while their eyes are planted elsewhere. The salesman bumps my arm.

"Watch where you point that, sweetie."

"How much?" I purr.

Her price startles. The salesman notices and offers a ten-percent discount. My integrity light is flashing—we're getting low here.

But a devil perches on my shoulder, nudging my hand wallet-ward. *After the day I've had, don't I deserve a reward?*

The two men give me advice on how to care for her, like dads instructing a daughter. I'm nodding as the sales guy swipes my credit card. And, okay, being called "honey" is making me feel young instead of irritated. I wouldn't mow down these good ole boys. If they gawk at the girls, big deal.

Do I submit to a sensible background check like a good citizen? Are you kidding? This is the "gun show loophole!" My Lucy is placed right in my nutty fingertips. Then I buy her a hip, shiny case.

I'm a well-regulated, one-gal militia—and I shall *not* be infringed! Or wear fringe…however it goes.

{Look for *Good-Time Girl,* available now.}